Mystics IN HELL

CREATED BY
JANET MORRIS

EDITED BY JANET MORRIS AND ALEX BUTCHER

Perseid Press
P.O. Box 584
Centerville, MA 02632

Mystics in Hell
Copyright © 2021, Janet Morris

First Perseid Press digital edition, April 2021.
First Perseid Press trade edition, April 2021.

Book design, A.L. Butcher
Cover design, A.L. Butcher and Roy Mauritsen
Edited by Janet Morris and Alex Butcher
Cover painting: – *Portrait of Sir Francis Dashwood, 11th Baron le Despenser* by William Hogarth by 1764, oil on Canvas
Mystics in Hell cover image copyright © Perseid, 2021
ISBN for E-book 978-1-948602-30-3
ISBN for paperback 978-1-948602-31-0

Published in the United States of America

RELATED WORKS:

Heroes in Hell

The Gates of Hell

Rebels in Hell

Kings in Hell

Crusaders in Hell

Legions in ell

Angels in Hell

The Little Helliad

War in Hell

Prophets in Hell

Explorers in Hell

Lawyers in Hell

Rogues in Hell

Dreamers in Hell

Poets in Hell

Doctors in Hell

Pirates in Hell

Lovers in Hell

To find out more about the series please visit:
theperseidpress.com

Acknowledgements

Janet Morris & Chris Morris: *A Frame of Mind*

Andrew P. Weston: *The Come Right Inn*

A. L. Butcher: *Abode of Woe*

S. E. Lindberg: *Fool's Gold*

Lou Antonelli: *The True Believer*

Gustavo Bondoni: *By Any Means Necessary*

Tom Barczak: *Excalibur*

Michael H. Hanson: *On the Run*

Andrew P. Weston: *The Sorcerous Apprentice*

Joe Bonadonna: *Colossus of Hell*

Janet and Chris Morris: *Strange Arts*

Contents

Mystics
IN
HELL

A Frame of Mind

Janet Morris and Chris Morris

"All live to die, and rise to fall."
– Christopher Marlowe, *Edward II*

"The stars move still, time runs, the clock will strike," muttered Christopher Marlowe, alone on a thundery heath blasted and deserted enough for even the most modern interpretation of *Macbeth*. His words weren't from Shakespeare, but from Kit's own *Faustus*. One more dusty quote, this one, among so many; one more impossible dream of a man, dead and damned. No stars sprinkled the bloody vault above, where Paradise held sway over all that was good and scowled at humanity's evildoings in the manifold hells below.

Kit stumbled, looked down and saw the upper part of a skull half embedded in the dirt and weeds. Caught by his boot's toe, it was, with every tooth in place. He wouldn't touch it, or stoop to own that toothy jaw. This was devil's work. Satan called the plays today, and every day, where Marlowe was concerned.

In *Faustus*, Marlowe had said, "Hell is just a frame of mind." Those few words had damned him beyond Mercy's reach, once Diabolos himself took umbrage at what Kit wrote.

So here he roamed, in hells empty or full of Old Dead and New, spun from moment to moment wherever the devil pleased. Kit had once courted souls here with whom to bide: Shakespeare and his players; J, the bible writer; Solomon the king; Orpheus and the *Argo*'s crew, as if Kit had enjoyed a mystic's mesmerizing power, some unerring sense of where comfort could be found.

But all of that was gone now, and some skull (please, not Yorick's) had hooked around his booted toe.

Even the coldest comfort was beyond Kit's reach on these desolate days. Ripped away from New Hell and Shakespeare and the afterlives they'd made together, wearing tattered doublet and linen, leather and hose, he trudged a ridgetop draped in heavy fog. Such fogs bore plagues from one hell to another: bubonic plagues, black plagues, poxes that could rot your lungs, later scourges that could cover you with boils or turn you to dust, to salt, to water, leaving only sand or slicks of mud behind.

He most missed companionship, souls to love on warm nights and wit to share onstage. He'd tried to stand between the Trickster and his favorite toy, Will Shakespeare, and thus attracted Old Nick's ire. So here he was, with no friend or even foe to share his pain.

On this blasted rise, with the fog rolling in, he looked around, before, behind, and saw . . . nothing. Infernity turned her face away, snubbing him.

He'd thought to oppose Satan, to spy for Erra, the Babylonian god of plague and mayhem; to sell a bit of soul to Erra, auditor from Above, and bolster resistance to Satan's rule.

But he'd misstepped, letting Will know part of his plan. And from there to Satan's ear came word of what Kit hoped to accomplish by serving Erra and his enforcers.

Thus here he was, alone; perhaps alone forever . . .

At that moment, his legs chose not to hold him, folding under him until he sat, dizzy and sore oppressed, afraid of the oncoming fog but equally afraid to flee it. But flee where? He needed help. He needed such prophecy and witchery as this hell might deliver. Sitting with a leg crooked beneath him, he pried and kicked the toothy jaws away.

The skull rolled and hopped, as if it had a destination in mind, careening down the slope. Was it sentient? Alive in any way? Even the habitat of a ghost? But no. Here were punishments custom-crafted for one who gamed too much with those far more powerful.

From somewhere came thoughts of Will Shakespeare, and more thoughts of Will, sweet-cheeked and honest-eyed, followed by a wisp of the First Folio's *Macbeth*:

"The weyward Sisters, hand in hand,
Posters of the Sea and Land . . ."

And out of the fog came three sisters. approaching in strange and wild garb, hair whipping about their faces, obscuring all identity, resembling creatures from some elder world. As frightful as the sight of Hekate they were. *Moerae*, were they? Maybe; maybe not, but as wyrd. Every limb and ort of them was wrapped in glowing prophecy, necromantical science. Such wraiths were far more mystical than hell commonly brought forth.

These knew destinies, they did; he could feel it. These were prophets; he knew it. Clothed in nothing and everything, they came. And they spoke without words among themselves, but clearly to Kit's inner ear. They made his heart throb. They caused every hair on his head and neck to horripilate.

And as they came on, they raised a swirl of winds that pushed him to his feet and downhill.

"Who are you?" Kit called, for they were coming right at him. "Are you the Fates?" *Or are you worse?*

For worse they might be, might have been, might be again—any or all. Though they headed straight for him, he still could see only their outlines, cowls and shimmers as they closed the distance. Faster now they came, blowing their way down the ridge, through the fog. And faster yet.

So fast they came at him that he went to his knees, regained his feet, then crouched, and squinted into the wind.

"Fair is foul and foul is fair. Hover through the fog and filthy air," he heard them whisper trochaic tetrameter, or heard the wind sough. Will always used that meter for supernatural speakers, witches and such. These were Will's lines from *Macbeth*, for certain. But was Will trying to find him? Or warning him off? Or neither? He missed Will more than afterlife itself. But would Will send such emissaries? More to the point, *could* he?

Right through him, they came. He felt no bump or lurch, no push, no touch of flesh warm or cold.

When they'd passed and got behind him, he rose, spun on his heels.

In their wake lay nothing more than a hard incline bathed in fog. No weyward Sisters here, no prophets of doom, no mystical allies or keepers of destinies.

But the skull rested there, downslope, as if awaiting him.

So he went that way, down and down, first walking, then running with arms waving for balance, until he reached the skull. He grabbed it in his fingers as he caromed farther downward still.

Skidding downhill, he angled his descent to slow himself. When he could, he stopped.

Catching his breath, he pressed the skull to his ear as if it were a seashell holding the sound of waves breaking on some primordial beach.

Within the skull, he heard something else: a distant watercourse or pulse of blood. Its faraway sound whispered courage, of which he had so little left himself, and with it came a shove from gusts at his back to prod him on his way.

These could not be pure devil-sent omens. Could not, because ringing next in his ears came the battle sounds of his own play, *Tamburlaine,* being performed someplace out of reach.

Skull to his temple, Kit ran on, farther and faster, homing on the sounds the bone whispered, hoping to get beyond this ridge of endless abandonment, ready for anything that summed more than the oblivious fog in which he'd been trapped so long.

*

Orpheus (augur, singer and seer) and Solomon (prophet, mystic, idolater and judge), stood together on the apron stage of Shakespeare's rebuilt Globe Playhouse, a polygon of twenty sides surrounding a three-story open-air amphitheater, and compared their weal and woe:

"The plagues have shut nearly every house. The Globe survives by playing to a third of its capacity," sighed Solomon as a phantasm of a gray cat bolted from stage left to stage right and disappeared with a mew and a hiss and a struggling bat flapping in its jaws. A graymalkin it was, some witch's familiar: a sure sign of evil afoot. Solomon ignored the omen and continued: "We're open at all only because Satan wants his plays performed, and Shakespeare insists that playgoers won't be sickened by the vapors here, or so the devil promises him. But you'll need to manage the music and sound effects, Orpheus—and no more running off to find your lost Eurydice. Every time you go hunting for that wife of yours, we lose the use of you. And you can't keep her from her fate: every time she's found, she's summarily lost posthaste."

Orpheus knew when to argue with Solomon. This was not one of those times. "I can't fault your logic, Solomon. Nor will I flout Satan. As long as the Globe needs my services and my music, I will be here. If the Globe closes, I'll search again for my wife, but the plagues change everything." With no plectrum handy, he reached down to strum his golden lyre, belted across his chest: a summation, a crescendo. "Now, about these apparitions . . .?" Orpheus jutted his chin toward the vanished cat before he sluiced brine from his face and down his chest. Since he'd last shipped with Jason on the *Argo,* he and the rest of the crew continually dripped salt water from every pore.

Solomon, full bearded, wearing his customary brown wool robe, rapped his oak staff three times on the wooden stage, until a shoot sprouted from the staff's top. "The apparitions? Three Fates, they are, at least when seen by us poor sinners: The Weyward Sisters, Shakespeare calls them. They show up for plays like *Macbeth*, written with parts for creatures such as they. There's nothing I can do to stop them from playing those parts, or even give them stage direction. They come. They act. They go. Some think that they apportion fates to each soul in the audience, those foolish enough to attend such productions and risk infection. Beyond expecting their visitations, what should I do?"

Orpheus swiped at his damp face and stared Solomon in the eye. "Do? Short of finding a baby to cut in half? Get

Marlowe back. You're more the mystic than I, these days, or so rumors say. Use your authority over spirits, creatures, wind, and water, over all obedient to your magic. Use whatever powers you wield to find Kit Marlowe. He's the only one who can modulate Shakespeare's pride, Satan's lusts, and the groundlings who stand here on rushes and hazelnut shells and speckle the cheap seats."

Solomon rapped once more on the wooden stage with his oak staff and strode away, evanescing as he did so.

In that storied playhouse alone, Orpheus shivered. High overhead, a wind picked up and moaned a lonely song he knew as it blew through the rafters of the near-empty Globe. He must be careful as he headed home. There he had hid his wife Eurydice, safe from prying eyes, safe as could be in New Hell, where everyone had much to hide and all to lose. Should he lose Eurydice again, in these times of plague and sorrow, finding her might be beyond his skill. But when he got to his Cheapside garret, Eurydice was nowhere to be found.

Again.

*

In the multifarious hells, plague and loathing dallied, obliterating one, terrifying all, destroying trust wherever they spread. Hellions feared the hideous deaths meted out by Erra and his personified weapons as much as they feared reassignment via the Undertaker's table. Everyone knew, no matter how bad things were in time without end, they could still get worse.

New death tolls, announced each Sinday, were followed by weekly lockdowns and lines of penitents hoping for mercy. The occasional breath of air on Sadderdays hardly helped.

Then matinees and cabin fever enticed the bravest out of seclusion to join audiences for Satan's Unreality shows and Trash Metal concerts until automatic rifle fire killed the applauding New Dead audiences even as they screamed for more.

In hell, screaming was nothing new. Nor death, since death for all time could only be had through obliteration of soul, mind, and body. Lesser deaths were simply down-payments on tortures to come and were followed by agonizing trips to the Undertaker's reassignments facility, his feared Slab A.

Exhausted hellions schemed and struggled to outwit their fear, hold tight to their loved ones when they could, and find the fabled manumission that yet might come from on high. But the rarity of success stopped no soul from trying. The courts were busy, hell's judges overwhelmed, and the guilty or innocent sentenced, ten to the hour.

Few here belonged in a better place. Most of those deserving were animals, searching for people they loved. Few, animals or humans, found their beloveds. Hell was not meant to reunite the lost, but to isolate and penalize the guilty. Internment camps hosted stories of cages for masses of latter-day damned. When babes were found among the doomed, these were usually souls sold young, souls of vile nature, or souls whose punishments included prolonged infancy due to prior offenses against the young.

Most times, when babes were found they were not baby sinners, but rather misplaced progeny whose antecedents remained unclear. When such youngsters might be blameless, they came to trial in the arms of judges such as Solomon, who in life once offered two squabbling women halves of an infant over whose custody they fought.

Today was such a case, and Solomon such a judge, sitting now in the cavernous Hall of Injustice.

As a judge, he unsheathed his law-giving sword. It glowed with fiery light as he pointed it upward toward Paradise, then sheathed it, indicating he was ready to hear the next case before him. The king then let his silence and his penetrating glare underscore the importance of this particular case until none in the crowd spoke or moved. Behind the press of spectators staring into the stacks of big wire cages were many who believed that the outcome of this proceeding would set precedent for others in the hereafter.

The case centered upon a nut-brown baby, a tiny, misplaced soul now mewling in Solomon's arms, one of a flood of such. These had resulted in part not only from the works of Erra and his Seven, but also from the simple fact that hell was overcrowded.

Solomon hiked up the black-haired baby in both arms and boomed, "Who claims this soul?"

The crowd shifted. Among that multitude in hopes of acquittal and a trip Above, three women yelled and shoved and ranted for Solomon's attention.

One of the three was pox-faced, one rheumy-eyed and coughing, and the last one overweight and toothless. "I do," said the first, claiming Solomon held her child, a babe shot and killed in a 21st century melee.

"I do," claimed the second in a raspy voice, saying the same babe was orphaned in later culture wars, and although its parents were here in hell, no one knew where, therefore the fault here was hell's bureaucracy, not the babe's at all. This woman had given birth to nine children and claimed that, being a mother so many times over, she was the best choice to succor this babe.

"I do," insisted the third woman, who claimed to be the babe's natural mother. She was short, ragged, and covered with colorful tattoos. This would-be mother testified that the child's father was lost somewhere in hell and pulled open her shirt to show proof by tattoos. The tattoos moved, depicting a mother with a black-haired baby; but no father could be seen.

"His daddy's lost *here*," said the short woman, pointing to her midriff. "You can see. This soul you're holding is my son."

The baby coughed and whined until something wet and warm dropped onto Solomon's chest and steamed there.

Still holding the babe with one arm, Solomon unsheathed the sword at his waist and waggled it at the women and the crowd. "We have one baby, and three claimants. Which of you will give up custody to another?"

"Not I," said the first.

"Never," said the second, pushing forward through the crowd.

"I will," said the third, the woman with many tattoos. "My son needs a mother. If his mother cannot be me, then choose another, Judge Solomon."

From the dome above, the dour light of Paradise licked up and down Solomon's sword. "I have made my decision. No need to threaten to cut this baby into pieces. Only one of you knew this infant well enough to know his gender and call him your 'son.' You other two: lying is a sin. We will decide your punishments next."

Those two lying women wailed as loud as the baby. Gray fiends in uniforms marked 'Police' came out of the crowd and grabbed them by their arms. The crowd yelled and hissed. Many shook their fists.

"Step forward, Mother," said Solomon to the tattooed woman over the crowd's angry voices. "Take your son and leave. This boy child is yours. May you bring him to a Sadderday matinee at the Globe when he's old enough to stay quiet through one of our performances. And remember this wisdom: 'Your own soul is nourished when you are kind; it is destroyed when you are cruel.' Hell or not, the basics still apply."

The king was greatly relieved to give the mother her baby, who had wet himself again in Solomon's arms and defecated on his brown robe. Which, indeed, was why he wore that color whenever he served in this capacity.

One thing Solomon had learned in hell was that people will tell you whether they are guilty or innocent if you simply listen.

But on this day, when he listened, he heard, "Fair is foul, and foul is fair. Hover through the fog and filthy air," a refrain from the Scottish play that chilled him when he heard it outside the environs of the stage.

So Solomon called a recess in his docket and struck the ground three times with his oaken staff to return him to the belly of the Globe.

Something was wrong, very wrong, whenever fair was declared foul and foul declared fair. But then, everything was always wrong in hell.

*

Kit Marlowe had a hole in the toe of his right boot where he'd first kicked the skull. At every step along his trek through this marsh, damp and cold invaded his foot the more. His wet toes chafed, rubbing against boot-leather.

He ignored his abraded toes as best he could, carrying the skull he'd found toward some unknown destination. Ahead he could see the pall a city makes when Paradise squats atop

it. That place would be as good as any, if there was life there-
in. Or afterlife.

The underverse by the riverside boasted no bird nor beast
nor anything alive. If 'alive' was the right word for what souls
experienced once they'd come to hell. Kit veered away from
the river, favoring dunes and tall grass, less abrasive to his
blistered toes than mud and gravel. Not long after, he flushed
a gray cat who snarled as it crossed his path and bounded
away. Graymalkin! A graymalkin seen was never a sign of
life, but often of death. "I come, graymalkin," he murmured,
mouthing the line uttered by the first witch in *Macbeth*.

But this was no longer the heath he'd left behind. And if
these manifestations came from Shakespeare, he welcomed
them. Next would come the thunder, lightning, or the rain.

But they didn't. The silence once more dashed Marlowe's
hopes of imminent rescue by Shakespeare.

Yet Kit well knew Shakespeare's *Macbeth*, and suspicion
grew in his anxious heart. Bad enough it was to be lost in
hell, but to be somehow sucked into Will's Scottish play, one
of the worst tragedies ever wrought? It seemed a surfeit of
penance for Marlowe's slim catalogue of sins.

What if Satan had devised a worse punishment for Marlowe, actually trapping him inside the play he knew so well?

Upon the heath? He'd been there.

Graymalkin? He'd seen one.

Kit limped onward, hoping to see no further sign of
witchery.

He yet had the skull. Did that count as witchery?

He'd been using the bony orb as a compass, and before
he reached the city it led him unerringly to a vast battlefield
covered in corpses and dotted with squawking ravens as far
as the eye could see. There he saw a bloody baboon dancing
on a dead man's chest. The baboon yelled at Kit, pointing its

hairy finger his way, then splashing its palms in the corpse's blood as he passed by.

Baboon? Now there's a third sign, if I choose to credit it. Was this yet another message from *Macbeth*? If so, its meaning remained unclear, beyond the fact that the second Sister had used a baboon in her cauldron's recipes.

Would this garden of death all around finally lead him on to New Hell, or where? He had to step carefully, not to tread on arms and legs and heads and mounds where intestines lay laced with flies swarming and buzzing.

For too long, he held his breath. He feared to find he'd nearly stepped on someone he'd known, someone he'd loved, someone he'd hoped to meet.

But none of those first corpses spread across the field belonged to wars he'd created, tragedies he'd wrought. He felt, after a time, that these doomed fighters came from his *Tamburlaine*, warriors lifted from his pages and dying anew here.

"I'm sorry," he said to this panorama of dead, but did not pause. He kept moving, the skull going slippery in his right hand.

When he came to the end of the war fought here, the corpses changed their nature: here they were bloated, but not bloodied. Here some were wrapped in shrouds, some naked. Not even the ravens or the flies wanted more than a taste of them.

What had happened here? A plague? Old or new, plagues promise the same result. Was Satan bringing him here to know the horrors of his oncoming destiny?

Hekate, queen of witches, had proclaimed to Macbeth that he would see apparitions that, by the strength of their illusion, would assure him that he was safe, when he wasn't. Would the same befall Kit?

Safe? When? 'When the hurly-burly's done? When the battle's lost and won'? This scene perplexed him worse. Kit moved faster, stepping among the shrouded and the rotting until he drew past them. In hell he had co-written with Will a twisted play, *Macdeath*, for the devil's amusement. And the devil had been pleased, though he and Will had been appalled to stage such a farce.

Was this diorama of death pleasing to the Son of the Morning? None of these corpses turned to salt or sand while he watched. The Undertaker didn't reach out to claim a one of them. Not yet. Kit trod that field like a dancer, now stepping here, never there. In the distance, he could still see a city, sprawling under Paradise's glower.

He kept his eyes on that city, kept moving until he recognized New Hell for what it was: a finer trap for a prouder group of damned still moving.

His right boot had filled with pebbles. Standing amid the sickly-sweet putrefying dead, he emptied it. Sand and mud and small stones cascaded to the ground. He pushed his sore foot into that soaked boot and stood on both feet, then limped onward, past the multitudinous corpses that had yet to find their way to the Undertaker.

He limped out the day, and limped farther, into Paradise's niggardly night. No one approached him. He limped until he saw Bankside, and limped to the front entrance of Will's New Globe Playhouse.

Its doors were barred; on them in red paint or blood someone had scrawled, "Closed for plague today. Deliveries at the back."

So he went to the back door and paused there. It was unlocked.

He hesitated, full of qualms at seeing Shakespeare again; at the least, they had much to discuss. His breath came short;

his throat hurt. His right boot had filled with yet more debris. Inside, he climbed the familiar stair and pushed through the attic door into Shakespeare's aerie.

No one met him there. Not a single bat spread its wings and fled his approach. The place was emptier than the ridgetop where he'd begun this trek, quieter than the heath and the battlefield and the stacks of the corpses in their vast graveyard.

He closed the door behind him, laid the skull on the table where he and Will had penned so many tales. He stood with most weight on his good foot, unsure what might come next.

After a while he heard a rustle of wings and smelled a fragrance like grace, like forgiveness, like joy. Unbearable.

He was slow to turn to face it, for he had smelled that smell before.

The farthest-fallen angel, beauteous beyond reason, took a seat across from Kit at Shakespeare's table and said, "Christopher Marlowe, I've been waiting. Sit down."

Kit sat across from Satan. The smell of deviltry wafted about him, entrancing.

"I have a bone to pick with thee," said Satan. The devil reached out and poked the skull Kit had found on the ridge. Somewhere aloft, a harpy hooted. Few animals were native to hell: among these were hell-toads, hell-bats, hell-cats, hell-goats and hell-owls, even hell-hounds and horses on occasion, but this hooting reminded Marlowe of the three Fates, Lachesis, Clotho, and Atropos. The weary playwright would rather have faced the three Weyward Sisters than this archfiend, more beautiful the longer Kit watched him.

Bereft of a retort suited to a chat with the Trickster, Kit still opened his mouth. At first no sound issued forth. Then it did: "A bone?" Kit croaked.

"A bone. Whence got you this skull? And why do you yet have it?" asked His Satanic Majesty and raised his right hand.

From between them, the skull took flight. As if thrown through the air it circuited the room and landed in the Adversary's hand. Black talons wrapped it tight. Satan stroked the skull. From the marsh beyond the Globe, a toad called loud: *Ribbit*! *Ribbit*!

Humanity's great Accuser sighed as if experiencing *orgasmos*. His ebon wings fluttered, then bated, then spread wide enough to block Kit's view of anything else. "I am waiting for your answer, soul. How did you get this skull and what business with it do you and Shakespeare have?"

"I went for a walk. By myself. Alone. On that walk I found the skull. I was bringing it back as a surprise for Shakespeare. It will hold a good many quills. I have no business with it beyond that. And Shakespeare is innocent in all this. He's not seen me nor —"

Three sounds came from behind Satan, sounds like umbrellas opening or closing or doors slamming shut. Behind the devil's wings, more huge pinions flapped. White-winged two were, and black the third.

Kit gained his feet and took a limping step backward.

Satan gestured to the dark one of the three summoned angels and said to Kit: "Wrong answer, Marlowe. Samael, Master Marlowe likes long walks alone. Take him where he can have one." The eyes of Diabolos burned into Marlowe like fire. "Let him walk until he's learned that no plague or Babylonian henchman has aught to offer such as he, until he begs my pardon."

The angel of death smirked and waved at Marlowe, bowing low to his lord with a swish of feathers. Like a mirage, behind Samael, Kit then saw a play ongoing, players in full costume, an audience pressing forward from the cheap seats. Here was a play about to start, with everyone he loved engaged. He heard the rattle of thunder made from sheet metal, and a cauldron bubbling.

Onto that stage came the three Weyward Sisters, chanting: "Double, double, toil and trouble/ Fire burn and cauldron bubble."

Kit nearly swooned, mesmerized. He wanted so to join the cast. He saw his precious Will, costumed to play Macbeth, waiting to go onstage when the second Sister would cry, "Open, locks, /Whoever knocks!"

And then all that was gone: no steaming cauldron, no three Sisters, no aerie where he and Shakespeare had worked so long and hard. Before him lay the ridge with fog lying over it like a blanket. And by his side stood Samael, wings flapping.

"But Angel . . ." Marlowe protested, "Let me recant. Take whatever oath pleases His Satanic Majesty. Now. And let me join my players, Shakespeare and the rest."

Samael cocked his head. Black wings bated, closed, opened wide.

"You wish to abase yourself before my master, renounce all other lords? You wish life in death? Then wish harder. Truer."

And before Kit could answer, could finally capitulate, the angel of death took to the foggy air and disappeared.

Kit looked along the ridgetop with its shroud of fog, and down at his feet. He should have offered his soul again to Satan when they were face to face. Or offered all he'd once had with Will, even. Failing that, he should have asked for something simpler. He should have asked for a new pair of boots.

He sat down there, on the cold hard ground. Satan could not be bested. This darkest angel had contested against the

Almighty and led a third of the stars in heaven to revolt. So futile, to take up arms against Satan, be those arms as simple as the truth. Even so, a moment in Will's apartment had restored his faith in love. And love he yet did.

Something rolled against his foot. The skull, or *a* skull, came to rest against his instep. Same skull? Who could say? What was it trying to tell him? If it could speak, what would it say?

For a moment he thought to stomp it to pieces. But what effect would that have?

He craned his neck upward and saw Paradise turn her face away yet again. If Samael did not come anew to goad him or to get him, he would find a way back to Bankside and to the shatters of his Rose Playhouse. He would start anew. He'd seek out J, the most beautiful bible writer and bringer of Mercy, and ask her help in finding the way to say the right things to the Trickster.

If only he'd never written that hell was just a frame of mind, he'd not have earned such a fate. He picked up the skull and stroked it. Might it be warm? He couldn't tell. He lay it by his knee once more.

And as he sat, bereft of all but remorse, out of the fog again came three weyward Sisters. One, the harpy, was crying, "'Tis time, 'tis time."

That omen chilled him to the bone. He curled up there, unable to do more. He hugged his knees to his chest.

He tried to ignore the spectres, but down upon him they swept, all three witches. And lifted him up, into the fog and out again, to Bankside, to New Hell in all its despair, and to the doors of the Globe Playhouse, where his heart most wanted e'er to be.

The three left him there, backstage, foolish but free, as they rushed onstage to play their parts. No friends of Satan, these Weyward Sisters.

Then he heard it, a final incantation from the second witch to his bruised and battered soul: "For a charm of powerful trouble, /Like a hell-broth boil and bubble."

Perhaps Kit could employ such a recipe for joy or powerful trouble, if he dared, although its results might be beyond his ken. After all, he had naught to lose and all to gain in an afterlife where fair was foul and foul was fair. So he would try it.

*

"I thought I bade you take Marlowe for a walk," said the Trickster to the angel of death as they stood on Pandemonium's grandest parapet. "He is a bad dog and must be tamed. Did you walk him?"

"Yea, my lord," said Samael.

To Satan's left unfolded the past; to his right awaited the future; and where he stood with Samael was this moment of reckoning, perhaps for some, perhaps for all in an underverse grown unmanageable. Mighty Diabolos was owner of all the souls overrunning his fiefdom. Here once more he saw that no creature as insignificant as Christopher Marlowe could possibly have made the latter-day hells shiver to their bedrock with calumny and rebellion. But shiver they did. It was time to bring not only Marlowe, a lowly spy, but Erra, his spymaster, to heel. Satan could obliterate Marlowe in a heartbeat, but Erra had been sent down by the Almighty. Erra had his champions Above, so Satan must tread carefully where Erra and his minions were concerned.

"Marlowe?" said Samael. "I did, sire. I took him for the walk as you ordered. Marooned him on the blasted heath—again,"

"Then why is Master Marlowe at the Globe?" Satan asked, exasperated, his dark wings rising and the rest of him close behind. "And there with so many of his cohort, partners in crime?"

"Fates!" Samael nearly spat. "These are those same Fates who pay you no heed, Majesty, and never acknowledge my commissions. They turn New Hell on end, playing fair where foul is law. Command me, beautiful prince. Let me obliterate this Marlowe. Let me extirpate Shakespeare for the pleasure of it, and consign all their plays to infernity's sewers. But first and foremost, let me kill Marlowe before his rebellious nature spreads like yet another plague." Samael pleaded with the devil as they stood spread-legged until the fumes arising from Phlegethon made them dizzy.

Satan took a deep breath. No sweet vapors could change his mind. "Tell me of these Fates."

"Yes, Majesty. The Fates may appear as witches, or as creatures from another realm. They answer not to us, nor even to those Above, but freely mix in the affairs of mortals and the dead, or even the doings of such as Erra. But do remember that where the Fates go, will come Hekate, goddess of witchcraft with all her wiles."

Since before the dawn of time, Samael had followed Satan, even into revolt against the Almighty and the eternal penance that followed. The devil could not, would not, demote his angel of death for being unable to govern the machinations of puny souls due their comeuppance. So he said to his stalwart, "Then make sure Marlowe attends the cast party. I will see to him myself, there. And come you, yourself, to see how even Fates and the rankest mystics can serve us.

Now go, Samael, and shower my mighty displeasure upon the damned!"

"With delight, Great Deceiver." In a thunder of wings, Samael arced upward into the fiery night. Satan stared after his minion, then down at the river Phlegethon, smoking below with a new stench, too sickly sweet by half and spreading wide. He must find some way to set to rights this debacle of impertinent damned and overreaching spirits. This woe had been composed in large part by Erra, the Babylonian plague god. And he and his Seven would answer for it.

*

The cast party for *Macbeth* soon overflowed its bounds. All had been warned to call it 'the Scottish Play' or risk incurring its legendary curse, first laid upon it when a working witches' coven decried Shakespeare's use of real charms and spells. To avoid misfortune, all invited to the opening night fête were required, once entering the playhouse, to leave again immediately, spin round three times, spit, knock once more on the theater's door and ask to be re-admitted.

But Kit had skipped such formalities. This production party would fare no different from the hundreds he'd survived. Or so he thought.

And thus far, all had gone as well as a play in hell might.

Last to arrive, Marlowe watched from backstage, and there found himself face to face with Hekate, who smiled as wide as forever and said, "Master Marlowe, O well done, I commend your pains, and everyone shall share i' the gains." Since those words were quoted from Hekate in the play itself, Kit was touched to the quick.

"Queen Hekate," Kit breathed, "we're honored. May I escort you round the cast party?"

The queen of witches stuck out her arm like a bird's and by her elbow he led her forth, until the three Fates could be felt around her. Not seen. Not known. But felt, like the breathing of the spheres. No one, he thought, could pay undo attention to him with a grand mystical witch by his side.

Cast and crew and patrons mixed, while Orpheus' musicians played for the house. Soon enough, Hekate was swept away among eager well-wishers.

Having lost her and the aegis she offered, Kit drifted to the apron stage. And from there, on the balcony above, he saw Will at last.

Climbing through rigging when he must, 'mongst props and costumery, Kit ascended deftly toward his last sight of Will. He must have blinked. He blinked again and no Shakespeare was there.

Kit turned to find himself a spot among Orpheus' ensemble in the balcony, but a velveted form with one wing spread and the other enfolding Shakespeare barred his way.

"Diabolos," Kit whispered, "I am here for Shakespeare's sake." He tried to catch the playwright's eye, to no avail, so spoke boldly: "Will, I have a gift for you."

Will made him no answer, nor looked his way, as if he were some figment, some ghost. Desperate, Kit stared hard in the Bard's eye but summoned no recognition there. *Will?* Beyond and above and all about the cast had gathered, so many friends from living days to these, eating and drinking here where Satan's caterer provided palatable food and drink. "Will? Devil, let him see me, hear me. Please."

"What do you offer, Marlowe, for some time with your so-called friend, whom you sold to me thrice over, spying for Erra and his loathsome thugs?"

"Greatest of Princes, I didn't . . . I mean, I have nothing to offer, with not a bit of soul my own." He wished as hard as ever he'd wished before, wished for J, emissary of Mercy in this foulest place, to tell him what to say.

As if hearing his thoughts, Satan said, "No Mercy will be enough Mercy. You sold news of me, spoke disrespect for me, and have even traded me your own plays, forever. What have you left? What will you give to me now, so that Shakespeare can once again see you, hear you, play with you in your attic lovers' nest?"

"What have I? I'll give you all that a soul might have," Kit said without thinking. "I am well supplied with nothing. Name it, Lord. What's mine is already yours, free and forever. Anything. Everything I have, under any guise, or any name. How can I make amends? The skull, that I found and brought hither? Would you take that in trade?"

Satan's eyes widened. "I'll have that skull you claimed for the finding." In the Adversary's hands, the skull appeared. And as they spoke, the devil stroked it.

What value then, the skull from the heath? Kit no longer tallied cost. He wanted with every fiber of his being only to see recognition in Shakespeare's eyes. "Yes, Devil. Yours the skull and every farthing I command to see Will as he is, as he should be, full of wit and story."

Satan lifted the wing he'd curled around Shakespeare. As if released from sleep, Shakespeare said, "Marley," and stumbled one step toward Kit.

"Not yet, Shakespeare. Bide and learn," said the devil, and: "To cavort and scheme and be with your Shakespeare once more, Marlowe, you will give me not only that skull of yours, but much more. You will continue your mad game with Erra and the Sibitti and turn every trick of theirs to my service. You will continue to play the spy for Erra and run to me like a puppy with Erra's every plan. Beginning now."

Spying for Satan was a cost Kit had never counted. He'd been hoping to reconcile with Shakespeare and reunite with J the Merciful, but saw instead a dread vision, a presentiment of Erra in his rainbowed vestments, shining beyond the devil's risen wings. Foreboding wracked him.

"Beginning *now*," Satan clarified, "you will continue as Erra's tattler, yet bring his every scheme to me posthaste. So not only the skull which once was yours but now, too, all chance of serving those Above is lost to you. Forever." Satan stepped to one side, and Samael stood there, grinning, writing words into a shimmering journal.

The angel of death intoned, "All Marlowe's givens now belong to our lord, Satan, forever and ever, until infernity runs out."

William Shakespeare shuddered, moved another step, rubbed his eyes, and said, "Marley! So glad you came. We've been missing you lately, your sharp wit and knowing ways." The Bard strode forth and embraced Marlowe like a lover.

Kit stood still, shocked through and through at Satan's revelations: that the skull the devil fondled was none other than Kit's very own, and more, that he must now run to Satan with all Erra's machinations.

And more.

Satan said, "Shakespeare, your dear friend Marlowe will play Banquo in all subsequent productions of *Macbeth*. We'll send someone around after each performance to collect Banquo's head and reunite it with Kit's person."

With a flash and a flutter of wings, the devil and the angel of death departed.

And that was a good thing, since Shakespeare was dragging Kit by the hand over to Erra, who was fully incognito, costumed as Lady Macbeth. The plague god smirked and nodded his welcome.

"We'll soon have you set up as Banquo, Kit. And still in league with Erra in your other game," Shakespeare gloated. He well knew what accommodation Kit had made to help the emissary from Above. Kit once had thought that path might lead to freedom. Now he knew better.

"Will," Kit said, "my only 'game' is love. Stay you by me, Shakespeare, for I have given every drop of my heart for thee."

"That's a good line, Kit. We must remember to use it."

Kit promised to do that, but he felt an ectoplasmic hand upon his skull as somewhere in hell the devil stroked it. And he shivered. When Kit next played Banquo, losing his head in *Macbeth*, it was going to hurt like holy hell.

The Come Right Inn

Andrew P. Weston

'Tis said the soul of mortal man recoiled,
To view Black Annis' eye, so fierce and wild,
Vast talons, foul with human flesh, there grew,
In place of hands, and features livid blue,
Glared in her visage, whilst her obscene waist,
Warm skins of human victims close embraced.

Not without terror they the cave survey
Where hung the monstrous trophies of her sway,
'Tis said that in the rock large rooms were found,
Scooped with her claws beneath the flinty ground.'

John Heyrick – 1797

Bruised, battered, and thoroughly despondent, Isaac Darkin lowered his head into his hands and accepted the inevitable. "I'm lost!"

He knew it. The hell-owl looking down at him from its perch knew it. And by now Bison, his trusty old mongrel waiting impatiently at home, would also be blissfully aware of that fact too.

Isaac could imagine his supper sitting on a plate at this moment. It wouldn't be there for long. Bison didn't eat like other dogs. Why waste time chewing when you could inhale food directly into your stomach? Pity, it was moldy thirteen-day-old blood-sausage and only slightly browned greens tonight. Isaac's favorite. And when Isaac Darkin didn't show up . . .?

It was Isaac's own fault. He'd insisted on one last hunting trip into the Sable Swathe before the acid rains blew in. You could never be sure how long they'd last at this time of year, and with the way things had been since the Sibitti had stirred up the unnatural order, you couldn't rely on CIN's weather forecasts either. Food was food, rancid or not, and he'd wanted to ensure his meager larder was well stocked before the storms hit.

Idiot!

Both he and his longtime associate and fellow highwayman in life, Louis Mandrin, had moved into the abandoned, beat-up old cottage on the edge of the largest forest in the medieval era of the Juxtapose level of hell only last year. The previous occupants hadn't liked living in proximity to the fey-folk from other realms who seemed drawn to the dark expanse, and had been so desperate to get away, they simply upped sticks and left. That raised not a glimmer of sympathy from Isaac. Though frozen at only twenty-one years of age, he'd been habituated by his experiences, before and after his condemnation, and had more than tripled his tally of killings since arriving in the underworld. That didn't mean he was complacent, of course. Murder was the number one pastime here, and Isaac came to appreciate the fact that, as hard as he was, there was always someone nastier out to take advantage.

As such, he and Louis made a pact early on. Stick together. Trust no one. Stay out of the way of other denizens. And never—*ever*—stray too deeply into Black Annis' territory.

Nobody in this part of hell knew for sure if the stories about the old crone living at the center of the forest were true. Some said the hag was a mystic. Others, a younger woman burnt at the stake for being a witch. Most thought the legend a tall story designed to keep busybodies and outsiders at bay. No matter which version people tended to believe, several details never wavered. Black Annis was not to be crossed; she had a taste for human flesh; and she would tan the skins of those she ate before wearing them around her waist.

One thing was for sure. Any of mankind's damned who were foolish enough to wander the hidden paths of the Sable Swathe were never seen again, in any incarnation the Undertaker might devise. And that was where Isaac and Louis' approach paid dividends, for, by and large, they'd been left alone.

Yes, they would spot the occasional Dread-Lock hovering around the outer fringes of the tree line now and again. Or more rarely, the shadow of something larger lumbering past the edge of their fields at night. Regardless, folks about these parts were more sensible than those in Olde London Town and the other, more developed parts of Juxtapose. Everyone was in the same boat, sentenced to an eternity of suffering without hope of reprieve. So, instead of complaining about their lot, denizens here got on with unlife and managed their own burdens to the best of their ability.

In Isaac's case, he's been cursed to hang himself to sleep every night. It was just as bad for Louis, who wouldn't 'live' to see the disgusting pall of Paradise each day unless he shot himself through the heart at midnight on the dot.

That being said, by remaining wary and always sure to stay within a mile of the unofficial boundary, the other forest dwellers cut them some slack. No, they weren't neighborly. If anything, they were rather distant and aloof. But at least things had been relatively peaceful for several months. A point that made Isaac's current predicament all the more annoying.

Having never ventured into the Sable Swathe, he didn't know what lay within. The trees in hell were hideously warped and parasitic in many cases. Sickamores, witch elms, blackthorns. And cat-o-nine birches that could strip the flesh from unprotected arms. A clear path could quickly become a confusing tangle of boughs and bushes, of undergrowth and ferns that nipped at the ankles and pulled at clothing. The swathe was densely packed and difficult to extract yourself from if you strayed too far.

And straying too far was never a good idea.

Well, now I know.

Several hours previously, Isaac had caught sight of a splendid stag in an unexpected clearing. It was still late afternoon. The forest was alive with hooded crow song, sickadas and the dazzling display of cutterflies, and the thicker clouds hadn't quite rolled in to obscure Paradise's grace. Chewing lazily on a mouthful of wilted clover, the stag presented itself to him, bold as brass, a vision of magnificence. With its bullish chest, freakish spray of antlers, and blood-red eyes, it stood defiant, staring directly at Isaac, as if daring him to shoot it.

Needless to say, Isaac was happy to oblige. It would mean stalking a little farther into the woodlands than usual but because he'd seen no sign of habitation nearby, he was sure the animal was fair game. Raising his bow, he'd no sooner taken aim, than the buck snorted brimstone from its nostrils, sprang into the air and charged. Taken by surprise, Isaac let fly, only to watch his arrow sail serenely past the beast's head. By the time he was able to snatch another one from his quiver, the stag was upon him.

Isaac tried to dive out of the way, but somehow his tunic became entangled in a face full of needle-tipped antlers, and he'd been dragged even deeper into the forest before being knocked unconscious.

Coming around only a few minutes ago, he'd found himself lying beside a weather-beaten track overgrown with thistles and razor-sharp bleed-weeds. Paradise had either waned or was about to. The developing gloom quickly congealed around him, reducing already scant visibility to next to nothing.

That's when the owl arrived. Hooting its displeasure, it watched indifferently as Isaac scrabbled painfully around on the forest floor, feeling for his scattered belongings and trying to clear his head.

A thin gap in the canopy followed the course of the path. Cutting its way through the trees like a scar, the break provided a meager light to see by. Overhead, purple-blue clouds clenched their brows and the first drops started to kiss the ocean of midnight-green, creating a sibilant hiss among the pitter-patter of rain on acid-resistant leaves.

Isaac quickly gave up. It was too dark. There was no way he would ever find his longbow or quiver in these conditions. Desperate for some form of protection, he ran his hands down his body and was relieved to discover his hunting knife still secure in its sheath and his travel purse still attached to the belt loop he always wore. It only contained a few diablos but they might go a long way in getting him home.

Continuing his investigation, Isaac was amazed by the number of rents and tears in his clothing. Some still housed the barbs and thorns that had caused so much damage. Gasping, he picked them loose as best he could and ascertained he was covered in a multitude of cuts and abrasions. So many that he doubted he'd ever be able to leech the numbing ache from his bones. *Stupid, stupid, stupid! Why did I have to push my luck?*

Running a thumb across his fingernails, Isaac checked to see how many had been ripped away. *Too many.*

When he dabbed the bloody tips against his tongue, an unsavory copper taste caused him to pull a face and spit.

The rain began to fall more heavily, making the woodland sound as if it were filled with myriad competing drums, each percussive rhythm vying to be heard above its neighbor. Nearby, a hell-toad started its twilight serenade, chiding Isaac as it relished the worsening conditions.

Seven shades of shite! "What the hell am I going to do now?" he shouted into the darkness, immediately regretting his rash outburst.

Up above, the owl shrugged as if answering Isaac's question before turning its back and abandoning him. He'd never felt more alone and held his breath, peering into the gloom for all he was worth, straining to pluck whatever advance warning he might from the tenebrous tapestry squeezing in to envelop him.

Then he had a crazy idea:

Ah, what the heaven! "Help!" he called. "Can anybody hear me? I'm not an intruder. My name is Isaac Darkin, a fellow denizen from the edge of the Sable Swathe. I suffered an accident before Paradise fled for the night and now, I can't find my way home."

As soon as he said it, he scolded himself. *As if anyone will hear me. Or listen. Or respond, unless they think I'm easy prey.*

Old tales came back to haunt him. In them, ill-fated travelers stumbled helplessly about in the inky blackness until fatigue claimed them. And once asleep, Black Annis would snatch them away to her cooking pot, adding their meat to her belly, their skins to her wardrobe, and denying the Undertaker his due.

Suddenly frightened, Isaac brandished his knife and edged slowly toward the only tree he felt confident enough to find. It seemed farther away than he remembered, but eventually his throbbing fingers touched wet and soggy bark. Breathing a huge sigh of relief, he leaned back against its wide trunk and slid down onto the moss in abject misery. Visions of a cozy hearth sprang to mind. By now, Bison would be stretched out in front of the fire, his belly full from Isaac's evening meal. Louis would be pottering about in the kitchen, polishing his pistol in preparation for their nightly ritual and wondering where in the blazes his usually dependable friend was. *Knowing him, he'll probably be twisting himself into a temper and try and shoot me as soon as I walk through the door.* He sighed and tried to judge the time. *At least I still have a few hours before I need to try and find something to hang myself with.*

Staring into a void and daydreaming about better things, it took him a moment to realize that he could actually see something ahead. At first, he thought it might be a floater in his eye. However, the faint blob of *nothing* continued to demand attention and gradually clarified into a pastel olive glow. The more Isaac looked, the more whatever it was bobbed in and out of the branches of a nearby sickamore like the pendulum of a clock.

Damn! It's so dark. I can't get a proper sense of perception. At least it's not a Dread-Lock come to feast on my fear.

The luminance got closer. As it did so, it was joined by another. Then one more. Further sprites appeared, streaming from behind leaves and thickets in a plethora of psychedelic carrot and viridian hues. A faint humming, similar to the drone emitted by bees when their hive is threatened, approached. In moments, he was encircled by a squadron of lightning-jacks, the likes of which he'd never seen before.

With huge black eyes, snapping mandibles and animated six-inch-long feelers, lightning-jacks were renowned for their foul tempers. And they could back up that temper with radiant orangy-brown bodies armed with clawed legs that were a bugger to get off once they'd hooked on, and fang-sized stingers that dripped iridescent green venom.

But these specimens were even larger and—if possible—more menacing, despite the fact they seemed content to thread intricate patterns in the air, as if urging Isaac to get up and follow them. The buzzing became more insistent. Isaac didn't know if that was due to his reticence to act or the steady increase in rainfall. All doubt was squashed when, after refusing to budge for a good few minutes, his newfound *friends* decided to take matters into their own hands. Several of the larger specimens, with tangerine flashes along their thoraxes, alighted on his arms, latched on, and commenced tugging at his sleeves. *No friggerty way! Perhaps someone did hear me after all.*

It seemed fate, or a more sinister malevolence, had made his mind up for him. *At least I'll be able to see where I'm going now. And really, what else am I going to do?*

Having struggled to his feet, Isaac was shepherded along at a dizzying pace. Thankfully, the sheer volume of his swarming escorts illuminated the path sufficiently to prevent him from stumbling too often. Nonetheless, exhaustion, adrenalin and an increasing sense of bewilderment soon had him panting for breath. The Sable Swathe was a maze of twists and turns that confused the eye and any comprehension of which direction he might be headed in.

"Stop!" he gasped, pressing the stitch at his side. "Please. Just for a moment. I'm not feeling at all well and need to go more slowly."

The droning increased for a moment, then fell away, giving Isaac the impression that a greater intelligence had exerted its will. He needn't have worried. When the lightning-jacks started up again, he was abruptly pulled sideways along a narrow game trail he hadn't oreviously appreciated. Blustering through a thicket of grumbleweed, he was then deposited on a wide path with a choice of three routes.

A cracked and peeling wooden sign, edged in fading gold leaf, sat in the middle of the little junction. It read:

The Come Right Inn
Only Two Shakes of a Lamb's Tail Away
Wailing Pies Our Specialty

Isaac's face lit up. A tavern! Who the devil would set up shop in a place like this?

He decided then and there he didn't really give a toss. *I'll have light, company and a degree of comfort in which to throttle myself to sleep.*

And just like that, the trees didn't appear so sinister anymore. However, he was a long way from home in the middle of what was purported to be Black Annis' territory. Respectful or not, he didn't want to push his luck where the fey-folk were concerned. Even legends could rear up and bite you when you least expected it here in hell, so the sooner he could get off the road, the better. In any event, untamed reavers might be abroad. Worse still, now that night held sway, it would be easy to run into a demon or even a soul-shredder hungry for more than blood.

Isaac felt the gash on his head. It was only just starting to scab over. One of them might be tracking me right now and I'd never know until it was too late. I've heard soul-shredders can prevent your essence from returning to the Undertaker.

He shivered at the prospect of simply ceasing to exist. No, risky or not, it would be even more dangerous to stay out in the open in such a dismal and desolate place. The Come Right Inn it is then. . .

. . . But how do I get there?

As if sensing Isaac's thoughts, two of the fattest lighting-jacks landed on his cuff. Lifting his hand, they gently lowered it onto the notice. It was surprisingly smooth to the touch and he ran his fingers along the grain. He caught a splinter, opening one of the deeper cuts on his thumb. A dark smear now stained part of the gold leaf. He bent to wipe it away with his sleeve, but a gleam of light caused him to snatch back his hand. Ringed in a verdant bloom, the bloody stain evaporated with a hiss.

Isaac's kaleidoscopic escorts acted as if that was their signal to depart. Within moments, they were whirling around his head in an ascending vortex. As they disappeared into the canopy, their inner luminescence winked out, leaving him in the dark once more.

He slowly circled on the spot, expecting something to jump out almost immediately. Oh great. What do I do now?

A musical tone drew his attention.

Not five yards away, a large red and white toadstool glimmered warmly in the shadows. By its radiance, he could barely make out the fringes of the central pathway. Aha!

He walked forward expectantly. No sooner had he reached it, than it blinked out. As it did so, another chime from further along the same trail announced the position of his next marker; this one, a scarlet and yellow specimen on the opposite side of the track. It swayed gently from side to side, dancing to music beyond his comprehension.

He quickened his pace.

As before, the ethereal beacon faded the moment he arrived. An accompaniment of splintering ice flakes tinkled forth, and a cluster of delicate midnight-blue mushrooms throbbed to life amid a freckling of glittering stars.

Gradually, the process repeated itself, over and over, until Isaac was swallowed by the all-encompassing maw of the forest.

*

At last, the track widened, the undergrowth and foliage fell away, and Isaac's destination appeared before him. A natural green phosphorescence filled the air. By its light, he saw four roads converging on a wide sandstone hillock in the exact center of the clearing. The hillock was guarded by an ancient oak and surrounded by a low, chain-link fence. A brightly illuminated sign stood proudly at the end of a dandelion-lined pathway. It said:

The Come Right Inn
Wailing Pies Our Specialty

I'm obviously at the right place then!
He'd never seen such a welcoming sight. Stoutly built of stone and timber, the tavern protruded from the hummock like a carbuncle and stretched up over three floors high. A gabled roof gave way to turrets at each corner. While most of the upper-story windows were dark, those on the ground floor thrown open in defiance of the weather. Not that it mattered, for a wide, wraparound porch lined the entire building.

A warm ruddy light spilled out into the night, together with the sounds of music and laughter, and the occasional clatter of cups. *But . . . but this isn't like hell at all?*

Turning full circle, a suspicion surfaced at the back of his mind. *Are the tales about the Sable Swathe even true, or are they a bit of skillful scaremongering to keep other denizens away from places like this?*

Enthralled, Isaac started toward the veranda and only then noticed a huge, overweight cat on the bottom step. Sitting motionless, her feminine, feline features gave the appearance of someone completely in command of an awkward situation. She studied him with obvious suspicion and the closer he got, the more her tail began to swish angrily back and forth, creating a wash of aniseed fumes.

"*Pssst, pssst, pssst!*" he called, holding out his hand in an offer of friendship.

Predatory amber eyes stared back. Shrewd and penetrating. With a graceful flick of her paw, she commenced washing her face, dismissing him as irrelevant.

"You'll have to excuse the Lady Porcupine," an unexpectedly confident and resonant voice declared from the shadows. "She can be a little prickly with people she doesn't know. Especially the damned of humanity. We don't often get your kind stopping by."

Startled, Isaac jumped and looked toward the top step. A sylphic silhouette remained shrouded in darkness close to the main door.

"I'm can appreciate that," he mumbled in apology. "It's quite a scary place to be. And although I've done my best to be civil toward my more . . . exotic neighbors, I've always kept my distance. Begging your pardon, lady, but I don't know your customs, and I've always found its better to be safe than sorry."

A chuckle, surprisingly deep and throaty rumbled out of the gloom. "Ah, yes. You own the croft that borders my land, don't you?"

She knows about . . . hang on? My *land!* This *is Black Annis?*

Sudden fear gripped him as a multitude of tales—all with bad and bloody endings—came flooding back. Yet something stymied the panic about to send him running blindly back into the viridescent maze. The woman's tone had been far from menacing, and if he judged her posture right, she seemed to be pondering something.

Thinking on his feet, Isaac replied, "That's right. My companion and I keep to ourselves, as I say. And if you're as astute as I think you are, you'll know I'm here by accident. Please, don't think me rude. I do appreciate the fact you sent your familiars to assist me, but I have to be back in time to hang my–

She lifted a long and slender hand to cut him off. "You need not concern yourself about such things while under my aegis. Though the Undertaker's reach is extensive, my service to the crown carries considerable weight. Weight and exclusivity sufficient to sway the fey and ward you from misfortune . . . if your spirit is willing, that is."

"If I'm willing?" Isaac didn't know what to say. "You mean you'd let me stay the night before venturing home?" He lifted his money pouch, "I'm not carrying a lot of coin, for I was out hunting. But I'm prepared to work off any debts I incur."

"Are you now? That's good news indeed," the voice replied, its owner stepping out into the light at last.

A striking, alien beauty stood before him. At well over six feet tall, her mane of raven hair fell about her shoulders like a shawl, accentuating the cobalt hue of her skin. Finely wrought features and an alert, almost feral posture gave her a regal appearance. Her dress was fashioned from homespun wool. And apart from her apron, which hung about her slender waist like a curtain of molten candle wax, everything about her conveyed a sense of quality.

The sternness of her ice-chip countenance was compensated for by a friendly smile and milk-white teeth. Bowing formally, she announced, "I am Agnes, your host, and I am delighted you happened upon my humble hostelry."

As if on cue, the sound of carousing from inside grew much louder.

Isaac was drawn to the ruckus, despite his reservations. "It would seem your patrons are enjoying themselves? Are you sure my being here won't dampen everyone's spirits?"

"On the contrary," Agnes replied, clasping him firmly by the shoulders and ushering him forward. "Your presence is expected."

Answering the inquisitive look on Isaac's face, she glanced behind her into the forest and explained, "We're mystical creatures here, one and all. What humans might view as metaphysical or paranormal . . . occult even, in the realm above. My minions are dotted throughout the Greshwin Weald—Sable Swathe, as you call it—to let me know who's coming to dinner. Most of my clients are a boisterous, if somewhat freakish, lot who also keep themselves to themselves and haven't seen a human in years. But fear not. While they're under my roof, they're consigned to behave on pain of obliteration. And to tell the truth, they're dying to meet you. Especially as my signature dish is back on the menu."

"Signature dish?"

"Yes, the wailing pies. As you can imagine, because of where I'm situated, and my odd . . . *reputation*, it's difficult to get the right ingredients. But we've been blessed tonight."

A distant rumble warned against expanding on such a blasphemous phrase.

Isaac glanced up at the canopy and dubiously rummaged through the scant diablos rattling about in his purse. "Will I have enough?"

"Don't worry…?" She resolutely ignored the accompanying echo of thunder and interrogated him with a frank and searching gaze.

"Isaac," he replied quickly, catching her inference.

"Then don't worry, Isaac. As I said, your presence here in this out of the way, damned neck of the woods is something of a novelty and everyone will want to celebrate. I don't get to spend much time at home, and you've ensured a large crowd has assembled. The least I can do is make your stay as pleasant and as comfortable as hell allows." She stepped in through the door and swept her arms wide, "Please, come right in."

"Thank you. That . . . that's very kind. I won't forget this." Stepping across the threshold, Isaac was assailed by a wash of light, smoke, and heat.

A huge open hearth dominated the center of the chamber. A variety of unknown meats turned slowly on a spit, hissing and crackling as the fat dripped endlessly down into the flames below. A heady fragrance of urine, hops and yeast added an aromatic, ammonia-tinged haze to the already succulent atmosphere, making him salivate as soon as he entered.

Agnes hadn't been exaggerating about her clientele.

On the far side, a long counter stretched across the width of the room, obviously serving as the bar, behind which a harassed-looking ogre tried to keep tabs on the revelers. Along its front, all manner of sprites, demons, and ghouls in various states of inebriation, cavorted, sang, wrestled or played pranks on one another.

There was even a limikkin among them, transforming herself into all manner of disgusting and sickening apparitions at the urging of her drinking buddies. Her manifestations were rewarded by raucous toasts, cat-calling and praise from friends and onlookers alike, and the occasional retching of those overcome by her best efforts.

In front of them, the spaces were packed with parishioners of all shapes and sizes. Here, an aged mystic with a long white beard, singed in many places, smoked an ornate pipe carved from what Isaac was sure was pure gold. After every draw, he exhaled an unusual purple colored smoke that wove intricate shapes through the air. It would circle him and worm its way inside one of his ears, causing him to swell and belch loudly. His eyes bulged on every occasion, turning a luminous shade of violet for just a moment, until he deflated back down onto his seat. There, on the very next table, a group of oversized Grumbles were playing a game of cards. Two of them were snacking on the contents of a satchel positioned on the floor between them. Whatever it was, they stuffed it repeatedly into their mouths, crunched loudly.

A group of marids and effrits had crowded around the fire. Elemental beings, they passed the time by teasing each other. The effrits would immerse their hands into the flames and set themselves ablaze, only to have their friends shoot them with jets of water.

Considering them closely, an old crone on a nearby creaky rocking chair cackled to herself. Whenever she got too carried away, the squeaking wood and her guttural laughter would reduce her to fits of coughing. Mesmerized, Isaac watched as the huge wart on the end of her nose danced across her face and onto her neck to get out of the way. Only once the bout had passed would it slowly begin to edge back toward its former position.

Some of the tinier fey were content to frolic in the shadows up in the rafters, shooting at each other with sprays of prismatic dust motes that sparked like lightning.

Isaac found the sight overwhelming. He stood there in the doorway with his jaws agape, unashamedly staring.

Then, all at once, they noticed him.

A huge cheer erupted from every throat, causing him to take a few steps backward. The air shimmered, and a tankard of frothing ale appeared in his hand. "Thish one ish on meee," someone yelled from the bar area. One of the demons was jumping up and down on its stool. Thinking it might be his mystery benefactor, Isaac raised his beer and saluted it.

The demon returned the gesture, only to lose its balance and disappear behind the counter to the sound of breaking glass and laughter. A huge club appeared in the barkeep's paws, whereupon the miscreant suffered a vicious beating to a chorus of "oohs" and "aaahs" from his friends. A loud implosion marked the demon's demise, and the saloon erupted in applause.

Unholy shit! Why have Louis and I never braved the Swathe before? This place is . . . it's as close to perfection as we'll ever get. He grinned and Agnes embraced him once more, shouting to make herself heard over the ruckus, "I told you they'd make you feel welcome, eh? Now, would you like to get something to eat or would you like to wash up first?" Giving him the once over, she added, "Not to be rude, but you stink and need a good long soak."

A bath. "Is it okay to order something and clean up while it cooks?"

"An excellent idea." She beamed. Ushering Isaac through the press, Agnes somehow found a vacant table near a rear door and miraculously slapped a menu down in front of him.

Glancing at it, Isaac was dismayed to realize it was written in ancient Hellanese, a language he'd never been able to learn.

Guiltily, he muttered, "Agnes, I'm sorry. I can't read this. Just tell me what you've got or make a recommendation."

Adopting a pose, she thought for a moment, lingering only to reach out absentmindedly and cuff one of the Grumbles around the ear for farting in her general direction, before replying, "Well . . . we have a selection of piss-wines from the Vale of Quenn. Very nice, very light. They only destroy a couple of brain cells per serving. There are ales from the slave mines of Tomrog. Watch out though, they're quite potent, especially for humans. On the food side, there are singing toadstools, mostly of the fly agaric and skullcap varieties. Guaranteed to screw with your nervous system or fuck what's left of your liver and kidneys; fricasseed cutterfly in beetle juice; a particular favorite of mine, hissing rockcoach. Oh, and we have bat on a stick, cooked to your particular preference. Our roasts include Perishiennes, fornicators and disgraced Blue Suits. But if you're not used to them, they'll turn your stomach inside out."

Isaac balked. "I don't want anything too heavy or spicy, if you don't mind. Not after the night I've endured." Then he had an idea. "What about a slice of that wailing pie you mentioned? It sounds rather intriguing?"

The room went quiet as all heads turned toward him.

"What?" he asked, abruptly self-conscious. "Did I say something wrong?"

"Not at all," Agnes replied. "It's just that humans *in-the-know* don't usually show much interest in our signature dish."

"Well, I'm not *in-the-know*." he snorted, defensively, "as this evening has clearly shown. If we're going to be closer neighbors, you need to let me make my own mistakes. This is hell, after all. The quicker I learn, the less painful it'll be."

One of Agnes' brows arched upward. Then she nodded, as if acceding he'd made a valid point. She turned to face the room and gestured Isaac's way. A roar of approval rang out to the accompaniment of table drumming and tankard thumping.

Shrugging her shoulders, she looked him straight in the eye and said, "Okay, wailing pie it is. How about we get you scrubbed up now?"

Isaac made to follow his host through to the bathrooms which were situated at the rear of the premises. On the way, he was forced to run a gauntlet of backslapping, handshakes, "bravos" and "good on yers."

This is like a dream come true. I can't believe how badly people have misjudged them. I'll have to bring Louis here tomorrow and introduce him to everyone.

The back rooms proved to be a surprise. They didn't exist. Instead, a twisting flight of well-paved steps descended into what could only be described as an underground grotto.

The roof was a dome of intertwined branches and vines that had wound down from the oak tree above. Those roots were lit from within by threaded strands of luminescent spider silk. The walls were a combination of warm peat and steaming moss, glowing with effervescent veins of gold and copper radiance. In the middle of the room, a hot spring bubbled invitingly, streaming with vapor trails that wafted a subtle sulfurous fragrance throughout the air. Despite the mist, the water itself was crystal clear. Isaac could see shallow depressions had been fashioned into the circumference of the rock below, obviously to be used as a means of seating.

"Oh yes!" he mumbled, staggering forward and divesting himself of his rags as quickly as possible.

A polite cough from behind reminded him he wasn't alone.

Using her fingertips, Agnes picked up his clothes and held them at arm's length. "I don't think you'll need *these* any longer?" she said, wrinkling her nose. "They're more holes than fabric now. Don't you worry, though. I'll sort you out with something much more appropriate. You'll see." As she turned to leave, she added, "And I'll have a refreshing drink brought down too. On the house. Can't have you nodding off, can we, when everyone's expecting you upstairs."

"Thank you, Agnes," Isaac mumbled, dismissing her fretting and fussing almost immediately as his anticipation for urgent respite mounted.

More exhausted than he realized, Isaac shuffled toward the edge of the spa. Dipping his toes into the water, he smiled. *Oh, that's marvelous. How did I know it would be the perfect temperature?*

Easing himself in, he settled down onto one of the seats and, after lacing his fingers together behind his head, leant back, ensuring to hook his thumbs over the lip at the edge of the pool. No sooner had he shut his eyes than his knuckles brushed against something cold.

Surprised, he craned his neck and discovered a chilled goblet containing some form of sparkling beverage had already been delivered. *Wow! That was fast.* He chuckled. *The service here is top-notch. I wonder where all the hype came from that said this place was dangerous?*

Isaac lifted the drink high and watched as beads of condensation trickled down the outside of the glass. *Probably to keep the riffraff away. Powerful witch or not, if word got out a five skull tavern existed in the middle of the Sable Swathe, we'd have endless queues of vagabonds and wannabes traipsing through and raising merry hell.*

He shook his head. *No, Agnes has created just the right atmosphere. The less attention the better.*

Raising the flute to his lips, Isaac took a long draught. The bubbles tickled his nose, and the flavor of rosehip, liquorice, and hemlock infused his taste buds. In an instant, his mind was flooded with memories of flintlocks at dawn; of braying horses and barks of alarm; of coiffured ladies and outraged gentlemen; and finally, with the sense of a brisk gallop to freedom with saddlebags full of plunder.

Sighing, he lay back again and relaxed. As his eyelids fluttered closed, he was sure he caught sight of a glowing pair of amber eyes staring out from the corner of the room. Lady Porcupine had come to watch over him. *She likes me after all.*

*

With infinite lethargy, Isaac labored toward consciousness. His tongue felt heavy and still tingled to the taste of the ingredients within his cocktail. Floating lazily in a viscous medium of contentment and bliss, he was in no rush to move. *The spring must keep things at a constant temperature, day and night. Although, to be honest, it feels a little warmer than when I got in?*

Fighting himself awake, he tried to sit up. For some reason, his arms and legs refused to obey. Something bumped against the side of his head. Turning, he struggled to focus on the object bobbing next to him. *A carrot? What in the underworld is that doing here?*

He took a breath and swallowed a mouthful of thick, rich gravy. *I can taste onions!*

Attempting to rise again, Isaac became aware of others all around him. *I . . . I'm back in the main salon from the look of it. By the fire. But . . .?* Agnes' face loomed into view, an expectant cast setting her features in stone. "Wha . . . what's going on?" he gasped.

"I'm sorry, my friend," Agnes replied. "But I did say I'd been expecting you since you stumbled into one of my signs in the forest. It's been a long time since any of mankind's damned has strayed this way. So long, in fact, that I thought I'd have to change my signature dish."

She smiled, showing milk-white fangs and stood to one side as the Grumbles Isaac had seen playing cards earlier crowded forward. Between them, they were carrying a very large, yellow-colored, waxy film. One of them still crunched away on a tidbit. He grinned and his bloody teeth revealed what he'd been snacking on all night. *Human finger bones?*

Isaac glanced down, and saw his limbs were encased in some form of jelly.

A cold and empty feeling clutched at his bowels. "Agnes?" he snapped, "What do you mean, *change your signature dish?*"

The Grumbles positioned themselves at his feet and started lowering the covering into place, pressing it into position as they went.

Is that pastry? "Agnes," Isaac squeaked, louder this time, "Why are you doing this?"

"For two reasons." Her muffled reply held a note of finality. "Firstly, I am what I am, constrained to abide by the tenets by which His Satanic Majesty grants me power. Though I live in solitude and well away from the condemned of humanity, your nature ensures some will always find a reason to come snooping. When they do, I am allowed to feed myself, absorbing vitality to maintain the guise that men find so disarming. But fear not, the skins I collect retain sufficient puissance for the Undertaker to make his golems. How else do you think he fills the ranks of his mortuary? Secondly, if you remember, you insisted on being allowed to learn from your own mistakes. And tonight, Isaac Darkin, you will."

The savory lid closed above him. Isaac heard the rasping of many hands as it was fingered firmly shut. Then he felt the liquid sloshing about as he was lifted and carried a short distance. Metal scraped on metal, setting his teeth on edge. *They've put me over the fire on a roasting jack.*

The background hubbub resumed as tables were laid and the patrons settled in to wait for their meal to cook.

Within a few minutes, the gravy started to boil. Unable to move, Isaac threw back his head and wailed.

Abode of Woe

A.L. Butcher

Smoke curled in languid shapes, a hypnotic dance of gray and white with occasional belches of green. Some said smoke in New Hell was alive, or what passed for the myriad forms of existence in His Satanic Majesty's domain. Anyone watching might have seen a grinning maw, or bright orange eyes for a fleeting moment, but generally it paid not to examine things too closely in hell, lest one discover another monster or another reflection of one's own earthly sins.

The two people watching from the doorway of their establishment had little regard for such happenings; they were far more concerned with the monster of hell-stone rising on their doorstep. It was a behemoth, and not a happy one at that. Both onlookers were well aware of the sins history accredited to them, but they'd been here long enough to try to make the best of perdition. It was the only way to survive with one's sanity partially intact. Inconvenience was rife in New Hell and attempting to avoid it a game played daily, with varying degrees of success. The red-haired woman with the wild eyes stared, as though seeing what others could not.

Being a prophet in hell brought visions which made even the bravest cower under the bed.

Cassandra, daughter of a king and prophetess of Troy, whose visions had foretold the fall of the city-state, pronounced, "I see mayhem on our doorstep. And death. Everywhere I look I see death, but it does not take a seer to foretell that."

She stopped, gazing into the distance, and her voice went low. "That building will fall, and if it does, we will be the gainers, Calchas. I see it as a shell, nothing more, a giant hell-stone monster sinking into the mud. And one that will bring the customers our way. No one will dare attack or question us again. We will find some sanctuary with the spitter-of-fire and the bringer of death."

Calchas shrugged, "It's hell, we are all dead, child. And that fool Henry Prince will bring strife to our door, without a doubt. Why the Department of Disassembly and Destruction granted him that misplanning permission I have no idea, but it's ruining our business. No one wants to game with that noise melting the eardrums. Look at the damned place . . . it's ugly. That's not even a real temple.

"It has no finesse; temples are here for those brave enough to venture down that particular route." Calchas was not convinced the temple would be easy to get rid of and shook his head.

He called to a figure scurrying past their door in soiled monkish robes. "Assisi — what think you of yonder building? It shall kill business, think you?"

The monk paused and kicked at something near his foot. "That it will – and bring the rats, and the hell-cats and all manner of beasties. I hate animals, but they love me," the old man grumbled. He glared at the partially built monstrosity. "Tis ugly. Everything in Hell is ugly."

"Probably, but what is there to do, Assisi?" Calchas asked his neighbor, eying the man with some pity.

"Buggered if I know," responded the old fallen saint, and went on his way, shivering at the thought of all the hell-creatures on his doorstep.

The Trojan prophetess scowled towards the mayhem and the large crowd lurking, with some amusement, at the proceedings. "They will never finish it, believe me." She stopped. That was her curse—no one ever did believe her. "Two egos that large can only bring destruction. Trust me, I know. It will be their ruin, not ours; but we must help it along."

The old seer squeezed her arm. "No, buildings like that don't simply go away. It will lurk like a bubo – neither one thing nor the other. That Prince fellow has charisma, I'll give him that. And Smyth-Pigott, well . . . he seems to have more followers here. See there: the ones to the north. More women, too. He claims to be the Chosen One, or so I hear. There are many of his ilk – misguided and foolish but dangerous. I remember when prophets truly had the ear of the, um, immortals. It was not for greed or glory. Well, not always," he amended thinking of Agamemnon.

"How does one kill such a beast? Those worshippers are not our customers—they think us the sinners, and corruptors of men's souls. That man Prince claims he is the new antimessiah. And that leads to investigations from those lower down. Everyone is on edge as it is," Cassandra said, wrinkling her nose. She'd encountered far too many people chosen by one god or another and it usually had ended badly. "The women are not so much trapped by the men, as bound to them. Concubines or slaves perhaps."

Calchas thought it over. "They are New Dead, not like us. Such men as they kept no slaves, at least not as we would have done, as our old masters did. Concubines, maybe; or temple women—if they had them. We had them in our day, simply more recognized and more honored.

"Slavery keeps many forms, Cassandra, and its chains surround us all, one way or another."

They stood watching, as workers scurried like cockroaches around the building, and the scaffolding creaked in the hell-winds. Men carried stones the size of dogs on their backs and bowed under the weight. Smoke rose from the molten brew spewing from machines; and the stench of brimstone, dement and sulfur pervaded.

"We may have to move again, which is a shame as I like it here. Clytemnestra doesn't know where we are, and the ghost of that poor girl Iphigenia doesn't taunt me as much," Calchas grimaced. They could put up with the clientele, who did not ask too many awkward questions, left with nothing yet returned again and again. There was an element of safety here—at least relative to the usual misfortunes of hell.

Wistful, he continued, "Maybe we should offer one of those new blood prophets some 'advice' to go away. Men like that believe any old crap."

Cassandra shook her head. "Two men cannot hold the same land at the same time. Two egos cannot both reside in the same space. That leads to bloodshed."

"There's always room for arrogance, for falsehood and the lust for glory and revenge, especially in this infernal place, child. Hell is built on the foundations of men's folly." Calchas had not been surprised to find himself in hell, after the crimes he'd committed to please a king and placate a jealous goddess, but he had been surprised to find himself in this hell of hells. Apparently "I was only following orders" simply didn't cut the mustard in the Great Hereafter and all men's hells were as one. Cynicism, Agamemnon and

Clytemnestra's henchmen and a troubled soul had led him to travel around the various regions of the manifold hells seeking answers. It was a shame he did not know the questions.

Knowing he did not believe her, Cassandra sometimes wondered why Calchas asked for her counsel, although she knew the guilt he bore. The demons which followed Cassandra were in her head and sent by gods from ancient times, jealous and fickle. Calchas understood better than anyone, and so they had found themselves on the same lonely and rather confused path in the afterlife and became firm friends. Once on opposing sides in life, in afterlife they had meandered onward together in death and were now set in their ways and one another's company.

A cacophony rose: hammering, shouting, swearing, the screech of masonry being hauled upwards by gears which screamed with effort. It was chaos. But in New Hell chaos stalked many byways, and the drumbeat of Hades was deafening. Calchas swore and motioned his companion back inside. "Go within, girl. Let's try and manage what business remains to us. We need a plan, my dear."

They returned to the gaming tables – the sound was not much quieter within. He rubbed his ears and shook his head again. He could not stand much more of this hellish racket.

"Maybe advice is exactly what they need, or a challenge. Yes, men like that long to appear in charge, and in control to their followers. They do not like to appear as fools," she mused, the light of a scheme firing in her eyes. "Has that man from the ministry been in recently? He would be useful. We can get them gone and that awful temple, both."

"I'll not have you risk a trip to the Undertaker. We will pack up and move." Calchas had seen that look on the young seer's face before and he didn't like it, Cassandra took risks. Deep within he knew she was right; Cassandra was always right. But he could never admit it. It would not be the first time they'd moved on.

"Oh, it won't come to that. At least not for me. The blood I see is rarely my own. Trust me," Cassandra implored. "I *am* always right."

Calchas opened his mouth to protest but as he gazed at the looming monstrosity taking shape yonder, he shrugged. "What have you in mind?"

*

"Damn it, I can't focus on the cards with that awful racket going on. Haven't you heard of soundproofing here?" The speaker yelled over the din, eying his opponent and grimacing at his cards.

"What?" shouted the other man—a large individual sporting a Che Guevara t-shirt, torn jeans, and a beard down to his midriff.

"*Soundproofing.* To drown out the awful racket. You gonna fold or what?" the first speaker asked.

"Soundproofing in hell? That's having an ice-pick in the ears—ask poor old Trotsky—or possibly molten tar. I've heard that one is in favor these days. Annoying noise is part of the torment," the first player's opponent responded. "Besides I can concentrate—I used to play drums for a heavy metal band, and I can't hear much except the drums. Always drums."

The *Fiery Cauldron* was not one of New Hell's most prestigious gambling haunts, but it was popular, or at least had been, with a certain class of damned souls. Calchas, once seer of Agamemnon, King of Mycenae, now presided over those who sought respite from infernity in cards and games of chance. There were plenty of lost souls who had a diablo to spare, or a desperation severe enough to gamble in such dens. The house always wins—especially in Hell—and his foresight led him to be good at business. It helped to be able to predict who would win and who would lose. At least, were he not following some fool's orders, he added to himself. That's where the trouble lay—obeying the obsessed, idiotic or arrogant, and well the former seer knew it.

The odds are not fair in hell's gambling dens, no one ever leaves with more than when they entered. So he'd been told but did not entirely believe it. Calchas paid his dues to the correct authorities, and for the most part they left him alone, and thus he left better off in part—he kept no apartment save the small rooms behind the main building. He was a man with enemies, and it did not pay to court more among hell's bureaucracy. He abided by such rules that did not make him suffer too greatly and hid among the low-lives and the desperate with his borrowed names, borrowed clothes and foresight of his own.

He was a prophet who made a profit, he chuckled to himself. At first, he'd thought to model the place along the lines of the gaming dens of Ancient Greece, but that was too obvious, and those were two a diablo, next to the Roman whore-dens and the Egyptian-themed hell crack-houses, so he'd kept it decorated with flames—which sometimes really burned – and bad wall-paintings. Hell was hell and so still the gamblers came. Day after day. Sin paid.

Calchas looked around the smoke-filled den. For now, it would suffice as a refuge from those who hunted them, and his own dark and guilty dreams were torment enough. He'd not admit it but the girl Cassandra, barely into womanhood, brought him joy and sorrow—what joy as could be eked out in this infernal pit. He'd told himself he'd murdered another man's daughter at the whim of a warrior-king; this lost girl had been daughter to a king whose city was razed and family killed because Calchas had not been brave enough to defy his gods or his king. She was his blessing and his curse—for every time he saw her, or they conversed, their entwined fates hung between them. Ilios. Troy.

Yet she did not blame him, or at least he thought she didn't. Cassandra had plenty of inner demons, dark emotion twisted within that young body. She'd lived in hell when alive and this place was not a good deal worse for her; at least here, he mused, she was not alone.

*

At the table, Calchas viewed his cards. Not bad. Not good but not bad. Calchas' opponent was a ministry man, formerly a clerk who had covered up his employer's fraudulent dealings for a share of the money to spend on slot machines and dice. He was a minor sinner, of the sort that populated the Hellispheres in their millions.

Calchas kept a cadre of spies looking out for Agamemnon, Clytemnestra and their allies. Such favors came not cheap and he'd used them to find this particular patron and offer him a 'too good to be true' deal. Of course, the details of the deal had not been given until after the mark gave his consent.

The seer preferred dice, but Red-Hot Poker was not a bad game. It helped to be a foreteller in such games, and he could read men well enough. He rarely lost, unless it suited their purpose.

He glanced over to Cassandra who was serving drinks, watched her intense looks and occasional smiles at patrons. With the tiniest of gestures, he caught her notice. She stopped at their table and muttered to the man, "Hold and yea shall be rewarded."

"Fold. I'm done," said the red-eyed man in the grey uniform of the Department of Disassembly and Deconstruction. "You took my last diablo." He downed the dregs of many terrible drinks and gazed mournfully at the pile before Calchas on the pitted table.

"Two pair—eights and nines." Calchas grinned, eying the pile of diablos, bags of blood, an ear and three IOUs.

"Shit. I had a royal flush, spades of course!" yelled the man who'd folded. "My boss is going to skin me alive." He paled, not joking.

Cassandra placed the drink carefully on the table, spilling the rancid beer in hell usually meant replacing the table, or putting up with the acid-holes. "You should have held out. Men never listen; too easily do they think themselves the victor."

"Hey, how about a deal? I can get you the means to expand or let you in on what your neighbors are planning. I'm a big man in the Department of Misplanning and Deconstruction?" The man felt around in the nearly empty case at his feet. "Lessee . . . in the area you got a dealer in fake relics—that's old Assisi; two coffee joints—by joints I mean drugs; a fortune-teller in number seventeen, and three empties, but you know that already. Oh, and the Abode of Woe. That's the big place on the waste ground. Some posh English fellow, Prince Harry or something, wants that. I guess you've heard the noise, can't miss it? Thinks he's the new anti-messiah or something, I can't see the Prince of Lies abiding that for long, but it ain't my problem. I just sign the forms. Wait! Some other chap wants it too—and the plans have both been signed . . . oh, dear. Two buildings on the same plot. That ain't going to end well. There must be some mistake, or underhandedness. There will be a heap of trouble for someone."

"Is that so?" Cassandra asked, grinning. "That will be inconvenient."

"You think? It is, but it happens more often than you'd think, miss. Bureaucracy in hell is hell."

Calchas nodded sagely. Ever since that false prophet from New Hell had decided to try his luck in this part of town and build his 'temple,' Calchas' takings had gone through the floor. It was far more entertaining to watch the mischief and arguments going on at the partially built Abode of Woe. "A deal? What can you offer us?"

Cassandra grinned wider, an idea forming that might end their business problems once and for all. She gently put her hand on the Department man's shoulder, "Ah, a bargain! Let us discuss terms like civilized folk. I can see a long and profitable future for you."

The man shivered, "I doubt that, love."

"I am never wrong," Cassandra said.

*

The Abode of Woe would, in another place, have been a magnificent building. Indeed, it had been, in another life and another realm, but hell's malevolent touch marred everything. The late Reverend Henry Prince scowled as Paradise's unreachable light filtered dimly through a man-sized crack in the roof of the half-built temple. "Not good enough!" bellowed the man who had founded the Agapemonites. "Work harder, you damned fools!"

Angrily Prince aimed a kick at the scaffolding, which groaned in pain. He looked harder at it. The posts were yellowing and the length of a man's femur. He curled his lip in distaste. No wonder it was struggling to hold the rickety tower aloft. Bone scaffolding was not what he'd ordered. But then, he reflected, one rarely got what one requested. A pile of blood-red stones caught his attention as they were unloaded from a wagon. His temple was bone yellow—he'd hoped for a godly white, but everything tarnished here. And the stone, if stone it was, had turned the color of ancient bones. After the third batch had arrived, he'd given up and accepted it.

"What are they? That's another mistake. You—What is going on?" Prince bellowed to the man unloading the blocks.

"Delivery guv'nor. Got the docket 'ere. Six thousand Bleedblocks—delivered to Reverend Pig. I guess that's you, Father."

"Revered Pig? Father? You idiot, I am not a Catholic, and I am not a pig. I am the 'Abhorred One', the Reverend Henry Prince."

The delivery man looked him up and down. "Well, someone has to take them. I have a collection of skulls to make, and then the Undertaker wants his library book returned." With that the man pulled a lever and the wagon dumped its remaining cargo onto the ground.

"I just deliver. Sell 'em, eat 'em or build your 'ouse. I don't care. I've got the docket that says deliver them 'ere and that's what I have done." The man clambered back onto his van and drove off in a cloud of foul exhaust.

Henry Prince swore after him, and then kicked at the gently oozing pile. "Damn." He couldn't think of anything else to say and stomped off towards the workers. The old man glared at the coveralled workers scurrying like rats at the site. Some were human but not all. Or had been human. He despised workmen, but he could not raise this building by his own hand or the will of the god he'd once professed to follow. As with every other damned soul here, the Revered

Henry Prince had to make the best of the worst job. It wasn't easy.

In life he'd been a man of some power and influence. His disciples had styled him 'The Beloved One', or had it been a name he'd given himself? Prince could barely remember after so long. It mattered little here. In hell's gloomy domains he had been given the title 'The Abhorred One' and that was also true. As he muttered about the shoddy cement spewing from the mouth of a device of suspect workings, and the awful stink of brimstone which pervaded the environs, Henry Prince reflected that love and hate were, basically, the same—albeit approached from opposite directions. A bit like good and evil, he thought. Though of course down here evil held the trump card every time. He'd preached of Hell's fiery domains often enough, and committed enough sins, if truth be told. Sins which hadn't been sins at the time—at least not to him. Those women had come to him willingly, they'd brought their money and virtue to present at the Prophet's alter, and who was he to argue? He had been the New Messiah, the Chosen Lamb—it had been the truth then, or at least *his* truth. Sin was subjective, he'd once believed. Now he was a sinner in Hell, and this riled him more. He was not only another regular man; he was meant for more. Few here knew his name or his legacy. But he intended to change all that.

He'd been diametrically wrong in his sermons. The light which had finally called him to the afterlife was hell-light. Many of his followers muttered about his sanity. As bound to him as he to them, for the most part they'd followed him here. For better or worse, mostly worse. Reverend Prince had been a self-proclaimed messiah on Earth, and he had not given up this delusion in hell—where failed messiahs were a dozen a diablo.

"Why do we bother, Abhorred One? The crack will have reappeared by the end of the week." The speaker was a weary woman clad in overalls stained with something unmentionable. In hell it was best not to ask. She was plain and haggard, the sort of woman who had been attractive once, but years of strife had stripped away that beauty and hope and left a shell. She hadn't wanted to build in this area; there had been some difficulty with the Misplanning Permission and so they'd ended up near a run-down casino and a shop which sold fake relics to fools. But no one told the Abhorred One what to do. Louisa Nottidge knew that well enough. They argued, day in day out. Neither yielding. The passive obedience that once she'd known had evaporated long ago, with hope and love in swift pursuit.

They'd managed to acquire two plots for the price of one and she'd wondered why. Now she knew. Prince had told her they deserved what they got, and she was afraid this would turn out to be true. Bureaucracy in New Hell was red-tape central, and nothing ever went to plan.

"Sister-wife, we must keep up appearances! I am the Chosen One—the Son of Go–"

Louisa Nottidge's hand clamped across his mouth. "Do NOT say it. Not *that* name. Not ever. How do you think that vast breach got into the roof in the first place?" She yelled something at the workers trying in vain to drag a tarpaulin over the gaping hole before the afternoon's acid rain arrived. He tried to pull the hand away, his face puce with indignation. Fingers scrabbling at hers and indistinct cursing made Louisa remove her hand. "To think I loved you once. I must have been a bloody fool. I gave you everything: money; my virtue; my reputation; and I left my family. And all for *this…*?"

She turned back to directing the builders. Hindsight was glorious, and bitter. And Louisa had bitterness in abundance. She'd been a good woman, a virtuous fool and loved unwisely—this was her penance. She hated him, but their lots were bound together. Yet years of stubborn failure had made her determined to succeed if only once. To be right, once.

"How dare you, woman. Know your place! I can have you sent to the nut-house again. I am sure there is one here!" Prince snapped, puffed out a thin chest, and the black hat he habitually wore slithered across white unkempt hair. Smoothing his moustache, Prince sneered, "You remember that place? Imagine one here—all the crackpots of history gathered together. I am still the Leader of the Abode of Woe. I am the prophet, the cursed one."

Louisa scowled at him, "You bastard. You ungrateful cur! I should have stayed in that asylum. Anything is better than an eternity working for you to build this infernal structure." She wondered if a Hellish asylum would harbor anyone worse than those who surrounded her here today.

"Are you still the prophet? That isn't what I heard, Reverend." The slight carried across the hammering and bashing of workmen bent on repair and thwarted at every turn. "I see the building is going as planned," the speaker snickered.

"Go away sister. You are not wanted here," Louisa snapped to the woman who had approached. Her eyes rolled. Could that woman leave nothing alone? This was all Louisa needed. Muttering a very unladylike curse, she prepared for the battle she suspected would follow.

Agnes Smyth-Pigott nee Nottidge eyed her sibling smugly. She considered herself lucky, or as lucky as one in the Devil's realm could be – *her* man was the true heir to the Agapemonites, the true prophet. Not like this old, failing, fading charlatan. "We were just passing."

"Ha! No one 'just passes' here. You came to gloat," Louisa replied. Once she would have defended her man with every core of her being. Now Louisa's mind was her own and bitterness tempered love as swiftly as water tempered iron. But she could not, would not be bested by that stupid girl. She would not be held to account by her own sister. So she replied for her own pride and not Prince's: "This is our property. The Abode of Woe. From the Temple of the Fallen Agapemonites, get you gone." She glared at her sister, and the man who accompanied her.

"We have the chitty stating this is our property—to be labeled The Temple of the Slaughtered Lamb. There has been a mistake! You are trespassing. Piss off." John Hugh Smyth-Pigott waved the paper angrily at Prince and his group.

Agnes nodded. "The Lamb speaks the truth." She glowered. "I am the real Messiah-wife."

Louisa shook her head. "At least my mind and opinions are my own."

"The mistake is yours, false prophet. *I* submitted the application first. The demon's stamp is clear enough." Henry Prince pointed at his one-time heir. "It is you and your band of charlatans who are trespassing."

Attired in the borrowed uniform of the ministry man, Calchas walked purposefully between the two arguing groups. He'd brought one of the fiends the Cauldron used for security along as support and the creature lurked to his right; its name-badge said, 'my name is Kevin, how may I help you?' The creature ill-fitted its suit, but it was a lesser hell fiend and they did not share His Satanic Majesty's taste in sharp suits. Kevin the fiend would enjoy this, he liked making humans squirm.

"Department of Disassembly and Destruction inspectors! There have been complaints from the neighbors here

about unruly behavior, sabotage, and general underhandedness. Now we know this is hell, but there must be some order
in the chaos, mustn't there? Now, show your permits."

Calchas waved a bloodstained copy of the Misplanning
Laws and Regulations—Edition 666. It was as thick as his
arm and the other hand clasped a clipboard.

Both men stopped their bickering and stared at the old
man, who looked vaguely familiar, but neither of them had
paid much notice to the neighbors, so they shrugged off the
recognition. He was an underling, a hired man and nothing
more to them. "Bugger off, this is private property," Smyth-
Pigott said, turning his back on Calchas.

"Well! How rude! Add to the tab 'resisting inspection, hindrance of HSM's ordnances and laws, and being a
cheeky so and so', Kevin. Isn't that six hundred and sixty-
five years cleaning the sewers under Perish's more unpleasant quarter? Or is it target dummy for the Vietcong? I can
never remember." Calchas peered at his clipboard as if he
was short-sighted.

"Six hundred and sixty-five years? That's an odd
amount—should it not be six hundred and sixty-six?" Reverend Prince asked, curious despite his anger.

"Satan is renowned for his sense of humor and unpre-
dictability—and has dropped a year for the expected good
behavior of the victim. Oh, wait. No, I forget, he thinks it's
amusing to make people wonder as they are naked and scrubbing demon feces from the tunnels, and wading neck deep in
the effluence of millions of damned souls…"

Prince held out his own building permit—"Inspector,
you'll find nothing amiss here."

Calchas peered at the permit, spending far too long examining every clause. "Ah yes. I see. The Badoe of Ewo?
What sort of name is that? Some demonic name? I think old

Crowley has first dibs on those, using it might be tantamount to copyright infringement. Add that too, Kevin. There's a special place here for copyright infringement—I believe."

Prince snatched back the document, "What? No! It should be Abode of Woe! It's a temple." He puffed out his chest and, eying his rival, declared, "I am the Abhorred One. The true prophet."

"Is that so? Prophet of what? Bad spelling? Terrible architecture?" Calchas winked. "A Chosen One. We've not had one of those for at least a week or two, have we, Kevin?"

The fiend shook what passed for its head and rumbled, "No, master . . . but that last one was quite tasty."

Calchas patted the fiend's hunchback and said, sotto voce, "We've talked about that, Kevin. You are not supposed to eat transgressors. At least not until we discover if they really are transgressors." He slapped himself on the forehead. "Sometimes I forget: everyone is a transgressor. But look at him, he'll be all stringy."

Kevin leered at the potential morsel. "Never had breakfast, master."

"No! At least not yet. Now behave or you'll go back to the pit—that one with the unicorn wallpaper."

The fiend shivered, and muttered, "Yes master, sorry master."

Smyth-Pigott thrust his building permit under Calchas' nose and tried very hard to ignore the fiend. "That charlatan Prince has no claim to this land. It belongs to me. I am the Chosen One. The reincarnation of Jes– er. The real heir. This interloper is false."

Taking the second document, Calchas squinted. "Smyly-Piggy. Really? Oh well, takes all sorts. Building a temple too, I see. That's convenient." He looked doubtfully at the half-built monstrosity taking misshape. "It doesn't look very sound. How deep are the foundations? Where are the materials sourced from? We can't have it falling down every other week. It's bad for business. Old Assisi is a bugger for complaints. Every other day we get one about something minor. We would do something about him, but the poor old soul has enough problems with the Hell-rat infestation. Oh . . . I guess you didn't know about the rats?"

John Smyth-Piggott stood, mouth agape at the insult and eyes flashing with worry. "Smyly-Piggy? How dare you!" He snatched back the paper and glared at it. "Oh. I should have known better than to trust a demon clerk."

His mind caught up with his ears. "Hell-rats? Are they a problem?"

Kevin licked his lips and slobbered. "Yummy."

"Not so much of a problem as a perpetual nuisance. Assisi was given a hell-cat but he's allergic, the poor bugger. And the cat ran away.

"These rats are great big buggers the size of your leg. You know the Black Death? Well, these charming fellows carry the Great Plague's more pestilential brother."

Holding out his hand, Calchas said authoritatively, "We digress. My associate here has to stamp these—in blood of course."

The pause was laden with the promise of more trouble. Neither man moved to hand over his documentation again.

"Cease! All building must cease, forthwith!" Calchas bellowed, trying to be heard above the din.

Louisa Nottidge waved her hands towards the builders and abruptly the sound and activity ceased.

"What is going on? We are behind schedule as it is." She eyed the fiend in his ill-fitting suit and Calchas with his battered case. "Oh crap: department men."

Calchas looked between the two men. "We have a problem here—you both own this land—and you both apparently have permission to build at the same time, on the same spot. One or both of you filed an illegal request. Worse, both documents are riddled with errors. What can I do? I shall be having a stern word with the operatives when I get back, I can assure you! But paperwork aside, we can't have both of you building different structures on the same plot at the same time, can we?

"Paragraph D: section X, subsection eight, part one point four A, line sixty-eight," rumbled the fiend.

"Ah, of course. Thank you, Kevin." Calchas patted the fiend's bulging arm, "I knew that."

Kevin poked at Smyth-Pigott's chitty with a claw. "Hey! This ain't a real document, it's fake. There's no seal."

"That is outrageous! I paid fair and square for that infernal chitty! Damned cheek!" Smyth-Pigott's face went puce with anger. "I am the Lamb, the Chosen One! How dare you insinuate such lies . . . fiend!"

Calchas theatrically held up the document, peering at it under Paradise's distant glow. "Oh. Yes. Kevin is correct. Now that makes things *very* interesting."

Peering at the paper again, Calchas continued, "Illegal use of His Satanic Majesty's property, and misuse of his domain for nefarious purposes. Theft of land—that's what this amounts to. Oh dear, it gets worse and worse. With the other charges—we are looking at very serious offenses indeed. The Lord of Lies is keeping a very close eye, and very clawed talon, on things during this audit from Above. Can't have it going all to hell, as it were, can we?" Calchas chuckled, quickly followed by a sound which resembled water pouring into a drain. Kevin held his sides as the humor shook him. Laughs were few enough here. The crowd of New Dead watching the proceedings shivered as one soul; demonic laughter was right to cause fear. One of the workers, who had stopped to watch the entertainment, squeaked and the wet puddle around his feet gave away his fear. Before his shame was noticed the man hurried wetly away.

"Subsection Eighty-Five, Paragraph C, line six hundred and three point one," Kevin rumbled, reminding Calchas of what was needed when the awful sound abated.

"Ah yes, the punishment." Calchas flipped open a tattered, blood-stained notepad. "It's the option of trial by combat, or challenge of battle. First blood wins."

"What does that mean?" Smyth-Pigott asked, wary.

Louisa stood open-mouthed. "A duel? What sort of justice is that?"

"Justice? This is hell, woman! There is no justice but rough justice, and no court but the court of the damned," Calchas bellowed. He remembered 'justice' as revenge for a stolen wife and a decade of war. He knew courts as the whims of warrior kings.

"Preposterous!" Reverend Henry Prince roared, for once in agreement with his rival.

"A duel? Oh yes, that word would suffice. The law is the law. You could try to find a lawyer. Satan knows there are plenty of that ilk here, but they charge blood and more diablos than you've seen in a year, at least the reputable ones do. And a disreputable one would charge you more than you want to give. And then there are the timescales." Calchas shook his head. "I suppose since Erra and his terrible minions are abroad, we could wait eons for those . . . gentlemen to become available. They are occupied on other matters at the moment." As one the assembly trembled with fear at the name of Erra and his seven personified weapons of destruction. Lesser Auditors had never invoked such fear.

"Erra? No thanks!" Louisa squeaked. Drawing herself up and mustering her courage, she spoke: "Get you to it, Henry. You are the Abhorred One—G...er fate will be on your side." For the first time in eons Louisa Nottidge smiled. The Reverend Henry Prince was an old man, and a lousy shot. His rival was younger, fitter and, she hoped, more adept. Henry would likely end under the Undertaker's brutal hand—which meant some respite from Henry's ego for her, at least for a while. Maybe she could do something about her sister at the same time.

Prince smoothed his moustache. What she said was, of course, true. He was the Abhorred One—a chosen soul. And that charlatan John Smyth-Pigott was nothing but an imposter. He had been a thorn in Prince's side in life and in afterlife he was even more insufferable. Eyeing his rival, Prince declared, "Yes, I agree to this duel, and the winner gets all rights to build on this site."

John Smyth-Pigott straightened. "That will be the solution to this debacle. And then I will be having stern words with the Department of Disassembly and Misplanning. We are English. We should not put up with this!"

"Kings, demigods, rich, and poor from Earth's great nations, those who deserve damnation and those who do not. His Satanic Majesty makes no distinction. Have you not realized that, John?" Agnes responded, her eyes filled with sadness. "We are all damned.

"Get it over with, John. End this now. The temple will be ours. We can send that cow, Louisa, away."

"The loser renounces all claims to the land, all claims to the temple?" Louisa clarified. "It's only fair."

Calchas refrained from commenting about the concept of 'fairness' in hell and simply said, "As you wish."

Surprised at his wife's reply, John Smyth-Pigott stared at her, then towards his rival. "Agreed. We will need an impartial witness; cheating is rife in hell. It's mandatory."

"You are not in a position to make demands," Calchas admonished.

"It's only fair. After all you have a stake in this—it's your department which has perpetrated the error," Louisa said.

Calchas shrugged as if it made no difference to him. "Well, you should have read the paperwork before you signed it."

Cassandra walked past, stopping to look at the awful construction. "There's a hole there, east of the door," she said helpfully.

Louisa remembered this young woman with the sad eyes and red hair. She had been a fortune-teller in the ancient times and had been chatting to some of the Agapemonite women. Pointing at the young seer she said, "She will do for a referee. She has nothing to gain."

"Referee? Is this some sporting venture? I am not skilled in such decisions." Cassandra spoke quietly, shyly; she looked bewildered.

"Miss, these men must fight a duel. We need an impartial bystander as witness," Calchas told her, as though he'd never seen her before.

"But what if someone dies?" she replied, feigning shock.

"That's the point. They have both broken the rules and ordinances of His Satanic Majesty's domain. The Dark Lord has other more serious matters to deal with and there is an old punishment of trial by combat. Will you do your damned duty?"

"The better man will be victorious." Agnes declared, squeezing Smyth-Pigott's arm. She had no doubt of it.

"Yes, those who use wiles and cunning, will indeed triumph. Those whose ego is greater than their skill will fall," Cassandra predicted, trying not to look at Calchas.

"Er, yes. Exactly. Now we will reconvene at Paradise-set, I suggest you make preparations." Calchas turned on his heel and left.

"The Abhorred One will be victorious! The Temple of Woe will rise glorious!" Henry Prince declared, trying to outstare his rival.

Smyth-Pigott stood close, arms crossed. "Pah. You are old and worn out. I shall be triumphant!"

The two men continued to bicker, each insult growing more complex, more heated. The three women who remained looked at each other in shared frustration. "Look at them, going at it," Agnes said, wondering what on Earth she had seen in the red-faced Lamb, but her curse reared up and she found her mouth saying, "But mine is winning."

"Sister, you are delusional." Louisa shook her head.

"I am not the one who spent time in the loony-bin," Agnes snapped.

Cassandra looked from one to the other, noting the sibling resemblance. "I do not understand."

Agnes replied, "That woman is my sister, she is sister-wife to the charlatan prophet Henry Prince—in life he founded the Agapemonites, but my husband is the true heir. And it's her fault we are in hell. She was the first, and the letters she smuggled spoke of an Eden. Our lives were dull. We had no prospects but marriage if we were lucky, and spinsterhood if not. Women then had few rights, and nothing exciting ahead for us. This was, I suppose, a form of rebellion. The Agapemonites offered freedom, and a chance to be closer to Go– Him upstairs. John was the chief disciple—and the heir. But all went sour. Louisa was sent . . . away. Our father and brothers were not pleased when we ran away. They would not, could not understand."

"You didn't need to follow. Always in my shadow, even when we were children," Louisa grumbled.

The raised voices grew shriller. The two former Agapemonites were playing the blame game and now all the workers stopped to gawp.

Louisa Nottidge rolled her eyes. "Egos the size of buildings, both, girl. Heed my advice, take no husband or lover. Listen not to prophets and zealots."

"This I know. Love in Hades is a fool's course. Egos and love mix not. Wars have been fought over men's pride, and the comely face of an unworthy woman." Cassandra's face darkened, and her eyes flashed with gloomy memories.

"Wait, you're Cassandra? *The* Cassandra? From Troy?" Agnes' jaw dropped.

Cassandra turned away, "Yes, I must go." With that she fled, unwilling to answer further questions from these two New Dead women, whom she thought had acted foolishly.

*

Paradise's dim light grew ever dimmer as the hell-lights began to glare with the blue glow of sulfur. It was an unforgiving light for the unforgiven. Word had got around, and crowds had begun to gather for the evening's entertainment. Calchas had started a book on the outcome of the battle, and the diablos were rolling in.

"Two to One for the Pig Man!" yelled a grifter clad in the sharpest suit of the evening.

"Seven to Four for the Prince!" bellowed another voice, shrill in the crowd.

Kevin the fiend grinned. He was having the time of his unlife; he'd read the small-print.

"Are they ready?" Calchas asked, eying the large and sinister cloth-covered mounds on opposing sides of the temple.

"Yep. Ready for mayhem, master." A smiling fiend is not something to stir the heart with confidence or joy and Calchas sobered. He wondered if he should feel guilty, but he had enough of that to last a thousand lifetimes and these New Dead had brought it on themselves. At least that is what he told himself and Cassandra.

"Ego fighting ego will bring no good for either. A temple built in haste to honor mere vanity and lies will surely fall to dust." Cassandra stared at the mounds, hoping these fire-spiting death machines would not bring them all to the Undertaker's door. Were they too close? She closed her eyes and let her mind wander.

"Will we be punished for this venture?" He'd asked, thinking too late they may have erred and voicing both their fears. He hoped nothing would backfire; plans in hell oft went awry. And he knew that sooner or later he'd pay the price for this deceit.

"This is Hades. Punishment is inherent. But I think not . . . at least not on this day. 'Rue thy former life, and revel in thy afterlife, for thou art damned.' Is that not the advice you once gave me? We are the damned. We must survive as we may. But those infernal and wicked weapons of the new-dead—Surely the walls of Ilium would have fallen on the first day." She paused, "Would we have fought with such demon-weapons of war?"

Calchas gazed over to the two looming cloth-bound shapes. "Probably. Priam and Agamemnon would have found some means to destroy one another, no doubt. Man's capacity for war outweighs his capacity for reason—and this place is full of the testimonials to that.”

“They will fall in dust as vain men are wont to do.” Cassandra told him.

“They won’t go through with it. It would be suicide. That building will fall down in the next hell-storm,” Calchas replied, doubtful.

They’d watched the crowd assemble from a reasonable distance. “Pack up. In case. And I will try to steer the mayhem from our door to be on the safe side, should the range of those war-weapons be enough to hit us. Make sure you are careful where you stand.

“Look there’s old Assisi. Out for the entertainment, along with everyone else by the looks. Let’s see—drinks are half-price.” Calchas would not let this opportunity pass.

Cassandra nodded, “Where did you get the fire-spitters?”

“Che Guevara owes me a favor. It might be useful to keep one—just in case. How hard can they be to use? Look, come there are our two brave heroes.” Calchas separated himself from Cassandra, still in the guise of the department man, and wandered over to the two Prophets.

“So, gentlemen, are we ready to settle this? Remember the winner gets control of that site, should it still be standing. The loser, or losers . . .will have more immediate issues to deal with.” Calchas motioned to the nearer of the covered shapes. “Who would like Big Bertha?”

The Reverend Henry Prince stared doubtfully at the shape. “That’s not a sword, or a firearm.”

“Give that make a Heck-Cookie!” Kevin chortled. He’d been milling and warming up the onlookers. With a flourish he tugged the cloth away—to reveal a howitzer, pointing towards the Temple of Woe. It was an evil-looking device, as were many man-made machines of death. “Humans, they do like to kill one another in all sorts of inventive ways! Welcome Big Bertha. She's a friendly girl!"

"And the other?" Smyth-Pigott asked, his voice tremulous.

They walked across to a lower-slung shape. "Gentlemen, meet Roaring Meg, the deadly maiden of the English Roundheads," Kevin chuckled.

"Not your era, I suppose, but they do the job. They are primed for combat. Meg has helpers: she fires but one ball at a time, yet she's a fiery lass and one of the more knowledgeable operatives of hell has evened the odds." Calchas held his palm out, containing dice. "Whoever rolls snakeeyes gets first choice, but Meg is a little slower, and older, and thus she fires first."

"What happens if we refuse this ridiculous plan?" Henry Prince could not take his eyes from the cannon.

"Refuse? I wasn't aware that was an option." Calchas feigned surprise.

Kevin murmured something in Calchas' ear, "My associate says it *is* an option but if a refusal is forthcoming then all rights are revoked to build now and for infernity, Sentence will be the six-hundred and sixty-five years of cleaning Perish sewers, and you must publicly affirm your rival as the true Chosen One, the true heir and the ultimate seer. And as both are equally guilty you will have to work together, and your women too, forever. If both refuse, then it must be done at exactly the same time. Whomever speaks first is deemed the greater coward."

Calchas knew men with such egos as these two possessed might well favor death, albeit temporary, and delayed vainglory over public humiliation. And he wondered if adding the women into the equation might sway things.

"How deep are these sewers?" Henry Prince squeaked; his face white.

"Between about neck height and above head height. The 'liquid' for want of a suitable term, burns and the other material combusts now and then, or so I understand." Calchas grinned; he was enjoying himself. He learned long ago that he was not a good man; misguided and unfortunate yes, but not good. Any semblance of goodness had bled away with Iphigenia's blood.

"You are a coward as well as a fraud!" Agnes Nottidge flung herself towards the Abhorred One. "You are a filthy coward. You deserve to be scrubbing shit for eternity."

Louisa stood still, mouth agape. She'd never heard her sister use such a word. "You foolish bitch, it's suicide. And what about us?" She turned to Calchas. "Surely we are not guilty. Let them renounce the claim and we will go from this place."

"Not guilty? This is hell, miss, *everyone* is guilty. If your men fight the duel then the women are free to go about their business; if not you are all neck deep in the poo," Calchas said. "Make your choice, we do not have all evening. The artillery pieces need to be returned."

John Smyth-Pigott looked at Agnes, then rolled the dice. "Snake eyes."

Henry Prince snatched up the dice, rolling them across the dirt. "Two and four."

"I'll take Roaring Meg," Smyth-Pigott declared and motioned Agnes and Louisa aside.

Once the death-machines had been revealed to the sound of gasps and gossip from the audience, everyone with an ounce of sense shuffled back or found a suitable vantage behind rocks or the higher levels of the casino. Field glasses appeared, passed hand to hand for a better view. Such entertainment was rare, and this damned crowd was determined to get their jollies where they could.

*

John Smyth-Pigott stood behind Roaring Meg, the sparks from the burning taper speckling his face with light. He eyed the cannon, bringer of death, and shook his head. This was madness. This was suicide.

"I fire first. If I hit him, he's a goner, and even if I miss, a man like that will piss his drawers and run. I am the Chosen One. I am the Slaughtered Lamb!" he intoned under his breath.

He wondered what 'evening the odds' meant. He was not a gambling man; gambling was, after all, a sin.

"I cannot even see him. This is ridiculous. The building is in the way." He tried to peer through the half-complete Abode of Woe. "How am I to fight a duel under these conditions?"

One of Meg's helpers, a late Cromwellian soldier by the name of Fairfax shrugged: "She brought down the walls of Goodrich Castle, which had stood for four hundred years. That badly-built structure will fall down soon as looked at. Meg is hungry for battle. She has been idle too long. If you cannot see your enemy, destroy his walls, then he'll be ripe for taking." Fairfax smirked. He did not bring John much comfort.

"You are behind the cannon, sir. Not afore it. Behind is good—in front is bad. I've seen Meg rip the arms and legs from a man. She's not a dame to be trifled with."

"Let's get this over with." Smyth-Pigott bent to light the fuse.

*

Doubtfully, the Reverend Henry Prince eyed the camou-flage-colored artillery piece. "It's not English," he said to the man clad in a German First World War uniform.

"*Nein, Sie ist eine Deutsche waffe,*" the man told him, proudly.

"I see," he said, not really understanding the foreign words but reluctant to admit the fact.

"German," the man reiterated in accented English.

This was madness. This was suicide. But he thought that such a weapon would likely bring much mayhem. At least he was on the safer side.

"And it will hit that man over there?" he asked the German artilleryman.

"Ja, will hit. Bertha—she hit building too."

As they spoke and Prince stared at the giant gun, he tried to ignore the nagging doubts which clamored loudly in his head. "Six hundred and sixty-five years cleaning up crap or *that* monster." The words were spoken aloud, and the young German looked at him "*Was*?"

"Oh, nothing. Just point that awful thing that—"

BOOOOOM!

*

Fire spat from the deadly jaws of Roaring Meg, who had earned her name for a reason. The cannoneer had had the foresight to borrow ear defenders, a man of the past utiliz-ing technology from his future. The roar tore through John Smyth-Pigott's hearing as a ball the size of a large apple flew past. The cannon jumped back, and the heat pouring from the barrel seared John's clothes.

"Bloody fiery hell!" he screamed as a smoking chunk of masonry tumbled from the wall of the Abode of Woe. Flame crept upwards, gaining speed as a crack grew and the tarpaulin smoldered.

"Did it hit anyone?" he shouted above the ringing in his ears.

*

Henry Prince heard the loudest sound he'd ever experienced, and his body bypassed his mind, threw him flat on the ground, and whimpered on his behalf. Lumps of stone and what passed for concrete showered around them. Smoke billowed and he saw a lick of flame.

"Fire it! Now!" Prince screamed.

Big Bertha roared!

The sound of her song shook the ground and flaming stone rained down. At the edge of the awful cacophony was a terrible silence—the silence carried by the bringer of death and by hearing being torn away. Henry Prince whimpered and hoped his trousers were wet with water, not something else.

The German artillery man chuckled, *"Sie ist gut, ja?"*

"You're barmy!" Prince muttered, his pale face turned towards the German, who was not only grinning but seemed immune to the noise and terror. He wondered if that was what war did to a man.

"I am the Abhorred One! I am the Anti-Messiah!" Who was he trying to convince? Himself? Prince pulled himself to his knees. "Did we hit him?"

*

Smoke crawled across the dome of the Abode of Woe. Chunks of masonry tumbled, and the tarpaulin flapped away, trailing sparks. Roaring Meg sang again and the building trembled.

Big Bertha, not a girl to be outdone by an elder sibling growled, spat and the ground cracked open and thundered.

"The Temple!" screamed Agnes, trying to peer through the smoke but too terrified to move to investigate.

A flaming ball roared past and buried itself in the earth. Clods sprayed over her, and knocked her to the ground.

The Abode shook as Bertha spat, and this time the artillery aimed over the dome.

*

In the smoke, with eyes streaming and ears ringing, Henry Prince saw the flaming ball of death far too late. The dodge only succeeded in the mortar hitting his shoulder, ripping off his arm and part of his chest. Had he been alive then the wounds would have been mortal, but death was not permanent in Satan's domain and as his blood spurted from the ruin of his body, The Reverend Henry Prince whispered, "I am the Abhorred One. I am the Anti-Messiah—the Abode of Woe will rise again—" With that his smoking, bloodied remains shimmered and vanished. A place was made for him in the Undertaker's unmerciful clutches.

The German artilleryman continued to grin, aiming another volley towards the temple. He cared not that the other man was gone. He'd been hired to exercise his favorite girl and take her out he would.

*

Roaring Meg was living up to her name, her bellow fearsome indeed. John Smyth-Pigott had no idea what was going on, except he still seemed to be alive. He could hear nothing but the whistling in his ears and he wondered if his hearing would return. "Is it over?" he yelled.

"How should I know? We usually carry on until we something falls over or we run out of balls." The civil war man loaded another. "That building can't last much longer."

"What? I can't hear you very well, man!" Smyth-Pigott had never been as unsure, or as afraid in life, or afterlife. "I'm going to have a look. Run out of balls? That happened as soon as that bloody thing went off!" he muttered, wondering if he'd heard correctly.

He staggered, dust splattered and smoke-wheezing towards the temple. There were shapes looming in the smoke and dust, but in hell it paid not to look too closely. "Hey, Department Man—happy now? Is this over?" he yelled towards Calchas and his horrible assistant.

The rumble as the temple finally gave way sounded far worse than even the artillery. It was the sound of a behemoth expiring. When the shuddering finally stopped Calchas braved a look.

"Whose feet are those?" he asked Kevin, who had been enjoying himself immensely in the mayhem.

"The Pigman, master. That one is still twitching." Kevin licked his lips. "Just one foot as a reward, master?"

"Go take a look around the other side, there's a good fiend, and maybe I'll think about it." Calchas shook his head at the mayhem. "Amateurs," he said.

Cassandra had walked from one side to the other, once the smoke of battle and mayhem had cleared. "I declare the

Pigman winner, much good may it do him! But he is still guilty and will serve suitable sentence. I suggest the minions take themselves away, lest the curse spread further. Drinks are half price, and the first winning bet is doubled—only in the *Cauldron* tonight."

*

The *Fiery Cauldron* had more patrons than ever—people came to see the ruins. Hell was for many, ennui incarnate, and it took little to amuse the locals. Someone was selling scorched rock as a cure for hell-piles and Calchas had not wished to enquire too far down that particular line. He'd advertised the odds of the temple staying upright and made a killing even after the two artillerymen had been paid for their time. The old seer had been afraid of losing this place. He smiled as his hand caressed Roaring Meg. Agamemnon and Clytemnestra's henchmen would think twice about attacking this place now.

Cassandra joined him on the threshold. "I told you it would be thus. The women have left—they have been persuaded to start their own community."

"Have they now? We have customers aplenty. Well done, dear girl." Calchas bowed his head. Although his lips could not say it, Cassandra had been right. Cassandra was always right.

Fool's Gold

S. E. Lindberg

*"Separate thou the earth from the fire,
the subtle from the gross. . . by this means
you shall have the glory of the whole
world."*
    *—Sir Isaac Newton (1700 CE), transla-
tion of Thoth's Emerald Tablet (a.k.a. Philosopher's Stone)*

*"It is best not to be born at all; and next
to that, it is better to die than to live."*
    *—Aristotle (354 BCE) on The Wisdom of
Silenus*

"Do you want to live like that?" rasped the speaker. It squawked like a sick bird. A long, down-curved beak lowered as it waded through the flooded chamber. Water moved from about its waist, sending a small wave toward the foliage curtain. The ibis-headed god leaned through the colossal petals. It loomed over the sprawled woman inside, whom it addressed.

Miss Carter floated on her back beneath the visage. Vulnerable on the lotus pad, she squinted to discern the figure's face. Remote torchlight limned the bird-face. Miss Carter coiled up in the fetal position. Vines wrapped about her arms, anchored her to the living slab as would intravenous catheters in a hospital bed. Instinctively, she rubbed her sore, pregnant belly. The baby within rotated as if to hide from the beaked doctor. She asked, "Doctor? Are you not finished with me?"

Liquid dripped into the subterranean cellar. The ethereal drops burned as if ignited petrol, issuing prismatic flames in the otherwise pitch-black vault: sodium yellow, cupreous green and ferrous blue. They collided with the watery surface. Each plop echoed.

The splashes reminded the waking Carter that she had been imprisoned on Level A of Osiris's temple, a rare architectural construct surviving in the Egyptian Realm of Duat. Anubis and the Undertaker governed here. The Lake of Fire, a body of bloody liquid, surrounded it. Osiris once used this temple to rejuvenate the dead. Satan's Undertaker had displaced that ancient god of rebirth. Now the Undertaker employed the facility as a satellite mortuary, resurrecting souls in grotesque ways. Yet this physician looked different.

"You are not the Undertaker. Who are you?" Carter asked.

The speaker answered with the rhythm of a quacking duck, "I am Thoth. Father of Alchemy. You may know me by my Greek name. Hermes. Squawk. I served Osiris. Once I flew from Duat to the living world. Passing mystical secrets to lesser beings." Thoth leaned against the flower's corolla with a golden staff comprising two entwined, winged serpents.

Miss Carter's eyes dilated. "Wow, you have a splendid caduceus. It must be worth a fortune."

Thoth replied nasally, "I saw the Undertaker remove the emerald that had empowered it. Smash it. He sewed the fragments into one of his victims here on Slab A. I could not stop him."

Scarce light pervading the chamber reflected off the staff and onto Miss Carter's glossy eyes. She asked, "You want me to have your staff?"

"No," Thoth chirped. "I hope we will aid each other. The Undertaker has wronged you. As he wronged me. If we team together, we can regain control. Squawk. You look confused. Do you recall who you were?"

Miss Carter massaged her face as would a blind person to measure its features. Her hair still receded such that she was arguably bald. However, a full mustache adorned her upper lip. The transgender Carter grunted as her abdomen pulsed with cramps. Whispering in her newfound, feminine voice between contractions, "I was. . . I am . . . Howard Carter. Archeologist." Miss Carter cradled her swollen belly as she sat on the lotus bed.

Thoth nodded. "The infamous robber of King Tutankhamun's tomb? That explains why you are in Duat. Anubis judged you. You had a corrupt heart. Squawk. It beats again. The Undertaker remade you as a woman."

Carter pondered on her current apparel. Her tweeds were hardly becoming on a fully ripened, pregnant woman. A bowtie accented her wares. She would have given birth in more comfortable clothing than snug wool had she a choice. "The Undertaker had a keen eye for quality. He wore a beautiful, bespoke Savile Row."

"Squawk. You are still the cunning Howard Carter. At heart."

She asked, "Did the Undertaker remake you too, give you that beak?"

Thoth's bill parted, an avian smile. "No. Instead, he robbed me of power. He and Anubis do not allow me here on Level A. And Anubis is on patrol. My time is limited."

"My time is too," Carter whimpered. She massaged her belly. "My boy wants out."

"You know the gender?" Thoth asked.

"I had a partner of sorts, a compatriot I met on the banks of the Vile River. Herr Doctor Ernst Haeckel, an ecologist of some renown. He . . . uh . . . he was fascinated with embryos and organic life, appreciating them over material wealth. His drawings showed that all life shared common embryonic forms, whether you be a pig, chicken, human or fish. Nitpickers claimed he forged data. Whatever, it is all the same to me. Who cares about such things when there are treasures to collect? Anyway, the Undertaker said that I was contributing to Ernst's reassignment by bringing his embryo to term. He stated that any scientist so obsessed should become the object of his fancy."

"It will be interesting. To see how the Undertaker remade your partner," Thoth said.

"Well, I will soon be rid of him." Pointing toward the vines threading her body, Miss Carter asked, "So, Doctor Thoth, are you going to free me before Anubis comes back on his rounds? Cut these vines?"

"Unfortunately, no. I cannot —"

"Ahh!" interrupted Miss Carter with a cry. A contraction seized her muscles. Or was it a baby Ernst banging and rotating from within? Babies were as rare as angels in hell and never normal, but Miss Carter was about to give birth to one. "Perhaps you could conjure a cigarette to dull my pain?"

Thoth leaned on the caduceus, fondling the empty setting at its apex. "The prongs that once cradled the most powerful stone in Duat is gone. Without the stone, I cannot perform alchemy. Squawk. This staff is worthless."

"Hardly. It is pure gold. I bet I could find a buyer," Carter replied.

"You will get more than money. If you help me repair it. Squawk. When Ernst Haeckel is born, both of your transformations will be complete. That will trigger your Reassignment, likely to the same realm King Midas went." Thoth sighed. "I implore you. Find the stone."

"A stone?"

"The Philosopher's Stone. It —"

Amniotic fluid gushed onto the slab. Carter lurched forward to embrace her knees. Between clenched teeth she swore, "Ernst, you little bastard. You . . . are . . . hurting me."

"His head is crowning," Thoth observed. "Your friend is very hairy."

"Can you . . . pull him . . . out?"

"Easy now. Push. Inhale through your nose. Exhale with your mouth as you push again. Allow your breath to flow continuously," Thoth told her, peering down his beak.

"Ahh!"

Thoth calmly encouraged, "Press. Relax. Press . . ."

Baby Ernst's bearded face appeared. Once his head was free, the body plopped out onto the slab. Had the umbilical cord been less resilient, the baby would have skittered off into murky water.

"There you are." Thoth handed over Ernst, the baby's gray hair matted and dripping with amniotic fluid. The cord remained attached. "Your boy's body appears malformed. And his face is bearded."

Carter cringed. "Cripes, he looks like a wet gnome. His head is enormous. Ouch, can we cut that? It's tugging."

Thoth frowned. "The cord? Soon, yes. But you must wait until —"

"*Wa-wa!*" Ernst screeched. He had the brain and skull of a wizened scientist, but his premature lungs and throat could hardly support words yet.

Thoth resumed, "As I was saying —"

"Wa-wa!"

Carter cradled Ernst. Blood soaked her wool suit. "My apologies, but my dear boy won't shut up. Commence, sir."

Thoth cleared his throat, but before he could talk, Ernst wailed again.

"This racket is intolerable," muttered the new mother. "Eureka! I almost forgot. I have a pacifier." Carter retrieved a gilded phallus from her suit pocket. "Suck on this." She inserted the sucker into Ernst's mouth. "Yes, Doctor Thoth, that was my member. The Undertaker figured I should keep my manhood. He told me as much when he started the operation. I am surprised he preserved it in gold."

"Yes, he has a knack. For being creatively mean-spirited," Thoth squawked. The demigod noticed the pattern of a lotus hieroglyph on baby Ernst's back. "Look here. He has the birthmark of a being remade in Duat, the Egyptian *sesen*. It is an emerald-colored lotus with golden flowers. It symbolizes cyclical rebirth, since the lotus flower rises with every sunrise and sinks at sunset. King Midas also received this brand. This bodes well. *Squawk.* Let me check your back."

Exasperated but excited to confirm if she had a birthmark laced with gold, Carter replied, "We'll have to take my suit-coat and shirt off." The pair took turns holding the baby as they undressed Carter's top half. Thoth confirmed the mark was present and equally brilliant.

"Understand, few are resurrected on the Slab A of Duat. You will start your next assignment branded with the special glyph. Like King Midas. His *sesen* should aid you to identify him." Thoth redressed Carter, wrapping the shirt and suit yet leaving them unbuttoned.

"Tell me more about this character. Cripes, am I leaking?"

"Midas was a king of Phrygia." Thoth handed her a handkerchief. "And you are lactating."

"I am cursed with donning premier suits that are forever stained and sopping," Miss Carter continued as she snuggled her newborn. "You will have to fill me in on what you know about this reassignment process . . . ouch!"

Having spat out the golden phallus into a puddle of filth atop the lotus pad, Ernst had found a free nipple to suckle. Carter retrieved the pacifier. Detaching her bowtie, she fashioned it as a tether for the pacifier, anchoring it to her suit pocket's flap.

"I thought breastfeeding was supposed to feel natural. This little bastard is gnawing on me. And his beard is scratching. Thank the Undertaker that Ernst has no teeth."

"Listen, Miss Carter. Let me explain while I can. If you bring me the stone. I can remake you. Are you familiar with alchemy? You could be a real man again."

While breastfeeding, Carter said, "Chemistry is more of Haeckel's domain. He would better converse with you, if he could." Ernst squirmed and gurgled loudly. "I think he can hear you at least. He grows excited."

Thoth addressed both. "Ah, it is simple. The emerald stone contains the power of transmuting matter's base elements into new objects."

Ernst struggled to speak. He wanted to exclaim: "*Herr Thoth, you could reverse this mockery of evolution. Ja wohl! You could turn me back into an adult.*" However, this plaint manifested in slobbering mutters.

"Had I the stone, I could transform both flesh and materials. Into whatever you wish," the Egyptian mystic explained.

Carter's greed drowned out her baby's burbles. "I recall now. You alchemists can turn things into gold!"

Frustrated, Ernst clamped down.

"Ouch, stop biting me!" exclaimed Carter.

"Who cares about gold? You dolt. Thoth could fix our bodies," Ernst declared silently. *"Let me remind you that you have sore breasts that need not be there."* He bit his mother again.

Carter slapped her baby. Then she wiggled an index finger as a stern warning. "Hungry or not, we won't be having that behavior." A handprint remained as an afterimage on Ernst's soft cheek. Mother Carter shoved the phallic pacifier back into his mouth.

Thoth hastily resumed his plea to deescalate the tension: "Alchemy is more about spiritual transcendence than increasing wealth. It is about the connection of corporal matter to divinity. This power originally powered Osiris's Temple of Rebirth. *Squawk.* When you leave here, seek my Philosopher's Stone. Retrieve it from King Midas and bring it back to me. You were once a tomb raider. Go find my artifact."

"I am intrigued by the prospect. Why don't you go?" Carter replied. "You are wise. Mobile, too."

Thoth's head lowered. "I cannot leave Duat anymore, but you two will."

"Let's say we partner with you, and we agree to find your stone. How do we get back to Duat?" Carter asked.

"Easy," Thoth rasped. "I have seen this cycle many times in the afterlife. When your body perishes in hell, your form will dissipate. Then it will reappear here. On Slab A."

"We have to die to come back?" Miss Carter asked.

Thoth contemplated Carter's reaction. "Close. Understand, you are *already* dead. Your body, the essence binding your soul, can take many shapes and can still experience pain. Your body's death in hell brings you back here. To be remade again."

"With every corporeal demise, the Undertaker will reanimate us?"

"*Squawk,* yes. It can be a torturous cycle. But, if you bring the Stone back, then I can retrieve it before the Undertaker gets to you. With it, I will be powerful enough to save you. I'll remake you both. We can retake Osiris's temple."

Carter knew they were in a superior position than this Thoth fellow. She negotiated for more. "What else do we get?"

"*What else could we need?*" Ernst tried to spit out the phallus to protest. This fool was going to ruin their chances at freedom.

Carter disliked the uncooperative wiggling, so she shoved the pacifier deeper into Ernst's throat to subdue him. "Doctor Thoth, I am thinking we'll need something that glitters."

"*Squawk.* I suppose if gold motivates you, then that can be arranged."

"Renewed bodies and as much gold as I can carry. Deal?" Miss Carter extended her right hand.

Thoth shook in agreement. "Once your bearded son and you separate, cord cut, your operations will be complete. You will be two whole beings. No more. Or less. That will signal the end of the Undertaker's work. You will dissolve from Duat and reappear in another realm in hell. Find King Midas there. He will have the same lotus tattoo as you. Retrieve my stone. Make your way back."

The creaking of a door opening across the chamber ended the conversation. Fifty yards away, a muscular giant entered the lowest level of the temple. Five steps on dry stone sounded, followed by splashing.

Thoth whispered, "Anubis approaches. I must hide. Best to you. For both our sakes." He left, and the curtain of petals closed.

A minute passed. With each second, a louder sloshing signaled the approach of the Undertaker's Duat Assistant, judger of souls, Anubis.

A curved *khopesh* blade penetrated the petals and drew them aside. An ebony jackal-head framed with a blue-faience pectoral peered within. At nine feet, Anubis stood a yard taller than Thoth. His *shendyt* kilt of flayed faces was level with the slab.

"*Woof*!" Anubis barked with laughter. "You two are adorable. Well, enough is enough. Time to send you away." He grabbed the baby with such force and speed that Carter could not resist. With a single surgical strike, Anubis sliced the umbilical cord. Blood sluiced across the blade. Anubis dropped Ernst.

Miss Carter reached to grab her baby. Shadows of the lotus blossom closed tight. Before she could catch Ernst, darkness consumed them. A tidal wave of nothingness washed over them, and celestial currents swept them away.

*

Miss Carter and baby Ernst spiraled in a vortex, surfing a whirling pool atop the gargantuan lotus pad. Bubbling currents ran against gravity. Torrents stripped away petals from the megaflora craft. The mustached mother lay flat, her left arm extended, her right clutching her infant. They twirled fast enough that sitting was impossible.

Chaotic, violent mists swirled around them as the portal spewed them into New Hell. Darkness gave way to a blistering crimson haze. Egyptian flotsam coasted with them. Turbulent eddies calmed. Their craft rocked until horizontally righted. As tides of vertigo receded, the pair realized they had risen to the surface of a river.

The hazy, sunless sky tinted everything red. Aggregates of floating, coagulated necroflesh churned about, creaming to the roiling surface as molten fat does on soup. A fog of putrescence limited vision. The stench of sewage nearly suffocated them. Ernst breathed in the fumes. Then vomited.

A blurry landmass emerged from the miasma as they glided.

The waters thickened into a slurry. Body parts and refuse from Duat concentrated on a marshy shoreline.

Carter abandoned Haeckel on the pad to seek solid footing. The golden pacifier remained attached to her bowtie. She waded through the muck with her shirt untucked. She stepped on countless submerged treasures. It seemed as if all the Sea Peoples to ever invade Egypt deposited their bronze here. Sharp, verdigris weaponry and armor complicated her path, wicked blades awaiting legs and feet like the teeth of some hideous sea creature. She grasped a hilt for leverage to pull herself atop a defaced sculpture. It snapped. Carter lost balance and fell between pitted blades. Another misstep promised impalement. She was forced to seek a path free of slippery algae, which also led her away from alluring fortune.

"That is a flooded museum!" Carter muttered, gaining the relative safety of a beach. She wondered what mysteries had been lost within. She tossed the hilt away. "And it all rots."

"*Muma*," baby Ernst wailed from behind. "*You could pick me up, fool.*" Doctor Haeckel paddled after his partner on his belly. He drew on his knowledge of anatomy and evolution. He knew the dimensions and ability of his current form and moved accordingly. Immature, bent limbs approximated the flipper-like, webbed feet of a turtle. Imitating one, he propelled himself. Decaying lily blossoms and ropes of bundled vines slowed his advance. To Ernst, the bog was more a zoo than a museum. Locusts from the Ramses era, *Schistocerca gregaria*, floated in clumps. Sundered arms and heads of *Homo mediterraneus*, both Sea Peoples and Egyptian, and Lemurian monkey-like men, *Homo netherterraneans*, bobbed as if trying to swim on their own accord.

Haeckel escaped the sludge. He slithered beside his mother. Exhausted, he spat insects out of his mouth and rolled onto his back.

"This is no Lake of Fire," Miss Carter looked outward at the expansive coast. "Duat is indeed behind us. But boy, this water is no less appealing. It corrodes all the artifacts." Having caught her breath, she stood to survey the landscape. Carter detected a hunch-backed figure sifting through the sand farther down the desolate beach. "We are not alone, after all. See there, beyond all that coiled wire? A lone beachcomber. Let us get this adventure started."

Miss Carter trudged forth, ignoring any pleas from her waddling son to be carried. Barbed wire threaded the shoreline. Several gaps allowed passage until she reached a dead-end of entangled coils. Carter ruminated on a path forward, allowing time for Ernst to catch up. She reckoned they were within earshot of the other person. Carter stood tall, stuck her chest out, and spread her legs akimbo as if she just scaled a pyramid's apex.

She waved across the field of wire. "Ahoy there, mister wayfarer."

No response came from the pan sifter. Slouched over the swirling sieve, the man sorted with his fingers, pushing aside locust carcasses. The sediment was thick with glazed pebbles and other ceramic relics. Three frogs voluntarily hopped out to splash into the river.

"Ahoy!" Carter called again.

The hunchback sighed while keeping attention for gold flecks in the sieve. *"Bonjour."*

"Ooh, a Frenchman. Are we in Normandy?" Carter inched closer, her open suit flaps dangled and exposing a mud-spackled chest without a brassiere. A lifetime of being an arrogant man did not prepare her to present her augmented body with any grace. Unconcerned, she twirled her mustache, waiting for a reply.

Phew, you are one ugly mother. And so is that pet. Is that a baby? The Frenchman became agitated. He had work to do. These clowns threatened to ruin his day. *Did they not understand their situation? They are itching to approach.* Holding his palm outright, he yelled, *"Arrêtez!* Stop."

"Monsieur, if not in France, where in hell are we?" Carter adjusted her stance. Her left foot compressed Ernst's bearded face into a puddle.

"New Hell, to be precise. Beside the Vile River. What the . . .? *Attention, ton bébé se noie!"*

"What?" Miss Carter cupped a hand behind her ear. Thirty yards of distance, coupled with the coastal noise of crashing waves, made the man's accented words hard to interpret.

The figure pointed to Carter's foot. "Your baby is drowning."

"Ernst! You need to watch where you crawl. You'll get hurt." Carter swooped up baby Ernst by both feet, then jiggled him upside down. "This is my boy." Miss Carter spanked the baby repeatedly. "Ernst Haeckel. A doctor of the sciences."

The last hit cleared Ernst's lungs. Cries followed spittle. "Waa!"

"*Un docteur?* And you, sir?" The man asked, curious about the half-naked, soaking, mustached woman and the ugliest baby he had ever seen.

"I am Howard Carter, the most renowned archeologist." She offered a nipple to silence Ernst.

"Howard?" *Strange name for a woman. She breastfeeds and so must be female, but such a thick mustache is out of place. The Undertaker worked her, or him.*

"I am Quasimodo, once the bell ringer of Notre Dame, now in the employ of —"

"Aye, you are a laborer," Carter interrupted. She lifted Ernst upright again and held him against her shoulder. Then she edged into the wire hedgerows. "Quasimodo, tell me where we are." Sparks danced on the wires, crackling as they crawled the metal skein.

"*Arrête de bouger*! Stop moving. You are in a minefield." The hunchback articulated slowly, "Mine. Field."

Carter halted. Eyebrow raised, she questioned, "Where? Field of mines?"

Quasimodo shook his head. "*Madame*, few souls exit from the Vile Duatenum," he waved to the maelstrom in the Vile River whence the duo came. "Best stay where you are. This field is one of the Sibitti's works. They are looking for those like you reassigned from Duat. Move much more and you will trigger something. Then *they* will come."

"Ah, the Sibitti. Walter Andrae, a compatriot of mine, adored Akkadian history. It would be grand to meet with the real seven enforcers," Carter told him.

"*Sûrement pas!* Are you mad? They are Erra's personified weapons! You do not want to meet them or their master plague god. You will be flambéed—much like those two," he gestured toward a concentrated bundle in a nearby trench. "A few weeks ago, that pair from Duat got ensnared. Then the Sibitti came. The encounter did not end well. They are trapped in the spider's web, indefinitely, and may never leave. They would have been better off if the Sibitti had completed their deaths."

Carter oriented Haeckel so they both could see where Quasimodo indicated. They looked down to see two figures entwined within endless coils. One hung suspended, arms outstretched. Threaded wire wrapped its jackal jaws shut. It wiggled as it made eye contact with Carter. It muttered incoherently from its metallic cocoon. Below it, attached rear to hip with the former, sprawled a female figure in bodacious leather. Her disfigured face looked skyward, burned beyond recognition. To baby Ernst, Carter whispered. "Reminds me of the belligerent pharaoh Hatshepsut, and her lover Senenmut. To think they were with us in Duat not too long ago. They look a bit overcooked to me."

With her free right hand, Carter nudged a wire to inspect further. *Snap!* An arc shot across her arm, leaving a line of soot. "Ugh! This fence is electrified."

Quasimodo prepared to run. "I tried to warn you. That is the work of the Second Sibitti. You must stop meddling. Go back, *s'il vous plaît.*"

Sensing the Frenchman had found wealth with his panning but did not want to share, Miss Carter inquired without departing, "So, what are you doing here on such a dangerous beach?"

"I am looking for the gold, madame. Many Egyptian treasures come ashore here. They are scarce, but wealth is in here, somewhere. My master, Doctor Victor Frankenstein, requires funding for his experiments."

Ernst jiggled with excitement. The devolved evolution-ist fantasized about a cure. *Doctor Frankenstein? The leg-endary surgeon who reshapes corpses and can reanimate them? Perhaps he could fix our bodies.* Haeckel tried to speak but merely spat. His lot in life, and afterlife, was to be misunderstood.

"Quiet, Ernie," Miss Carter hushed her baby. "I sense a deal in the works."

Ernst sobbed. His entire body ached. His gums especial-ly. The German scientist thought, *"All you heard was 'gold.' We need to find the Philosopher's Stone, enable Thoth, or a surgeon like Frankenstein, to fix us."* This dissent manifest-ed as audible cries.

"Shh. Cease your babbling, now. I am trying to have an adult conversation," Carter grumbled and waggled a finger again.

"You better get your mind on track. Get me out of this body." Ernst clamped down on the appendage.

"Ouch!" The finger retreated. "You are teething!" Cart-er groped for her gold member, found it still attached to the bowtie compressed between her body and baby Ernst. She fished it free. Before she could insert into Ernst's mouth, the glare of Paradise reflected brilliantly from the pacifier.

Quasimodo's eyes lit up. The hunchback swore he saw a curvilinear, metallic tube. Then it disappeared into a mouth. *Does that baby nurse on an ingot of gold? Perhaps this new mining craze shall measure up to its rumors.* "Is that a golden buttcoin?" He asked, a grin creasing his misshapen features.

Carter tried to pull out her former member to display the artifact openly, and to further discussion, but baby Ernst would not release it. Haeckel glared quietly while sucking. Curved teeth had just breached his gums. The fangs jutted out of his lips at peculiar angles, like tusks. Fastening his jaws tightly eased the throbbing.

"The pacifier is phallic, not fecal." Miss Carter met the Frenchman's stare. "A Buttcoin, you say? Entertain my curiosity."

"You have not heard?" Quasimodo retrieved a disk-shaped coin from his pocket and held it up. "See this diablo? This currency may be worthless soon. Scabby necro-flesh is everywhere. Bone diablos are worth a bit more. But such things do not matter. The new gastrocurrency offered by the Mortuary Mint promises to replace them all. Personally, I have not seen a single buttcoin yet. Hellizens can collect and donate body parts, those plagued by Erra especially. That will buy time for mining the waste lagoon. It is much like a lottery. The more flesh you bring, the more time you get to search. There are no guarantees, my friends. Only hope."

Miss Carter envisioned the rush for gold. "Why are you here, Monsieur Quasimodo, and not at the Mint?"

The hunchback spat out a laugh. "Me? I would rather pan silt than shit." Quasimodo contemplated: if he could get that pacifier from this imbecile, then Victor Frankenstein could fund countless endeavors. "So, what motivates you? Perhaps we can make a trade?"

"I . . ." Carter began, pausing since Ernst squirmed. Carter corrected herself, *"We.* We are looking for King Midas."

"The one with the golden touch? You seem destined to mine the new lagoons then. As in legend, Midas is rumored to turn flesh into gold. Regardless, he definitely works at the Mortuary Mint for the Undertaker."

The antiquarian returned, "Buttcoin mining seems promising." *However, if we get the Philosopher's Stone, we can mint our own coin.* "We have loftier ambitions. We seek audience with the king himself."

"Are you fools? Midas is the one manufacturing Buttcoins. The Mortuary Mint is a fortress. You will never break into Satan's new treasury."

"Penetrating such architecture is my specialty. I just need to find the building. Getting inside will be trivial, I am sure. If you help us on our mission, we can compensate. Trust me, I'll soon have more than enough money to finance your master's experiments," Carter proposed while leaning toward the wire again. It hummed with potential energy. "Just tell me, where is the Mortuary Mint?"

Zap!

The ground rumbled. Wires jiggled, waved.

"Have you no bounds? I told you—the Mint is a fortress. Not even the Sibitti can get near to that place. You will never get inside. *Zut,* you are imprisoned now anyway! There is no going around these trenches. You are dolts for testing the traps. The Akkadians come for you now. *Bonne chance, good luck.*" With haste, Quasimodo hobbled away from the beach. He shouted back, "If you escape and need help adjusting to New Hell, find me up there." Quasimodo aimed his arm upward, to a gothic manor resting atop jagged cliffs. "I live in my master's manor up in Golem Heights."

Distant thunder intensified. It pulsated as an air-raid siren would, rising and falling in tone, growing steadily louder. The audible curtain hit them before the source was visible in the rippling sky.

The earth convulsed.

Carter and Haeckel bounced in the air, then collapsed on their rears. Plumes of putrid dust atomized. All became awash in an ochre tinge. The dense mist shorted electrical pathways. Energy danced from coil to barb in streaks of pulsating lightning. The duo closed their eyes from the intense flashes, so they did not see the first flying wraith gash the earth with his gleaming sword. Nor did they see the second appear to control the energy which had called it. But they could feel the ground slope and sink beneath them. A pit opened. They fell downwards.

Sliding tumultuously, they missed sight of the circling wraith who had carved the land beneath them. Hovering as if gravity had no pull, the lanky humanoid spiraled, circumscribing giant circles, dragging its elemental sword. The First's blade did not contact the ground, yet the surface below retreated, contracted, as if it were elastic meat freshly cut. At the crater's depressed center rested those who triggered the trap. Haeckel balled, his pacifier half contained in his mouth. Miss Carter sat. Her hands worked her mustache back into shape.

Eventually the dust settled. Above Haeckel and Carter, two robed figures hovered in the air. Tattered streamers fluttered in the wind. Hoods drooped over visages devoid of substance. Limned with Paradisaic gleam, the pair floated, wingless, as would drifting jelly fish. Indeed, the wraiths appeared as swaying, invertebrate forms. Both floaters held hilts of marvelous swords; the one on the left held a blade that shimmered like mica; the other, a weapon radiating electricity such that its blade had no proper form. Carter instinctively held her breath, fearing that she was truly submerged, about to drown on the riverbed of the Vile, looking upward at ethereal watchers who intended to murder them.

"Be still," commanded the First.

The Second's tattered clothes sparkled blue, discharging and recharging while snapping like whips. He extended his hands, which sprouted lengthening tendrils of light. These raced in the air, keeping their tethered connection to the hands, extending over Carter and Haeckel, branching and reaching, wrapping around skeleton and muscle. Palms turning up, the Second raised its two puppets. The baby rotated with a wrist twitch; its marked back became visible: a green lotus with a golden flower branding its young hide. Carter's posterior faced the wraiths. With the rise of a middle finger, an arc split Carter's suit; her *sesen* showed.

The Second's intonation was a notch kinder than the First. With a voice that sounded stifled and crackly as an antique telephone connection, the relatively gentler bringer of doom spoke: "He is the First. I, the Second. We are sons of heaven and earth. We serve only Erra, lord of pestilence and destruction. We are part of his seven weapons, the Sibitti, here to cleanse hell, ensuring the damned get their due."

"Enforcers! Splendid, just like the ancient Babylonian tablets read." Carter said, awed.

The Second continued, "Erra has instructed that hellizens do not have wealth, yet a new economy emerges. We are here to destroy Satan's newly minted gold. Understand, the damned should only deal in the currency of plagued flesh and rotten bone. All here shall be poor, forever."

Carter promptly, yet discreetly, shoved the opulent pacifier deep into Ernst's mouth to ensure no gold showed. "Are we suspects? We have not been involved with minting currency. You are powerful, so you probably know that we are innocent."

The Second continued, "Satan toys with us and his responsibility. Erra's plagues affect the damned, but now there is a means for some to profit from it. Satan and his Undertaker enlisted an individual from Duat to forge a new currency. He can transform plagued flesh into gold. Obelisks transmitting alchemical energies deter us. We will shut down the operation by sending in moles."

"Us?" Carter asked.

"Any souls from the Egyptian afterlife should suffice, but few emerge from the Vile Duatenum to enlist. You are eligible, but not obliged. The last two did not accept our deal. We can always wait for the next ones. Our traps alert us when candidates arrive from reassignment."

Carter extolled, "Hatshepsut and Senenmut? They were fools not to accept employment. I excel at raiding temples, and my compatriot is even better at tracking living things. We are your men … woman and baby."

"Then you are contracted as our servants. Many hellizens can enter the targeted grounds, but only those marked with the Duat lotus can enter the heart of the treasury. You should have complete access. The alchemy of that *sesen* glyph protects the mastermind, the Phrygian King Midas. Bring us his body alive."

Midas! Did he say Midas? Carter squeezed her baby and whispered. "Hear that, little Ernie? We have competitive buyers! Good fortune follows us." Then she addressed the supernatural beings, "What's in it for us?"

The First motioned to end Carter's existence by raising his sword, but the Second had a measure of patience and ceased the execution. "Temporary freedom from our wrath. Otherwise, you can join those two burned in the trenches."

"Let's do this." Carter stood.

The Second sheathed his weapon and brought both hands together. Teasing energy between his fingers like a cat's cradle, he pulled ropes of lightning from his fingertips. The skein undulated and enlarged, levitating away from its creator, swelling to accommodate Carter and Haeckel.

"Hold on to those cords. We will fly you to the edge of the Mortuary Mint."

With invisible wings, the Sibitti levitated, as if gravity ignored them, even repelled them. They shot upward. The First kept his sword unsheathed and ready. The Second dangled his sword, which anchored the electrical container of the passengers; his cargo followed within the luminous cyan net.

Carter simultaneously cradled Ernst and the ethereal threads. Every contact between flesh and energy tingled. Her suit smoldered in streaks but did not catch flame. "Cripes, my Savile is ruined."

*

The maelstrom of the Vile Duatenum receded from view as the four figures rose. Their ascent granted a bird's-eye survey. Carter noted a hobbling figure, the hunchback from the beach, making his way uphill from the Vile River shore towards the Victorian manors of Golem Heights. This surveillance was short-lived since they flew fast. Nothing stayed in focus for long. The Sibitti followed the river until it spilled into the Netherterranean Sea. Above them Paradise frowned, and below, on the surface of the polluted sea, sanguine shadows of the Sibitti raced. A boiling wake trailed the shades of the First and Second. Bubbling waters boiled fish and swimmers alike.

To amplify the cataclysmic assault and make traveling more entertaining, the First lowered his sword point. He and his blade were fine-tuned weapons for recrafting landscapes. Even while being hundreds of feet in the air, the sword's power reached to part the waters, exposing the river bottom. This split the Vile down its center. Liquid walls rose to wondrous heights, frothing at their edges, sweeping in great rolls towards the entire, serpentine coastline. Dozens of surfers rushed to ride the alluring tidal waves, which had been absent for time immemorial. They assessed the water's temperature too late as their boards melted and bodies vaporized.

The Undertaker's system accepted them for reassignment as the tsunami rolled inland, cleansing hundreds more. So swift was the tide, the flux of dead souls saturated the Mortuary's intake.

An azure haze surrounded the watching Carter and Haeckel. Being under the Sibitti's arrest, hanging from the spherical net attached to the Second afforded privileged protection versus those damned below. Trails of dust and electrically charged gas traced their path. So fast they flew, the ionized air crackled in a continuous, deafening roar.

"Can you see that?" Miss Carter smiled while crushing Ernst. The cacophony muffled her words. Still, baby Ernst could understand his partner's glee. Their destination was obvious, spectacular. The Sibitti flew around the flooded edifice to reveal the lay of the land.

A causeway extended from the coast two furlongs offshore, leading to a filled caldera. Thirty-six granite pharaohs protected the outer circumference in defiance of the surrounding elements. Each anonymous colossus stood seventy-five feet tall. Carved stripes depicted sacred headcloths, *nemes,* framing the defaced scalps. False, braided beards and bare chests marked them as young, strong pharaohs. Each had arms outstretched to form a wall of connected, crucified gods. Between each reaching hand, brilliant green energy sealed their embrace. The ring of giant pharaohs topped a glazed barrier of turquoise faience; the ramped bulwark descended into the Vile. Flocks of ibis perched and flew about haphazardly. They decorated the statues with guano flecked with gold; they splattered the porcelain-like rim.

The First's sword cut around, around, and around. Every pass of the Sibitti issued another surge. Waves rammed the colossi and the ceramic rim, then broke into white, frothy showers. Mud slid back into the Vile River repelled from the bastion of monuments. Each swathe of the blade scored a chasm outside the caldera, yet the edifice held strong. Somehow the Sibitti's forces did not penetrate the Egyptian engineering, or the alchemical energies exhibited at the Mortuary Mint, yet the tumult did flush the causeway clear of hundreds of hellizens who had been trekking across.

The outer colonnade of pharaohs shielded the interior, concentric rings of obelisks. These stood like naked, dead tree stumps within the caldera's brown lagoon. Clouds of locusts and flies added to the swampy atmosphere. Emerald-green electricity danced from obelisk tip to obelisk tip. These trails of energy traced an intricate circuit, all routing energy to and from, a singular centerpiece. A ziggurat supporting four huddle colossi formed the central battery. The pinnacle showcased the posteriors of seated pharaohs, their double crown, conical pschents rose as antennae, their ancillary pairs of serpentine uraei, rearing cobras, functioned as anodes and cathodes. Filaments of jade-hued plasma undulated from crown to crown. Neon-limelight suffused from the space between the statues as if they were incandescent bulbs.

The Sibitti and their Duat contractors descended toward the coast. Carter discerned a rail system of mine trolleys. It snaked around the central pyramid, up the ziggurat ramp, to the base of the seated colossi, then looped downward. Trolleys full of body parts went up, and empty ones came down. The materials in the carts fed the alchemical machine. The four enthroned statues in the center processed the fleshy donations. Whatever alchemy occurred in the structure, it also produced crude, oily liquid that leaked from the colossal anuses. Marbleized, red veins in the granite orifices appeared as inflamed hemorrhoids.

The two Sibitti remained levitating over the entrance to the causeway. They had no intention of lingering. Carter and

Haeckel swayed inside the electrical net beneath. Blue light contrasted with the green flares in the background. With cold brevity, the Second reiterated the mission goals. "Enter the pyramid. Disable the barrier. Provide us Midas, alive."

The Sibitti left unceremoniously, letting their cargo drop onto the causeway. The lightning net discharged, recoiling into the Second's blade. Carter and Haeckel smacked onto the wet faience that encircled the Mortuary Mint. They arose from a turmeric-colored slick, splattered in pungent slop.

Diarrhea welcomed them. It wafted in hazy clouds teeming with flies. It puddled beneath their feet. There was a whole lagoon filled with it flanking both sides of the causeway. The lake itself bubbled with molten poop. Four fountains shot from granite posteriors, hundreds of feet high, to aerate the waters. Soupy stool gushed out in pulses.

"There lies hope." Carter smiled, rising to stand on a cerulean tile. She focused on their towering destination at the end of the avenue bridge. "Ah, even defaced and turned away, I recognize the one honored there. The excessive, multiple versions of the same entity give it away. His posture and legs too. Those are depictions of our old friend, Ramses II, the greatest of all Rameses, posed as he was before the Great Temple at Abu Simbel. Except, his thrones here are ceramic rather than rock. And each of his hovering asses sprays a jet of poo."

She brushed off her tattered, stained suit to survey the landscape. The Sibitti's presence had cleared the area nearby. Tortured bodies blown by wind and thrown onto quaking ground wiggled until they collapsed. Many vaporized. However, hands, feet, forearms, and ankles bumpy with pustules splayed about, their reassignment delayed. Hellizens approached Carter and her baby reluctantly. Beachcombers recollected the appendages stricken with Erra's disease, riddled with pox. Those who gathered their fill reformed a queue on the causeway, waiting their turn. They headed to the central ziggurat. There was only one entrance.

Mother Carter picked up her son and joined the line. She underestimated how strenuous the flight here was, not to mention giving birth. Having clutched the Sibitti's net intensely, and for so long, her biceps cramped.

"Ah, I can't carry you." She looked for a resource to help move the baby. Carter noted that the prospectors in line carried body parts by many means: in backpacks, in grocery carts, and even balanced in bags across shoulder yokes.

"When in Rome," Carter placed Haeckel down so she could get an abandoned wheelbarrow. Two oars served as handles. A single tire supported the rusty basin's front. Opaque waste covered the bottom. Tilting it on its side failed to remove the viscous slop. Baby Ernst wailed for attention. "I understand you are anxious to proceed. Me too." Carter turned the wheelbarrow upright and dropped Ernst inside. *Splat.*

Baby Ernst flopped around as they rolled forward, his flipper-like hands too stubby to gain purchase. Haeckel rocked the basin. So short, he could not see where they were going. The toxicity and flavor of gases varied, sometimes rife with ammonia, other moments with sulfur. The sky above was awash in a green haze emanating from the globe of sparking currents arching over them. His jaws ached. A dozen fangs now breached his gums. The malleable pacifier was not satisfying. *"Help me,"* he tried to say; what he did say was, "Hmmm. Mmm."

Miss Carter navigated the land-bridge's divots with all the skill one would expect from a lady of high status. Once a gentleman leading operations over grandiose archeological digs, she usually hired natives for this type of work. Now her hands blistered. Her mind stewed on getting gold, and she considered just dumping Haeckel—he was just slowing her down. But until she made it to Midas, she may need another from Duat. There were many opportunities ahead, but vital details had yet to present themselves. Could they league with Midas, stay inside this protective bubble and snub the Sibitti? Perhaps she could go solo, obtain the Philosopher's Stone, and make her own gold?

Whatever the case, Carter needed more intelligence. She considered striking up a conversation with the prospector leading them. Buckets of pox-swollen hands balanced either side of his shoulder yoke. Four compact shovels bounced and clanked from a belt. An upside-down pot appeared as a helmet. Being so prepared, the individual must have had experience. However, baby Ernst spat out the golden binky and wailed before Carter could start a conversation.

"Shh. I am trying to strategize." Carter stopped the wheelbarrow to retrieve and reinsert the pacifier. Ernst's pointy teeth had riddled it into a bumpy mess. Carter squealed, "You butchered my bauble!" Then she smacked the bearded baby. "This is why we can't have nice things. If you threaten my mission, then mark my words, I'll dump you in an instant. Now start acting like an adult." She crammed the pacifier in her vest pocket and shoved the cart forward. Ernst bounced several times and quieted momentarily.

Carter eased her advance as she noticed the miner in front had turned to stare. A gray beard dangled like Spanish moss. Did he notice the golden pacifier?

The miner said, "Pardon."

Ernst continued to wail.

"Why won't you shut up?" Carter muttered. She had no intention of letting him further mutilate the gold member, so she held back the pacifier. Yet she had to quiet the infant somehow. "Cripes! You are drawing attention. I can't concentrate with this tantrum. Now, stop your childish behavior!"

"Pardon me, sir. I mean, ma'am. I have to inquire," the prospector said while chewing on cud. "Are those real?"

Carter glanced at her exposed bosom. She was not accustomed to covering it, nor was she accustomed to her suit being in such rags.

"I mean the ensemble, sir," he kept both arms on the yoke, spit again. "Savile Row?"

"Indeed, it is," the androgynous Carter adjusted her ruined outfit. She grew suspicious, raised a brow.

"No worries. I'm not hitting on you. There's a tailor in Port Boil who sets up those lucky enough to find gold. Winners don't always come back. Did you win already? Yours looks a tad worn."

She shrugged. "First time mining. Maybe I'll get lucky and use the gold to get this one fixed. Or have a new one tailored. Heck, I may get a whole new wardrobe. No, I *will* get them."

"Now you're talking like a Forty-niner! Most of us here seek gold as we did in California, back in the day. We know some tricks, but it's easy to be fooled." The prospector spat again, then munched his choppers, searching for grit in his cud. His incisors and canine teeth appeared as broken shards, consequences of biting into minerals to determine if they were hard, pyritic fool's gold or genuine, soft gold. "Wish this shitty chew were tobacco. Anyway, most of us here're greedy, ya know?" He snorted.

Carter watched with admiration toward hundreds of Forty-niners who sifted, mined, and hunted for golden nuggets beneath the showering fountains. Thigh deep in the lagoon, they wore pots and colanders, ladles and sieves as armor. The miners' movements issued a din of clanging metal. Several people manufactured sluice troughs to spread out the liquid. All were in hell for their avarice from raping the land of California, pushing out native dwellers, exhausting the environment of precious resources and bringing countless criminals into pastoral farmland.

The prospector continued, "Just like the Gold Rush, you get all sorts of folks tagging along, serving various sins. Slackers. Beggars. Envious louts. Yep. Lots of sin to go around. See that huddle over there?"

To their right, a dozen individuals mud-wrestled in the mire. They formed a twisted mass. One could only see backs and legs. All squiggled like a muddle of piranha during a feeding frenzy. "They do look . . . beside themselves," Carter said.

"They're Sixty-niners. They want 'coin like the rest of us, but they get distracted, aroused by the slightest thing. They're here for the lust more than gold, you get me? They never stay in line long enough to pass the gate. Often, they are peddling sex for the lucky miners who found gold. Gold-digging tramps."

"Well, I'm here strictly for the mining opportunity," Carter said, hastily.

"Mining Buttcoin is not as easy as it looks. Be wary, if you succeed, all the others out there will close in. Be subtle, I tell ya."

They advanced a few steps as the prospector continued, "Once you pay the gatekeeper, you get to mine. The more body parts you give, the more he lets you dig." The toothless miner's eyebrows curled, and his right eye squinted as he summed up Carter. "Your cart looks empty. Ye got anything to donate?"

Baby Ernst's head rose from inside the wheelbarrow. Dingle-berries dangled from Haeckel's orange-stained beard.

Carter shrugged and nudged her head toward the baby.

Ernst frowned in protest. He tried to escape the wheelbarrow to no avail.

The prospector laughed. "Not sure how much time you get for a donation without plague. You'll have to see what Silenus says." Spit.

Carter smiled. Silenus? Of course. In Ovid's poetic *Metamorphosis XI*, Silenus tutored the wine god Dionysus and had several escapades with the Phrygian king. Carter rolled with the information, "That drunk?"

"Aye, his reputation precedes him. He's the only one manning the gate, so when he passes out, the entire operation shuts down. Inefficient, as expected in hell. Anyways, once you get to his pylon, you pass along the . . . uh . . . baby, and then get to sift shit."

"Yee ha! I am rich!" A distant miner held an ingot shaped like a French loaf above his head. It glistened. All in the lagoon instantly focused on the meteoric nugget. It was solid gold. Then a whip of emerald-green electricity appeared like lightning, streaming from the towering obelisks, and zapped the Buttcoin.

The charge knocked the miner off his feet, breaking the circuit and sending him below the surface of diarrhea. He rebounded to stand, blackened. Relieved to have survived, he danced in the cauldron of sewage. Envious Forty-niners blitzed the idiot. Countless orgasmic Sixty-niners stampeded through the lagoon. A wave of limbs and cartwheeling whores consumed the winner. An orgy ensued. Several ibises retreated from the madness, fluttering to safety atop the Rameses. Everyone on the causeway stared, hypnotized by the erotic mayhem.

An ibis flew overhead, squirting a small dose onto Carter's suit. She muttered, "Cursed seagulls!"

From inside the makeshift stroller, Doctor Haeckel disagreed. *"They are* Threskiornis aethiopicus, *African ibis.* Dummkopf!*"*

The aerial attack was well timed. It awoke Carter from watching the pornographic celebration. "Greed trumps lust," she said aloud to affirm her conviction, lifting the wheelbarrow's handles to roll to the front of the line. She ran to the trapezoidal threshold of the ziggurat's pylon, her baby peering over the cart's front, and entered.

*

Buzzing fluorescent lights flickered from the ceiling. Their green light suffused the limestone antechamber. A teller reclined behind the counter of the barred kiosk. He was an immense man with a bulbous nose. His naked, wine-stained torso had all the traits of a well-fed pig. Rolls of belly fat hid his privates from view. Pointy ears stood erect in a wrap of curly hair flanking a bald pate. Arabesque tattoos of gold and green ink covered his shoulders and snaked their way to his concealed backside. Clusters of swollen purple grapes, fresh real grapes, overfilled his hands. He tossed grapes into his mouth as if they were in abundant supply. Indeed, many fell from his grip and rolled on the tile floor.

The teller spoke, "Welcome to the Mortuary Mint, the amusement park for the money-grubbing damned. You look new. Are you prepared to mine buttcoins in the great Ramesside Bowl?"

Miss Carter parked the cart beside the counter. She sighed as baby Ernst rattled the wheelbarrow. He tried to climb out, only to slide back down.

"There is a cost to bank here," spoke the teller. The man glanced over the counter, retrieving a *kantharos*. He took a drink of wine from the dual-handled jar while looking through the bars at the wheelbarrow. "Do you have a donation of flesh, blood, or bone to deposit? Place what you have on the scale." He pointed toward a large rectangular plate in the floor featuring an analogue gauge atop a thin pedestal.

"You are not dropping me off!" Ernst howled. *"Carter? I'm going to get you for this. Carter!"*

"Actually," Miss Carter smacked Ernst to silence, "we are not here to mine."

This response stunned the teller and the German doctor. What was Carter up to? Haeckel yearned to stand, see more, and join the conversation.

"We are here to work," the pretentious antiquarian clarified.

The tall, fat man stood, swigged from his cup, and slurred, "You work? Here, at the Mortuary Mint? I alone work for the Undertaker. Well, me and one other. But he is tied up at the moment." An emerging belch swelled his cheeks.

"We work with the Undertaker too," Carter lied. "You have coworkers now, Silenus."

Silenus burped. His breath smelled intoxicatingly wonderful, especially in contrast to the ubiquitous smell of waste outside. "Do I know you?"

"Not personally. But we are in the same gang." Miss Carter turned to show her back and reveal the lotus mark. Carter then lifted Haeckel by his hair to feature the same symbol. The babe dropped with a thud back into the cart. "I am the Howard Carter, master of antiquities, and my child here is Doctor Ernst Haeckel. The Undertaker sent us to you from Duat. You, sir, deserve a break. As do we. The damnable Sibitti chased us here."

Silenus replied, "No worries. Those weapons of Erra cannot break the alchemical seal around the Mint. If we keep the engine running, we will be fine. All right, come over to the body scanner. Bring your baby."

Carter picked up Haeckel and began walking toward a turnstile.

"No, not that way. That leads to the lagoon. Come this way." Silenus pointed to the opposite side of the room to a cylindrical booth decorated with flashing electrodes. "I'll activate the scanner. Only credentialed materials made by the Undertaker will pass. Strip yourself of unsanctioned artifacts. When it opens, just step inside."

Silenus hobbled to a new terminal, his knees bent backward, and his feet elongated. "Remove your shoes, belt, and all clothing. Place them in a bin. There is a fifty-dram limit on all liquids. Furthermore, your biological constitution, your person, must be from Duat. If your *sesen* is authentic, you will survive. Else, you'll be electrocuted."

"What's a dram?" the archeologist asked. "Is that a currency?"

Silenus ignored her.

Baby Ernst wanted to reply but could not. *"A dram is a measure of volume used by alchemists and scientists. Eight drams is a fluid ounce. Fool!"*

Miss Carter folded her tattered, ripped, stained, burned, soaked-in-crap Savile Row, put it in a bin, then placed her gilded penis on top. A cartoon depiction with hieroglyphs directed how she should stand. She picked up her baby, entered the cavity, sprawled her legs and held Ernst aloft between her hands. Then she waited for the device to activate. After a minute, nothing happened. "Am I standing correctly?"

Silenus studied Miss Carter's androgynous body. "Ah, I drifted off for a moment. You reminded me of my old consort, Hermaphroditus. He was a beauty. Look here, I have him tattooed on my back." Naked Silenus rotated to reveal the full spread of his tramp stamp: a womanly face and breasted humanoid with male genitals caressed the sesen stem as if it were a dancing pole. Silenus laughed. "Well, that may be the last sight you see in your current form. Look forward now. Here goes."

Pulses of brilliant energy flashed. Emerald electrodes lit up the subjects. *Zap, crackle. Pop!*

The pacifier smoldered atop the singed suit; the gold had arced since it was conductive. Carter and Haeckel's naked forms remained unscathed. Their bodies proved compatible with the alchemical, green energy. The process not only confirmed that they came from Duat, but it sterilized their bodies and their clothing in the bin.

"Huh. I expected you to disappear." Silenus took another swig and smiled. "Well, it looks like I have company. You're good to come through."

Miss Carter redressed in her rags and picked up the squiggling Ernst. She kept the pacifier, reluctant to give the prized possession to the ungrateful baby.

A ruckus emanated from the causeway entrance. The pylon threshold filled with eager miners. A prospector called, "Yo, Silenus? Where're ya going?"

The bulbs flickered again.

Silenus took measure of the dimming lights. He closed the kiosk and locked the turnstile. Addressing his new co-workers he said, "They'll wait. Trolley's nearly full, anyway. Time to feed Midas. Come, I'll show you how the Mint works." He pushed a mine trolley full of body parts, limping awkwardly behind it. He headed up the ziggurat ramp in a zig-zag fashion.

Carter followed, her arms aching. It was painful to watch the inebriated Silenus struggle, and more painful to carry a heavy baby. "Fellow Silenus, I will get that cart for you." She assumed ownership of steering the minecart, then dropped Ernst into the plagued necroflesh. Ernst burrowed into the pile. He gnawed on bones to ease his teething.

"You two are eager to work." Silenus smiled.

In short order, they reached the top of the ziggurat. Four colossal versions of Ramses II faced the center of the functional atrium. A common central funnel held atop the statues supplied liquids to a feeding tube lodged in Midas' mouth. The morbidly obese king hovered at the statues' waists, suspended; surrounded by a gibbet of green energy—eerily reminiscent of the Second Sibitti's blue net. Arcs of electricity shot out from the plasma globe that was Midas' glowing form toward the antennae on the Rameses' headdresses.

"Ah, King Midas!" Carter exclaimed and waved. "Greetings!"

The floating king rotated, as if a beached whale. The feeding tube and distance obscured any communication. Midas twitched his donkey-shaped ears, comically extended by the Undertaker as punishment for the king's poor taste in music. Midas's eyes bulged and teared, seeking mercy.

Silenus explained, "Legend had it that King Midas could turn anything to gold—just by touching it. In hell, he can turn flesh into gold. That's because the Undertaker implanted the Philosopher's Stone inside the king. Now Midas ingests plagued flesh, digests it, then egests metallic stool. Somehow this process can launder the plague Erra gives to hellizens." The teller imbibed some wine to wet his throat.

Silenus pointed up to the giant bowl held by the Rameses. "See the hopper up there? The trolleys feed it. There is a stone pestle inside, not visible from down here. Midas creates the electricity for the shaft to rotate and grind the mix of pus, blood, and bone. A slurry exits out the bottom drain of the mortar and funnels directly into his stomach. Then the

magic happens. Midas digests. Look, he is having a movement now."

The four urinary catheters filled with sparkling gold piss.
Similarly, four branched rectal tubes wiggled as pearlescent
liquid moved inside them. These collected the feces that
drained from Midas into, and through, the crotches of the giant Rameses.

Suddenly Midas gasped, arching his back. He wheezed
agonizing throes as his throat bulged. The king wiggled
while stuck in the network of energy, and bound in the manifold of tubes, as surely doomed as any prey in a spider's
web. He gurgled and choked. His stomach flooded with air.
The portly belly inflated, so the folds disappeared, and he
floated higher as if he were a colossal parade balloon. Then
gas cleared his tracks. Air pockets raced through the droop-
ing tubes. Huge sputtering farts resonated from beyond the
atrium. Four squatting Rameses emptied their chutes with a
fanfare of flatulence, literally passing gas toward all four car-
dinal directions.

"Yep." Silenus drunk. "The hopper is empty. He's taking
in air. Time to feed him. Push the cart over there beneath the
pulley. Connect the chains and draw them. Hello?"

Carter did not respond. She was star-struck. Sparkling
gold twinkled from Midas' grand underside. The heart, or the
butt rather, of the Mortuary Mint was beautiful.

"Howard Carter?" Silenus inquired.

"Ah, yes." Carter awoke. She rolled the fodder trolley
containing Ernst to the pulley station. Carter was too awed
by the golden spectacle to remember Haeckel's whereabouts.
She connected the hook and pulled on a chain to activate the
system. Up the minecart went, jerking and creaking with
great speed.

Ernst hardly noticed anything while nursing a bone. He realized too late that he was rising. He climbed his way to the top of the flesh. *"Help!"* Ernst attempted to yell. *"Get me out of here*, dumme Mutter. *"*

The cart reached the top, then rotated automatically. The contents, baby Ernst included, dumped into the hopper. Rotten flesh buried him. Struggling to swim in the primordial soup, it was as if the evolutionist was being born again. The mixing shaft threatened to pulverize him. Ernst clung to the pestle to escape being shredded, his body pressed tight, his feet dangling over the drain. As the fodder thinned into a slurry, it sucked downward. Fighting the drag, he inched his way up the shaft, spinning all the while. Finally, he was parallel to the rim. He lurched to the hopper side, desperately hoping his tiny hands could find purchase.

His stomach slammed the rim. Folded over the edge, with his oversized head on the exterior, he balanced. Without Carter's gold member to soothe his gums, he clamped his jaws onto the stone rim.

Ernst looked beyond the bowl. Midas' belly glowed green. The king's translucent skin barely concealed dozens of stone fragments inside. They lace the entire digestive system! The king's eyes rolled back while sucking on the tube incessantly. As the king ate, his belly glowed brighter and brighter. The consumption triggered some reaction, emitting green light and producing golden waste. It would grow darker as Midas grew hungry again.

The ecologist watched this cycle of ingesting and brightening, emptying and dimming, many dozens of times. Ernst counted the number of trolleys dumped to monitor time. Silenus and Carter did the minimal work to sustain Midas, feeding him regularly and reducing New Hell of plagued flesh. However, they spent most of their time feeding each other grapes, snuggling, and philosophizing. Occasionally, their voices carried so Ernst could hear.

"This is a grand vintage. I never tasted anything so sweet in life or hell." Carter reveled posing as an Undertaker's assistant. She and Silenus talked of wine as they drank from pedestaled cups, maintaining a superb level of intoxication. "Hell is getting better all the time, at least for me."

Silenus returned, "The best thing for a man is to not be born at all."

"But if he is born, then what?" asked Miss Carter.

"Well," Silenus burped, "then the best thing to do is die. As soon as possible."

They toasted and extolled 'cheers'.

Carter doesn't even know she left me in the cart. She basks in the glow of gold, drinking, while I roost in pus-soaked corpse flesh.

Trapped atop the hopper had a benefit: being elevated so high enabled the German to see the atmosphere. A Sibitti storm shot overhead. Its sonic wave reverberated off the Mortuary Mint's dome force-field. Trails of cloud and smoke traced the wraith's flights. *At least I am safe from the Sibitti, but I can't stay like this forever,* Ernst snorted. *We were to retrieve the stone, then die. Thoth would regain his power, then fix us. He could reverse the Undertaker's meddling. Dammit, Carter, serve Thoth, or the Sibitti. Not just yourself.*

Ernst munched the hopper to hone his teeth. *Time to take care of myself. Adapt or die, I must. The strongest survive. That is simply natural selection. It is kill or be killed. Ouch!* His incisors cracked the stone surface. Fragments cut his gums. Ernst spat out blood and smiled. *I have teeth. And jaws. And I can move. I am not powerless. If my teeth can damage stone, then they can easily chew soft flesh.*

As his teeth grew, so did his nails. Clinging with clawed fingers, the doctor descended the feeding tube emerging from the hopper. Vertigo swelled his brain as Ernst clung with his head lower than his legs. Nauseous, he opened his mouth and regurgitated. The moment passed as he closed his eyes until his balance resumed.

Pretentious chuckling rose from way below. Murmurs of Carter's heroic tomb raiding droned on as Silenus lay in a heap, passed out. Lounging at the base of the atrium, the two looked much smaller from up here. Neither saw the serpentine baby crawl toward the king's face.

Baby Ernst made intimate eye contact with Midas. The scientist studied the forlorn visage: sunken eyes, puffy cheeks, extended mouth swallowing a flexible tube. Haeckel hypothesized: *Green light emanates from Midas. He does more than transform diseased flesh into gold. He makes energy too. The Philosopher's Stone is inside him as Silenus showed on his tour and evidenced by the nexus of electricity. The alchemy within the Stone can make both material wealth and spiritual energy. Yet Midas' energy secures his imprisonment. He does not know how to work it, so he is a slave to it. His torture will persist until someone removes the Philosopher's Stone. I must free him for his sake and mine.*

The king wiggled with anticipation as the baby approached. Ernst crept meticulously. Any misstep and he would fall, crash into limestone tile, and end his current existence. Then he would return to Duat without the stone. Inch by inch Ernst stalked, clinging with all four appendages to the feeding tube as if he shimmied on a tightrope. Emerald-hued lightning shot from Midas to the antennae higher up. As within the pylon security scanner, the *sesen* protected Ernst from these bursts.

Hungry for the Philosopher's Stone, and driven by a teething frenzy, the infantile Ernst chewed on the feeding tube. The tube severed. It snapped and flapped around, freed.

Minced food sprayed down. Bile and necroflesh rained onto the two Mortuary Mint workers. Awakened rudely, Silenus wiped cruor from his brow. The teller looked up from the source.

"Not good." Silenus burped. Attempting to stand and run simultaneously, he slipped en route to the pulley system, perhaps thinking to climb it. His *kantharos* cracked as it hit the floor. Lavender-colored wine puddled and soaked its owner. The old man did not have the wherewithal to upright himself.

Carter glimpsed her son slithering. She yelled up, shaking her parental index finger. "Stop it! You come down here. Right now, mister."

Ernst hissed and focused on Midas, who struggled to speak words. The king inhaled forcefully, then gagged. Glittering bile poured out his nose with a ragged exhale. Gulping desperately, Midas instructed, "Take it. End me." Then he stuttered, "Please."

Ernst slithered immediately onto Midas' squishy abdomen. Brilliant uranium-green veins extended through the pale belly. Exercising his animal instincts, Ernst gnawed on his subject. In life, he had steered away from performing vivisections, but now he barbarically executed one using his teeth as crude scalpels. Chew, then spit. Repeat. In this fashion, the devolved doctor mined the body of Midas as elegantly as the Forty-niners sloshed through diarrhea sieving for buttcoins. Ernst delved past the blubbery shell, sinking headlong into the abdominal cavity.

The primary urinary catheter broke free from the immobilized, jostling Midas; the tube hung awkwardly since it remained connected by four branches to the Rameses.

Electrical streaks crackled across the air chaotically, short-circuiting, burning and flashing. Smoke curled from the rubber conduits. Higher up, atop the statues, the electrodes on the pschents flared and sizzled. Then snuffed out. Everything darkened. The hum of the grinding pestle ceased. The entire energy shell protecting the Mortuary Mint flickered. Sphincters from the four colossal Rameses flatulated one last, synchronized puff. All powered down.

The archeologist paced beneath as the plinths beside her cracked. All she could do was watch from the sidelines. "Curses! Haeckel, cease your madness."

Out of sight, the baby gnawed away on the king's internal organs. They revealed the Undertaker's master craftmanship. He had turned Midas' entire digestive system into a biochemical reactor. Dozens of faceted stones, green glowing fragments of the Philosopher's Stone, adorned the internal tracts.

Anywhere Haeckel could discern a glow, he focused his burrowing: kidney stones in their titular location, gallstones in the bladder, and gastroliths in the intestinal tracts. Baby Ernst collected these. Chomping and spitting out flesh, he selectively swallowed the alchemical stones. With each piece removed, the power fueling the Mint failed more. Haeckel stole the sources empowering the Mortuary Mint.

The energy net over the Ramesside Bowl collapsed. No longer supported, Midas' body fell with Ernst inside. Fecal and urinary tubes spanning the interstitial space between the Rameses caught the bloated prisoner. King Midas hung like a broken piñata, spilling entrails as he swayed just over head. Ernst plopped out of the belly to land on a cushion of blubber.

Overhead, thunder boomed, and blue lightning flashed. The Sibitti storm approached again.

"The First and Second are back," Carter muttered. "We are going to have to ensure they know we did this on purpose." She moved to pick up Ernst, compelled to shake sense into the boy, but the rumbling ground interrupted her.

The First slashed his sword at the lagoon. The entire Ramesside Bowl quaked. Obelisks toppled. Swipes of the First's sword struck tangent to the curvature of the faience rim. Brown sluice flushed from the giant bowl into the Vile River. Finally, the four Rameses fell backward into the lagoon. Midas dropped completely to ground level. The enormous mortar flipped over to cover him and the unconscious Silenus. After the dust settled on the sundered monuments, countless Forty- and Sixty-niners screamed until the First slaughtered them.

Meanwhile, the Second hovered on invisible wings over the entry pylon. He repeated aloud to all whom he sentenced: "Erra commands, New Hell shall be called the house of poor, but you have made it a den of thieves." Blue lightning branched from his sword to cast aside scores of prospectors seeking wealth from the temple.

The First floated from on high while the Second levitated up the ziggurat ramp. They converged on the central temple top.

Miss Carter waited. She stood proudly in her ruined suit, appearing as a partially unwrapped mummy. She was prepared to fabricate a believable lie while presenting Midas' golden body to the Sibitti.

Meanwhile, Ernst struggled to speak out to the Second. He attempted to yell, *"Kill me too!" I just need to die now. Get back to Thoth.* His underdeveloped vocal chords failed him, drawing on the attention of his malicious partner.

Carter noticed a green tinge to Ernst's cheeks. Was he sick from eating poisoned flesh? She could not have him interrupting now. Hastily, Carter whipped out the golden pacifier and inserted it. "Shut it." Then she picked up her baby and held him tight. Ernst was considerably heavier after eating Midas' innards and the Philosopher's Stone. Ernst's arms and legs seemed to have evolved too, growing a few inches each. Carter whispered a rant while she could, "You ruined it all. And, ah . . . man. Really?"

Ernst had worked out a squirt of poo onto Carter's ragged suit. Enraged, Carter wrapped her hands around Haeckel's burly neck and squeezed. "You, insolent animal. Stop Haeckel-ing me!" Then her keen eyes caught a sparkle. The shit stain was twinkling. Her emotions flipped in an instant from violent anger to pride. "Oh, wow. Jackpot! I know what you've got. You won't be dying now. You'll be coming with me."

The floating wraiths approached.

Carter bowed dramatically. "Welcome, most powerful Sibitti. Contained under that dome are the men working Satan's Mortuary Mint. Our job is complete."

The Sibitti lifted the overturned hopper to inspect the entrapped Silenus and Midas. Indeed, they found the signature sesen on the Mortuary Mint workers. The alchemy of the site was absent now, since there was no trace of green electricity and the Sibitti walked unabated on the grounds. These imbeciles proved successful.

"Mission accomplished." the Second said, floating before Carter and Haeckel. "You have done well, so we grant you several minutes to leave the premises. You are free to walk New Hell, but not free from serving us. If we ever need beings that have the Duat marking, we will find you. Now go."

Unsupervised, Miss Carter picked up her partner and ran away from the ruined caldera. Being newcomers to New

Hell, Carter knew only of one place to go, Golem Heights to find that Quasimodo character.

Then, without ceremony or pause, the First stabbed Midas and Silenus. Both bodies sublimed into ether, disappearing before they could bleed a drop. The Sibitti departed with godspeed into the air, pleased and still unaware that the power of the Mint lived on within one of their contractors.

*

Hellizens watching the Sibitti rampage for entertainment from afar also delighted in witnessing the retreat of a bare-breasted transgender dragging a deformed child.

"Come on, doctor, we are almost there," Miss Carter dragged Ernst with a leash made from remnants of her suit, mere rags now, rolled and tied end-to-end with knots. Herr Doctor Haeckel crawled on his four limbs as fast as he could, his matted beard dragging on the ground. Dried chunks of Midas' organs still clung to his cheeks. He growled while trying to bite the leash. Hastily crafted as they retreated from the Mortuary Mint causeway, scraps served as a muzzle—the gold pacifier acted as a bit. The left sleeve wrapped around the toddler's rear like a makeshift diaper. It bulged.

Having recalled the location of the French bell-ringer's mansion in Golem Heights, Carter stepped up to the wide, double-door entrance to Goblin Manor. She knocked and heard a commotion inside. The door creaked ajar. Quasimodo recognized the visitors.

Before conversation could begin, shrieking winds burgeoned on the horizon. From this vantage, they all looked over the alleyways of Port Boil to the edge of the Vile River. Cobalt-blue lightning crawled illuminated the atmosphere beneath Paradise.

"Sacrebleu! Please, leave here before the Sibitti come. You must go." Quasimodo slammed the door.

Carter pounded the knocker. "I am not going anywhere. If you want me to leave, then you'll have to listen first. Otherwise, you'll have the First and Second on your doorstep too." She waited now for the Frenchman to calculate her conviction. Ernst squirmed. Shadows and light flickered through the door's peephole.

Eventually, the door opened a tad. "What happened to your suit?" asked Quasimodo from behind the locking chain.

"I admit, my attire is looking distressed." Miss Carter adjusted to support the child on her left hip. "It has been eventful lately."

The hunchback continued his assessment. "Your childish friend has a decorative diaper. It looks most fancy. Is it . . .?"

"Yes, indeed. A Savile."

Quasimodo nodded, impressed. "Cloth is arguably better than disposables."

"Nonsense. This wool is chaffing my privates!" Bit in mouth and unable to speak words, Ernst contributed to the conversation with a long, belligerent toot. A plume of emerald gas coalesced beside them, then exploded into electrical sparks.

"Your friend, the *docteur*, can pass gas better than any adult. You must have your hands, and suit, full of shit. Now, what do you want?"

"It is not what I want, but what *you* want. I can supply you with the finest buttcoins. No need to mine it on the edges of the Vile River or the Mortuary Mint."

"But the Mint blew up. We saw that from up here!"

"Far be it from me to be disingenuous." Carter opened the flap of Ernst's diaper and revealed a golden nugget. "It's not like I am cold-calling your door selling cookies, cleaning sprays, or lawn service. That's not an egg he's hatched. That's genuine buttcoin. I am offering you a sample."

"That nugget must be worth one-hundred thousand diablos! It must be a counterfeit."

"It's authentic. Look closer." She extended the full diaper, showing it through the gap by the doorframe.

"Excréments d'or? Golden feces?" Quasimodo reached out to collect the diaper and zap! Emerald light flashed. The hunchback extinguished his smoldering sleeve. "I shall leave that with you. I must get my master." He left the visitors outside.

When it opened again, thunder crackled across the sky. Light gleamed upon a towering, eight-foot-tall creature of a man. The scar-faced doctor loomed over his hunched servant. Fresh gore splashed his lab coat. Clearly, they had interrupted an operation. Purple veins shone through paper-thin skin around a mesh of chicken wire enclosing an exposed brain. "My servant claims you have found the golden fleece?"

"Feces, *mon amie,*" Quasimodo interjected. "Master, I said golden *feces*!"

Victor shot his servant a harsh look and gestured to close the door.

Miss Carter spoke fast in her huskiest voice, "Name is Howard Carter. Dealing with antiquities is my specialty. My boy here is the renowned evolutionist Doctor Ernst Haeckel. You, sir?"

"Doctor Victor Frankenstein, anatomist." He sighed. "What do you want from us?"

Carter grabbed the glossy, metallic slug and bit into it. Imprints remained. "I need a discreet place to set up my operation. Then, if you can supply flesh, I can get you more of this." She tossed the ingot in the air.

Victor grabbed and inspected it. He glanced at Quasimodo approvingly. "Flesh is scarce. Bodies disintegrate when
killed in New Hell, but I would assume you understand that."
Victor Frankenstein educated Miss Carter: "These bodies we
are given in hell are composed of variations of organic matter: necroflesh, moribones and mortisblood."

"I just need the plagued type. The type folks were bringing to the Mortuary Mint. Can you source that? My child
needs to eat, understand? We need his gold."

"What would prevent us from taking your partner, feeding him ourselves and then mining 'coin without you."

Ernst's cheeks swelled with frustration. Electric threads
shot from his Duat birthmark to that on Carter. The shredded
Savile Row singed as well as Haeckel's beard.

"Unless you are from Duat, I wouldn't touch him. Besides, we all have our own arts. You appear to be a medical
doctor. I deal with material wealth. Let us work our crafts
and help one another. Deal?"

Victor smirked. Finally, he would have funds for his research. "Quasimodo, take our friends here to one of your
dens in Port Boil. Let us give this a try."

"*Oui,* my friend."

*

Port Boil was no Egyptian Valley of the Kings, but it was
beside a river and Howard Carter fancied it as equivalent.
Whereas the topside Valley along the Nile hosted dozens of
pharaohs' graves including the tomb of King Tutankhamen,
Port Boil featured sewage-doused streets littered with the ap-
athetic damned, gluttonous heathens and lazy beggars. Populated sections spawned pubs, drug dens, and brothels. In this
labyrinthine ghetto, Quasimodo found a discreet location

indescribable from its neighbors, a district of fast-food res-
taurants torched to the ground.

"Over there was Stake & Shake, and on that corner an
Unlucky Fried Chicken. But this is the site that should work
for you." The hunchback stood as a dwarf beside the defining
statue. Forged from a fire-resistant ceramic, the restaurant's
mascot stood tall atop the burned rubble: a ten-foot-high,
cartoonish boy holding a platter of intestines, his belly eviscerated such that coils of sausage spilled over his red check-
ered pants; a multi-tiered crown adorned his head. "He's the
Burger Boy King, with his innards out. See, this was an Innards Out Burger joint," the Frenchman said. He pointed to
the menu placard which appeared from a pile and that read:
Tender Fingers, Pus Fried Nuggets, Curly Colon Fries, Irri-
table Bowel Patties; all marked with 'zero calorie' nutritional
warnings.

"So, you propose I set up operations out in the open, next
to the Boy King?" asked Carter. She held her baby tight, raising a brow.

"*Non, mademoiselle,*" the hunchback replied. "Of course
not. Look under the debris." He lurched forward and nudged
aside a deep-fryer to reveal a descending staircase. Sooty
beams, congealed pus, and ashen trash clogged it. Together,
the two adults unplugged the threshold. At the bottom of the
steps, a rectangular antechamber four by six fathoms opened
before them. One wall hosted a series of metallic doors. Quasimodo started shifting disheveled heaps of paper crowns
and napkins to clear a path. The two stacked stockpiles of
condiment packets to the side.

"Safes?" Miss Carter gasped, envisioning banks of hidden wealth. She squeezed Ernst. He gagged behind the
muzzle.

"You are close, *mademoiselle*." Quasimodo turned the handle to the nearest. A cloud of sulfurous rot roiled out. Undeterred, the party toured the inside of the abandoned, defunct meat cellar. "These freezers full of inventory are yours to eat."

In the first freezer, wires dangled from a caved ceiling. Crimson light from Paradise diffused through the roof. Three poles penetrated the hole.

"There is flesh here! Canned and ill-preserved."

"*Oui*, processed foods that contain no nutrition and shall never expire. They are, more than likely, infected by Erra's plague, too. This food should suit your specifications. If you stay underground, no one should know you exist. Out of sight, out of mind. I shall return in time." Quasimodo left.

Carter applied her mastery to remodel the basement into sacred grounds. Securing the entry was the priority. Maintaining the rubble camouflage, she cleared away the remaining refuse on the steps, lodged two metal panels and manufactured a latch out of a wooden plank. Likewise, she cleared the room. Soon, the primary cellar was befitting of a royal burial chamber, the adjoining freezer and ancillary chambers promised to become treasuries. In the first freezer, Carter modified the grated shelving to form a playpen for the budding Ernst. She set to work building her wealth.

"Open up little fellow," Miss Carter extended a steel spoon into the improvised kennel. A pimpled strand of intestine wiggled on it.

Ernst pressed against the grating. He swiped at the spoon, and the morsel shot as if catapulted.

The androgynous captor collected the stray meat with her fingers. She offered the silage again.

Ernst's mouth snapped at her fingers.

"Ouch!" Carter backed away, sighed. "You know, you could cooperate. Hunger strikes do not become a gentleman. Seriously, show some civility, doctor."

The devolved, German evolutionist retreated into the corner of his kennel. He squatted, clenched his jaws, and held his breath. Green light illumined from his belly as the stones worked their magic. Grunting, huffing and puffing ensued.

"Oh, poor baby. Are you constipated?"

Green-cheeked Ernst pushed harder. With explosive, gaseous fanfare, the bowel movement ended. A golden pellet shot down into the straw.

Carter did not hesitate to collect the treasure. She had taken to grooming the litter box religiously to gather any golden feces. She placed the nugget in an array of others laid out on the floor.

"So much wealth, and yet it covers so little of the room. I need more from you, my dear partner. It is time for you to eat again. Oh, do not feign that you are not hungry. You may not need real sustenance in hell, but I saw you eat into Midas' belly with immeasurable conviction. Now you have the power he had. You must want to use the Philosopher's Stone. Otherwise, why claim it?"

"To give it to Thoth, idiot!" Haeckel motored about his kennel avoiding the spoon. *"Let me out of here. You cannot hold me captive. I am a being. Not some animal!"*

The reply sounded like babbling nonsense to Carter, but the language was taking better form. It was almost discernable.

"Now stop muttering and rolling about. Cripes." Carter followed her partner around the cage with a spoonful of mashed innards to no avail. "Fine, your obstinance is easily met." She retrieved the rusty poles from the ruins. She inserted them into the cage such that Haeckel could no longer rotate. Then, she tugged on the scruff of Haeckel's neck so that his mouth opened, raised.

The doctor gurgled. Then the innards-slurry poured down his throat. He choked it down.

I must be true to science, to the purpose of alchemy. I will not make gold. No. Instead, I will remake, myself. As Haeckel focused his energies toward developing his own spirit and body, the stones within blazed. Potential energy increased, so Ernst glowed. The static electricity discharged in a bright green flash.

*

Time droned on. Miss Carter typically stayed in the proper cellar, arranging and playing with her gold. Columns of well-stacked buttcoins fell over into an amorphous, wondrous heap. This left the immobilized dwarf unsupervised. Being dead, Haeckel had no actual need to eat, drink or sleep. Imprisoned, he was no better off than Hatshepsut and Senenmut who remained ensnared in barbed wire, in a trench, alongside the Vile River. If only he could die again to be remade by Thoth, or even the Undertaker. For now, Haeckel could do almost nothing except listen. Occasionally, the walls would shake as storms passed over New Hell. Certainly, the Sibitti maintained their flybys.

Doctor Haeckel did what he could: ruminate. Midas had created energy somehow with alchemy, not just gold. Could Ernst electrify the wires dangling through the hole in the freezer's top? He set to experimenting. Willing his body to create energy was nonintuitive, inefficient, yet eventually productive. Alchemy needed necroflesh and the Philosopher's Stone. He learned to make his intestines glow after consuming. He could generate small bolts of electricity on demand from his anus, but they did not launch in any specific direction and were only short bursts.

He wanted to extend his reach, gain freedom. He had no choice other than to work with the materials on hand. He sent tendrils of green sparks to electrify the cage. They arced to the ceiling. Haeckel felt the freezer's shape through the ether. It tickled all his nerves. He felt peculiar harmonics. *Voices? Radio stations?* Wires jiggled and danced until one lashed like a whip onto the steel manifold around him. The signals pulsed every instant the circuit broke. Then it held constant: *Zzzz, zap!* The room glowed green.

Words flooded through the conduit to stream into Haeckel's brain: "We continue our incessant fund drive on the Perdition Broadcasting System . . . until we reach our goal, we will rerun the classic Abbott and Costello's 'Who's on First' skit continuously."

The first hour was entertaining, but then it repeated ad infinitum. Haeckel could not turn it off. He heard this many, many times. He repeated both characters' lines in his head, merging them: "Well then who's on first? Yes. I mean the fellow's name. Who. The guy on first. Who. The first baseman. Who. The guy playing . . . Who is on first! I'm asking you who's on first . . . Who's on Second?"

Ah, the First and Second. Silly American baseball humor. My torture is far from funny. I need to get back to Duat. Get to Thoth. He can transform my body. But I cannot leave here. Perhaps . . . the First . . . and the Second . . . perhaps they could free me?

"Wow, you are lighting up." Miss Carter had approached, startling Ernst. Lightning traced onto her, split into a dozen streams, then dissipated. Unfortunately, Carter was immune to this shock. Thankfully, it disconnected the wiry antennae and the connection to PBS. Abbot and Costello quieted.

The discharge also dislodged the golden pacifier from Ernst's mouth. The muzzle kept it from falling too far. Haeckel was free to mutter, "*Zuerst.*"

Miss Carter rushed to the cage. "What? You are learning to speak? What did you say?"

"*Zuerst. Zweite . . .*"

"Wurst? That's Deutsche for sausage!" Carter misinterpreted the German for 'first' and 'second.' She continued, "You are hungry. I'll fish up some wienerwurst." She started to retrieve the meat when a visitor knocked on the door. She shoved the golden pacifier back into Ernst's mouth.

"*I tire of you shoving your penis into my throat.*"

Miss Carter left toward the antechamber, "Quasimodo comes. Your sausage is coming after I deal with him."

The Frenchman stayed atop the steps. Haeckel could still hear the exchange from the basement.

Miss Carter said, "Here are your buttcoins, as promised."

"Only three, *mon amie,* not five?"

"If the suit you brought me fits, I'll give you the rest. Hmmm, yes. Forty. Thirty. Thirty-six. My measurements exactly."

"You look stunning, madam."

Miss Carter replied, "Splendid. Pass along my sentiments to the tailor. Here are three additional buttcoins."

"Three more!" Quasimodo smiled. "Victor will be most pleased. He can finance several experiments now."

They arranged to meet periodically and said farewells. Carter sealed the entry, prancing into the basement in her new Savile Row dress-skirt. Carter tucked in her fresh buttoned-down shirt into her curveless cut, straight skirt, then shifted her breasts to conceal them behind the coat flaps. These were unstained wool garments assembled from over a dozen other dresses. Gathering fine, unadulterated fabric swatches was a costly endeavor. The patchwork was seamless. Yet, only a few buttcoins covered this craftmanship, and she had a whole secret hoard.

A second freezer was full now. Buttcoins and fecal sluice spilled into the cellar. The chemical Law of Conservation of Mass applied. For every dram of necroflesh that Haeckel ate, he generated a commensurate volume of gold. The cellar was getting full. As if a dragon, Carter rolled atop the hoard, letting the metallic nuggets tumble through her pudgy fingers. Then she donned a paper Burger Boy crown, anointed herself pharaoh of the underworld, and approached her imprisoned son. Overcome with ecstasy from being fully self-actualized, she had forgotten about the sausage request.

"As pharaohs live past death, so do I," Carter twirled with her paper crown and her repurposed Savile dress.

"You are in hell, idiot, with billions of others. Death becomes you. All of us," Haeckel railed internally.

Tossing coins all about as if confetti, she exclaimed, "I create gold!"

"No, I do! Out of my asshole, danke schoen. *You torture me for it!"*

Carter ignored Haeckel, ranting, "I am a king, and queen. I am rich. Rich!"

"Dumkopf! *There are more powerful entities than you. That paper crown is no Egyptian pschent. That gold is literally my shit."*

Unable to interpret that, Carter continued educating his compatriot. "History is what I make of it, and it will remember me well. You, Doctor Haeckel, witness the beginning of the Carter Dynasty."

"Are you mad? What are you doing now? Painting?"

Indeed, Carter decorated the walls with intricate graffiti. Divine muses and an inflated ego inspired her. She rushed from freezer to cellar, to the other freezer, and back again. In moments, horizontal lines outlined the forthcoming bounds of four murals. Streaks of tomato ketchup delivered through a plastic straw spelled the hieroglyphs. Mustard yellow filled in sections of two-dimensional stick figures. The edible paints hastily splashed onto her gray suit.

Miss Carter inspected the stains and cackled. "I may have to buy another!"

She sketched out the four panels, the first capturing her accomplishments in life, especially the finding of KV62, the tomb of King Tutankhamun. The subsequent panels showcased her exploits in hell. The second covered the excavation of the Duat Nile Delta, including championing a defense against the piratic Sea Peoples, entering Anubis' Hall of Two Truths and passing her challenge of the Scale of Truths. The third, covered the navigation of the underverse's Lake of Fire and excavating the pyramidal temple of Osiris to find the god's lost penis. With limited vantage, Ernst only saw the fourth panel. This showed the Pharaoh Carter in a suit and pointy beard atop a pyramid of coins. Ernst knew Carter left him out of her version of their history together. Haeckel frowned.

"No worries, friend. I included you. This toad represents you. It is symbolic of your love for the things on the Nile Delta. Remember playing in the mud with them? I had to use relish for the coloring, which is not colorfast, but it will have to do."

"*Frogs plagued the Nile during the great plague under Ramses II, not toads. You forge history with more embellishment than I ever expressed with my hand-drawn data.*"

"You look displeased. I'll just erase it." Carter washed the relish toad away.

"Have you no honor in documenting the truth? Do not omit me!" Sparks flew from the cage to the coins, forcing them aside and sending them twirling and bouncing. Haeckel considered: *There must be many, many more coins outside this room. I know how much I egested. And gold is conductive. Now is the time to act.*

Ernst spat out the gilded phallus of Howard Carter. Tendrils of green lightning discharged to follow it, reaching out from Ernst to the pacifier, and clinging to it as it reached the floor. It passed its charge to the trails of coins. Energy sizzled. Ernst concentrated harder and harder, pushing all his potential, cramping his stomach, working his intestines and mind, urging whatever nascent alchemical power he had to release. Lightning streamed out his anus. Alchemical energy danced from coin to coin, popping like kernels of popcorn. Heat from the reaction fused many coins. The explosive nature of the transformation shot hundreds into the ceiling. As if someone ignited a stockpile of munitions, the entire hoard of gold energized and created thousands of short circuits. In just milliseconds, several million arcs constructively amplified.

The place blew.

The roof of Innards Out Burger peeled away. Buttcoins and condiment packets fountained upward in a mushroom-shaped cloud, paused nearly a furlong high, then rained upon the ashen district of Port Boil. Globs of ketchup, pus, mustard, and mortisblood splattered the pavement.

"You are ruining everything, you bastard. Curse you, Ernst!" In a smoldering, stained suit and singed crown, the self-declared Pharaoh shouted, "You are why I can't have nice things!"

Haeckel smirked since the golden phallus flew away in the chaos, and, more importantly, the sky rumbled. Thunder raced from a distant horizon.

"Where did my penis go?" Carter yelled in frustration at her boy. She did not expect an audience, and gasped when two floating, wingless wraiths zoomed forward as if the air itself formed invisible palanquins. Effortlessly and precisely, the personified weapons of Erra made way to the Innards Out Burger.

"*Zuerst. Zweite.*" Haeckel said aloud. "Who is First? What's on Second." He laughed in his cage. The end was near. A new beginning awaited.

"You called. We came," announced the Second.

Miss Carter said, "Uh, erm. Yes, yes. We, erm . . . found a hidden stash of gold. We thought you may want to dispose of it."

The Second cut to the chase. "It looks as if *you* create wealth now. Hell is not a place for that. You must work for the Undertaker."

"Uh, no. Actually, we do not," replied Carter.

The First cared not for antics or lies. The Sibitti with the earthen sword took flight, flew around the premises. Each swathe shot turbulent air toward inorganic buttcoins. The coinage melted on impact or shattered into dust.

"No, not my gold!" Carter inhaled deeply in disbelief, shock. She wrung her hands through her hair. "Cripes, Haeckel, can't you repel them or something? Midas could. Do something!"

The Second drifted toward the freezer wherein Ernst remained pinned. Blue sparks crackled about the Sibitti's form and sword. Any incompatible, emerald electricity subsided from the caged victim. Haeckel controlled the Philosopher's Stone as much as he could. He kept all its fragments powered off.

The Second understood and dismantled the kennel. To Carter, he said, "Even with Midas gone and the Mortuary

Mint in ruins, gold currency still circulates in hell. You are the source. I am here to eliminate wealth. I am here to nullify the power that manufactures gold." He picked up Haeckel and floated upward.

"Noooo!" Carter instinctively leaned against Burger Boy King for support. She collapsed beside it, sinking to her knees while wailing. "No. Not my baby. That's my baby. Please don't take him. I need him."

"I know what you did, greedy man." The Second held the mutant Haeckel aloft by the beard so that his neck was accessible. One slice took the head clean off. Haeckel's decapitated form and head dropped separately. His bearded face smiling, his body twirling for a split second, and then . . . *poof* . . . . The body parts disappeared.

Carter balled in the fetal position. "No, no, no! I had it all."

Then a shadow loomed over her.

It was the silhouette of the First.

And then . . .

*

Ernst Haeckel opened his eyes. He saw only the texture of a lotus pad beside his head. He could not move.

Thank the powers that be, I am back in Duat. Then he remembered that a blade had separated his body. *That pile beside my head must be it. Someone already cut into it. Where is the Stone?*

Brilliant green light diffused into the foliage surrounding the floral operating table. The sepals opened wide. Several humanoid figures stared down at Haeckel's head and body. One held the golden caduceus, the tip of which was illumined with the Philosopher's Stone. The light was so bright, Ernst could not discern who was present beside it.

The one holding the staff had an extended nose. A beak? He asked aloud, "Thoth?"

The silhouette growled a laugh. Its canine snout clarified as Ernst's eyes adjusted. It wore a kilt of flayed skin, made from eleven Ramesside faces.

"Anubis?" Haeckel queried.

"Yes." growled the Operator of the Scale of Truth. "Just close your eyes; the Undertaker is here to operate."

A Caucasian male in a Savile Row suit leaned on the winged staff. He was not Carter. This one had a full head of oiled black hair. And his breath smelled terrible.

"Undertaker?"

The Undertaker picked up the doctor's head with one hand and spoke to it directly, face-to-face. "Ernst Haeckel, you are a meddler, aren't you? You could learn a thing or two from your partner Carter. He at least supported my plans. However, you sabotaged my Mortuary Mint, disrupted the work put in place to stem the accumulation of flesh plagued by Erra. You must adore the Sibitti, but they annoy me. Impressive meddling deserves equal attention."

Ernst's head was placed back on Slab A.

"As a scientist, you deserve to know more about the power of the Philosopher's Stone," the Undertaker said. "The art of alchemy began in Egypt, and the powers of it sustained Osiris's Temple of Rebirth. The power to transmute, to reform, and to reassign is a wondrous science. It is equally useful to work materials as flesh or one's identity. And I use it more adeptly than that bird-brain Thoth ever could. Your next form will embody my wrath."

"What happened to Thoth?" the ecologist's head muttered, glaring at the caduceus.

The Undertaker understood and laughed. "Why, did you not see? His body shares the slab with you."

Another operation began.

The True Believer

Lou Antonelli

Quashing hope is the most common and tedious chore for demons, and it seemed this assignment would be no exception.

Reports had reached certain hellish ears of a damned soul who needed some special attention. This soul needed a personal visit from a demon. And so he would get one.

As the demon flew towards the precincts where he expected he would find his victim, harsh sounds reached his pointy ears. The demon knitted his brow and listened more carefully.

It was language.

A particularly harsh guttural sound of this language floated up through the steam and fumes. Sometimes it sounded like a hellhound clearing its throat.

The demon began his descent.

As he flew lower, words became audible, and then the meanings of sentences.

As he alit, he realized this was the language the damned in this precinct spoke, cried out and cursed in.

Afrikaans.

German is a harsh sounding language, and then its neighbor—both geographically and linguistically—Dutch sounds that much worse.

Afrikaans, the language that evolved from the mother tongue that the Dutch-descended settlers spoke in isolated South Africa, is harsher and more guttural still. Arthur C. Clarke opined it was the harshest language in the world to curse in, and that innocent bystanders had been injured in the course of a heated argument in Afrikaans.

The demon curled his lips in pleasure. The language sounded so harsh that he found it delightful.

He folded his wings and then smoothly and seamlessly took on the appearance of one of the bystanders, in this case an innocuous bywoner—a poor white South African sharecropper.

Such a person would not get a second glance in New Preterroria, the South African Boer precinct in New Hell. This demon wasn't interested in attracting attention. He'd been given a job to do and wanted to do it as fast and efficiently as possible and get back to his favorite crag.

The "city" he walked through was of course a hellish afterimage of is prototype on Earth. The streets were wide but dirty, and rows and rows of jacarandas now glowed an ominous purple, as their original blue hue was tinged by the red of Paradise above New Hell's glow.

Here and there were disturbing signs of efforts made by damned souls at maintaining order: a wall painted here, a fence repaired.

"Silly," muttered the demon. These helpless souls tried to emulate their home, and it bothered him because it might indicate they retained some kind of hope.

Which he will crush. That's why he was here.

He sneered at stupid hints meant to maintain bourgeois normalcy and wondered in some fashion—for demons are not deep thinkers—whether the man he was looking for was responsible.

Reports had reached HSM as he sat behind his desk that there was a New Dead man who denied the finality of his damnation, who in fact, still spoke of salvation. He had not been an insignificant figure in life, and indeed had led the Republic of South Africa for many years.

He was well-educated, a doctor of psychology, and later a newspaper editor. Subtle and crafty, controlling South Africa behind the scenes for many years, he was forced into the open by the passage of time when he assumed the prime minister's post, There, he survived multiple assassination attempts before being ambushed and finally killed.

Now in hell, he remained recalcitrant. That's why the demon was on his errand.

In the distance, the hellish emissary saw the outline of the South African Government House outlined by flames and obscured by smoke. As he walked, he saw many of the New Dead Boers on streets raking leaves, picking up trash, and doing menial chores as their Black *baas* watched, while the good Boer *vrouws* served as nannies and household servants.

The role-reversal evened the score for centuries of household servitude they had imposed on the people whose land they stole and settled.

It was only Petty Apartheid, the most visible and obvious example of the system of racial oppression that pinned down the native African population.

Grand Apartheid—the co-option of the nation's resources and economy in the service of the descendants of European settlers—saw the black man labor below the ground mining gold he would never own, harvest food crops he would never eat. All maintained by rule of law and enforces by large and officious bureaucracy.

The ruins of that bureaucracy were obvious to the demon as he walked into the lobby of the government house. Flames flickering in dark corners. Broken light fixtures illuminated papers blowing across the lobby, the remains of once-important executive orders. Singed rubber stamps littered the floor amidst the occasional three-ring binders.

The demon saw a set of ornate doors at one end of a hallway. Light outlined them from within. He walked purposely onward. When he reached the end doors, he grabbed one handle and yanked.

The doors were locked.

The demon pounded hard on the doors. They began to splinter. One door suddenly swung open.

"May I help you, sir?" He was greeted by a man who looked very British but sounded very much like a native Afrikaans speaker. He had a bristling russet mustache and hair and wore a neatly tailored Savile Row-type suit with an old school tie over a crisp white shirt.

"I'm here for Hendrik Vewoerd, the South African politician."

"Do you have an appointment, sir?"

"What?" the demon roared. He raised a flaming fist to strike the man down, but a voice came from behind him.

"Clive, let our visitor inside, I'm not preoccupied," boomed a voice from within.

The man at the door looked up at the demon. "I am his personal assistant, Clive Darby-Lewis. Allow me to introduce you."

"I need no announcement," said the demon as he pushed the man aside and strode into the office. On the far side of his desk, the former Prime Minister of South Africa was already standing—with a genial smile and yes, a twinkle in his eye.

Six feet four inches, stood the well-proportioned man with sandy blond hair and glacier- blue eyes, Dr. Verwoerd wore a striking well-tailored suit, 1960s era, and a narrow tie. He smiled broadly as he gestured towards a seat for his guest.

The demon crossed his arms on his chest and fumed at Verwoerd's pleasant and genial air. He stomped up to the ornate desk and planted his feet.

"You seem cheerful enough for one of the damned," the demon said.

"I have been told that I am a cheerful fellow," said Verwoerd. "May I sit?"

The demon nodded. Dr. Verwoerd sat behind his desk and clasped his hands on its leather surface.

"To what do I owe this honor?" he asked.

"I have a few questions to ask. You do know where we are, correct?"

"The afterlife, of course."

"This is not the afterlife, this is hell," snarled the demon.

"Is not hell the afterlife?" asked Dr. Verwoerd.

"*This sonofabitch is clever*," thought the demon.

He pointed a sharp finger. "Hell is your afterlife, and you don't seem to be suffering as much as you should." He paused. "There are reports you still speak of salvation. You do know you are damned for all infernity, correct?"

The genial expression vanished from Verwoerd's face, which now appeared like that of a dominee—a Dutch Reformed Church minister—who was disappointed with a student's answer in Sunday School.

"No, I do not, sir," he said wagging a finger at the demon like an irate schoolmaster.

"I know my people—*die Volk*—are the Chosen. That's why we were given the land to settle and prosper. That's why we succeeded and surpassed all the trials placed before us from Above while on earth, including the Great Trek and defeating the black savages at the Battle of Blood River. That's why we were able to build up a prosperous and modern nation that was the envy of the world.

"What you call damnation is just another setback we have encountered, nothing more than a particularly onerous set of sanctions," he continued. "We have overcome all the trials we have encountered before, and we will overcome again."

The demon sat, stunned, eyes wide. He had heard defiance before, but this son-of-a-bitch believed what he said!

Verwoerd half turned in his chair and pointed to a large black and white photograph on the wall. It showed him on stage at an outdoor event, tall, erect and smiling behind a microphone.

"That was taken at a National Party political rally in Cape Town in 1966," he said. "You see that banner behind me? I believe that. Even if I am damned for all eternity, which I do *not* believe, I will not be a hypocrite in death."

Verwoerd was an intelligent man and correctly surmised the demon could read all languages. He watched as the demon scanned the message:

"Glo in jou volk, glo in jou self, skep jy jou eie toekoms."

The demon roared his response: "Believe in your people, believe in yourself, make your own future! Such drivel! You're nothing more than a self-important charlatan! Your stupid platitudes may have fooled millions on earth, but they are meaningless here! How dare you spout such sanctimonious bullshit!"

Dr. Vewoerd rose. "They are not platitudes. They are . . ."

"Enough!" roared the demon. Your 'people', as you call them, were the dregs of Europe who went abroad rather than face ostracism and poverty in their homeland. They stumbled into a more primitive people, killed and subjugated them, made them into little more than slaves to drive their nation-building. You disguised their racial oppression with all sorts of high-sounding verbiage, but in so many ways your people served my master, bringing hell on earth to those black people while they were still living!"

All the alleyways and streets in Preterroria echoed with the demon's rant.

"You and your chosen people are in hell. Get that through your thick skull! This is not purgatory, you dous—insulting him in his native tongue—This is hell and hell is final. There is no escape, there is no redemption, and I will visit a most terrible punishment upon you!"

"Do as you wish," said Dr. Verwoerd. "While I am here I am subject to your wrath and punishment. It is part of the eternal plan."

The demon knew he should not react to such goading. He took a deep breath and pointed a sharp talon at Verwoerd.

"I will say this: my master reigns over many people who were deluded Christian mystics above, but you are the only one I know of who chose to call himself a politician instead of a prophet, seer, cleric or saint."

Verwoerd chuckled. "That was my third career. I was named a professor at Stellenbosch University when I was twenty-six. In middle age, I was a journalist and edited the National Party's newspaper, *Die Transvaler*. I became prime minister when I was fifty-six."

The demon was stunned by how little impact his words had made on this already damned soul. He took a half step forward and inhaled.

"Doctor Verwoerd, fire and brimstone are too good for you, and as deluded as you are, I doubt they will make an impression."

With a nod of his head the demon extended his wings. "I have a most appropriate punishment for you."

He walked around and behind the prime minister's desk and threw open the double doors to the balcony that looked over New Preterroria. He turned to stare at Verwoerd.

"I will say it has been interesting."

As he took flight, the powerful gusts blew open the office's doors and Darby-Lewis ran to him.

"Well, Clive, he's gone, and he didn't touch a hair on my head," said Verwoerd. "Despite this purgatorial punishment that has been meted out to us, he finally can't destroy us, can he?

Verwoerd waited a few seconds and then hearing no reply, turned to face Darby-Lewis, whose eyes were wide.

"What is it, Clive?"

"He's done worse than destroy you, sir." He gestured to a side wall, where a mirror hung over a decorative table.

Dr. Hendrik Verwoerd—the Man Who Invented Apartheid—walked over to the mirror to see a tall, handsome, very black African man staring back at him in utter shock.

By Any Means Necessary

Gustavo Bondoni

Umberto Eco pressed his eyelids together. The metal slab beneath him told him all he needed to know: it hadn't been a dream, or if it was, it wasn't over.

Think. The last thing he remembered was the hall of pendulums. The place was nearly dark, but he could remember it contained hundreds of massive weights in motion, whizzing one way and then the other, their patterns of interaction growing more and more complex until, by the end, he couldn't predict them. Finally, one of the spheres slammed into him with a crunch and sent him flying into the path of several others. Dead on the slab.

Before that, a gaggle of students, failed papers in hand, had lynched him, and the endless sun of an island without time had scorched him to nothingness. Worst of all had been the crazed monk who'd force-fed him an entire manuscript. It must have been poisoned—it should have been poisoned—but Umberto Eco had felt no ill effects other than the fact that the paper tasted much worse than it should have. Finally, the monk tore out Umberto's eyes and set him on fire.

With that memory, fear of blindness came upon him and he snapped his eyes open. It was almost comforting that he saw the face of the gray creature above him.

"You're ready to go now," the voice said.

None-too-gentle hands pushed him off the table, and he landed on the ground with a bone-jarring thud. Dry laughter echoed as he struggled to his feet.

The elevator. The obscene woman and her monstrous, pendulous . . . He fended off her half-hearted advances and exited onto a field of dry grass. The last few times this had happened, he'd been killed horribly and almost immediately. But something felt different about this time. It didn't feel like he was about to die, or whatever passed for death in this place.

Until he saw the man.

The man was death on the hoof. Tall and broad-shouldered, his posture screamed military. He walked with the swagger of someone who knew he was the most dangerous person for miles around . . . No mean feat, considering where they were. Expressionless gray-brown eyes surveyed the scene. A deep, ugly scar curved from his clean-shaven chin to his left ear. His bearing was perfectly complemented by his dark gray uniform, devoid of insignia but redolent of the Nazis of Eco's youth. A German-looking pistol hung, holsterless, from his belt.

The man headed straight toward Umberto Eco, who shrank back but, having nowhere to go, went nowhere.

A hand the size of a dinner plate closed around his arm. Umberto had to look up, way up, to meet the man's gaze.

"You Eco?"

"Y– ye– yes," Umberto stammered. The man seemed somehow familiar, but that was ridiculous. If he'd met the guy before, he would have had nightmares about him every night.

"Good. Do you know where you are?"

"I . . ." Seeing that the man made no immediate move to hurt him, Umberto got a hold of himself, calming his heart, his lungs, his shaky limbs. "My best guess is hell."

"Good guess." The man looked at him sternly. "And I don't want to hear anything about how you don't deserve to be here. No one cares."

"Oh, I never thought I might go to heaven. Didn't expect to come here, but that's only because I never really believed in hell. I spent my entire career laughing at other people's credulity." He chuckled and his fear made his tongue click. "I guess the joke is on me."

"Yes. I've heard."

That caught Eco's attention. "Why would you have heard of me?"

"This isn't the place for such talk," the man replied. His tone brooked no argument. "Come with me."

Umberto went.

*

"I am Otto Skorzeny," the man said.

As he tried to place the name, Eco looked around the bar. It was a bar you would expect to find in Naples or Palermo: a seaside bar in a seaside town. Wooden tables, wooden chairs, tile floor, a window out of which you could watch a man being thrown to a pack of jackal-like creatures by a group of men who appeared to be taking bets on how long he'd last. It was as dirty and hot and muggy as one could want.

Then the name struck home.

"The Nazi commando? The one who rescued Mussolini?"

Skorzeny grimaced. "Not my finest hour, but . . . Yes."

Eco swallowed as he recalled the rest of the man's history: Unrepentant Austrian Nazi; SS trooper; commando; war criminal and, it was reputed, an assassin for the Mossad later in life who kept busy killing his former friends and comrades. Best to make him happy.

"How can I help you?"

The Nazi didn't answer. Instead, he looked once around the room and leaned in. "How have you been enjoying your stay?"

"Here? I haven't really had time to look around. Every time I get off the ugly guy's slab, I'm immediately involved in some painful termination of whatever passes for existence in these parts."

"Yeah. It's like that for a lot of new fish." He looked around again, eyes darting to each occupied table and shadowed corner. "I can shorten your transition, show you around, keep you in one piece while you learn the ropes."

It was Umberto's turn for suspicion. This was a man not known for his altruism. All to the contrary, in fact. And how many true altruists would end up in hell, anyway?

"And the price?"

The satisfied ghost of a smile crossed the man's features. Or perhaps it was just an effect caused by the flickering light, which seemed to be off as often as it was on. "They told me you were smart. I am going to use you as bait."

"Bait?" Eco pushed his seat back, ready to run if necessary. Better to be shot in the back by that Luger than devoured by some infernal creature. He'd dedicated a good portion of his life to the contemplation of medieval images of monsters. One could say many things about the minds of middle-age men, but one thing was for certain: they had a much better grasp of hell than did most modern folk. Now that he knew Inferno (or infernity) existed, he was much less likely to chuckle at the sea serpents in the corners of their maps . . . or to accept being used as a snare for one of their cousins. "Bait for what?"

"For who, not what," Skorzeny replied. "Do you still have your earthly memories of a woman called Blavatsky?"

Eco spat and leaned closer. "The charlatan?" The only Blavatsky he knew of was a 19th century occultist who'd been the principal purveyor of nonsense and drivel for certain parts of the European upper classes. Her speciality then, was combining misreadings of ancient texts with other, equally mistaken, interpretations to create wholly new levels of idiocy.

Skorzeny shrugged. "Perhaps, but she apparently has some real ability as a medium . . . and that is a very useful trait here. I want to talk to her."

"I still don't understand why you need me," Eco replied.

"Because she's not an easy person to contact. She spends all her time in the seventh circle."

"The seventh circle actually exists?"

"I guess you'd say that. It's a basement in the Pentagram. They also call it Satan's Skunkworks. She's a researcher." Skorzeny told him.

"Blavatsky is a researcher? That makes about as much sense as Dante being . . . I don't know . . . a computer engineer instead of a poet." Umberto decided not to speculate about the possible meaning of Skorzeny's smirk and quickly continued: "And if you want my help getting into her presence, I wouldn't do you much good. I never met the woman, and if she's heard of me, I doubt she cares much for my opinions."

It seemed so strange to be discussing someone who'd died forty years before he was born. . . But it was better than being killed painfully again. By Eco's count, this was the longest he'd survived the snares of the underverse since first coming to hell.

The smirk became a full-formed smile. "That's the beauty of it. She hates you with a passion you don't get in hell all that often. I won't need to go see her. As soon as she realizes you're here, she'll come for you." Skorzeny drank deeply of the beer in front of him and made a face. "Drink up. It tastes like baby piss."

Eco did, and it did. He pushed his glass aside. The man in front of him seemed a hard man, not the kind to indulge in silly obsessions centered around the occult. But then again, he was the ultimate Nazi: unrepentant and still at the center of some intrigue. Blavatsky's mumbo-jumbo had played a large part in inspiring Nazi Aryanism, so the man must want her for that reason.

But to do what? Raise an army of true believers to establish the Aryan race and its white-separatist dicta as the dominant force in the netherworld? What use would that be?

"And what if I don't want to be bait?" Eco said.

Skorzeny laughed. "Trust me. You want to be bait."

The laugh never reached the Nazi's eyes. A chill formed in Eco's stomach. He was saved from having to answer by an interruption from an unexpected source:

The lights flickered off and stayed that way for some moments. When they came on there were three of them at the table: they'd been joined by a man with hypnotic blue eyes and wild hair.

*

"Damn it. Can't we ever get decent power generation in the Pentagram?" Helena Blavatsky spat as the lights went off and on and off again.

"Hell is hell," Guido Von List replied. It was a mantra with him.

She cursed and glared at the monitor. When the screen flickered back to life, she nodded in satisfaction, convinced she was responsible for the return of electricity.

The screen showed a man seated in a chair from several angles. His glasses were bent and his expression appeared to be that of the deepest resignation.

Von List nodded towards the screen. "Jung is ready."

Helena giggled. "He doesn't look happy about this. Good."

They turned back to the table beside them. A long, wide oval of highly-polished wood, it took up most of the conference room. Hooded men and women sat around it, apparently blind to what was happening around them but listening expectantly. The hoods were there for a reason: the anonymous figures represented a collection of the most powerful spiritualists and mediums she had managed to grab—and she didn't want them to recognize each other.

Of course, if they were as good as they claimed, they already knew who all the other seated people were.

The seats at the head and foot of the table were open, and Blavatsky and Von List sat down. They each took the hands of the person beside them. The ritual began with no preamble.

"Guardians of the Greater and Lesser Gates, once again we implore your help. If you're listening and willing to hear our requests, give us a sign," Blavatsky intoned.

The tabletop was littered with large prisms of cut glass. At first, she'd insisted upon using crystals, but had soon realized that glass was just as effective. And much cheaper. Better to face whatever horde came through a portal in a botched summoning than be confronted by a single one of Satan's accountants.

The hairs on her arms stood on end, and a soft humming filled the room. It was working!

Moments later, one of the crystals began to shine with a soft pink glow. She suspected the colors meant something, but had no clue what that might be. Yet pink light always heralded an interesting show.

She wished she could tell Jung that he was in for something heavy, but that was impossible. Everything in the room was likely to be torn to pieces when the monsters came through . . . .

They'd learned that the hard way. The first time they'd run this particular ritual, fully expecting a drag-out, knockdown negotiation with the gatekeeper spirits, they had been shocked when a portal opened immediately, right next to the table.

No one in the room had survived for more than a few seconds, and the Undertaker had lodged a formal protest with the Pentagram about the amount of work he'd had to do to put them all back together.

In hell, getting the Undertaker to complain about the state of dead bodies was a major achievement.

So Carl Jung had been volunteered for the duty. His eternal mordant criticism of Helena's life's work was eternally being rewarded as it deserved.

In the monitor, a floating square of mist appeared in front of Jung, whose features morphed from calm resignation to abject terror. He screamed and screamed—silently, since the sound had been muted.

The portal solidified and Blavatsky strained her eyes to see what would come through. Only she had a decent view of the screen, as befitted her position as the leader of the research team. But that was moot, since the hoods worn by the rest of them precluded sight anyway. Van List had his back to the screen, but he wouldn't dare ask for anything more.

A thin tendril of light emerged from the portal and felt its way tentatively around the room, causing Blavatsky to snort in frustration. Tentacles again? Why did it have to be tentacles? Surely there couldn't be that many dimensions overrun by tentacular monstrosities, could there? In an infinite set of parallel worlds, worlds of spirit and matter, there must be more than this. The one time they'd summoned something else, it had turned out to be demons from Satan's Engineering department. They'd been extremely annoyed.

Still she watched, fascinated. The line of light wrapped itself around Jung's neck and pulled. She giggled as old Jung jerked and thrashed like a marionette controlled by an epileptic. Then she smiled: though she never tired of watching tentacles tear a soul to shreds, this summoning had suddenly taken a promising turn.

The rope of light unwound itself from Jung's neck and stretched, becoming both thicker and more transparent at the same time. A figure appeared in its place—the torso of an elfin woman mounted centaur-like atop the body of a lion. She was soon joined by other mashups, equally strange to her eyes but each, somehow, terrifyingly natural.

Beings of light, of course, could become any shape they chose.

She held her breath. Timing was everything. If she waited too long, the creatures might escape the way they'd come in, or they might dissolve because some quality of the astral energy in hell was wrong for them. But she wanted to be sure she could get as many of them as possible, and that meant timing things perfectly.

Her nerve gave out once five of them were in the room with Jung.

"Break the circle!" she cried and released the hand of the man next to her. The portal disappeared.

Now came the tricky bit. Could the creatures survive here? Could they be contained? Would they realize that the path back to their own plane had been cut off and go berserk, tearing Carl Jung apart in the process?

She hoped so. That was always fun to watch.

Von List joined her at the monitor and they toggled the view to show a single image, full-screen.

The lion-woman exploded into mist and, for a second, Blavatsky thought they'd screwed it up and the creatures wouldn't be viable. But then the entities re-formed and began to prance frantically around the hermetically sealed room that Blavatsky's team had prepared for them. This movement became more and more frantic as they tested each corner for a way out.

There was no way out. The room had been built solid, with a single window-sized opening which had been bricked and mortared once Jung had been poured through. It was also protected by magnetic fields, electric fields and warded with as many talismans and sacred objects as Helena had been able to find after scouring hell from top to bottom. There were quite a few of those, most of whose workings and intended purpose she had no clue about, but better to have too many than to need one and not have it.

The creatures of light went nuts. They turned back into tendrils, crisscrossing the room faster than the eye could follow. Smashing into the walls hard enough to make the image shudder. They might have been made of energy, but they certainly packed a punch.

Finally, all five of the creatures coalesced around the only thing in the room they could affect: the hapless form of Carl Jung, still alive and conscious. The figures began to circle him as if studying the strange offering they'd been given. He must have been found wanting, because the speed of their swirling gradually increased until the forms became a funnel cloud around the seated psychologist.

Faster and faster they twirled until a tendril of the spinning mass darted inward and touched Jung. A piece of clothing fluttered away.

A second tendril tore off another patch. A third broke Jung's skin as droplets of crimson blood sprayed into the air.

That did it. Like sharks in a feeding frenzy, the tendrils came in furiously, growing ever closer and ever faster until it looked as if Jung had been fed into a blender. The spray became a fine mist of blood particles suspended in the air. And when those finally fell to ground, the man, his clothes and his chair were nowhere to be seen.

Von List watched the scene slack-jawed.

Helena smiled. "Perhaps he should have held his tongue while he had the chance," she said. "Now he doesn't even have one."

"Should . . . should I call in the containment team?"

"Yes, List. This lot should prove interesting if those morons can hold onto them this time. Do me a favor and remind them that they have been chosen for this duty partly because they have superior training but mostly because they're completely expendable. If I see anyone making a special effort to stay off the Undertaker's table, I'll have them killed more slowly and painfully than anything mere energy beings could possibly deliver."

She turned to the screen. She always enjoyed watching the gore of her second-most-virulent critic sloughing down the walls. It was satisfying to know that, while he'd embarrassed her in life, she was making his infernity much more awful than anything he'd done to her.

Staring at the pools of blood, Helena had achieved a state of near serenity when a uniformed man walked in. He was short, wore a neatly trimmed mustache and a green uniform that sported a patch with the word "LACKEY" stitched on.

"Excuse me, Madam," he said in a voice at once obsequious and enthusiastic.

"What?" She growled at him. She hated being interrupted when viewing Jung's remains.

"I have news. That Italian you've been asking about is here."

"Here in hell?" she inquired.

"Better, Madam. Here in New Hell itself. He was reported at a bar near the docks."

"These Italians are all the same. Head straight for the whorehouses."

The man made no answer to that, apparently thinking speculation was either above his pay grade or below his dignity.

Blavatsky didn't care. Lackeys weren't there for their conversational skills. "Come on. We've got to go grab him. Call out the strike team. Better split them up, too. Send a few men to the Mortuary. Don't want old Jung wandering off while we're otherwise occupied, do we?"

"No, Madam."

*

Fierce, wild blue eyes stared out at them from within a shock of black hair that covered their visitor's head and chin. An unkempt beard reached halfway down his chest.

"I come with you, too," he said. It wasn't a statement, wasn't a request. The voice seemed accustomed to command. Then he realized that this must be the soul of Rasputin.

Umberto flinched away from the apparition but Skorzeny appeared entirely unfazed. "Grigory. I heard you'd been visiting with the Undertaker. Can't say I was surprised. Anyhow, you've come to the wrong room. They keep the girls upstairs."

"I not here for girl." The voice was a growl. "I want find Cagliostro."

"Heard he got wasted. I certainly don't know where he is now."

"Yes. But he not appear out of Mortuary. I want find him soon."

"You're still bugging the wrong crew. We've got nothing to do with that. Now scoot," Skorzeny ordered.

"I come with you. I find Blavatsky." He spat out the last word.

"What about her?" Skorzeny asked.

"Has . . . How you call it? Figurine. Small statue. Help me find Cagliostro. I help you with Blavatsky."

"Oh, yeah? How will you help?"

Eco watched them negotiate. When he'd met Skorzeny, he didn't imagine that anyone could be more magnetic than the Austrian Nazi. But this new soul had a nearly hypnotic quality about him. Perhaps it was the blazing eyes, or the way his voice fell into a rhythmic cadence as he mangled the English language.

That made Eco wonder: why were they speaking English in hell? He would have thought that such a young language would have had trouble establishing itself there. Why not Greek or Latin or Chinese? Koine Greek had established itself much earlier . . . But hell extended into the future as well as the past, and privacy in language represented a sort of primacy in culture as well as in thought. Or so he surmised. He would ask . . . later, when he found someone who might know.

As for the soul of Rasputin facing them, Umberto had few doubts. It appeared that, before they killed him again, the powers-that-were in hell had decided to torture him by exposing him to all the unscientific destroyers of spirituality and religion. First Blavatsky, now Rasputin.

Still, he wouldn't be bored.

"I protect you if she tries occult attack. Your soldiers not know how to protect. I do."

"She won't have time to think. We'll hit her before she can react," Skorzeny said.

"Perhaps."

A long silence ensued. Eco, out of habit, sipped his beer. It had been bad enough cold, but now that it was warm. How had it grown so warm, so fast? It tasted nearly identical to blood-laced urine. He pushed it aside again.

Skorzeny sighed. "Damn it. All right. You can come. But you do what I say, when I say. Understood?"

Rasputin glared, but nodded. "Da."

The Nazi stood and, without a word, headed towards the door. Eco followed with Rasputin bringing up the rear.

The street (if you could call the semi-paved collection of mud, ruts, potholes and the occasional dead animal a street) meandered through a part of hell that Eco had not yet seen. Thus far, he'd been killed in bucolic settings and monasteries but what they were walking through now was most undoubtedly a city. Or at least the dockyard slums of one.

He shook his head. As a student of history, he had little trouble identifying the buildings they passed as a muddled cross-section of architectural and social constructs from throughout the ages. A medieval blacksmith negotiated terms inside his dark forge with some guy in a legionnaire's uniform driving a jeep. Helots and harlots and hillbillies mixed with the expected results. Several altercations turned lethal—or at least as lethal as things could—within the first few moments of their walk. The feeling here was that existence was cheap; thrills were taken where they could be; and sanitation didn't apply.

Even more than the mix of buildings and people, Eco marveled and snickered at the mixture of underworld lore around him. In one square, a demon was calmly devouring some luckless soul, feet first so he could get the full hellish experience, while across the road, a crowd had gathered to watch a woman tied to a metal cylinder slowly being burned to a crisp by the fire that heated the base of the tube. Eco recognized it as one of the tortures from a Chinese hell. The smell of cooking meat made him wonder when he'd last eaten here, if he ever had.

The bustling crowd also featured a colossal three-headed dog that ran down anyone too slow to react and mauled them; as well as what appeared to be a good chunk of a Mongol horde, sans horses. And suddenly he realized that the reason occult texts were so muddled in the world of mortals was that the underworld itself was tremendously mixed. He wondered if the Vikings had a gigantic hall of feasting on some barren peninsula in the northern nether hells.

Despite the raucousness, no one got in Skorzeny's way as he marched through the throng, where a path opened magically before him.

The wharf area gave way gradually to an industrial-age slum until the Nazi called a halt in a quiet part of town. "Let's sit at that bar," he suggested, pointing to a tavern with actual glass at the window and, in a fiscally suicidal move, tables on the street.

Rasputin raised an eyebrow but said nothing. Umberto followed suit; at least the drinks should be better there.

The drink, some kind of red aperitif in a fancy bottle, tasted like piss laced with diarrhea: Brown swirled through the yellow.

"What the hell is wrong with the drinks here?" Eco said, spraying the foul liquid from his mouth onto the floor.

"The drink is part of the punishment. You've led a sheltered afterlife so far. Many of the damned have an insatiable appetite, and I guess the Devil laughs at them when they drink," Skorzeny replied. "Consider yourself lucky that you can excrete what you eat or drink. Many cannot."

Hell. It made sense, in its own perverted way.

"So, what are we doing now?" Eco asked, looking around doubtfully.

"We're waiting for your old friend Blavatsky to show up. The Pentagram is just up that hill, so she shouldn't be too long."

"She probably doesn't even know I'm here. Why would anyone in hell take note of me?"

The Nazi considered. "People that need to find each other endure great hardship to do so, especially if they'd really, really rather not. Wellington and Napoleon are neighbors, Brutus and Caesar are back together. You get the idea. You can't hide your destiny even among hell's teeming billions. I'm not sure how it works, but it does."

"And you're betting on that?" Umberto said.

"Of course not. I bribed one of her flunkies to tell her you'd be here. I also told her that you'd be here alone and unarmed. That should bring her out here with her guard down."

"I think you no succeed," Rasputin muttered.

As if to contradict the wild-eyed mystic, a commotion sounded in the square outside. They turned to look:

Blavatsky marched towards them at the head of a group of fifteen large men in black uniforms.

Skorzeny yawned. "Told you so. Caught her off guard."

"That's off-guard?" Eco wondered. "What about the heavies?"

"She never goes anywhere without them. Usually twice as many," Skorzeny told him.

"Have you got a plan to deal with them?"

In response, the upper story windows of the houses along the street sprouted gunmen in place of the women flaunting their wares. A barrage of gunfire swept the lane. Most of the uniformed men fell immediately, but four took cover behind a stack of barrels and returned fire. A man in one window screamed and fell, theatrically clutching his neck, landing on the cobbles below with a sickening crunch.

Skorzeny sighed and pulled out his weapon. Before anyone realized that the group at the tables were party to the fighting, the Nazi had dispatched all four with neat shots to the heart through the back.

The noise died down, leaving Blavatsky and an earnest-looking man with a receding hairline and a dark beard that rivaled Rasputin's. He was standing alone in the street. Witnesses, neutrals and passers-by were notable for their sudden absence.

"Hello, Helena," Skorzeny called out. "Why don't you join us?" He kicked a chair away from the table and motioned to it.

Blavatsky huffed, stomped over, then sat and glared at him. He grinned at her until she spoke. "All right. I know who these two are." She pointed at Eco and Rasputin before turning back to the Nazi. "The scum of the underworld, especially the Italian. So, I already have a bad opinion of you. Will you try to change my mind?"

"You wound me to the very soul. Here, I've dedicated my life to serving men who followed your doctrines, and this is how you treat me?"

She rolled her eyes. "Oh, no. Not another Nazi."

Skorzeny grinned. "My name is Otto Skorzeny. And yes, I was an enthusiastic member of the party." Then he narrowed his yes. "But only when it served me. Now, I'm a law-abiding denizen of the latterday hells."

"You have a funny way of showing it." Blavatsky scowled.

"Again: only when it serves me. While the Devil holds sway, I prefer not to cross him. But what if I can escape his clutches? Then, we shall see what is right and what is wrong."

Blavatsky laughed. "If you think that's possible, all you're doing is setting yourself up for a very unpleasant afterlife."

Skorzeny appeared unfazed. "That's what the Allies thought with their little cell in their war-crimes trial. That didn't hold me too well, and I lived my life exactly as I pleased after that. Well, except for that unpleasantness with the Israelis, but I soon cleared that up. After all, it's not as if I ever cared who I killed. Jew, Christian, American, German: what difference does it make? The only ones I really enjoyed knocking off were the French." He laughed. "They make the most satisfying noises." Then his eyes grew hard again and he placed the Luger on the table. "But all of that is beside the point. I'm not asking for your approval, all I need from you is that you help me get past Pentagram security."

"They'll shoot us all," Blavatsky said.

"Not if you help."

"Still, impossible."

"Don't lie to me, Helena. You know as well as I do that soldiers never shoot top brass. So get me in. If you don't co-operate, I'll kill you as slowly as possible." He chuckled. "I've been practicing my slow killing."

"I can take it." She stared hard at him, unfazed.

"Then I'll shoot this worthless piece of mold," he gestured over at Von List, "in the nuts and ask you again once I've done it. I'll enjoy that."

"And if I help you?"

"Once I have what I want, you go free," Skorzeny said.

"Can I have Eco?" Blavatsky glared at the Italian.

"No. Once we're done, he goes free, too. Catch him if you can."

"Wait," Umberto said. "You have Blavatsky. Why can't I go free now?"

"Insurance. As long as you're around, she won't run very far even if she manages to escape. Now, enough chatter. Let's get moving."

"They're going to shoot us all, you know," Blavatsky said.

"Don't be so gloomy." Skorzeny looked cheerful at the prospect of a good firefight.

No one retorted.

Skorzeny led them up the hill towards the Pentagram parking lots. It was, as Eco had imagined, an octagonal building that squatted shining atop a hill overlooking the city. Eco wondered if the prevalence of puns was part of his particular punishment or whether it was the result of elements from the living world being reflected onto the coils of infernity. Or could it be spooky action at a distance? Did physics create the duality of creation, twinning what the mind of humanity believed with their errant expectations? Maybe the mortal realm was reflected here just as hell was reflected in the literature of the living while Paradise, unreachable, condemned the sinners from on high? Or perhaps the manifold hells were simply created by humanity's expectations and the dead no different in the hells they expected than they'd been when alive. After all, Satan and his angels had fought a war for heaven—and lost. And ended here . . .

The day was dimly lit with the ruddy glow of Paradise, unattainable and smug, and Eco heard shells exploding off in the distance. He wondered who would be at war after death, and why. But then he remembered both the crowds they'd passed through and the ambush. War, said the living, was hell. By the same token, maybe hell was war? He needed to think about it.

But that would have to be some other time. Skorzeny marched his group—the men who'd been upstairs during the ambush had joined them—right up to the armored main gate and pressed a large red button.

Hell's bells rang somewhere inside, and Eco grimaced. Even doorbells appeared to be designed for maximum discomfort. It was, he admitted, a much more creative interpretation of hell than Dante ever foresaw. Once again, the old adage about truth surpassing fiction proved true.

A panel slid open, just wide enough for a head to appear. "Go away."

"We have business inside," Skorzeny replied.

This gave the doorman pause. He studied them. "You look like a bunch of Nazis to me."

"And you don't let Nazis in?"

"Of course we do. A lot of our most important souls are Nazis. But you bunch are the wrong kind of Nazis," sneered the doorman.

"Madame Blavatsky will vouch for us," Skorzeny replied, as that worthy was pushed to the fore.

"Commander." The voice suddenly held new respect. "Should I let them in?"

"Yes," Blavatsky said. "They're here on official Occult Division business."

"Very well," the voice replied.

The door opened outward and they had to step back smartly to avoid two panes of armor, a meter thick. When the opening was wide enough for two men to pass abreast, the doors came to a halt with a grinding screech. Lackeys flocked to inspect it and amid much cursing, declared it well and truly stuck.

"That was good," Skorzeny told Blavatsky. "Now get us into the occult levels and you'll soon be rid of us. If we do this right, there will be no evidence you ever let us in."

The main gates opened up to a courtyard, the perimeter of which was formed by the walls of the octagonal office building. They headed towards the nearest door, a couple of hundred feet away.

No one was expecting the shell.

A huge explosion rocked the courtyard, breaking windows and showering them with dirt and stones. The group hit the deck. All except for Eco, who was still trying to understand what the hell had just happened, and a couple of stragglers who'd caught the full brunt of the explosion and were now dissolving their way onto the Undertaker's queue.

When no further shelling was forthcoming, everyone stood. Skorzeny's men drew their weapons, and when a squad of soldiers in Pentagram uniforms appeared to investigate, the rattled Nazi commandos opened fire.

"Don't shoot!" Skorzeny commanded. "That was probably a Cong shell! Stop!"

But no one other than Eco, standing right beside him, could hear. The Pentagram troops joined in the firefight, turning the cacophony deafening.

Finally, Skorzeny threw up his hands in disgust and, pausing to grab Blavatsky, ran for the armored gate. Someone was trying to close it, but to no avail; it groaned. Eco followed mere steps behind as bullets whizzed through the air above them. Fortunately, the commandos had managed the keep the defenders pinned inside the building, which meant they couldn't fire at the retreating group effectively.

That changed when Pentagram troops made it to the slot between door halves. The guys inside the building must have got their act together. They were, judging by the way they swarmed forward, extremely angry at the intrusion.

Skorzeny led them back down the hill, around a wooded area and into a park.

"That's Decentral Park," Von List yelled.

"Yeah, so?" Blavatsky commented.

Whatever the occultist replied was lost among another barrage from defenders.

They redoubled their speed until they entered the park. For some reason, the well-manicured lawns were interspersed with overgrown shell holes.

Equally unfathomably, the troops chasing them reached the border of the park but seemed unwilling to go any farther. A couple of arguments and at least one fistfight broke out within their ranks before they retreated.

Eco watched them go, relief at their retreat warring with uneasiness about what had caused them to desist.

Skorzeny walked over to a picnic table, most of which had been blown to pieces by something, and sat on the only remaining piece of bench. "All right. Plan B. We'll have to open the portal outside the Pentagram."

He turned to Blavatsky. "Can you do that?"

"Of course not. We need our equipment, my team of mediums and —"

"She lies."

Everyone turned to look at Rasputin. In all the excitement, Umberto had completely forgotten that the man was there.

"She and Von List can open a portal anywhere they like. This is hell. It's easy. The walls between the worlds . . . How you say?" He rubbed two fingers together. "Thin like paper."

Blavatsky's glare promised dire retribution, but the Russian monk didn't appear to care. He kept talking. "If they cannot do so, I show them how."

Umberto wondered just how powerful Madam Blavatsky might be in this particular fiefdom. This was more than just academic interest, of course: he knew she had it in for him. But it appeared that, temporarily, at least, Rasputin would be drawing most of her ire.

"I'll do it," she replied. "But tell that bumbling amateur to keep his hands to himself."

Skorzeny grinned. "Perfect. I saw some big houses on that ridge over there, between those two stands of trees. How about we commandeer one so we can work in peace? We don't want your friends from the Pentagram stumbling onto us, now do we?"

They'd barely taken three steps in the indicated direction when one of Skorzeny's commandos with ten men in tow

screamed in pain and horror. He had fallen into a shallow pit
four feet deep. When his companions rushed over to see what
had happened, they saw that the floor of the hole was lined
with sharpened spikes placed perfectly to impale the feet of
anyone who happened to fall in.

It looked extraordinarily painful, but Eco was much more
interested in how the pit had been concealed: a long flat piece
of some light material had been covered with grass and when
the man had stepped on it, it pivoted in the middle to drop the
quarry onto the stakes.

"Damn the Cong," Skorzeny grunted. "And you shut up.
You'll bring them down on us." A single bullet from the Nazi's Luger silenced the screaming. "Now, where were we?"

Skorzeny never got to finish. A fusillade from one of the
trees sent them to ground, where they crawled along a slight
rise towards the trees. Shouts in a language he didn't recognize—and Eco spoke five modern languages as well as Latin
and Greek—echoed across the seemingly empty park and
received a response from unseen voices spread beyond the
ridge.

"All right. Run!" Skorzeny ordered.

Grabbing Blatavsky, the commando leader set the
example.

Spurred by the certainty that each step would be his last,
that hot metal would tear into his back at any moment, Eco
ran like he hadn't run in years. Had his trip to hell made him
a young man again? Perhaps, or it might just be that people
shooting at him was a first-time experience that gave him
wings. As a semiotician, he'd almost never been shot at.

Men fell on either side, but the core group managed to
reach the tree line and, crossing a manicured yard that in-
sanely pressed right against the Park, they hid behind the

mansion's wall, close enough to one edge that they could bolt around it if cover became necessary.

A quick head-count told Umberto that he'd been lucky to get out alive. Most hadn't. Rasputin, Skorzeny and Blavatsky had survived, crawling in front of Eco while Von list dragged himself behind. There a solitary commando crouched, apprehensive.

"Where's Guido?" Blavatsky wailed.

"Here," Von list said from the ground.

"What's wrong with you?" she asked.

"They shot me in the ass."

Skorzeny laughed. "Couldn't have happened to a nicer boy-toy."

"Screw you, Nazi."

The big commando bent and without apparent effort pulled Von List to his feet. "The only reason I'm not going to shoot you again, somewhere where it can do more damage, is that I might need you. I think your lover-lady might cooperate if I begin to pull out toenails or crush testicles with a hammer. But if she doesn't, you're going to wish you'd never been born. Now, let's get inside."

"Not that house," Rasputin said.

"Why not?"

"It's Napoleon's."

"Crap. And I know that one over there is Goebbels' house. He doesn't want to see me. Let's go this way." Skorzeny headed past.

The Nazi dragged the protesting Von List down a long suburban street which sported only minor shell damage until they came to a house with unkempt grass and a pile of newspapers on the porch. "This should do nicely."

Skorzeny marched up the steps. He tried the doorknob and, finding the door locked. Why would anyone leave a door unlocked in hell Eco wondered? Then he simply shot out the mechanism and walked inside.

"Ah. I see we've arrived at the home of some paragon of good taste," he said when he finally found the light switch.

The décor appeared to consist mostly of shrunken heads and rugs made from the pelts of several large animals including humans.

"This place will help us," Rasputin declared. "The vibrations are correct."

"Yeah, I can see that," Skorzeny replied, barely giving the accoutrements a glance.

"No, no," Blavatsky said. "It's all wrong. We should find a new place."

"Nice try, but you're not backing out on us. If you do, your boyfriend and I are going to have a nice long sit-down."

Von List scowled but wisely said nothing.

"Glad that's settled. Now what do you need?"

"We need a room with a big table and several exits," she said.

"Exits?" Skorzeny asked.

"Trust me. You never know what might get through a portal," she warned him.

"Yeah. Us," Skorzeny smirked.

"I mean from the other side."

They searched the house until they came to what must have been the dining room. It held a table suitable for twelve.

"Ugh," Umberto said. "Who'd want to eat with those heads looking down on you?"

"Who'd want to eat anything in hell in the first place? The décor can't make it any worse. And besides, it matches the rest of the house," Skorzeny said. "We'll use this room."

"No, no, no! Too small! Not enough escape routes." Madam Blavatsky turned purple.

"Just relax. We can deal with whatever comes through. Now, do you need any of these talismans?"

Blavatsky studied the agonized shrunken faces and the beaded and feathered fetishes around her. "Nah. They're so close that their mere presence should be enough if any of them are actually good for anything."

Rasputin, for his own part, was studying an item that looked like a pair of feathered maracas tied together with leather thongs. "Do you mind if I steal this? It help me find Cagliostro," he said.

"Suit yourself," Skorzeny replied. "But you can't leave until the ritual's done."

Following the medium's instructions, they sat and held hands—except for Von List, who was forced to stand by the pain in his nether regions. Blavatsky began to chant, and Eco rolled his eyes. He'd read dozens of descriptions of her mix of French, Latin and Russian, with a little German thrown in when in need. They'd been bad enough in writing. Hear this gibberish spoken aloud made him wonder how, even in the 19th century, where people were willing to believe just about anything, this obvious fraud had induced anyone to listen to her. And yet the evidence was there: imbeciles had flocked to her in their millions, and continued to do so after her death, as evinced by the importance her works held for the Nazi party.

As Blavatsky worked herself into a frothing frenzy, so unlike the way he'd imagined Victorian seances, the hairs on his arms stood on end. He willed them to stop; this was childishness.

Eco couldn't keep himself from jumping halfway out of his seat when he heard a sudden crash and the breaking of glass as the crazy lady reached a climax. Only Rasputin's iron grip on one hand and Von List's on the other prevented him from running off.

Blavatsky appeared not to notice the commotion. She finished her chant and looked expectantly at a spot in the center of the table slightly above their heads. She wasn't disappointed: a form of mist, roughly rectangular in shape, appeared where she stared. Its surface rippled, illuminated from within.

Eco couldn't believe his eyes. This was stupid.

Then it hit him that, perhaps for him, hell would be the place where charlatans saw their beliefs come true and wielded actual power, while scholars were dragged along behind Nazi war criminals.

"No one move!"

The voice—harsh, shrill, unexpected—startled them all. Even Blavatsky stopped staring at the space over the table and turned to see soldiers pouring into the room. They were all armed with rifles and dressed in the uniforms of the Pentagram.

"Hands on the table where we can see them. Right now!" someone barked.

Eco hastened to comply and realized that even Skorzeny had relaxed. There were too many of them to fight.

The troops advanced on the Nazi and his surviving commando first, handcuffs at the ready.

All hell broke loose.

A clustered mass of tentacles shot from the mist floating over the table. Two of the soldiers were impaled immediately and a third brushed aside. The others began to shoot the tentacles, desperately trying to fight them off.

Skorzeny sprang into action. He shouted, "Anyone who doesn't want to stay in hell forever had better come with me now." And he jumped into the mist.

Rasputin dove through after him, all thoughts of Cagliostro apparently forgotten as this unparalleled opportunity overcame everything. To Umberto's surprise, Von List hobbled onto the table and followed.

Blavatsky screeched: "Guido!" and stood, then stopped. Umberto realized that she didn't actually want to leave hell. He understood all too well: here was a place where her teachings weren't considered purest mumbo-jumbo, but worked; a place where she was respected, even feared.

And yet, her love for Von List somehow moved her. She took a step towards the portal . . . And it was her last. Two tentacles converged, one wrapping around her neck, the other taking her by the ankles. They tensed and, with a sickening breaking sound, Blavatsky's head tore away from her neck, taking what seemed like several yards of veins and other assorted body parts with it.

The sight galvanized Umberto. He followed the last of the commandos through the portal. After all, no matter what might be on the other side—and those tentacles, he reasoned, probably weren't a good sign—it had to be better than hell, right?

It wasn't. At least not on first sight. Source less light from a purple sky illuminated a blasted landscape of barren hills. Bundles of tentacles several times the size of men ambled around, most heading towards the portal.

"They're coming this way," Eco cried.

Skorzeny didn't look too concerned. "They're attracted to the exit gate. Once we move away, we'll be safe enough. At least it looks that way to me."

"Aren't you worried that even evil balls of tentacles hate this place so much they'd rather be in hell?" Eco said.

"No. They don't know that's hell over there. They're just investigating. And I say that no matter where we are, it's better than hell by definition."

As they retreated to better ground, or at least ground farther from the portal, Eco counted heads. Of the group that had assaulted the Pentagram, only five of them remained: Skorzeny, Rasputin, the surprising Von List, the last of the commandos and Umberto himself.

"Do you realize what we've done?" Von List said, mad glee pouring from him. "We've broken through the walls of hell itself, escaped the final frontier. First we learned that death wasn't final and now this. We've turned humanity into immortals, into gods."

As if to show him what the universe thought about that, one of the tentacled balls chose that moment to appear from around a corner in Von List's path. He was torn to pieces, along with the luckless commando. Gore flew in every direction as the team retreated. Umberto threw himself in the same direction as Skorzeny, trusting the commando's instinct more than his own, and thanking his lucky stars that they'd let Von List get a few steps ahead of them.

Skorzeny led them to the steep valley between two mounds. "All right. We're here, somewhere. Wherever this is. I'll do my best to keep us alive, but you'll also have to pull your weight." He gave them a satisfied look. "At least you're both experts on the occult, and I think that will be key to opening the door to wherever we can get to from here."

Eco thought of the purple sky. "What makes you think we'll be of any help? I was a skeptic, more interesting in finding the holes in other people's craziness than duplicating it. And Rasputin . . . I always thought he was more of a politician than a mystic."

"Well, you're the only crew I've got, so we might as well make the most of it. Or we could just stay here."

"We should return to hell," Rasputin said.

"Return? Can't. The portal just closed." Skorzeny struck a pose. The man actually seemed to be enjoying himself. "So, my dear advisors, which way should we go?"

"That way," Rasputin said, pointing.

"What? Why do you say that?" Eco asked.

"We must move away from the sun. Or the light or whatever. All civilizations put their death worship away from the light. Spirits of the dead are key to opening portals between worlds."

Eco suddenly felt more respect for the Russian monk. "You know, he just might be right. There's a lot of precedent for having the underworld in the west. The ancient Etruscans . . ."

"Are a bunch of smelly barbarians who are still angry at the Romans for knocking them off their perch. I've met them," Skorzeny said. "But if you're agreed about the direction, we'll go that way."

Eco looked down at a sharp push as he turned to follow the Nazi. He screamed with agony that made even his earlier deaths seem almost civilized in comparison. A long, scaled tentacle, covered in blood, his own blood, was waving around in front of him. It looked like it had sprouted from his chest.

He tried to call for help, but his voice bubbled with blood. He felt as weak as a baby, and only the agony of his torn flesh kept him conscious. But even the torturing fire burning in his chest couldn't win that battle. Darkness began to envelop him.

The last thing he saw before his eyes closed was the figure of Skorzeny cresting a rise, Rasputin in hot pursuit.

*

The slab?

"How can this be?" Eco asked, a mixture of hope and anguish filling his voice and making it whinier than he'd intended. He opened his eyes.

Bright light and an unfortunately familiar face made him shut them again.

"We'd escaped," he said plaintively. "Hell has no more grip on our souls."

The laughter, low-pitched, echoed like something in a tomb.

"You thought to leave hell? Judging by where you came in from, you only succeeded in reaching a storeroom level." There came a rustling of parchment. "Apparently you were in a place where Satan keeps an assortment of malformed demons. Why you wanted to go in there is anyone's guess, but there you have it. You're free to go. Well, free is a relative term, of course." The Undertaker chuckled.

Eco stumbled out into the hall with the elevator. For once, the Undertaker's laughter didn't bother him. Eco laughed as he imagined Skorzeny, visions of glory and freedom filling his mind, scampering around in what was, essentially, a glorified broom closet. How the Devil must have been enjoying that!

He would have given much to be able to see the look on the Nazi's face when he awoke in the Mortuary after the tentacles finally got him.

On second thought, it might be wisest to get as far away as possible before he arrived. Skorzeny, he assumed, would not be in the best of moods.

The elevator door opened. Eco was almost happy to see the welcome woman. She grinned her revolting cronelike grin and beckoned him forward.

Almost.

Excalibur

Tom Barczak

Caustic and mewling, the little imp descended to the roof of the small shack at the center of hell's switchyard, where fires burned on every horizon. The ever-changing rails crossed perilously, often moving, unexpected but deliberate. Toppled cars and engines exploded with the force of bombs so regularly that no soul took the train in hell unless they were made to, which of course, this being hell, they often were.

Which is precisely why the Infernal Master sent him here to investigate a rumor about a bargain about to be made. Because at this very moment, two souls, once three, and soon to be three again, were known to be here, in this very switch house to be precise, which by intent is never manned, and in hell, where two or more are gathered, there are always two things that must occur and in their right order: first a deal, and then dismay.

*

"He's coming," Lafayette Ronald Hubbard whispered.

Hubbard pulled himself back across the dried and broken floorboards of the shack. Bits of asbestos tile splintered beneath his hands. The splintering kept him alert, at least. He could no longer feel anything below his waist. He had blocked all feeling away. It was a pain that no longer necessary.

"Wait for him" He winced at Aleister Crowley, who still squatted over Parson's corpse.

Hubbard had already heard the one they waited for approaching, long before Aleister even could, or would, acknowledge Rasputin, what with the particular limitations he held. Aleister, though a man of great vision to be true, chosen by the god Horus himself, his erudite vision was coupled with a most juvenile sense of the Will, the great power that all souls, wittingly, or unwittingly, served.

Aleister stood up from Jack Parson's ignoble naked corpse. Parson, the one who'd first introduced Hubbard to Aleister in life, his throat now opened up, his body sprawled out upon the chalked pentagram scrawled across the floor, was already dissolving to hell's ether and the Undertaker's wants.

Aleister grimaced as he wiped the blood from the dagger and his hands onto his pants. Parson, of course, never had any pants, not here in hell anyway. The twat never even put a fight either, just standing there with his dick in his hand waiting for his sacred whore Babylon to appear. A spell had to be used to summon, so an offering had to be made. Parson just didn't know it would be him, and not just his seed, as he'd thought. And well, Parson had never been that important to begin with.

Bellowing catcalls soon sounded, distant, far outside the shack, although steadily rising as they drew near.

The one summoned had arrived.

Aleister hastened for the door.

"I like to remember, at times like this," Hubbard stopped Aleister, "how, for a brief, dark, age, the Will was silent to us.

It eventually woke up, of course, rising upon the illumination of past incorporations. It's sometimes too easy to forget that the Will is an eternal and perpetual thing, counting many others as its vessels. Each one of them had risen upon the ashes of those who had passed before. Osiris, Rasputin, you, me. Now here we all are, or nearly all, together again in punished flesh if not in perpetuity itself." He smiled shrewdly. "I had never once thought that it would be hell that would present to us such an opportunity as this. But, as they say, here we are."

Aleister flashed his thelemic smile at Hubbard. "How unfortunate for Rasputin that he got his cock back."

"Yes," Hubbard smiled. "Very."

"Ha ha ha! I'm here you stupid bastards!" The unwitting mule bellowed from beyond the door.

Aleister dried his hands against his pants once more and reached for the knob.

"Wait," Hubbard told Aleister again and, like a dog on a lead, he obeyed. But also like a dog, when excited he sometimes pulled too much on his lead, lest someone take away the scraps set out before him. But this was no scrap; and well, timing is of course everything. "Wait is what I said to do."

Aleister bowed his head where he was. Through the open holes in the ceiling and the roof, the rusted light of hell illuminated the man's bald pate. Sweat beaded there from the infernal heat of Paradise, always out of reach. Creases of impatience, a conflict of wills, of his will and the greater Will that they all served, traced their way across his countenance.

"A moment more," Hubbard commanded once again, but more softly this time. He settled back at last against his small pallet by the wall. "Do you remember when you wrote once that I was a swindler, and that Parson was a fool?"

Aleister looked back at him, all the more uncomfortable now; all the more nervous; searching desperately through the memories of his life for anything but the painful and awkward truth of which he'd just been reminded. He knew by now who his better was. He knew who it was that had done what he had never been able to do. He knew who it was that the Will had ultimately chosen.

"You are no swindler," Aleister told him, his chin raised in proffered humility and respect. "But he was always a fool for you."

"Yes, yes he was," Hubbard acknowledged in response. He smiled. He waved at the door with his hand. "Now. Now would be perfect."

Aleister pulled the door open.

Rasputin stood just beyond the open door, a giant filth of a man wavering on unsteady feet, nearly falling inward from where he stood infirm on the tracks. He was grinning from ear to ear, a bottle in one hand and his hard member in the other. Blood already stained the corner of his mouth and his long beard, blood from his lacerated innards, shredded by shards of glass, part and parcel of hell's brew.

Trains roared by behind Rasputin, far too close, and too loud for anyone to hear the audible and distinct snick of two more sets of tracks changing vector just down the line.

"Grab it," Hubbard commanded in a whisper nobody but himself could hear. But the Will heard and commanded its servant: "Now."

Aleister obeyed, reaching out and seizing Rasputin just above the balls.

Rasputin looked down, then up, scowling at Aleister. Then he shrugged.

"Why do you keep me . . . waiting!" Rasputin yelled, leering past him. "And where are the girls? I want sex magi–"

Rasputin's words ended, along with most of his body, which was abruptly smeared across the front of a steam engine whose track had just been changed.

Aleister stood there shaking, stunned, Rasputin's severed cock in his hand, the sap of its hellish incarnation draining out from it. He was too shocked to appreciate or take advantage of the significance of the power that he held, of what had in life once been his. The wind and roar of a passing train only a foot away fell silent as if in homage to the artifact. And yes, to the moment itself.

"Give it to me," Hubbard promptly commanded Aleister, before the magician could regain his senses. "Now."

Aleister turned towards him, the reincarnated vessel of the god Osiris, and the source of Rasputin, Crowley, and Hubbard's power in life, in his hand, and brought it to him.

Hubbard's breath caught in his throat.

"Excalibur," Hubbard whispered at last as he received the severed penis of Rasputin away from Aleister. "At last."

Excalibur: the one word; the one thing; the one answer to everything; the one word whispered to him in life as he had lain in the dentist's chair on the edge of death; the one word of power that could drive men mad. That was the name of the unholy grail before him, the same one he had wielded successfully over so many servants in life.

And if so it was in life, what power he would wield with it here in hell.

He stroked it in his hand, Osiris' vessel, bestowed first upon his son, Horus, and then passed down to mankind. He rubbed it against his face, touching it to his lips. It reeked of the unwashed power of the gods. Part of him very much wanted to consume it. But not all things were meant to be devoured. Some things, the greatest of things, these were meant to be wielded, and so it would be with this, as commanded by the Will.

He said at last to Aleister, "What is power if one does not seek it?" He tugged at the bandages beneath his waist. "What is freedom if one does not dream it? What is the punishment of hell if one does not accept it? I tell you, they are nothing. They are but motes of ash. Now come to me and witness true magic."

"Our victory," Aleister mewled. "The time for a new Aeon has come at last."

"No," Hubbard said.

He pulled the last of his bandages aside and slammed the base of Excalibur down onto the open bloody wound where his cock had been. The pain of life, power, and the Will tore through his very existence. Some moments last longer than others. In the last of this one, the spirit of Horus loomed over him.

"Mine," he sighed as the second train exploded through the switch house taking them both.

*

The imp lifted regretfully away from and the grime, death, and despair coating the corbeled arches of the Undertaker's hall. But then it settled back again. It felt oddly guilty in doing so, as it was most certainly not what he'd been instructed to do. It'd been told only to confirm the receipt of the phallus by the Undertaker. It had not been asked to do anything more. It already knew what was going to happen anyway: what always happens here, here at the place of the beginnings of endings.

But for some reason, this time it wanted to see it for itself.

The indescribable scrape of rusting steel-shod boots marked the Undertaker's approach, along with the all-too-ironic whirr of the bone saw, considering what he was about to remove. Hubbard's scream had risen immediately, as soon as he'd awoken, even louder as he heard the bone saw. His fruitless writhing against hell's restraints marked his awareness once more of his fiendish punishment and his pre-ordained fate. It had ended the same way nearly every time before. Six hundred and sixty-five times before, to be exact.

The imp often had been told by its master that if heaven made things new, then hell was set up on permanent repeat. So what was in a number anyway?

Still, it was odd that this time the Undertaker needed a bone saw.

The imp stopped mewling and licked its thin cracked lips. It looked nervously around. But there was nothing, other than the slow whirr of a faulty bone saw and Hubbard's screams. The other slabs, where souls in hell were customarily reincarnated, lay empty, an anomaly to be sure. But then it smiled, understanding something at last. Something was different. Something had changed. The damned fool of a soul named Hubbard had made it farther this time than ever before. This time the talisman had fastened and become one with Hubbard's flesh.

The bone saw cut, its heat cauterizing flesh as it went.

The imp licked its lips again. Deeper and slower this time. It could almost taste it on the air, drifting up to him on the wings of Hubbard's burned flesh. It was sweet and unlike anything the imp had ever tasted before. Nothing in hell could compare. Oh, how delicious and precious was the fruit that the Will and patience bore.

The imp opened his mouth, drew back his lips, and chewed, becoming one with the Will of hell.

On the Run

Michael H. Hanson

*Don't be satisfied with stories, how things
have gone with others. Unfold your own myth.*
– Jalāl ad-Dīn Muhammad Rūmī

"Damn," Dogen yells, "damn these rocks."

Mina Crandon looks back at the bald and stolid Dogen,
frowning at the sight of the jagged black shards of stone that
cover this path, tearing at all their feet and ankles. As sharp
as blades the rocks cut through everything.

The three of them, adults who appear to be in their mid to
late thirties, walk slowly and steadily through a heavily shad-
ed mountain valley. This particular corner of hell is as torturous as it is secluded. Heavy sulfurous cloud cover, thick
skin-slicing foliage, and multiple spiky cliffs hide the purpose of these three damned pilgrims, which is all well and
good, but the price, oh the price . . . .

"Isn't pain just another path to eventual enlightenment,
my friend?"

"You know where you can shove your enlightenment, Madame Crandon," Dogen snaps, his mild

thirteenth-century Japanese accent barely noticeable amidst his idiomatic English.

"Now, now," a third voice speaks up, "let us save our weapons for real combat."

The speaker, a short, lean man of dark sunbaked skin, wearing a ragged turban on his head and a disintegrating Dhoti about hips and upper thighs, leaps out from behind a boulder. He sports a wide grin on his face while tucking a reed flute under the wrappings around his waist.

"Combat?" Mina asked.

"I have just finished a successful communing with nature," Rumi says, "one not oft permitted in hell. Though not a victory, I consider my action as having struck a moral balance."

"More of a zero-sum conclusion," Dogen groans while adjusting his shabby brown robe, "considering we're downwind of your impromptu toilet."

This last has them all chuckling darkly as their trek recommences.

Though time is a concept usually laughed at in hell, all three of these mystics agree upon one single assessment . . . they have traveled upon this path for several weeks. During their horrible afterlives, each has found and embraced the dark magic that often bleeds from the infernal landscape to create virtual clocks within themselves, something as much a curse as a blessing, as knowing how long they have been in hell often increases their eternal torment.

*

Two days earlier they sat in a small circle and debated their circumstances. "I don't care how many times we have discussed this," Mina states firmly. "We shall do so again, and right now."

"Were you this impetuous as a living soul, my dear?" Dogen asks.

"Our memories have been altered," Rumi says. "How many times we do not know. Perhaps dozens."

"Perhaps hundreds," Mina ventures.

"Yet we know that we are in control of our destiny," Dogen says, "because of our powers."

Mina closes her eyes and opens them quickly, instantly revealing brightly glowing green orbs. Her visage does not startle her comrades, who have witnessed her powers on many occasions. Mina's astral vision was superior among the three, as the other two each had specific powers that Mina could not equal. Hell was more than a wasteland of tortures for the three mystics. It was an endless oasis of dark mana that they had learned to taste to their occasional advantage.

"No dimensional pathways or markers lead to or from us."

"I told you my masking spells were without fault," Dogen chides.

"And I have looked to both future and past," Rumi says, "with no indication of 'he who will not be named' having any awareness of us."

"I do not remember exactly how we met," Mina says. "I was fleeing a mighty explosion, and then a vast army of flying demons. A dust storm, magical I believe, suddenly came upon me. I lost consciousness, and when I awoke, you two were on the ground beside me. Though I had no memory of you, I could feel we were familiar. Our paths have crossed many times."

"Yes, yes, yes. We've discussed this over and over," Dogen spits. "I was being flayed to pieces in the Hell of One

Thousand Torturers when an explosion of blinding white light drowned my senses before I woke next to both of you."

"And my story remains the same," Rumi says. "I have the vaguest memory of charging toward some doorway, when huge globes of flaming death swept down upon me . . . and then I awoke with you."

"Though we knew not of each other," Mina says, "our trust had us exposing our powers to each other. My own I only discovered during my second life in infernity. As a living soul, I was a charlatan. Only here did I acquire the arcane knowledge and eldritch energies I yearned for when alive."

"We joined our senses and realized we are on a quest to attain talismans that will allow us to escape this pit," Dogen says.

"Yes, the vision was quite clear. Given to us by . . . the blessed one himself, I am sure." Rumi waved his hand skywards.

All three look upwards at this last statement, squinting against the distant but painfully beautiful incandescence that marks the mesmerizing borders of Paradise.

"Still, our memories," Mina says, "if we're wrong, and are being toyed with—"

"A thousand ifs, a thousand whys. They are all for naught. Let us embrace our destiny, for beginning, middle, and end are all one. The path to enlightenment has already begun and ended. We merely must embrace it."

"Let us trust in our powers and each other," Dogen says. "Besides, our memories might be the smallest of wounds acquired during many adventures and successful acts of survival across hell's endless lurid landscapes."

"Agreed," Mina says, "to the talismans!"

"Agreed!"

*

Though the sun neither rises nor sets, Mina, accessing her internal thaumaturgical clock, feels that another week has passed when they come upon the landmarks of their vision. Finally leaving the terrible valley, the three journeyers face a seemingly endless plain covered in shining white limestone. In the distance they spot three spires, each jutting upwards, piercing the clouds themselves. Moving their hands in various arcane gestures, and mouthing spells in different languages, they each enhance their own visions to rival that of an eagle.

"I am meant for the far-left spire," Mina says, indicating a jet-black structure that glistens like polished obsidian. "I hear its eldritch song in the back of my head. It is a siren call that I cannot resist."

"I have the honor of the right tower," Dogen says, nodding at the far right and the reddish-brown monstrosity that appears to have been cut from a massive single piece of desert sandstone. "The mere sight of it has lit a fire in my breast. It burns with a yearning that will consume me if I do not reach it soon."

"And mine is the middle way," Rumi says, smiling at the largest of the three gargantuan structures, an unholy façade that appears to be a vast splinter of translucent quartz.

Miles upon miles slip by as they walk for over two days until finally, they are within hours of their destination.

"We must separate," Mina says. "The vision we all shared when we awoke together at the beginning of this journey told us that upon gathering our three talismans, our new journey will begin. Remember, for a glorious series of moments we were all dressed in iridescent gowns and the choirs of angels flowed through our bodies like pure love. Three glowing doves carried the talismans and dropped them at our feet. Surely that is our ultimate destiny, to leave this horrible place. Good fortune to us all."

"Let us embrace our destinies," Dogen says.

"I empty myself of desire," Rumi replies.

Eschewing handshakes, head nods, and hugs, the three turn from one another and walk swiftly toward hope and escape.

*

Dogen Zenji, also known as Dogen Kigen, Eihei Dogen, Koso Joyo Daishi, and Bussho Dento Kokushi during his fifty-three years of life, had died from a particularly painful case of syphilis. He had acquired the unforgiving venereal disease after overpowering a peasant gardener at the Daibutsu Temple north of Kyoto. It was merely one of the multiple personal sins he had kept secret from the world at large, and so was not at all surprised when he had arisen in Nirya, the Buddhist hell. On Earth he had been a famous Japanese Buddhist priest, writer, poet, philosopher, and founder of the Soto school of Zen in Japan. In these nether realms, Dogen was only one more pathetic sinner reaping his supernatural punishment.

Leaving his two mysterious colleagues behind, Dogen approaches the gaping cave like opening at the base of the sandstone tower. Within feet of the shadowed arch, Dogen centers his mind and focuses on the concept of Uji, i.e., Time-Being.

His lips part and he whispers:

"Fifty-four years lighting up the sky.
A quivering leap smashes a billion worlds.
Hah!

My entire body looks for nothing.
Living, I plunge into Yellow Springs."

Dogen enters the base of the sandstone tower. He is prepared for the coming trials. He walks into shadows and drowns in blinding white light.

*

Rumi, also known as Jalal ad-Din Rumi and Jalal ad-Din Muhammad when alive, left his companions with the merest of qualms and focuses on the fast-approaching diamondlike tower. During his life and long after his death (as many mortal souls were wont to inform him in this infernal perdition) he was a lauded poet, jurist, Islamic scholar, theologian, and Sufi mystic. Rumi had lived the latter half of his life as a Persian ascetic, one who sought to see the truth in life and provide sermons for the betterment of humankind.

When he died at the age of sixty-six in Konya, Sultanate of Rum, Rumi was not all that surprised to awaken in Duzakh, the endless Well of Hell, and an eternity of tortures performed by the great destructive spirit Ahriman and his demons.

Rumi knew that his earliest years as a Jurist, spewing out unfair and malicious Fatwahs on a whim before his eventual Sufi's enlightenment had damned his soul beyond the grasp of any glorified supernatural forgiveness.

A small archway at the base of the crystalline tower becomes apparent and Rumi whispers:

"On the seeker's path, wise men and fools are one.
In His love, brothers and strangers are one.
Go on! Drink the wine of the Beloved!
In that faith, Muslims and pagans are one."

Rumi steps beneath the sparkling archway and enters the crystalline tower knowing that he seeks an essence the same as himself.

*

Mina Margery Crandon, adjusting her brown trousers and faded white shirt, strides toward the black obsidian spire without hesitation. Unlike her two famous companions, Mina's sins were widely exposed during the last years of her mortal life. Although she continued to make a living by conning middle and upper-class suckers with her fake seances, the newspapers of the day were only too happy to document a wide variety of investigators and committees that systematically attacked her supernatural claims.

Her greatest hatred was reserved for that pompous stage magician Harry Houdini. Not long after Sir Arthur Conan Doyle himself had lauded her amazing abilities, the insufferable Houdini had swept in to expose her greatest tricks. After dying of alcoholism in nineteen forty-one, Mina was shocked to realize that the Almighty, the devil, and eternal punishment were all real.

During her endless tortures, however, Mina quickly came to a fascinating and almost wonderful realization. Here, in hell, mystical powers were real, and after hundreds of horrible subjective years shuffled from one demon to another, from one damned location to another, her inquisitive mind solved the hellish riddles of netherworldly magic. Stealing minute amounts of it between demon interrogations she secretly grew her inner powers and experimented with them. It was not long before she escaped her shackles and began her adventures throughout infernity.

A small doorway suddenly appears at the base of the black tower. Just before she enters it, Mina whispers a series of words, like a litany, to balance her thoughts and sharpen her focus, "Automatic writing, psychic music, direct voice, séance, materialization."

Mina steps into darkness.

*

When the blinding light slowly bleeds away, Dogen's eyes resolve to view the hollowed-out interior of the tower. He stands upon a vast polished floor. In the distance, on the far side of this interior expanse, he spots a sparkling beacon of red light. He knows it is his destination and starts walking toward it.

Without warning, plants sprout all around him, growing rapidly and soon towering over his head, making it difficult to move forward with speed. Dogen realizes they are giant Higanbana, Red Spider Lilies whose blossoms are not unlike strips of bloody human flesh. A sudden movement above him causes Dogen to jump to his left. One of the terrible flowers, jagged teeth at the center of its blossoms, has nearly swallowed him whole. Several more move toward him from all sides.

The closest lily opens its maw and a voice screams forth:

"Accept your damnation false priest," its high-pitched voice wails. "Your teachings were all lies, your actions pathetic, and your sins innumerable!"

Dogen slows his heartbeat and does his best to cast off body and mind. He speaks a single word, "Bussho."

As the carnivorous flowers lunge, they grow semi-transparent and seem to move right through him, as if he is made of mist, or they are. Again they leap upon Dogen, but cannot strike or mark his flesh. He moves forward like a spirit through a graveyard vault.

Dogen smiles while moving steadily toward his distant goal, and speaks slowly,

"The very impermanency of grass and tree, thicket and forest are the Buddhist-nature."

*

Rumi walks into thick vermillion light that somehow feels like it has mass so that it presses against his flesh like a sandstorm. Squinting, he moves on, leaning forward almost forty-five degrees, refusing to give up. As the scarlet light dissipates, Rumi's pace increases. In the distance, he spots a flickering sapphire light and believes he has found his ultimate destination.

Before long he realizes that the red winds are now forming into dozens of vicious tornados, roughly ten feet high. Each one tears into the ground below and bites up chunks of rock, spewing them every which way. Twice Rumi ducks flying debris as he breaks into a zig-zagging jog.

Without notice, the terrifying tornados stop their haphazard movements and bear directly down on Rumi.

A scream erupts from the nearest tornado, and Rumi realizes it is a voice:

"False philosopher," it yells, "why do you fight your damnation? So many innocents died under your command. There is no redemption for one such as you!"

Rumi closes his eyes and lets his breath out slowly. "You dance secretly inside my heart where no one else can see."

Rumi begins to pirouette, swirling a full three hundred and sixty degrees. In moments he is spinning like a top, appearing as a blurry pale brown whirl of light that rushes forward and tears through the surrounding ring of faltering red tornados. Dozens more appear but each time they spin in to intercept, Rumi's whirling dervish form rips through the impediments almost effortlessly.

The sapphire light beckons.

*

Upon entering Mina finds herself facing an apparently endless parkland graveyard. Green grass and granite and marble headstones stretch outwards in concentric rings of burial plots. Turning around she notices that the door and the walls that surrounded it have disappeared. It is as if she'd been transported to another realm.

"A nice illusion," Mina speaks, "but I am in the dark tower, and the only way out is forward."

Mina takes a whole minute to scan her horizons until a flickering milky white light catches her eye. It is the source she seeks. She strides forward.

Moments later the grass and soil about her begin to crack and erupt. Dozens, then hundreds, then thousands of rotting corpses crawl forth and stand up from their graves.

Horrific visions all, Mina barely grants them a glance as she strides forward, unerring.

It takes a few minutes, but the ghouls soon take notice of Mina's singular form and shamble toward her from every direction. She breaks into a slow jog and for many minutes finds it an easy enough task to avoid the clumsy horrors.

Each one has a slightly familiar visage, and when one gets close enough, it wails in barely understandable English:

"You took my last pounds," an elderly woman yells. "I died starving, waiting for my husband's promised fortune."

"You made my wife commit suicide," a man screams, "thinking our dead daughter was waiting for her on the other side."

Each accusation piled upon the last and threatened to drown Mina's ears.

After what feels like an hour, the numbers of walking spirits grows so large that avoidance becomes impossible. A mass of several thousand creatures forms a solid ring around Mina and squeezes in on her.

When the inner circle closes within a few feet of her, Mina tilts her head back and yells: "*Spiritus manus!*"

Five large and glistening membranous hands, each several times the size of a human appendage, appear in the air around Mina. As she jogs forward, two of the floating hands form fists and punch forward, savagely knocking over ghouls and clearing a path for her. The three other hands cover Mina's flank and brutally slap away anything that gets within clawing distance of her body.

Mina is soon through and past the horde of walking nightmares as she continues her jog toward the distant milky light. She takes no chances, and keeps all five of her teleplasmic hands close, in case of further surprises. Nothing is going to impede her progress.

*

Dogen has crossed a vast distance, avoiding a horde of vicious carnivorous plants, and is now within a few dozen feet of a standing eight-foot-tall, uncut ruby jewel.

When he is but a few feet away, a massive wall of flame springs up all around it. Deep laughter rumbles from above. Dogen tilts his head back and stands still, amazed at the sight of a beautiful emerald-colored dragon, the source of this raging, self-sustaining flame.

"Good luck, priest," the dragon says over its shoulder as it flies away, "your petty Dharma is no match for my bane's breath."

The heat is punishing, but Dogen forces himself to stay close as he circumnavigates the entire border, confirming there is no weakness or simple access point to this barrier.

After a moment's contemplation, Dogen smiles, closed his eyes and takes in a deep breath.

"*Avalokiteshwara*," Dogen says, and then steps forward into the flames.

The pain is overwhelming as the all-consuming dragon fire tears through his flesh. Just before his first stumble, an icy sensation strikes him as if from within, and moves outward, instantly stopping the pain. A moment later Dogen can feel his flesh healing and re-growing as if he is being washed in cool pond water.

Opening his once-charred eyes, Dogen perceives that his body is garbed in a robe of water that floats a mere inch or two from his skin. Through the watery shroud, he can see that he is still within the wall of fire. And thus, he begins walking forward, girded by icy cold water and protected from further maiming. Minutes later he strides to the other side of the fiery wall and stands before the giant ruby gem. Dogen slams his right palm against the shiny stone, which immediately shatters into a thousand shards of scarlet light.

*

Rumi's spinning slows as he takes human form once again. Turning around, he sees that the majority of red tornados which attacked him have been destroyed. Those others that remain are only tiny vestiges of what they once were, and no longer threaten danger.

Turning back toward his destination, Rumi realizes that the flickering dark blue light that beckons him is coming from a towering sapphire crystal twice his height.

Before he can get within yards of the massive stone, a small skulk of jackals appear from nowhere and surround the large treasure.

One jackal, the biggest, opens its jaws and a voice erupts:

"Sufi fool," it laughs, "you have no power here."

Rumi pulls out his Ney and begins raising it to his lips as he steps forward.

"How doest thou know what sort of king I have within me as companion?" Rumi asks.

The jackals growl, stretching their jaws wide and revealing vicious teeth.

"We will tear you apart and eat you," the lead jackal laughs, "and shit your soul out in pieces."

Rumi's stride does not falter, and he speaks once more before pressing the flute to his mouth: "Do not cast thy glance upon my golden face, for I have iron legs."

Just as the jackals all coil their muscles to leap, the first fiery threads of music flicker forth from Rumi's flute, for the notes are indeed small swirls of red flame, sounds made manifest, as lovely in vision as they are in sound.

The jackals, having begun their charge, feel an instant lethargy strike their minds and bodies, and they slump to the ground, struggling to growl and keep their eyes open.

Rumi, now among them, strides between the sleeping forms until he stands facing the blue stone.

He stops playing and slams his right palm against the gem which explodes into hundreds of shards of sapphire matter.

*

Barring the occasional zombie-like form that charges, Mina finds the last few miles of her jog unimpeded, perhaps suspiciously so. Frowning, she quickly realizes that the eerie milky light beckoning her is a massive polished white moonstone gem, over two meters in height.

Closing the yards that separate her from destiny, Mina stops in her tracks as an undulating skin of translucent green matter rises from the ground and forms a tall wall around the moonstone.

Mina raises both her arms and points all her fingers at the barrier. "*Ectoplasm lamna*," she shouts.

Thick rips appear across the rippling green wall which sways as if in great pain.

"*Obice lacerabis!*" Mina further incants in Latin, focusing her will against this frightening impediment.

Large chunks of ectoplasmic matter fall from the wall and burn upon striking the ground.

Mina places her two hands together and pantomimes tearing something apart: "*Mori murum!*"

The last of the barrier flares into flames and drops to the ground, where it curls and turns black.

Mina walks across the blistering ground and turns up her nose at the awful stench. Without hesitation, she slams her left palm against the moonstone which shatters into thousands of pearl-sized points of light.

*

Simultaneously, all three mystics find themselves standing before a river of glowing molten lava that stretches forever in two directions. Overhead, mere feet above them, thousands of batlike creatures fly about, threatening any-thing that dares enter their realm.

"Look!" Dogen shouts, "An island in the lava."

"Yes," Rumi replies, "I see an altar."

"Our promised talismans," Mina adds, "but any attempt at leap or flight will be blunted by these flying vermin."

"I can give us a way in," Dogen says fiercely, "but it will only last a few minutes. You must not stumble or slow, or we are all lost."

"Do it!" Mina shouts.

"Sixteen Rakans," Dogen chants, "a celestial rock bridge I command."

Instantly, sixteen multicolored clouds swoop from high above and dive into the swift-moving lava river. Moments pass until they reappear, each carrying a glob of quickly cool-ing rock which they pile on the riverbank and the far shore of the island, easily two hundred yards distant.

A few minutes later the rock bridge is completed, a six-foot-wide flat arch with no sides or railings.

"Now!" Dogen yells.

All three commence running across the solid structure, Mina in the lead, Rumi second, and Dogen bringing up the rear.

At the midpoint and apex of the bridge, several of the low-flying creatures dive at the mystics, colliding with Mina and Rumi, knocking them off balance and almost pushing them over the edge if not for the steadying hands of Dogen who pulls them back and pushes them forward.

"Quickly," Dogen yells, "the bridge is losing its strength."

While sprinting down the last third of this magic arch, all three feel the vibrations flickering back and forth. The fright-ening sounds of rocks cracking, and splintering fill the air, and they somehow manage to run even faster.

All three sprint off the bridge and onto the rocky shore just after it breaks apart and splashes into the lava river.

An explosion of red light blinds them, but seconds later they can see again.

"That scarlet blindness," Dogen says. "It has somehow weakened me. I no longer can feel the netherblood in my veins."

"I also," Rumi replies. "In fact, I seem to have been stripped of my flute."

"I feel like I am missing something," Mina adds, "as if my third eye has gone numb, or asleep, but none of this matters. Here is our reward."

Gasping, the three walk toward the Greek temple that sits upon a sheer-sided hill, nearly two hundred feet high.

A bubbling moat of purple fluid surrounds the base.

Mina glances upward and instantly notices the lack of batlike creatures.

"Quick," Mina says, "hug me close."

The two men comply, and Mina wraps an arm around each man before shouting, "Scandens tribunal!"

All three levitate straight upwards. Seconds later Mina and her fellow mystics arrive at the entranceway of the open temple.

Stepping inside, they see a flat circular altar made of polished marble. Upon it rests three items.

They rush forward, instinctively knowing which talisman was fated for whom.

Mere feet from their prizes, a wave of the flying demons appeared. They are struck from all sides and knocked to the ground.

"My teleplasmic hands," Mina cries, "they have been stripped from me."

Long painful gashes open on their backs as they struggle forward.

"I cannot raise the image of the Buddha in my mind," Dogen yells.

It takes minutes to cross just three feet, but the bloody and wounded threesome touch the base of the altar and pull themselves up to sitting positions.

"I tried to shroud us with the elements," Rumi gasps, "but failed. Forgive me, my friends."

Dozens more of the vicious flyers start striking them from behind, scoring their backs.

Dogen reaches forward and grasps a fist-sized jade tiger.

Rumi places his right hand on a silver sculpture of a bull.

Mina picks up a diamond-tipped wand carved from ironwood.

All three turn away from the altar and thrust their objects upward. Instantly, thick bolts of lightning explode outward and fill the air. In ones and twos, and then dozens, then hundreds, the foul creatures are thrown from the air.

The three mystics slump back against the altar, gasping and groaning from their many agonizing and bleeding wounds.

"My vision ended here," Dogen says.

"And mine," Rumi adds.

"And mine also," Mina says, "I think we should place the talismans together, and simultaneously state our desires before we pass out."

"Yes," Rumi says, "I would avoid even one more resurrection on the Undertaker's slab."

They touch the three talismans against one another, and shout in one voice, "Paradise!"

An explosion of white light surrounds them.

*

Mina's eyes slowly open. She cannot move. All around her is a gauzy translucence that presses from every direction. She opens her mouth but cannot exhale. Neither does anything rush into her. After several panicked moments, she realizes she is not suffocating. At first not hearing anything, she soon begins to sense a sound, not unlike a distant roaring wind.

Is this paradise? she thinks. *Is this the moment before rebirth to heaven, or merely the doorway to a purgatory, one more step towards the eventual promised realm?*

Slowly, oh so slowly, the cloudy parameters of her sponge-like cell become clear . . . almost transparent. What Mina witnesses sends the coldest chill up her spine.

She is somehow perched upon a high hill, perhaps a mountain. Stretching downward and to either side is a vast glistening valley, covered by thousands of white shining jewels.

A sound to her left coaxes her into forcing her head in that direction. To move even a couple of inches might snap her neck, but she is granted instant recognition. Pressed up to her left, in clear jelly cell, is Rumi, unconscious, but groaning. On instinct, Mina twists to her right until finding herself face to face with an unconscious Dogen.

The realization floods into her forebrain. Mina looks downward again, finally comprehending her vantage, for streaming in every direction are not white jewels, but thousands upon thousands of mortal souls, legions of the damned suspended in gelatin coffins not unlike a vast bee brood of unborn pupae.

Time Foam, a scaly voice echoes in her head.

"What?" Mina asks, managing to speak. "Who?"

You all have been damned to this arcane valley, the punishing voice continues, *encased in my ingenious new torture, a punishment for two unforgivable crimes in my domain.*

"What crimes?" Mina asks.

Remember, the voice says, *before you first met Dogen and Rumi. What do you remember?*

Mina struggles with her mind, and then suddenly her memories appear. She is running with a vast crowd of other damned souls, dashing forward and onto a massive bridge and through a fantastic arch that spans hell itself as if Paradise could be reached from there. And just as quickly as it came, the vision floods from her mind.

You suffer in hell for righteous reasons, Mina Crandon, the voice says. *Redemption is not your reward.*

"Rumi and Dogen," Mina gasps, "they were among us refugees?"

You? Refugees? How quaint. No, though their crime was just as egregious. Both had been employed by a, oh what to call him . . . let us say a mystic far beyond the powers of you three fools. Rumi and Dogen were hired to use all their powers to try to shield the existence of an underground theatre in the city of Pandemonium, one which dared to pirate all of my most vicious and precious tortures.

"And we three share the same torture," Mina gasps.

An unanticipated side-effect of proximity, the voice adds, *one not planned as you each are condemned to a solitary virtual pantheon of failed journeys. But reading your mind, I see that working as a group only made your false sense of hope that much more powerful. Oh yes, such a truly delicious emotion is your horror and despair is to me, Mina Crandon. And now, my dear, it is time to recommence this grand cycle of perversity.*

It is then that Mina sees him. His Promethean size was hidden from her sight earlier, as his vast form blends in with the cliffs on the far side of the gigantic valley. He is a silhouette as tall as any mountain, with jutting ram's horns as big as skyscrapers and massive black unfolding membranous wings that threaten to erase the sky. Large flaming orbs draw nearer and a gargantuan red hand with black claws reaches toward Mina.

"Nighty, night, Mina," Satan says with a chuckle that rumbles like an earthquake.

Mina's screams follow her into oblivion.

The Sorcerous Apprentice

Andrew P. Weston

That old sorcerer has vanished,
And for once has gone away!
Spirits called by him, now banished,
My commands shall soon obey.
Every step and saying
That he used, I know,
And with sprites obeying,
My arts I will show

–Johann Wolfgang von Goethe
The Sorcerer's Apprentice

That old sorcerer has vanished.

The thing you have to understand about hell is that, no matter your rank or station, there are always plenty of opportunities to find yourself on your knees.

Sometimes, that can prove rather entertaining. Hell is a varied and wonderful playground, after all, arrayed over many different circles, all of them filled to the brim with brown-nosers and suck ups, crawlers and ass-lickers. And I, as Satan's Reaper, get to amuse myself by pulling the legs off such insects and compounding their suffering, either by questioning them directly along with my fellow bounty hunters, the Hell Hounds, or by submitting them to the most inimical form of interrogation there is at the hands of my Inquisitors.

At other times it can prove something of a nuisance. It's not often you'll find Daemon Grim on his hands and knees, rummaging around beneath the bleachers of one of Jahannam's most ancient tabernacles, as I was at this very moment. Unless I'm on the hunt, that is.

And if my hunch proved right, I'd just spotted a clue that might help solve my latest case.

Argent purity peeped back at me, glinting out from the shadowed recesses of the ranked pews like the mirrored sheen of a crow's eye. *Hello? Whatever that is, it's tucked in tight, out of the way on the floor, right under the locking bracket of the furthest bench. You wouldn't know it was there unless you were flat on your face and had a reason to be looking.*

Hunkering further down on all fours, I probed under the leg panel and reached forward until my fingers brushed against the telltale aloofness of cold steel. Victorious, my arm retracted to the sound of metal softly grating across stone, a private fanfare heralding the revelation of my discovery to plain sight. *Jotûn's saif? Ah, shit! My suspicions are confirmed, then. It never rains . . .*

With all the dignity I could muster, I sat back on my heels, laid my overly large find on the seat covers behind me and made haste to stand. Once upright, I commenced stretching my spine from side to side until I was rewarded with a series of satisfying cracks—a necessary exercise since my efforts to replace the Veil keeping heaven and hell apart had resulted in a number of injuries, slow to heal.

While some of those injuries had been grievous, the vast majority were relatively minor. One of the most aggravating of those minor maladies was the fact that I now seemed prone to a condition I'd never suffered from before: an occasional tightness between the shoulder blades. Odd, for the sensation felt as if something was missing; something that had left several of my vertebrae slightly out of alignment.

Mind you, I can't complain. I've endured trauma after trauma over the centuries, so there's bound to be a bit of wear and tear. So long as I keep regenerating where and when it counts, that'll be fine by me. Such thinking reminded me of the implications regarding the recovery of the Jinn warrior's weapon. *At least I'll never wind up like poor Jotûn or Garôk.*

For good measure, I triggered the Bãlefire within, and sent its healing remedy surging through my veins. As it took effect, I turned on the spot to take in the unearthly beauty of my surroundings.

Seamless, immaculate, primal and untainted by the ravaging dominance of Hatamâh—*that which breaks to pieces*: the most revered and mysteriously complex of all the Gates within the Al-Jinn circle of hell, the Hall of Shattered Dreams was a breathtaking marvel to behold.

Cloven from solid rock, the edifice was huge and fashioned in the likeness of a celestial sanctum, a cosmic temple confined to a space more than half a mile long.

Open to the firmament, the main parade was lined on either side by immense columns of smooth marblelike granite that sprouted so far into the heavens that phoenixes made their nests amongst its lofty pedestals. I could see them now, wheeling about on remote, unimaginable thermals against a malevolent burnished sky. Every now and then, their distant cries pierced the ether, challenging my right to be here.

Lower down, ranked balconies and ornate buttresses lined the space between those pillars. Balustered stewards all, each guarded landing filled floor to ceiling with bookshelves overflowing with tomes and manuscripts containing long-forgotten ancient wisdom and knowledge.

Everything possessed a refined quality, a woven, many-layered texture that not only generated its own form of light, but a sense of overpowering antiquity. First impressions made it clear that this place was made to last, and would no doubt be the only thing still standing when the arch of time itself finally fell. *Time . . . No matter how long you live, there's never enough of it.*

On the last occasion I'd set foot in this place, I'd been hunting for clues to help ensure the Veil between realms retained its integrity. While I'd been successful in my endeavors, I'd found more, much more, than I'd bargained for: Strawberry Fields, or a simulacrum of her, encased within one of the largest trúllefeng crystals I'd ever seen.

The exigencies of my assignment meant I'd been forced to leave Strawberry behind before I'd had a chance to free her. Not a problem, for I'd left her in the care of a pair of Jinn ogres from the Incendia Blade of Jahannam: Jotûn, the First Fist of that regiment, and one of his female lieutenants, Garôk—along with my promise to return forthwith.

Unfortunately, my mission to save the Veil had left me wounded and my energy reserves sorely depleted. Stripped of the heavenly and earthly mastery that made me unique among the denizens of the underworld, it had taken some time for my ruined equilibrium to adjust to the sole presence of the Bãlefire. As such, my recuperation had taken longer than anticipated.

That had been a month ago. A mere ten days in Jahannam, where temporal dominion held greater sway. Even so, it was ten days too long. For upon my return, not only had Strawberry and the gem in which she'd been interred disappeared, but of Jotûn and Garôk, nothing could be found.

Or at least, nothing could be found up until a few minutes ago.

There's never a good time for bad news. Retrieving Jotûn's saif, I called out to the Jinn commander, Gauntlet Nishôgh, who was busying himself directing those officers overseeing the various elements of our search. "Nishôgh, you're going to want to see this."

At more than eight feet in height and wider than a bull on steroids, the Gauntlet cut an imposing figure. The mere fact he was wearing gold and onyx armor encrusted with myriad miniature representations of the screaming supplicants of Saqar—the vilest and lowest of the Gates of Jahannam—did nothing to lessen the impact. For me, it was the way he sported additional battle spurs on his ten-inch tusks and horned boots that served as a final confirmation that here, right here, was a creature who would chop you into fleshy ice cubes to garnish his blood-punch as soon as look at you.

Nishôgh's voice sounded like hot coals sliding off a serrated shovel. "Janīn bearer, you have something at last?"

"I'm afraid so." Hefting Jotûn's scimitar, I cocked a thumb toward the pews at the front of the transcript, "I found it beneath the seating area of the middle aisle. It must have slid under there when . . ."

"When?"

"When the First Fist met his end."

Those soldiers close enough to hear our exchange stopped what they were doing to stare. The forms of several of the younger ogres rippled, revealing momentary flashes of burning vortices or smoking specters.

"*Fenôme je* (Fuck it)!" Bristling with barely suppressed rage, the Gauntlet stomped toward me, chiming with every step and emitting energies potent enough to kindle sparks. "You suspect foul play then, as opposed to direct intervention from Hatamâh itself?"

"I do. Though I'd only known Jotûn and Garôk for a short time, I found them to be stalwart companions, competent and totally reliable. Regardless of my own opinion, Hatamâh had accepted their presence as well as my own; otherwise we would not have been granted access to this site in the first place. Once here, I began my investigation but was forced to leave prematurely to counter a serious threat manifesting within my own realm. An irritating hindrance, to say the least. However, Jotûn assured me both he and Garôk would take care of my former lov . . . er, Chief Inquisitor, or arrange for suitable guards to be stationed about the Hall in their stead until my return. The mere fact that they didn't neither speaks volumes. They wouldn't have willingly left without taking suitable precautions or notifying you first. Agreed?"

"Agreed."

"Add those details to the subtle spoor I detected when I first arrived here and . . .?"

"Spoor?"

Expanding my consciousness, I reached out to out Nishôgh's mind, adjusted the resolution of my acuity, and homed in on the elusive tincture I'd noted, secreted away within the atoms of the air around us. "My senses are more refined than yours. Even so, I'm sure your people haven't failed to notice the atmosphere within the sanctuary? Despite Hatamâh's predisposition toward destruction, everything here is incredibly vibrant and invigorating. I get the distinct impression nothing is allowed to taint the purity of this place or its surrounding environment. Regardless, I perceived the fading resonance of decay the moment I arrived. It's very faint, but someone died recently. The mere fact that the Al-Jinn don't dissipate immediately for reassignment as the denizens of latterday hell do, suggests that whoever killed our brother and sister went to great lengths to sanitize the scene. That's why I've been digging around in all the hard-to-reach nooks and crannies."

Thunderheads congealed beneath the overhang of Nishôgh's brows. "But who would dare the wrath of the Blades of the Left-Hand Path? Such an act would guarantee a sentence both fatal and foul upon those foolish enough to—"

"*Over here!*"

Strident, the sudden declaration cut our conversation dead.

A lone Jinn soldier had been examining the albino oak-sculpted tympanum surrounding the feature rose window overlooking the sepulcher. Leaping from his position more than thirty feet up, he crashed to the flagstones below in a wash of vaporous flames and held his fist high.

"Deshân (Sergeant)," the Gauntlet roared, "Do you have anything to report?"

"Yes sir. I think I might have found something quite significant." The officer bounded toward us, his aura crackling with anticipation and excitement. Reaching our position, he skidded to a halt and opened his paw to reveal a miniscule, gray nugget sitting in the middle of his plate-sized palm. "I saw the frame near the bottom of the wooden trellis that had been damaged. After I'd dug about inside with the tip of my dagger for a few seconds, *this* fell out."

Clearly unimpressed, Nishôgh stooped to peer at the proffered item before voicing his concern. "You call this tiny thing a *significant* find?"

Because of the height difference, I couldn't quite see the offending article and found it necessary to pull the sergeant's hand a little lower. I was glad I did, for I recognized the nature of the twisted lump of metal almost immediately.

Nishôgh caught my expression and acknowledged it. "Reaper, you look as if you know what this is?"

"That's because I do. It's a slug from a Hell-Brass 6.66 Magnum. Solid silver from what I can determine . . ." I inhaled. The bittersweet tang of dark magic stung my receptors. "And it's been hexed all the way to heaven and back."

Both ogres appeared a bit confused by my response, so I thought it best to expand on my answer in a way they'd understand:

"Though your people are among some of the most puissant I've ever come across, several of the other, less noteworthy realms possess projectile weapons that can even the playing field. If Jotûn and Garôk were taken by surprise, a Hell-Brass Magnum would have been more than sufficient to negate their superior size, strength and aggression."

I plucked the spent bullet from the sergeant's grasp. Rolling it backward and forward between my thumb and forefinger, I emphasized, "This *insignificant* little thing came from such a weapon. Don't be misled by its harmless appearance."

Turning on my heel, I beckoned them to follow me back along the nave toward the altar. As we walked, I added further details to clarify the situation: "Your man retrieved this from what . . . thirty to forty feet up? That suggests whoever killed Jotûn and Garôk must have been standing . . ." I raised my opposite hand and made the shape of a finger-gun in the air. Using Nishôgh's height as a base reference, I calculated a likely angle of attack and kept adjusting it until I was sure my assessment would be accurate, ". . . round about *here*. See?"

Seasoned warriors, both soldiers became focused upon the mental task of following the imaginary line of the bullet as it travelled along the length of my arm, through its phantom target, and away toward the distant casement.

I waited a moment for them to finish, then rounded off my hypothesis:

"The trajectory suggests that whoever the assassin was, he or she must have been close to my height. Aiming up toward the most vulnerable part of the body—the head—would put the bullet smack bang where the sergeant found it. We're fortunate that window decoration is one of the few things made of a wood like substance, otherwise I doubt we would have found anything. You've seen how resilient the stonework is here."

Nishôgh was clearly infuriated. "How . . . ? But . . . ? Who would possess such a weapon in Jahannam? We don't journey to your world. And those humans who do stray here are quickly apprehended and don't last very long."

"That's what I would like to find out. We did have one or two miscreants who used to possess gadgets that allowed them to intrude just about anywhere. But they're out of the picture now." The problem knot between my shoulder blades started to ache again. "Still, that's not to say someone else got their hands on such tech and been up to no good?"

The Gauntlet's visage darkened. Flames danced in his eyes. Clenching his fists, he growled, "Such a travesty is intolerable. Unthinkable."

"And unforgivable," I added. Playing to the occasion, I shadowed Nishôgh's gesture and allowed sulfurous fumes to vent from my tattoos. "Not only is such an act a transgression of the precepts governing our treaty, but it shames our realm before the blood is dry on the parchment."

Thinking on my feet, I came to a snap decision:

"With your permission, I would like to assign a team of our top sulforensic examiners to assist in this case. Sadly, they lack the fortifying essence of the eternal flame and don't possess the vigor I am endowed with. However, I am not without influence and should attract sufficient volunteers to ensure a most thorough investigation takes place before they expire."

"You would send your compatriots to their deaths? And they would be willing to sacrifice themselves?"

"Though the latterday levels are mostly filled by verminous scum, there are those of a superior quality still eager to serve in the name of the dark lord. And it goes without saying; their reassignment would incur his Satanic Majesty's blessing. If we adopt suitable working parameters, they should be able to go over this place with a fine-tooth comb and uncover things we have miss . . . ? Are you alright?"

Nishôgh leaned forward, fascinated by my face. Reacting instinctively, I moved and wiped my lips, only to discover that the Gauntlet adjusted his position in an attempt to get a better view inside my mouth. "What? Have I dribbled or spilt something?"

"Not at all, Janīn bearer," he mumbled in reply, "it's just that I never realized that the denizens of your many worlds possessed hairy fangs that would require grooming?"

The penny dropped.

Despite the urgency of the situation, I burst out laughing and bared my teeth for inspection. After the Gauntlet had taken a good look, I explained, "My apologies, we don't. It's just a figure of speech we use to suggest the idea of being thorough."

A verdant flash from the top of the steps next to the altar announced the arrival of an unexpected visitor. I turned to find my latest recruit, and still something of an enigma, Heinrich von Nettesheim standing there.

In the short time Nettesheim had been with us, he'd picked up the honorific '*The Sorcerer*' on account of his uncanny affinity to wield the extraordinary potential encapsulated within the *third way*.

A remnant from the Time of Sundering, the 'third way' was, in fact, an echo generated by the sequestering of heaven from hell, for the power of creation—Holy Spirit—had polarized over the centuries into two forms: G*d's Grace and the Bãlefire.

Residual pockets still existed where the disparate sovereignties overlapped, and it was into this lofty medium that a handful of individuals in Satan's service could delve when the need arose. Though I possessed nowhere near the skill of Nettesheim or his associates, I was one of them. Or at least, I had been before the entire sum of my divine and earthly potential had been stripped away during the regeneration of the Veil. But that's another story.

And truth be told, I'd been a little reticent to try since then in case it didn't work.

Nettesheim didn't seem perturbed in the slightest by the scale or strangeness of our surroundings. The moment he'd materialized in full, he nodded briefly in my direction and stepped toward Nishôgh. Snapping to attention, Nettesheim then placed his right fist to his heart. "Hail, *Akhdûr* (Gauntlet). Heinrich von Nettesheim at your service. As former Knight and captain in earth and hell's armies, I now serve as Hell Hound to His most Despicable Highness, Satan. May your house and the Incendia Blade always find honor in battle."

Nishôgh stiffened and adopted a more reserved posture. Returning the salute, he intoned, "Greetings, Heinrich von Nettesheim, Hell Hound and warrior. It is gratifying to see you know our ways. I am Nishôgh, Gauntlet of the Incendia Blade of Jahannam under Shield Omniûs. May your blade always stay sharp."

Nettesheim bowed, "A pleasure. My colleagues and I have heard a lot about you. Though I wish we could have been introduced under better circumstances, rest assured, my pack members and I mourn the loss of the brother and sister we never met. We hope this joint investigation soon uncovers the identity of the culprit, and trust you will allow us the honor of being present at their execution?"

The Gauntlet's face brightened in evident surprise. "Why yes. It would be gratifying to have you present as public observers."

It was intriguing to watch my Hound at work. *I can see why Nettesheim was used extensively as an ambassador in his day. The man's a natural at fostering communication . . .*

Formalities over, Nettesheim looked toward me, an expectant cast in his eye.

And perceptive at seizing opportunities to engender trust, it would seem.

"The Al-Jinn are creatures of exceptional honor," I declared aloud. "I am sure the Gauntlet will treat what you have to say in his presence with the strictest confidence?"

Nishôgh glanced between Nettesheim and myself for a second or two and his shoulders lifted with ill-concealed pride. Lowering his great head in deference to my statement, he murmured, "My discretion is assured."

Nettesheim took that as his cue and ushered us closer together. Dropping his voice, he whispered, "We've had a major breakthrough regarding the ongoing plague."

"You have?" *At last, something's going right.*

"Yes. As I intimated a few weeks ago, it's not only telestic in origin but specific in the way it aggressively targets emotions. There are only a handful of individuals who could accomplish such a thing. Well, guess what? Whoever was responsible has been busy, and seems to have mutated it into a more vigorous strain."

I was a little concerned by Nettesheim's enthusiasm. "We've only just rid ourselves of two of the biggest pains in the ass to ever walk the underworld. Even the Undertaker is loath to retrieve their residue from the Hub to start playing with them. Why are you so gleeful of the fact some idiot is keen to take their place by unleashing the mother of all infections, especially if they've succeeded in making the damned plague even more virulent than it was before?"

"Because they had to return to the primary insertion site in order to do it," Nettesheim crowed with a flourish, "and we know where that is now."

Not privy to the trials and tribulations that were my everyday life, it was obvious the flow of this particular exchange was causing Nishôgh something of a headache. I thought it prudent to put the brakes on for a few minutes while I brought him up to speed.

Fortunately, details of this specific problem were rather scant and it didn't take me long.

When I'd finished, Nishôgh appeared truly shocked by the extent of the escalating unrest. "I never appreciated the degree of disorder you suffer," he grumbled. "It seems you're going to have your hands full for a while?"

"Not if we play our cards right," Nettesheim interjected, rejoining the conversation, "because now we've located the source, I've had some of my former associates working on a viable solution. And we think we have an answer."

Seeking clarification, I probed, "By, *associates*, I take it you're referring to other mystics like yourself?"

"That's right, Nettesheim responded, "mystics, conjurers, sorcerers and shamans. Call us what you will. It doesn't matter. As I say, we think we've hit on a way to immunize denizens against the contagion's effects."

"You have? But that's marvelous news. How soon do you think you could devise a suitable delivery system?"

"That's what we need to discuss, Daemon. I have no doubt the moment we neutralize the threat, our mischief maker will move to counter. Now, bearing in mind *who* it is that's responsible, and factoring in the changes you've recently undergone, we don't want to make our move until we're sure we're ready."

"We don't?"

"No. For not only is our perpetrator an accomplished artisan of magic, she has some very powerful friends, to boot."

"I see . . ." *And suddenly, I feel very old and out of my depth.*

Juggling a multitude of factors in my head, I came to a characteristic decision.

"As you'll come to appreciate, His Infernal Majesty likes a proactive approach, so I always encourage my teams to display initiative and deploy our resources accordingly to ensure we retain the advantage. Though you're the newest of us, your experience in such matters far outweighs the rest of us combined. What would you recommend?"

It was gratifying to witness how Nettesheim's maturity came to the fore at that moment, for he didn't feel the need to argue or labor the point. "I suggest we reconvene later this evening? Taking temporal variance between our two realms into account, that'll give me almost forty-eight hours to ready our people and prepare a suitable intelligence package from which to deliver a briefing. It will also give you two time to arrange suitable replacements to act as liaisons in your absence."

"I'm invited too?" Nishôgh was genuinely stunned.

"Of course. . ." Nettesheim hit me with a subliminal telepathic query, just in case I felt he was overstepping the mark. Taking my continued silence as affirmation, he forged ahead, "In the interests of our fledgling treaty, it will be a fine opportunity to welcome you to the Den of Iniquity. You'll meet the rest of the Hell Hounds and Inquisitors, and we can apprise you, firsthand, of potential enemies and the danger they represent."

"Then I am honored to accept. Thank you."

"The honor is all ours, Gauntlet," Nettesheim replied, "for once our enemies realize we are allied to the Al-Jinn, the mere thought of having to face the Blades of the Left-Hand Path should prove rather worrisome to them."

Nishôgh's chest puffed out like a prize fighting cock at the compliment—a heavily armored, cyberpunk version, but a fighting cock, nonetheless. I seriously expected him to start strutting his stuff at any moment. *Well played. Nettesheim's a definite envoy in the making. If His Satanic Majesty ever starts trying to corral me into playing the diplomat again, I'll know in whose direction to point.*

Nettesheim must have picked up on what I was thinking, for a brief look of discomfort clouded his features. Tensing, he stepped away and began drawing power. "If you don't mind, gentlemen, I'd best be off. Places to go and things to do . . ."

And with that, he spun an intricately refined upsilon field and disappeared.

That's it, I called after him: *You can run, but you can't hide . . . ambassador!*

I turned back to find Nishôgh studying me closely. Feeling like a schoolboy caught stealing candy bars from the tuck-shop, I mumbled, "Is everything alright?"

The sound of boulders being compressed in a car crusher wheezed from his lungs. The Gauntlet was chuckling. "I knew from the moment I identified the sacred flame within you, the fates of our peoples would become intertwined, Janīn bearer. It is also heartwarming, witnessing the way you encourage progress by delegating authority. That takes courage, especially in an environment where everyone is usually most concerned about themselves."

"Courage be damned. Come hell or high water, I'm judged on results. That's all that matters to my master. And Nettesheim's forgotten more about the skills and tactics we'll need to address this issue safely than I'll ever know. I'd be an idiot not to follow his lead. Though I must admit, like you, I'm itching to see how he intends to remedy the situation with the limited resources at our disposal."

Come old broomstick, you are needed.

Tick—tock. Tick—tock. Tick—tock . . .

The resonance of the grandfather clock counted down the seconds until our meeting would begin, its two-tone cadence vying for dominance against a constant crackle and occasional angry snap issuing from the open hearth nearby.

Flames from that fire cast a flickering radiance about the rest of the room. Roused from slumber, shadows cavorted merrily along the grain of the black walnut furnishings, causing eyelids to droop and the larger letters adorning the spines of many of the thicker volumes gracing my library to dance from side to side like sprites.

Despite the passing urge to doze, the atmosphere within my study was tense and sober. As well it should be, for my entire command staff were in attendance to give their backing to a policy that would hopefully rid the latterday levels of hell of a problem now mushrooming beyond pandemic in scope.

While there was still time, I skimmed the length and breadth of the table and studied each person in turn, thankful they were here and glad of the experience and wisdom they'd be able to offer:

To my immediate right sat my new Lead Hound, Yamato Takeru. The former prince of a first century Japanese dynasty, Yamato was also a legendary ninja killer with an uncanny knack for manipulating the elements. As patient and level-headed as they come, Yamato was the only person I knew who was capable of controlling the damned soul who had ended up as his partner, Champ Ferguson.

An infamous Confederate guerilla fighter during the American Civil War, Champ was as boorish as he was crass. The thing was, he was blessed with superlative tracking skills. So much so, that not even Erra's auditors had been able to elude him—though he'd paid a high price for such success, ending up in a Sibitti torture cell for months on end.

Midway along the table, my lover, Charlotte Corday, lounged across two chairs, deep in meditation. Remembered by the world above as, l' ange de l'assassinat (the angel of the assassination), she was the woman responsible for the murder of Jacobin leader, Jean-Paul Marat during the initial stages of the French revolution. We simply knew her as the 'Lady Gemini,' on account of the hideous ministrations of the Undertaker which had left one side of her face looking like withered parchment.

Supremely swift and stealthy, Gemini had the acutest senses of us all, and was a prodigious talent at compelling obedience from others, with animals and insects being particularly amenable to her will.

Stood apart at a separate, makeshift rostrum next to a neat stack of clip-folders and a holographic projector, stood the man—and sorcerer—himself, Heinrich Cornelius Agrippa von Nettesheim. Master of all trades and Jack of none. A true polymath if ever there was one, as reflected by his list of established credentials: occultist, theologian, astrologer, magician, alchemist, physician, legal expert, diplomat and soldier. Watching him put the last-minute touches to his briefing, I failed to discern the slightest sign of nerves.

Good, we'll need that confidence and self-assurance in the mission ahead.

Opposite my Hell Hounds, the Inquisitors filled their side of the table.

Farthest away, Leonard Skeffington, a previous lieutenant of the Tower of London, sat quietly, wireless ear buds firmly affixed, humming a tune and tapping his fingers against the armrest of his chair. His deceptively polite and reserved manner hid an intensely malicious streak that he often used to good effect when interrogating prisoners, for his cruelty was fed by an insatiable fascination to watch people suffer.

Beside him, Myra Belle Star—aka Black Velvet—a notorious outlaw from the end of the nineteenth century, stared blankly into the fire. Her calm disposition gave nothing away. I wasn't fooled. Here was a woman who would execute anyone: man, woman, child, even kittens, as readily as clip her nails.

And she loved to clip, did our Myra, as indicated by the volume of necklaces strung about her neck, each one bedecked with those bodily tokens her victims had been forced to relinquish as they submitted to her most invasive ministrations.

Next to her was Dr. David Livingstone, former warden at Cadavers Lunatic Asylum across in New Hell and now my new Chief Inquisitor. He sat quietly, taking in everything. Astute and down-to-earth, the good doctor had swiftly established himself as something of a go-getter and a man whose scientific bent gave us an edge when dealing with anything involving technology, no matter how abstruse.

Closest to me on my left were Baron Ferenc Nádasdy, a sixteenth century Hungarian nobleman, and his wife, Elizabeth Báthory. His Satanic majesty had made a rare exception in allowing this married couple to continue their relationship here in the underworld, but we all knew why. Elizabeth was nuts, plain and simple. And Ferenc was the only one she regularly responded to. Her mind was like an old stacked filing cabinet that had lost its contents in a bad tumble down the stairs, and now had monsters nesting in the debris. There were times when her scattered wits worked in perfect alphabetical order, and it was on those rare occasions she was able to offer eerily insightful advice. But mostly, the world's most prolific serial killer of young women liked to play in a fantasyland of pain and blood, all filed neatly under 'F' for frenziedly fucking feral. And usually, she liked to play naked.

We seem to have been particularly blessed this evening, for Elizabeth had taken an instant liking to Nishôgh from the moment she laid eyes on him only an hour ago. Slinking off to her rooms, she had returned, dripping in gold bangles and anklets and bedecked in silk, chiffon and lace, like a female genie from a popular 1960's comedy show I'd once seen. Seating the Gauntlet on one of the sofas, the only furniture large enough to accommodate Nishôgh's bulk, she then proceeded to lavish constant attention and endless drinks upon the bemused ogre, who clearly still hadn't quite worked out what to make of her.

I was particularly grateful for the fact Nishôgh seemed to prefer Indian Blood Peach Brandy to Diabhalvulin 18, as he was knocking the stuff back using an ice bucket for a glass; heroically, with no perceived side-effects whatsoever.

The grandfather clock clunked, whirred and struck eight. Everyone stopped what they were doing to listen. In the distance, Little Ben could be heard supporting its tiny cousin with peals reverberating at a slower, deeper pitch. As the dual chimes faded, Nettesheim used the occasion as a prompt to bring the meeting to order.

"First of all, I'd like to thank everyone for coming." He gestured toward the Al-Jinn commander who was busily engaged, cradling a pail of brandy in one hand while fending Elizabeth off with the other. "Especially Nishôgh, Gauntlet of the Incendia regiment of the Blades of the Left-Hand Path, whose people have been dragged into our shitfest through no direct fault of their own.

"As I'm sure you'll appreciate, there's never a convenient time to *drag* anyone away from their work. So, I'll crack straight on and keep this briefing as short as possible." Nettesheim paused to hand the stacked files he'd prepared on to those persons sitting closest to him, Gemini and Leonard. After selecting their own copies, they passed the rest on down each side of the table.

As the dwindling pile of dossiers worked its way toward me, Nettesheim pressed a button on the control panel of the holo-emitter and the full-color profile of a young, rather demure looking woman appeared in the air before him. Allowing it to rotate through three hundred and sixty degrees, he waited for the image to face forward once more before fixing it in place. Clearing his throat, he declared, "This is our target: Teresa Sánchez de Cepeda y Ahumada, a onetime nun and saint from the Ávila region of Spain.

"From an early age, Teresa was blessed with the quixotic ability to alter the scope of her consciousness sufficiently to comprehend and manipulate the higher states of reality. A rare and perilous gift, especially as she was an advocate of the teaching that love can influence all things for the better. Naturally, such a prize drew the attention of Satan who, after realizing the extent of her aptitude, began appearing to her in dreams in an effort to subvert her faith. Long story short? It took time, but in the end, Teresa was duped into condemning herself.

"Don't fool yourselves. While she might look all sweetness and light, she's one dangerous lady to cross. Once condemned, Teresa swore she'd get even with the devil by spreading her message of love here in hell, among the damned. Our dark father scoffed at such a threat, believing it the bitter, empty tirade of yet another naïve wretch . . . until he discovered this woman could still reach the hearts and minds of those truly contrite. Then he locked her away from the public domain and began moving her about his many prisons scattered throughout the length and breadth of the underverse.

"Even so, rumors of her presence and promise of the redemption she offered abounded, and people began seeking her out. It was a foregone conclusion such knowledge would reach the ears of Erra and the Seven."

"Have we been able to ascertain when such a leak is likely to have occurred?" I asked, keen to learn anything that might help me better understand how Erra and his goons operated.

"I'm afraid not," Livingstone replied. "If I were to hazard an educated guess, they most likely came about such information in one of two ways. First, we know the Sibitti were in league for a time with Chopin and Tesla before you crushed them. It may be the Seven have simply exploited contacts forged during that time. However, let's not overlook the nature of these sons of heaven and earth. From what we've been led to believe, they devour their victims and *read* that person's history by witnessing events as perceived through the subject's own eyes and ears. They can even recall what an individual has said, done or thought on every occurrence, through into the future. How simple it would be for an enforcer to retrieve the knowledge of Teresa's likely whereabouts while ingesting the hapless protestations of those they audit? The Sevens' understanding would be flawless, for they can translate the truth of a matter by perceiving exactly what each victim believes. An edge I'm sure they've exploited on countless occasions.

"However they did it, the fact remains that it most likely resulted in Teresa's release from Wormblood Scrubs just under six months ago. Although all witnesses to the incident (two prison guards and a visitor) were mindwiped prior to their deaths and reassignment, other bystanders outside the prison reported seeing what they believed were angelic creatures brandishing fiery swords ascending into the sky wreathed in electrum light. If that's not indicative of Erra's deacons of destruction, then I don't know. . . ?"

"The how's and the when's aren't really important," Yamato interrupted, chopping the air with his hand. "Not anymore. If this Saint Teresa has been working with Erra all along, we need to understand *what* she did that led to the disruptions we're seeing now. And how any of this links to her threat regarding a message of love?"

"Good point. I'm glad you asked," Nettesheim replied. And he was too. I could see it by the eagerness and the

look of anticipation—one conveying almost reverential respect—illuminating his face at this moment.

Leaning forward, he activated the holo-emitter and projected two opposing scenes into the air. In the one on my
left, a 3D representation of the boiling cauldron that was the
primary hydraspace node leading directly into the latterday
levels of hell loomed large. To my right, a strange, many
branched funguslike blob wallowed about within a shining
ectoplasmic medium.

Referring to the snot droplet, I voiced the question that
must have been on everyone's lips. "Why the fuck are you
showing us the contents of the Undertaker's handkerchief?
Was he suffering from a particularly bad case of hell-flu?"

"Many a true word has been spoken in jest. Hang on a tic,
and I'll explain." Nettesheim grinned, enlarged the phlegm-
filled picture, and continued, "What we have here is the
mother of all esothermatic viruses. Now, before you all start
jumping in demanding to know what the heck I'm talking
about; let me put it in layman's terms . . ."

Producing a laser pen, Nettesheim commenced pointing out the various features of the gooey nebula. "From what
we've determined so far, the sticky zones *there* and *there*,
seem to be biochemical in nature. That means they create a
physiological reaction within the subject. However, it's this
glowing mass, *here*, that interests us, because of its ethraclastic and psychosomatic properties.

"Basically, this thing thrives on anagogic energy. If that
energy happens to be in close proximity to strong emotions,
then all the better. Why? Well don't forget, nobody in the
underworld is entirely physical. Except for a certain few."
I didn't miss the glance Nettesheim cast my way. "The vast
majority of the populace possess only a pseudo-memory of
what they once were. A necromantic quasi-ghost body, if you

like, generated by the all-sustaining crux of hell: the Bãle-fire. This is important, because from what we've been able to determine, not only was the original contagion attuned to the distinct parametric current predominating the latterday circles, but it was also planted directly into the cosmic hub anchoring New Hell in place. It . . . how can I say . . . *ad-opted* the theurgic frequency by which New Hell operates; synchronized to it; and through it, blended to its denizens as well. Such a strategy would ensure a most expedient means of dispersal, for New Hell is a major travel terminal, directly linked to every other realm."

Bugger me senseless! *That's ingenious.*

I wasn't the only one to think so.

Ever sharp, Livingstone had also picked up on what Net-tesheim had been trying to emphasize. "So, you're saying the original viral strand was engineered with New Hell in mind, and that once released, the bug adapted to each latterday realm it came across, as well as those damned inhabiting it?"

"As ever, doctor, you are swift and perceptive. Yes, New Hell's hub was ground-zero for an ever expanding, ever cus-tomizing contagion that is nigh on impossible to keep a track of."

"Why is that?" The doc's eyes were shining with bare-ly suppressed enthusiasm. "How does this beauty actually propagate, then? What mutagenic properties are incorporat-ed within its template? Can it facilitate the cross . . .?"

"Let's keep this briefing on track, gentlemen," I inter-ceded. "Remember, we're here to counter a growing threat. Not wax lyrical about its scientific masturbatory value. Your additional waffling will only succeed in putting Champ to sleep."

My comments came belatedly. Champ's head had al-ready craned over to one side. And from what I could see, the first trace of saliva was just beginning to work its way from the corner of his slackened jaw.

Fixing Nettesheim with what I hoped was a stern enough look, I warned, "Stay focused, but by all means, feel free to answer the second part of the doctor's question. *How* is this thing actually spreading?"

Nettesheim didn't miss a beat. "Ah, this is the part that truly reveals Teresa's ingenuity and finesse. We know her construct is airborne, and that it can be spread by touch. Fair enough, and somewhat obvious, yes? But there are also the ethereal and psychic aspects to consider. The infection is somehow able to attach itself to the emotional nucleus of the predominant feelings being experienced by its host, before mutating those sentiments into something atypical. Something rabid and unnatural. And I think that's why she chose the quality of love to begin her little plague. Think about it. Satan has seen to it that one of the most basic of human needs—perhaps the most crucial—that of intimate companionship, has been denied the vast majority of his subjects. Even we who stand among the elite have to follow certain rules, or have the privilege withdrawn. Is it any wonder, then, that hell's subjects, spurred on by the slightest provocation, would take things to the extreme? That's why I likened this virus to a pathogen. It's designed to elicit a specific behavioral response: the urge, the inbuilt need to feel wanted and loved, and to see it tangibly demonstrated.

"But hell is populated by the dregs of human society. Their attitudes are impelled by the darkest of desires. And what holds sway in their secret hearts will predominate in outward expression: hate, for those who are spurned; lust for those who succumb to their carnal cravings. As you might expect, the ceaseless supply of scorpions and spiders at the devil's disposal guarantees submission proves fatal for every subject. And we haven't even touched on the consequences their willingness to flout one of Satan's most serious taboos will have on their inevitable reassignment."

"So *that's* how it spread so easily," I mumbled, half to myself, half aloud, "and why so much of the rioting ends up as one mass orgy. Human emotions are fickle at the best of times and easily influenced. People are quick to resort to violence, even against those they say they love."

"And don't forget," Nettesheim added, "as a mystic, Teresa would have been well aware of the approaching Soulstice. She timed her attack to capitalize on the inimitable resonance of the Ascendant itself. The resultant catalyst would have been amplified, and guaranteed to cause maximum disruption."

The Ascendant? Of course.

The extent of this so-called saint's skullduggery suddenly reminded me of a phrase the First of Seven had expressed during our last encounter, just over a month ago at the Statue of Lost Liberty, in New Hell. Using Gemini as bait, he'd drawn me to that location in the hope of wreaking revenge for a previous slight against his brothers. Before we'd gotten down to business, he'd referred to Gemini herself, and then said something odd. Something I hadn't understood at the time.

Recalling the event, I measured his words more closely:

"This fragile creature, for instance. Such a bright and perilous predator in so diminutive a guise. Fortunately, we are now accustomed to such contradictions . . ."

He'd sneered while the rest of his brood had laughed, privy to their own private joke, before concluding. "And credit where it's due, she was a formidable opponent. For all her delicacy, she begged no favor and we gave no quarter. Alas, our being impressed won't save her."

So, he must have been alluding to their secret arrange-
ment with this Saint Teresa. No wonder they seemed more
smug than usual. It must—Hang on?

Out of the blue, a hitherto unconsidered factor hit me. So
surprised was I that I voiced my concern aloud: "Heinrich,
why do you think that none of us here have been infected?"

The smile on Nettesheim's face revealed he'd been expecting such a question. "We probably have, Daemon," he
replied, meeting every gaze in turn, "but we're lucky in that
the effects have been muted sufficiently for us not to notice."

Not to notice? I had to ask. It was plain the others wanted
to know too. "And why would that be?"

"From what we can ascertain, there are two probable reasons. The first is the predominance of the Bãlefire. Not only
are the environs around the Den of Iniquity one of the richest
sources of hell's sustaining lifeblood, but each of us here carries a flame of the original pyre within us. You know as well
as I do that it empowers, elevates and sustains us. It looks as
if it also acts as a universal remedy against other forms of
deviltry." He nodded toward Nishôgh. "You'll probably find
that all the Al-Jinn possess a similar buoyancy. After all, the
eternal fire of Jahannam burns inside them. And Jahannam is
sentient, don't forget; it articulates the power of the Bãlefire
in its own unique way. The Al-Jinn might call the everlasting
flame, Janīn, but it's one and the same thing. An antithetical
expression of G*d's Grace, and a kick-ass protection."

"You said there might be two reasons for our immunity?"

"Yes, I did." Stepping around the hologram and into a
clear space, Nettesheim again made a point of holding the
attention of everyone present for a moment as he answered:
"Think of what else differentiates us from just about every other denizen of hell. We're entitled, yes. But so are the
Blue Suits and Devil's Children, who hold benefits far more

gracious than those of the rank and file. So, what is it that distinguishes the Hell Hounds and Inquisitors as virtually unique? More privileged, even, than the Devil's Own?"

Everyone stared at each other with blank expressions. The answer must have been so obvious, so in our faces, that we were missing it.

Fortunately, Nettesheim didn't keep us hanging for long: "I'll tell you," he said. "Sex."

An entire squadron of brows on either side of the table flared as the eyes beneath them popped in unison. An instant later, they subsided, one after the other, as the light of comprehension winked on like a set of runway strobes.

"Do you see?" Nettesheim raised his voice to emphasize the point. "The mere fact that we are allowed to engage in sexual congress may have proved a hidden devilsend. It isn't as big a deal to us as it is to virtually everyone else, so the virus is unable to elicit the necessary emotional response to gain a foothold."

"That's all well and good," I countered, marking an obvious oversight to his line of reasoning. "But if this plague is adapting as you've already suggested, into a new and more virulent strain, there might come a time when our natural resilience is insufficient to counter its effects, yes?"

"Exactly right! Thus, the urgency to act. And the sooner the better."

"So, what do you propose we do?"

"Simple. Use our heads. If we adopt a four-pronged coordinated line of attack, the solution should be straightforward."

Nettesheim turned first to my Chief Inquisitor. "David, I'd like you to set your staff the task of overseeing the uncapping of each and every bane-well running into the main repository beneath the battlements. By this time tomorrow night, Bālefire levels should have risen dangerously high.

But don't worry. Before it reaches critical mass, you'll have targeted the citadel's esobolic mirrors to transfer all that excess potential here . . ."

Leaning toward the table, Nettesheim entered a long sequence into the holo-emitter's keypad. The scene of the hydraspace node within the cloud expanded and zoomed in to show the arcane processes taking place at its core. A set of coordinates commenced flashing on and off across the bottom of the picture.

Referring to that sequence, Nettesheim resumed his instructions: "Hitting that spot will saturate the entire zone with Bãlefire and create the perfect environment in which to plant our embryonic countermeasure. Once it's gestated, we won't have to worry about it further, as it will propagate in a similar manner to the contagion its targeting. All we have to do is endeavor to give it sufficient time to mature. In *that* regard . . .

"Yamato? Champ, Gemini and yourself are to secret yourselves away within the natural folds of the Sheolspace continuum and maintain a discreet watch while Daemon and I move to insert the antidote directly into the matrix. That part of the process might take some time as we need to infuse it with sufficient vitality to ensure it not only grows, but becomes a thriving, self-sustaining organism. While I'll leave the specifics of your assignment to you, please don't forget: you'll have a limitless source of energy beaming your way from which to fashion your defenses and—if required—your attack options. As stealth and speed are a priority, especially during the early stages of the operation, I'd hope you'd consider employing Gemini's natural empathy for covert movement into your stratagem."

"And what of my people?" Nishôgh probed, swishing the ice in his drink loudly, before draining the remains of yet another bucketful of brandy in one gulp. "I doubt that you would have gone to all this trouble to invite me here if you weren't intending to make use of the Al-Jinn legions?"

"Quite right, Gauntlet," Nettesheim breezed on, taking the query in his stride. "We'll need you to assemble your entire Blade and ready them for war. Don't fret about the logistics of such a mobilization or the reactions this might engender among the populace. No one will know you're here. A special representative from Juxtapose will accompany you back to Jahannam equipped with a temporal mitigator to make sure our efforts are synchronized. Then, once your troops are ready, she'll start moving them through, a Link at a time, and secret them away in the training courts in the lower levels of the Den. From the outside looking in, it'll be just another day of pain and suffering in the latterday joy that is the Reaper's domain. If there *are* any of Erra's spies sniffing around outside the walls, they'll gain no inkling of the army building beneath their feet."

While I liked what I was hearing, a certain detail within Nettesheim's report gave me pause for concern. Sitting forward, I snapped, "And who is this mystery *representative* you speak of? If she's capable of entering and leaving Jahannam at will, I'd like to meet her beforehand, especially if you're intending to bring her into the castle's environs."

"Then, with your permission?" Nettesheim and I locked wills. He didn't seem embarrassed by his assumption that I would agree to everything he'd devised without complaint. When I didn't respond immediately, he qualified his request further: "Daemon? You *did* grant me charter to plan as I saw fit? I'll need to grant her safe passage through the Den's defenses. I can't do that without your help."

I let him dangle for a good thirty second before acquiescing and sending him a telepathic passkey code. Then I leaned back in my chair, interested now in seeing how things would develop.

Swiftly didn't begin to go anywhere near describing what happened next.

By the time I'd blinked, someone had already joined Nettesheim beside the holo-projector. Tall, willowy, and dressed from head to toe in a shimmering cyan colored cape that sparkled through all the colors of the forest, Nettesheim's friend was a striking beauty to say the least.

Sharp features and high cheekbones accentuated an immaculate, if slightly blue-tinged complexion. In turn, the smoothness of her cool skin provided the perfect canvas for ruby lips and the flood of coal-black tresses that spilled from the hood of her cowl in a wave. Unblinking, ocean-spray eyes stared out from layered folds. So hard, so aloof was her demeanor, that I was sure this woman must possess liquid nitrogen for blood.

I sounded her mind, lightly, and my probe was met by a glacial, well-constructed shield. *Hmmm. If she's been used to a cloak-and-dagger lifestyle in the service of His Satanic Majesty, being forced into the open like this in front of strangers won't be making her feel any comfier . . . I know!*

Standing, I made my way around the table to greet her. The closer I got, the more I sensed the presence of cunningly concealed power. Power of distinctive stripe. *Oh yes, she's definitely another exponent of our exclusive club.*

Fleeting, a flash of recognition passed between us, along with a clutch of stray thoughts.

Thank Beelzebub for that! Now I know for certain he remains one of us. We were concerned his foray into the Veil might have stripped him of the access that the third . . . allied . . . viable candidate for . . .

All too soon, her private musing passed beyond the scope of my ability to hear. Even so, I was relieved to note she visibly relaxed in my company. Barely perceptible, her expression softened. *Excellent, let's capitalize on that good start.*

"My lady, without fear of creating the wrong first impression, I'm sure I need no introduction." Reaching up, I pulled the hem of her hood forward until her face became lost in shadow. "And neither do you. While you are here, you have my assurance that none will dare pry as to your identity." I raised my voice and called out over my shoulder, "Is that understood?"

A smattering of mental and vocal affirmations filtered back.

I turned and beckoned for Nishôgh and Gemini to join us. When they'd gathered round, I continued, "As you'll be working closely with the Blades of the left-Hand Path, I'll let you and the Gauntlet get acquainted in private. My Hell Hound, Gemini, will assist you in this regard by escorting you both down to the staging area. You'll get a better sense of the lie of the land that way, and the extent of the wards we have in place there. If either of you come to think of anything that will enhance the transfer of troops, let Gemini know, and she'll ensure it gets done."

Finally, I spoke directly to Nishôgh himself:

"Nishôgh, make a note of telling your warriors about the variance between Jahannam and the latterday circles before they come through. The vibe here is somewhat lighter, and much more exuberant. While I like what Heinrich proposed, I would suggest you start deploying them now, as opposed to waiting until tomorrow. That way, each troop will have time to acclimatize and prepare themselves. Gemini will show you where the interface ports are in each chamber. They give direct access to the Bãlefire's elixir. Make use of them. I want your people hyped up and raring to go the moment Nettesheim gives us the word."

Addressing the trio, I concluded, "Are you clear on what each of you has to do?"

Three heads nodded in unison.

Standing aside, I allowed Gemini time to usher her charges from the room and turned to survey those still remaining. Everyone appeared frozen in place.

Ah, I'm not the only one entwined in the enchantress' web.

Clicking my fingers loudly to draw their attention, I said, "You've received your assignments. Don't you all need to be somewhere?" For good measure, I reinforced my statement by allowing my tattoos to flare, briefly.

It took a second for my meaning to sink in, then the room exploded into action as Hounds and Inquisitors alike sprang from their seats, intent upon the business at hand. I reached out and snagged Nettesheim's elbow as he passed, "Not you, Heinrich, we need to speak."

It seemed to take an age for the final person to depart, but at last the door clicked shut, leaving us alone.

Astute to people's feelings, Nettesheim spoke first. "Did I take things too far by inviting another mystic here without running it by you first? If so, I apologize. I'm used to doing things. I'm not used to answering. What I mean to say is—?"

"Forget it." A hand on his shoulder cut Nettesheim's protestations dead. "I know you had to put things together on short notice, so I'll let it slide . . . this time. You'll soon come to understand that the Bãlefire which sealed your soul to service doesn't lie, so I trust all members of my team implicitly. But your woman friend is a different kettle of fish. I don't know her. And though I appreciate Satan would have provided her file if he wanted me to be aware of her role in his pleasure, she's still a variable factor. I sensed her power, you know, while I was up close. She masked it expertly, but I could still tell she's strong. Very strong. So, it begs the question, why aren't you using someone like *that* to help you plant the Trojan instead of me? I'm new to all this third way shit, remember? Untrained and untested. And I haven't really tried using it since the Veil, so . . . ?"

This time, it was Nettesheim's turn to grasp me by the arm. "That's simple. I need your brute strength, old boy, and the legend that comes hand in hand with your presence."

"Huh?"

"The Sibitti have faced you before and know the consequences of rushing in where fools fear to tread. What's more, after the Lost Liberty incident, they're aware of those like me who can employ the authority of the third way. There's no doubt they're wary of us. Can you imagine the impact if they *do* turn up? When they discover the Reaper has become one of us? I tell you, it might make the difference between a shipwreck in a shitstorm of woe and coming home safely."

I had to admit, I liked Nettesheim's way of thinking. He seemed to have covered every aspect.

But this is hell, and things rarely go to plan.

What a flood that naught can fetter.

So far, things had worked like a charm.

Far, far below us, Nishôgh's army of six hundred Al-Jinn warriors had assembled without a hitch, filling the catacombs beneath the Den of Iniquity with nightmarish apparitions to freeze the soul. Divided into their strange triangular fighting formations, each troop (or as they called it, chain) now waited, armed and ready; hyped up to the eyeballs on adrenalin and the Bãlefire's invigorating distillate.

As one of the richest sources of the underverse's life-blood, the Den had proven the perfect environment for our final staging area. Its subterranean vaults and halls often reminded me of what Yellowstone National Park, topside in the USA, might resemble if its cave systems were riddled with antimatter as opposed to plain old magma.

The primary and ancillary chambers had filled to bursting within hours and, true to form, Dr. Livingstone had made certain his team was on the ball. No sooner had all that raw and unadulterated mayhem-waiting-to-happen redlined, than he'd channeled its might to where it was needed most. Not forty minutes ago, I'd watched, elated, as the coaxial temporal foci governing the entire latterday network had been supercharged beyond my wildest dreams.

It had been a breathtaking experience, for the froth and flux of the Sheolspace medium was frightening to behold at the best of times. But now that the Bãlefire had been introduced, it was like Nirvana for crack-heads.

Opposing celestial majesty exploded and imploded all around me, bound to the dynamics of everlasting mutual annihilation. Energies sufficient to shred galaxies and shatter gravity's grip itself clashed over and over, extirpating the stuff of matter as it conceived spacetime anew within the gulf of a nanosecond.

Within this maelstrom, three of my Hell Hounds stood guard, secreted away within a sequential fold in reality, while Nettesheim and I labored to undo the harm wrought by one of the most fragile flowers I had ever laid eyes on. Or more accurately, Nettesheim labored. I tried to look *don't-fuck-with-me* enough to frighten any unexpected opposition we might encounter into pissing themselves silly.

Unfamiliar with the finesse required to competently manipulate the third way, I was here to provide that extra bit

of power—a boost, if you like—that Nettesheim could uti-
lize to complete his ministrations all the quicker. And as he'd
worked, I'd watched and learned at the hands of a master,
while still chafing at how long it was taking.

We were open and exposed, and the thought of being
caught in a place where simply being rendered unconscious
could be the end of you was making me jittery. Examining
our surroundings for what must have been the umpteenth
time only made things worse. Tidal sheering was sufficient
to yank small moons out of orbit. And the warped physics
would turn you inside out in an instant if you weren't prop-
erly shielded. *Good grief! What's taking so long? I thought
my strength would have helped Nettesheim get this done, already? I mean, how long does it take to give an injection,
even if it is an esoteric one?*

It was as if Nettesheim had heard me: "That's just about
got it! Now all we have to do is wait."

So concerned was I in my own misgivings that Nettesheim's matter-of-fact assertion took me by surprise. "Eh?
You mean to say you've only just released the Trojan?"

"Yes. It's taken all this time to embed the initial delivery package. I mentioned earlier, I had to keep feeding it our
combined life energies until it pollinated and was ready to
germinate. Take a peek."

I did and was amazed to see that the final template had
all the appearance of a macrobiotic snowflake, only many
times larger than those you'd usually find in the northern-
most wastes of Niflheim.

Glistening with colors beyond the human spectrum,
it possessed more than two score identical fronds, each of
which had been etched in gradually reducing and evermore
intricate geometric patterns. The deeper I looked, the greater the detail. And as I followed that finely wrought fractal

tracery down to the subatomic level, I was stunned to realize there seemed no end to the scale of the microscopic divisions and subdivisions unfolding before me. *Unholy shit! It's like staring into the fringes of an entirely different universe! I really have got to make more of an effort to uncover the secrets of the third way. There's a whole world of wonder that I'm missing.*

"And now . . ." Nettesheim's voice pulled my awareness out from the infinitesimal depths of the paradigm, barely in time to witness our baby being sent on its way.

". . . let's set our antigen to work."

The conjugation blazed. Activated, a silver-green shooting star sprang toward the cosmic plexus distinguishing latterday hell from every other realm in existence. Nascent with potential and crackling with purpose, it settled over the surface of the anchor like a sentient web. Following the leanings of its cryptic programming, the construct tasted and tested everything it encountered, only to spawn appropriate countermeasures in its wake.

Where it passed, a multitude of variant strains bloomed away, each one homing in on the precise parametric currents governing the different levels. In moments, the causality nodes linking those subzones together thrummed with oyster and olivine tones. Then the new Trojans, carrying freshly mutated antibodies, flared once and disappeared from sight.

Whoa! Is it supposed to do that?

"We did it." Nettesheim muttered, more to himself than to me.

"We did? Then . . . then it's going to work?"

"Indeed it is." Nettesheim slapped me heartily on the back so hard I almost spat up a mouthful of spinal fluid. "We should begin to notice a difference within two or three hours. Four, tops."

Well screw me blind. Things have *worked like a charm.*

I should have been happy. But for some reason, I couldn't shake the foreboding that gathered about me like an approaching stormfront. My nerves frayed, listening to imaginary nails scoring deep furrows across a chalkboard. An empty hunger gnawed at the pit of my stomach. Danger swirled from myriad conflicting eddies. To top it all, the space between my shoulder blades started to ache, a worrisome niggle that had nothing whatsoever to do with my colleague's over exuberance. *I don't like this*!

"Are you alright, Daemon?" Nettesheim must have picked up on my mood. "You seem a little preoccupied?"

Something was closing in. Something that muted the background roar of the orphic broth surrounding us as it filtered out the light.

I inhaled and two glowing ninjaken-style swords appeared in my hands, one empowered by the glorious might of the Bãlefire; the other by a jewel that had once graced the *Sword of Dauntless Strength*, a Zion forged blade and now my only link to a level of authority that had once been mine by right of inheritance.

Exhaling, I charged both weapons to full capacity. I honestly didn't know if it would be enough.

Hear your doom.

Shadows congealed along the edge of my peripheral vision. Like photonegative images of those fragments seen within a kaleidoscope, they shifted, releasing a voiceless impulse of suspicion made manifest.

Four entities folded out of the spaces in between. Three of them I recognized instantly in spite of the dusty raiment covering their features, for their auras were hard to ignore: the Second, Fifth and Seventh of the Seven.

They'd brought a tiny little creature with them. Dressed in a nun's habit, she gave the appearance of someone who would be more at home crocheting doilies for a country fete than at a major nexus between realities.

That's Teresa of Ávila, *the mighty mystic? She doesn't seem old enough to . . . I mean, who'd turn to someone as young as she for advice?*

No sooner had I considered that thought than I realized what my dark father had done. *Ah, I see. Her threat to spread the repulsive message of love would have moved Satan to change her appearance before she was incarcerated. People are shallow. Most would take one look at her and wonder when she was going to graduate from university and get some real life experience before advising them on what to do. Very clever.*

Though the enforcers hadn't moved, the saint was a paragon of feline alertness. At first, I thought her attention to be firmly fixed on Nettesheim as he forded the arcane swells in an effort to reach a space from which he could mount an assault. But I was wrong. She must have been scanning the fuck out of our immediate vicinity, for she suddenly shrieked and leaped forward, claws bared.

"Do you think me stupid? Inexperienced and blind?" Ávila screamed. A glacial jade nimbus encompassed her right hand. Lashing out, she raked her fingers left and right, up and down. "I'll not let you undo everything I waited so long to set in motion."

I flinched, reflexively, expecting reprisal. But I wasn't her target.

"'Ware our ambush!" Nettesheim bellowed.

Gamboling to one side to give myself room, I glanced toward the pocket of Sheolspace where Yamato, Champ and Gemini lay in wait—only to watch, astounded, as a layered emerald net wove into place across its entrance.

Yamato! My telepathic warning thundered along his private mode: *Get your asses out here. Quickly before . . .*

I was too slow.

Responding to my command, Yamato attempted to exit the hide-a-way, only to find the threshold barred by a flexible web of frigid synchronicity. The fabric of hydraspace flexed and bulged mightily in answer to his increasing efforts to break free. Alas, it appeared that nothing he could do would breach its parametric nature.

"They're trapped. How are we going to get them out?"

"Let them wait," Nettesheim yelled, closing swiftly to intercept. "In the meantime, I'll deal with the saint. She is highly skilled and more robust than she appears."

"Do you need a hand?"

"Not from you, my friend," Nettesheim assured me. "I fear you may be otherwise engaged, all too soon."

A prelude to sorrow, Nettesheim's words were prophetic, for no sooner had he engaged his prey than a glittering, knife-edged juggernaut fell on me.

Bugger me. That was direct . . . and fast!

In a way, I was thankful for such tactics. Ever since I'd lost my heavenly and earthly attributes, I'd felt lacking in some way: diminished; insufficient to the task, especially against fiends like this who were forged as tools of vengeance and destruction.

The Fifth hadn't given me any time to dwell on my negativity, and in the space of a heartbeat, I was lost to the cut and thrust of this latest encounter. An exchange fueled by necessity as much as hate, for it quickly became apparent that this enforcer's attentions would be as furious as they were relentless.

My tattoo's flared, invoking the trigger that enveloped me within a polymimetic palladinium panoply. Thus protected, I bent like a reed in a tornado, every-which-way-at-once, concentrating on keeping my mind fluid, open to the ebb and flow of power and technique, my only answer to the omnipresent gyre attempting to shred me from existence. A surreal experience, for so fleeting was my adversary, there was nothing to see of him except for an ever-changing blur of dazzling, razor-sharp motion.

I greased the air in response, my exertions adding to a duality of intent filled with viper strikes and light-footed evasion; hammer blows and ringing ripostes; whirring advances and guarded retreats. Evenly matched under such circumstances, our exchange stretched on as an ever rising clangor that set the surrounding rarified gases alight.

Through a gap in the mêlée, I spotted Nettesheim and Ávila: Eyes shut, forehead to forehead, they faced each other with fingers interlaced. Somehow, they had managed to position themselves directly atop the latterday node, a precarious perch from which Charybdis vortices in abundance attempted to rip them free.

Seriously? Do they think they're engaged in a think-off or something? I was hoping—Oof! A shockwave reverberated along my left arm, numbing me to the elbow and reminding me of more pressing concerns. *That was too close for comfort. I'd better take control of the situation before this bunch decides to revert to their recent strategy of attacking all at once.*

It was as if my foes had been waiting for the moment I'd try to summon the Phage.

No sooner had I reached for the Bãlefire within, than the gyroscopic blender flailing at me from all sides glowed blue. A magnesium flare ignited, hot and urgent, searing the back of my retinas. Then an unseen rival joined the fray, for something that kicked like a bucking mule struck me full on the temple, jolting me to one side with incredible force.

Momentarily stunned, I floated in a morphine-laced dream and envisioned myself as a flaming comet, falling across a black glassy sea illuminated by sonic ripples as heavy as sin. When it came, the thalassic splashdown shattered my skull and yanked my perceptions back into the present.

Mother fucker!

My muscles felt strangely hollow, yet leaden at the same time and reluctant to respond. Then sparks flew and pain lanced my side as diamond tipped talons skittered across my exposed flanks.

I felt that despite my armor? A timely lesson that rang through loud and clear. *Get a grip, Daemon. You aren't what you were and these aren't your average minions. There's only one thing they respect, and holding back isn't it.*

A growl sent a surge of Bãlefire careening through tendons and ligaments alike, flensing my system of dross and the malaise hampering my reactions.

Satisfaction laced with contempt tinged the cosmic milieu, and the Fifth withdrew, revealing the true culprit behind his temporary success. *The Second of Seven? Unholy shit! He must have discharged the full might of his fidelity through the metallic essence of his brother to catch me out. Impressive.*

Though regret clouded his beauteous features, I was under no illusion as to his intent. The most communicative of his ilk the Second might be, but he was still a living weapon, a creature animated by the spirit of contention.

Kudos. I raised my primary ninjatō in salute and attempted to use this brief lull to determine how best to proceed.

If only I'd had time.

Such nobility was lost on the Seventh, his short fuse ensuring any thoughts of magnanimity were expressed in an efflux of magmanimity. The welkin about me bruised red, then orange, yellow and white in pyretic succession as he rushed to brand me with an iron heated in a sulfurous wash of revulsion and ire.

Nevertheless, the most heroically endowed of the Sibitti was wasting his time. Of all the elements, fire was most akin to my own nature. And not just any fire, either, for the flame coursing through my veins empowered me with the blistering passion of hell's own unquenchable fury. Recognizing this, the auditor saw sense and resorted to a more physical form of expression.

Our swords met in an incendiary exchange that fried the air in volatile decrees of violence. Over and over, again and again, metal slammed against metal; forging a scraping, chiming, grating dissonance of discordant rhythms that chafed the nerves and heightened awareness. Despite all that, I felt invigorated. I also thrived on the heat of battle and, for once, the Seventh seemed content to let his skills do all the talking, affording me the opportunity to assess Nettesheim's progress further.

From what I could see, Nettesheim's contest of wills with Ávila appeared to be devolving into something more brutal, for though they still clung to each other with a desperation bordering on delirium, both wore a patchwork of cuts and contusions, some of which stank of wild theurgy.

The method of their challenge inspired me.

Aha! That's *how we'll end this affair. Erra's enforcers are merely the icing on the cake. It's what's underneath the decoration that's important. And while I'd relish the chance of testing the full extent of my new resilience against them, they aren't the real issue here. We need to prevent Ávila from reactivating her contagion. So that means we need to stop . . .*

Initiating a complex two-handed advance, I managed to catch the Seventh flatfooted and forced him backward until I had an unobstructed view of my true quarry:

. . . her!

As I looked on, Nettesheim managed to adjust his grip and force the saint to her knees. He nodded once, and Ávila's head snapped back. Blood spurted from her nose and she cried out in pain.

Yes, my efforts would be better spent running her through while she's distracted.

Seeing this turn of events, the deadly trio moved to reply. Their swords began to shine, brighter and brighter, and my skin prickled in the presence of coalescing power.

I judged the distance between them and my new pet project. *But how do I hold these fuckers at bay long enough to get to her?*

Back at the nexus, Ávila seemed to be rallying remarkably well until a storm of verdigris cinders erupted about her form. Spiraling inward like a swarm of esoteric fireflies, the embers stuck to her body, whereupon she began to burn. Her clothing smoldered and started to smoke. Her skin blistered.

More importantly, the auditors stalled in their advance.

And there was my answer.

On the last occasion they had met, the Sibitti had been wary of Nettesheim's ability to manipulate the energies of the third way, for its constitution could cause them grievous harm.

A slow smile spread across my face. *And they don't know I can access it as well.*

Even so, I had to exercise extreme caution, for the third way was a medium left over from a time of antiquity when heaven and hell were sequestered—the Time of Sundering—an age when holy spirit was warped into the supernatural realm's equivalent of matter and antimatter: or as we called them, G*d's Grace and Bãlefire.

The result of that polarizing transmogrification created an exuberant emulsion, ubiquitous in nature, threading the very fabric of the spacetime and Sheolspace continuums in a symbiogenic existence. Forever enraptured upon the fulcrum separating creation and annihilation, it was hidden away within everything: the subatomic particles of the air we breathed; the forms we inhabited; and even the arcane planes between realms.

I recognized a major drawback to my plan immediately. While I might be able to dip into this seemingly omnipotent reservoir, I had nowhere near the strength, range or dexterity of Nettesheim and his mysterious lady friend back at the Den.

But my soul-auditing buddies don't know that.

Resorting to my basest instincts, I opened my soul and delved into the wex—the void spanning what is and isn't, and what yet might be—and scooped a tiny portion of this most vital fundament into my fingers.

A mistake! I felt as if I'd thrust my entire arm into a nest of pissed-off fire ants. *Azazel's balls!* Without ceremony, I flung my ill-gotten gains into the intervening space between us as fast as I could.

From my perspective, it appeared as if a verdure sun had peeped out from behind the disc of an occluding planet: blinding.

I threw up my arms to shield my eyes. Caught unawares, Erra's deacons acted as I hoped they would, recoiling in horror and granting me a small window of opportunity to act.

A small window was all I needed.

The slightest thought set me fording the aquamarine chop like a Roman war galley on collision course with an overladen prison ship. Still intent on harming each other, neither Nettesheim nor Ávila were cognizant of my approach.

But someone was.

As I swooped in for the kill, the conductive atoms of the nebulous environment about me began to spit and crackle. Plasmic tendrils danced along my breastplate, vambraces and pauldrons. *Bugger. The Second must have recovered more rapidly than his brothers. I forget he can read me better than can the rest of his kind.*

Committed to my attack, I did the best I could to defend myself:

Altering my grip, I thrust my secondary ninjatō, the one powered by the gem from the *Sword of Dauntless Strength*, over my shoulder and down my spine, so that its denying substance would protect my back. *That should be sufficient to absorb anything Thunderfart can throw my way until it's too late.*

Content, I angled round to ensure Ávila wouldn't see me coming.

Thankfully, Nettesheim did. Now alerted to my presence, he unloaded a rush of dark sorcery into Ávila's slight form, blasting her free of his grasp and sending her cartwheeling toward me.

Adjusting my path, I raised my primary weapon and readied the blow that would rid the latterday realms of her influence once and for all. *One—two—three . . .*

I chose my moment . . . *Now!*

My intent left a sizzling scarlet ribbon in its wake.

However, in the instant before the ninjatō tasted flesh, I was pounded from behind by a coruscating bolt of lightning that etched refulgent images across my mind and set my muscles to spasming. The thrust of my strike was arrested. *Jesus H Christ, will the Vidium crystal be able to handle shots like that?*

A puppet to inertia, Ávila's momentum and trajectory brought her spinning onto my extended blade. So keen was its razored edge and so preoccupied was I in riding out the irresistible surge of electricity, that when we collided and commenced an erratic orbit of each other, I didn't realize the full extent of what had happened.

Nor did I get the chance to, for another fulminous concussion struck me, this one far stronger and more prolonged.

Robbed of my ability to act spontaneously, I was tossed like a rag doll, and smashed into Ávila. Together, we somersaulted toward the cosmic plexus in a tangle of juddering arms and legs while our nervous systems contended with the ravages of countless millions of volts.

Yet I needn't have worried. An infinitely delicate ruby tracery appeared on Ávila's throat, extending from one side of her neck to the other. *Ha! I must have cut her?*

Sanguine pearls followed as the wound gaped, widening in an intoxicatingly sedate fashion, so that her head peeled back between her shoulder blades.

I was about to crow with delight, when everything happened all at once:

Still tangled, we struck the principal node dead center, prompting a release of anagogic energy that all but vaporized my brain and arrested my obsidian heart. Needless to say, the Second chose that moment to unleash another fulgurous burst, something that felt like his most devastating assault so far.

Helpless to do anything except take it like a bitch, I watched through slitted lids as Ávila's body glowed white hot. Then it exploded, catapulting her head off and into the polychromatic vista of hydraspace like a grotesque firework.

If I could, I'd have roared with laughter. But I needed to be able to breathe to do that. And truth be told, I had no cause to gloat anyway, for a discordant hum now demanded my attention. *What the fuck?* The subsonic buzz quickly built into a pining scream that split the ether and escalated in pitch beyond my ability to hear.

My blood ran cold.

The last time I'd heard such a complaint was during my battle with the Angel Grislington within the Colonnade of Eternal Reflections when I'd destroyed his weapon, the *Sword of Celestial Arches*.

I knew exactly what was coming, and there was nothing I could do about it. *Oh please! This is getting beyond ridiculous!*

The Vidium jewel protecting my back hissed . . .

Cracked . . .

And inevitably ruptured.

As had happened too many times before, I was propelled aloft on the incandescent wings of a dragon riding pyroclastic thermals and transposed into the bedlam existing where time ends and nihility begins; a many-latticed unreality of opposing majesty, where crushing and eruptive invocations resulted in a mindless cycle of never-ending chaos.

Bound to hell, there was only so far my immortal husk could fly.

Sure enough, an insidious influx manifested beneath me, preventing the ultimate emancipation. Then the underverse's gravity claimed me once more and the terrible drop into darkness began.

As the rate of my descent increased, a practical thought intruded:

Perhaps I ought to invest in a parachute?

Brood of hell, you're not a mortal!

As his sons of destruction gathered before him, Erra discerned a brighter mood—poorly concealed—emanating from their collective consciousness. Refusing to rise to the bait, he made haste to screen his own thoughts and maintained a neutral outward expression.

Leaning back in stately repose, Erra's fingernails drummed out a steady fourfold tattoo upon the skull embellishments of his divan. Forewarned, droves of cockroaches and centipedes scurried from eye sockets and nasal cavities alike and into the relative safety offered by the barrow of rent limbs, shattered bones and eviscerated remains that served as the royal throne mound, where they could lose themselves among the myriad other carnivorous life forms eking out an existence in the presence of imminent death.

Content to wait upon their master, the Seven lingered: silent, composed, lethal.

At last, Erra deigned to grace them with his attention. "And how did this latest venture play out? Was our venerable saint able to thwart the Reaper's machinations?"

Spokesman for his kin, the First stepped forward. "Alas no, my lord. Her light was extinguished beyond hope of reprieve."

"A pity. I hankered to taste the depth of her professed contrition once she had outlived her usefulness."

"As did we all, my liege. Still, our disappointment at the loss of such fare is tempered by the *enlightening* circumstances of her passing."

Ah, now we come to it. "It is? Pray, expound your meaning more clearly."

"We were correct in our estimation. Having expended himself mightily to prevent catastrophe at the Divide, Grim served some unknown, arcane purpose as yet hidden from us. The very crux of his three-fold vitality was altered; stripped somehow. Though less than he was, he is without doubt more fully an offspring of hell than ever before."

Erra still refused to hope. "He is less than he was?"

"Most certainly."

"And are his deficiencies sufficient that they might be exploited?"

"Most definitely."

Such confidence. Perhaps, too confident? "Not that I am delighted by such news, you understand. Even so, I am reticent to give way to joy just yet. Why are you so sure?"

"Because the Second was able to wring a victory from yesterday's debacle."

"A victory, you say?"

"Yes, my lord. Though the Second, Fifth and Seventh were forced to leave the field in the presence of . . . vigorous resistance, *that* didn't occur until after Grim was vanquished by a combination of other factors which played into their hands . . ." The First paused to convey a detailed summary of events directly into the plague god's mind.

As Erra perused the particulars on offer, he had to admit that the implications were ripe with potential. *Regardless, while Grim's soul is bound to that of Lucifer's little empire, he remains a formidable adversary.*

Aloud, Erra continued, "It would please me to see you devote your efforts to determining a means by which Satan's favorite spawn might be laid low. He is vulnerable now, and having achieved his aims at the cosmic anchor, will hopefully feel inclined to extend his recuperation to include a period of rest and—You have something more to add?"

"Forgive me, Sire, but I do." The First's excitement was most unexpected. "It's simply that the episode within the cosmic hub may not have unfolded in the way Grim and his minions planned, and we have Ávila's death to thank for that. Having spent the entire evening verifying our findings, we can now confirm . . . ."

*

A Wyrd tree basked in sublime tranquility at the center of an ash-dusted ornamental garden. Its ruby leaves shone like veined lanterns, blushing the surrounding hedgerows and shrubs with a warming infusion of rose-gold permanence.

Glowing embers fell from the heavens above, their sulfurous presence highlighting how congested the sky was. Every now and then, broad bands within the cloudbank burned hot, giving the impression that unseen giants were at work in their smithies, forging mighty weapons of war.

Around the edge of the sanctuary, massive sepulchers and ornate vaults cast their shadows over a parade of smaller cenotaphs and plinths, memorials marking those plots where ancient sentinels once maintained a lonely vigil, their stony hands resting upon the pommels of inhumanly long swords and obsidian wings folded against the chill of eternity.

Ghostly reminders of an era that no longer existed, they were gone now; intangible witnesses to a prophecy long in the making and finally fulfilled. Hard choices had been made, and only wraiths of regret remained, through which dappled flakes played in carefree abandon.

The soft crunch of boots upon icy cinders intruded as a lone figure walked the pristine parchment of the path. Hooded in black, her footfalls were light, and left an indented score along its length.

Without a word, she approached the remains where one of the guardians had stood in the southwest quadrant, and lingered before a blazing glyph as it hovered, seven feet off the ground. Pale fingers drew back her cowl, and burnished jet-colored hair that blazed like quartz in a waterfall cascaded around her shoulders. Her countenance paid testimony to the harshness of her afterlife, for a livid scar ran down the center of her face, policing the no-man's-land between the beautiful and the hideous.

For all that, she was attractive, possessing a stark, vibrant quality that smoldered with passion and a deep unity with her environment.

The unknown woman climbed the remains of the pedestal on which a champion had been positioned, and studied the slowly revolving sigil for a moment. Whatever it was she read there would remain a mystery forever, for she deemed it appropriate to act.

"Yes, you've been away from us long enough."

A look of determination tightened her features. Stretching up, she cupped her hands, and whispered, "Daemon? It's time to wake up, can you hear me—me—me—me?"

Somewhere an anvil chimed, the rhythm of the hammer striking it as synchronous as it was repetitive. Its resonance dimmed, the tempo muting as sound transposed into pure sensation. Thudding reverberations rose to dominance, a timbre that made me feel as if my cranium had been used as target practice for cannonballs fired at close range.

"Fuuuuck me!" I groaned through teeth so tightly clenched I could have ground diamonds to dust.

"Daemon?"

Inhaling deeply, I tried to move, only to wince and fall back in pain. "Oh Christ, my head feels as if it's held on by a thread." I reached up to massage my neck, and a nearby clap of thunder added its unwelcome tympanic applause to my already scrambled senses.

As the turbulence rumbled off into the distance, a persistent *someone* urged, "Daemon, you need to wake up."

Whoever was speaking might as well have been making "blah-blah" noises. Their words didn't really register or make sense. All the same, their tone suggested a degree of urgency would be in order, so I did my best to sit and take notice.

A different voice, this one deep and masculine, interposed, "Ah, I see. You're still a little out of sorts. Allow me; this should perk you up in no time."

Lightning, green and forked, played across the insides of my skull. The smell of ozone lingered. With grudging reluctance, I blinked my eyes open. The scene swam for a moment before clarifying into the familiar surrounds of my bedroom. Two faces loomed above me, one ruggedly handsome but clearly not my type, the other, a harlequin mask of feminine contradiction.

"Heinrich. Gemini." I grated, "What the hell have I been drinking?"

Then it all came crashing back: our mission to the cosmic anchor; Nettesheim's antivirus; Teresa of Ávila's response, her own personal retinue of Sibitti auditors included; the drama of battle joined while our reserves were effectively neutralized; the saint's pyrotechnic demise; being broiled alive, thanks to the double-whammy delivered by a ruptured cosmic node and the Second of Seven combined.

All in all, just another day at work in the service of the dark lord.

For good measure, I took the time to prod myself from top to bottom to ensure everything that should be was still there. I'd been without flesh before, and I didn't really care to repeat the experience. "How long was I out?"

Gemini piped up first. "Twenty-six hours, give or take."

In response to my look of surprise, she trailed the back of her knuckles along my exposed arm in a more than friendly manner, and murmured, "You're my big strong boy. Nothing keeps *you* down for long." and then more quietly, "I'm pleased to say."

Clearing his throat to draw attention, Nettesheim interposed, "Hmm, you really are a robust sort of fellow aren't you, and still something of a paradox, it seems?"

I eyed him dubiously. "Pot, kettle, black. Spot the connection? Anyway, what happened?"

"Well, I don't know what you remember, Daemon, but despite Erra's walking arsenals, you managed to take out Ávila. The trouble was, the Second's thunderbolt propelled both you and the saint onto the exposed coaxial foci . . . and *boom!*" Nettesheim made an expressive gesture and flared his fingers wide. "The charge vaporized Ávila's body and blew her head clean off. Pretty awesome to watch, actually, especially as it'll take the Sheolspace medium some time to dissolve her remains."

"And me? How did I end up here?"

"You? You caught the flashover, along with an additional stab in the back, courtesy of the Second, an assault so ardent; it destroyed the *Sword of Domocles'* power crystal." Nettesheim shook his head. "I thought your goose was cooked, for sure. I mean, you must have absorbed sufficient energy to keep the Department of Infernal Energy and hellextricity grids of New Hell, Perish and Juxtapose running for the next year. But then the markings on your armor blazed through all the colors of the setting sun and . . . I don't know, you seemed to swallow it all down without a single one of your pubes being singed. Extraordinary!"

"I'm glad the thought of my semi-electrocuted 'nads kept you entertained. What happened next?"

"Next? That's it! You were knocked unconscious. I didn't think it prudent to hang around discussing the finer points of your hardiness with our enforcer friends, so I sent the call to summon Nishôgh and the cavalry."

I snorted, "Azazel, I'd have loved to have seen that."

"It was most impressive," Nettesheim conceded, "though I thought we might end up having a riot on our hands. No sooner did the Incendia Blade manifest, than the Sibitti obviously thought it the better part of valor to make a hasty, tactical withdrawal."

"Ouch!"

"Yesss. Rather ungentlemanly if you ask me. Deprived of their sport, the Jinn got somewhat feisty, and it took Nishôgh quite a while to calm them all down."

Remembering the natural aggressive exuberance of the Al-Jinn from my previous visits to Jahannam, I had to smile. *Now that would have been a sight to see.*

Nettesheim continued, "Anyway, without anything to distract me, I managed to release Yamato, Champ and our Lady Gemini, here, and sent everybody home."

"You did? I take it our attempt to neutralize Ávila's contagion was successful?"

His face fell. "I . . . We don't . . . It's hard to . . ."

"Just tell me."

"My countermeasures were working like a charm, Daemon. But when Ávila's body fell against the node, I think her dying essence corrupted it somehow. You knew her original virus was ethraclastic in nature, with both biochemical and psychosomatic nucleotides?"

"With physiological, emotional and telestic qualities? Yes, go on."

"Well, it appears that certain aspects of her heart's deepest desires were transferred into the core of the temporal foci where they then bonded to the nucleus in some way. While my antigen will reduce the effects of her interference, I doubt very much it will last against the scope of her love."

For love conquers all. Bugger! Flopping back down onto my pillow, I took a few moments to contemplate how I was going to explain all this to the boss. *Yet another black mark for him to hold against me . . . until he chooses to remind me of it at the most inconvenient time, that is.*

"So, what are we going to do now?" Nettesheim's question was loaded with all sorts of implications. "Hell, what *can* we do?"

I saw only one real option. "*We* are going to be spending a lot of time together during the coming months, my friend. The Sibitti now know my stature is reduced from what it was. I've no doubt they'll try and profit from that. Even so, they'll find me a tough nut to crack. One that I hope will only get tougher." I met his gaze squarely. "And that's where you come in."

"It is?"

"Yes. It's clear these sons of heaven and earth fear the potency of the third way, so I'm going to take advantage of their misconceptions. But to do so, I need your help. When it comes down to sorcery, *you* are the master and I am the apprentice . . .

". . . Let's just say, I expect you to do more, much more, than merely put me through my paces. The next time I bump into those smug bastards, I want to be competent enough to roast them where they stand. Do you feel up to the challenge of training a new student in amongst your other duties?"

"And then some." Emerald flames danced in the depths of Nettesheim's eyes. "When do we start?"

"I was thinking right away. The Sibitti aside, we've still got unknown assailants and gem thieves to catch."

"Hang on a moment, Daemon," Gemini interjected. "How are you going to do that when one of your swords was destroyed?"

I understood what she was getting at immediately, and grinned.

"Relax, my secondary ninjatō was merely a polymimetic extension to the weapon I've always used. A doppelganger if you will, empowered by a Vidium gem to maintain its integrity. Now it's gone . . ."

As I spoke, I extended my hand toward my weapon's cabinet and issued a mental summons.

Something small and cylindrical; something possessing a silver-gray sheen topped by a garnet like jewel, slammed into my palm. A thought extended my staff of office into a more familiar guise, blade deployed.

"Your scythe!" Gemini squealed, "Its back the way it was."

"Of course," I growled. "And now that I'm truly of hell, what better instrument to wield in the task that lies ahead of us than one that strikes fear into black hearts throughout the length and breadth of the underverse?"

Leaping from my bed, I called on the sweet mastery of the Bālefire, invoking a palladinium response from my armor. Thus adorned, I stitched the air with atramentous promises.

"Yes, it's about time our denizens were reminded of what my being the Reaper is all about."

The Colossus of Hell

Joe Bonadonna

"The danger of the past was that men became slaves. The danger of the future is that man may become robots."

—*Erich Fromm*

Who am I? What's my name? What the hell did I do to end up here?

Eternal questions that for this lost soul shall remain forever unanswered.

"Here he comes—the Man with the Tangerine Tan!"

Laughter and ridicule dog his heels like the Hounds of Hell on the hunt. The sidewalk is riddled with pools of vomit that bubble and hiss, forcing him to sidestep each one as he schleps his way down Gorgon Street, a minor thoroughfare of Port Boil, far beyond the limits of New Hell City. Rivulets of puss and urine course along the curbside, emptying into sewers and storm drains emitting noxious odors that sting his nose and burn his eyes.

"Look out! It's the Bleached Bastard!"

"The Ginger Troll walks among us!"

Fucking intellectual libtard!

"Hey, don't insult him. You know he likes to be called the Orange Ogre."

Laughter and insults hurl at him from the mouths of the damned that follow him through the mud, filth and refuse clogging the streets of Port Boil.

"If he touches you, it's the Mortuary for sure!"

"The Orange Ogre will get you if you don't watch out!"

"Get the fuck out of my way!" Ogre growls at a plague victim covered in warts and carbuncles crawling over his body like some new form of insect life. He gives the infected soul a shove, causing him to slip on the curb and step into a thick puddle of industrial waste that melts the damned fool's necroflesh and sends him off to the Mortuary.

"See what I mean?"

But few pay attention to what has just occurred. The dead and the damned are inured to such commonplace sights.

"Mates, he's just another cockwobbling turd!"

More taunts, more laughter and more ridicule hound Ogre as he shambles down the sidewalk. If there's one thing he truly hates it's being mocked and humiliated. On the other hand, he hates to be ignored, too. His Afterlife seems to be an infernal commentary on the life he once led, whatever that was.

Shoving aside any soul who gets in his way, he hops monkeylike over a pool of steaming bile wherein float scorpions, dung beetles and the swollen and rotting bodies of kronofrogs. He coughs and chokes on the sickening miasma that fills the air with the reek of brimstone, sulfur and feces.

Port Boil was a mess. Although the flooding had begun to recede there were still plenty of lost souls infected with the contagions that had not yet been eradicated. No vaccine, no inoculation had any effect on Erra's plagues; they must simply run their course. Plague Zombies roamed the streets and alleys, falling apart like sandcastles and fading away, only to pop up again in the Mortuary to suffer hell's version of resurrection: Reassignment.

Ogre trembled at the memory of his most recent stay as a guest of the Mortuary. Three times since his fall into hell he had crossed the wrong rogue, pirate or lawyer and had paid the price by ending up on Slab A at the mercy, or lack thereof, of the Undertaker and his Deputy Assistant, Gorgonous. He wished those memories would fade into oblivion like all the memories of who he once was before his immortal soul was consigned to eternal damnation.

Turning the corner to head down Basilisk Boulevard, the Orange Ogre shuffled along, his hairy knuckles dragging the ground.

Half-drowned buildings leaned over streets and sidewalks piled with waste and refuse. Ogre witnessed torment and suffering on every corner of that boulevard of hopeless dreams. Devils had their way with poor damned souls, sodomizing them with red-hot pokers and cattle prods, torturing them with flaming whips, flailing knives and a variety of tools, weapons and devices that would have made Torquemada giggle with pleasure. Agonized cries and pitiful pleas for help and mercy echoed down the boulevard. But the hellizens, whether infected or not, paid no attention and continued on their dismal way. Every lost soul knew better than to interfere with a devil and its victim.

"*Deja paso al hombre olvidado*—make way for the man who has no memory!" shouted a small Mexican cowboy.

"Go back to your shithole, fucktard!" Ogre lashed out with one hairy fist and knocked the man down. He left the caballero lying in a puddle of sickly-green mud crawling with maggots and vipers.

It was true, however, what the cowboy had said. The Orange Ogre had no memory of who he was and who he'd been in life.

But Satan knew. Oh, yes, Satan knew.

In life, the Orange Ogre had been a bully, full of bluster and braggadocio, when in truth he was nothing more than a craven coward. Never had he gotten his hands dirty, but they were nonetheless washed in the blood of others. Once he'd been a wealthy but shady business tycoon who had no friends, often cheated his partners, took credit for the success of others and blamed everyone else for his failures. He was a misogynist, a pedophile, an unbalanced huckster, an adulterer and a narcissistic, psychopathic liar. He conned a nation, betrayed its allies and embraced its greatest foes—all for the sake of his vanity, ego and money. Petty and vindictive, arrogant and insensitive, he tumbled into hell because he'd broken more of the 613 commandments than anyone else who had ever lived. If a contest were to be held to select the worst sinner in human history, Ogre would take first prize. He committed sins that would even shame Satan.

In hell, however, Ogre was just another soul doomed to an eternity of torment and punishment, a mere footnote in the netherworld. Surprisingly enough, he had grown a bigger set of balls in hell and was no longer the coward he'd been in life. Perhaps this was because being dead, he no longer feared dying, although he tried and often failed to avoid the Undertaker's cold table. Three trips to the Mortuary were three trips too many. Nothing of his former life remained to him, not even his own name.

How many wives and mistresses did I have? Was I powerful and important? Did I have children? Was I loved and respected? Or was I feared and hated?

All memory and knowledge of his life had been erased from the chalkboard of his mind.

Throughout all the circles and levels, nooks and crannies and corners of hell, no one knew his name or who he had once been. There was no record of his past life; there was no DNA database or blood tests, no fingerprints or retina scans that might reveal his true identity. And all that, too, was part of his eternal punishment . . . the loss of his identity.

"Hey, Ogre boy!" a black woman wearing the uniform of a Marine officer shouted at him from across the street. "It ain't such a wonderful afterlife, is it?"

Every wayward soul Ogre passed on the street laughed at him. Although he saw many grotesqueries and deformities among the denizens of hell, no one laughed at *them*. They laughed only at him. And that, too, was part of his eternal punishment: the constant assaults on his pride.

"Eat shit and die, you lowlife dog!" he yelled back at the Marine.

The woman laughed as she continued on her way, reminding him once again that his entire afterlife was a futile quest to regain the memories that had been taken from him. For him, hell was an infernal version of *It's A Wonderful Life*. But Ogre's afterlife was a twisted reboot of the scene where the character of George Bailey gets his wish—that he'd never been born. For all intents and purposes, the Orange Ogre was a man who had never been born, but a man who had sinned and died, nevertheless.

Without further incident he continued on his way, thinking of the fortune that awaited him. Having made enough money in hell from questionable business deals, he now wanted what money could often buy: revenge.

"Brother, can you spare a diablo?"

Ogre stopped in his tracks, accosted by a legless Asian war veteran strapped to a wooden cart and using his hands to propel him forward along the sidewalk. The beggar was a mess of open sores, scaly skin and puss-filled eyes.

Another asshole infected with the plague! "Suck ass, chopstick dick!" Ogre kicked the legless Asian's cart and sent him rolling down the sidewalk, where he bounced off the curb and into the street, only to be crushed beneath the wheels of a waste-distribution truck.

Crossing Behemoth Avenue and turning down Judas Drive on the way to his final destination, Ogre paused in front of a Spawn Shop. There, in the black glass of its front window, he cringed at his reflection.

The color of Ogre's skin was as orange as the fruit itself, his eyes as bright as those of someone infected with hepatitis. On top of it all, his body boasted a rash of boils, carbuncles and pustules. He wore a green suit, brown shirt and plaid tie from Baalmart, and an old pair of golf shoes Gorgonous had nailed to his feet on his first trip to the Mortuary. Clothes may make the damned, but they could not conceal the fact that he was among the infected. To top it all off, the Undertaker had shaved his head clean of his long, unruly white hair. Upon his second sojourn to Slab A his flat, flabby ass had been removed. An unusually sympathetic Gorgonous then slipped him a bottle of VileAgra, so he could go home and masturbate. But after taking the first and only pill, Ogre's dick fell off and was gobbled up by a hellrat. Then, on his third trip to hell's mansion of mayhem, the Undertaker removed his tiny hands and replaced them with those belonging to an orangutan.

Rounding the corner of Belial Way and heading down Libertine Lane, the Orange Ogre heard a voice cry out: "Hey, fellas! It's that jagbag jerkwad who cheated us!"

I'll sue that bastard for public slander! Ogre promised himself.

He spun around and saw a trio of bully boys he recognized right off the bat: three hellions he once cheated out of a lucrative real estate deal in Hellywood, before the coming of the floods. Carrying switchblades, wrenches, chains and baseball bats wrapped with barbed wire, the hellions looked like they had stepped right out of a 1960s' era motorcycle gang movie.

"Let's dust the son of a bitch!"

"Yeah, a nice little stay at the Mortuary will do him good."

While he may have grown a bigger set of balls in hell, the Orange Ogre made it a habit of intimidating only those who were alone and much smaller than himself. Now there were three angry souls facing him, each one taller and more menacing than the last. Without giving it a second thought, Ogre turned and ran away across the street, down Dead Man's Curve and into Crud Alley, which proved to be a poor choice, for the alley was a dead end.

There was no escape. He was trapped.

"I'm gonna rip this piss-loving cocksucker's head off!"

And with that, in an instant, the trio was upon the Orange Ogre. They beat him and clubbed him and knocked him to the slimy ground of the alley. They cut him and stabbed him and even tried to bugger him with their baseball bats.

Ogre cried out in agony, called out for help. But nobody listened. Nobody cared.

*

The infernal Prometheus, that's who I am, Doctor Victor Frankenstein tells himself.

Damned to hell for daring to emulate the Almighty by creating life from the spare parts of dead bodies, Victor adjusts his blue stocking cap to make sure it sat snugly in place upon his great head. The cap conceals the chicken wire that Gorgonous, assistant to the notorious Undertaker in hell's Mortuary, had used to replace the top of his skull, leaving his brain free for everyone to see. But this isn't Victor's head nor his own body, for his brain is encased in the skull of Adam, the monster he built out of cadavers and had successfully brought to life. As for Adam, Victor's unholy misbegotten son . . . his brain resides in the head of the infamous doctor.

Victor inhales smoke from a Sulfarillo, then exhales slowly, blowing smoke rings into the air. He sits on the stoop outside his home, thinking and watching. He feels safe for now in Goblin Manor, which perches high atop the Golem Heights on the outskirts of New Hell City, overlooking the swollen waters of the Vile River. Be that as it may, he knows only too well that safety in hell is a fleeting thing. While all is quiet now on the infernal front, massive flooding can strike again without warning. A dozen new strains of Erra's plagues can morph into two dozen more. And the Flux, disrupting the whole fabric of infernity, still persists in tearing apart the hellscape, destroying landmasses here and creating new ones there.

All along the riverfront of Port Boil below, Victor spies the damned rushing about. Some sail away on boats towards new coastlines that emerged as floodwaters receded. Other hellions seek shelter in dried-up sewers, hoping against hope to escape Erra's plagues. Lost and mystified souls search in vain for missing friends and loved ones separated from them during the disasters. Others search for a way out of hell. Displaced souls wander about the streets, lost and alone, having been shunted to a hell where they knew no one. Forever tormented by the consequences of his actions in life, Doctor Frankenstein strives to atone for his sins and his crimes by helping those who come begging his aid, but he cannot help them all.

As for himself, Victor has survived it all, by whatever luck or grace may exist in hell. He weathered the Flux and the flooding, remained free of contagion, and thus far has escaped the Purging. But he cannot escape the nightmares that haunt him.

By hell—what have I done that is not of my own making? I truly deserve to be among the restless and eternally damned.

Visions from his dreams dance in his head, even now, as he sits there wide awake. They cavort like drunken demons. Snapshots of memories from his former life spark and fade in his brain. Memories of his mother's death by Scarlet Fever plague him still, her death having caused him to bury himself in his experiments to help him deal with his grief. More visions . . . of Henry Clerval, his childhood friend, strangled by the monster he created; of his younger brother William, also murdered by the Creature; of Justine Moritz, his brother's nanny, who was framed by the Creature and wrongly hanged for Willy's murder; of his father, who died shortly after the horrible death of Victor's wife, Elizabeth. Moving pictures of Victor's final moments in life haunt him still: the face of Captain Walton, who rescued him and took him aboard his ship at the North Pole after he collapsed from exhaustion and hyperthermia while hunting for the Creature. Victor has never forgotten his last words to the ship's captain . . . "to seek happiness in tranquility and avoid ambition."

But where is my brother Ernest? What became of him?

And then there is Elizabeth, his beloved Elizabeth, strangled by the Creature on the night following her marriage to Victor. If any of them exist somewhere in hell, Victor has never been able to find them. And perhaps that, too, is part of his eternal punishment.

These hands . . . these hands killed them all just as surely as if I had committed the crimes myself. But these are not my hands, not the hands of my own body. These are the hands of a corpse, of a dead man I brought back to life—the Creature whose body I now inhabit as my self-imposed penance for the evil I brought into the world an eternity ago.

As for Adam, with whom he made peace in hell ages ago . . . *Would that we could be together through this hellishly trying time. But I fear flood and Flux may have displaced him and his inamorata, Galatea.*

Heaving a sigh of longing and regret, Victor rose to his feet, brushed dust and lint from his denim coveralls and glanced at the crimson vault hanging high over New Hell, with the Light of Paradise gleaming and glowing, taunting and teasing the damned with the promise of a heaven that can never be attained.

Then he saw them, gliding across the blood-red skies on invisible wings—Erra, the Babylonian god of plague and mayhem, and his Seven Sibitti warriors. Majestic, beautiful and terrible to behold, they swept across the sky: Erra, the wrath of eternity, and his seven champions, come to deliver punishment as they see fit, where injustice has been unfairly distributed, for hell is still under audit from on high. Dreadful in their dusty raiment, they wore cloaks of human skin decorated with braided scalps. Their swords dangled from belts fashioned out of human entrails. Pouches made of scrota hung from those same, grisly belts.

In the distance, hellizens of Port Boil screamed and ran for shelter against Erra and his seven personified weapons. The Sibitti shimmered in their dusty cowls, eyes aglow and swords at hand.

From a pocket, Victor pulled the spyglass he used aboard the *Snark* when he and his companions had sailed hell's oceans in search of the Isle of the Damned. Thus, he watched what was taking place on the streets of Port Boil and the outer limits of New Hell City.

Plague Zombies, infected souls and Old and New Dead still free of the contagion—all fled in terror from the wrath and punishments of those merciless warriors sent from Above to audit hell and punish all. In some places, the streets and sidewalks cracked wide open and damned fools tumbled into unknown depths. Ice froze others, who fell and shattered like shards from a broken mirror. Lost souls dissolved into sand, while holy fire turned others into black ash. Lightning blasted untold numbers of the eternally condemned. A juggernaut of sharpened steel blades and razors rolled through the streets, butchering hundreds of hellions who tried in vain to escape. A rainstorm from the crimson vault above caused great flooding, washing streets and sidewalks clean.

And then they were gone, Erra and his Seven Sibitti, gone as quickly as they had come, on invisible wings that stirred the wind and sent debris flying in all directions.

Glad that it was all over and having witnessed more than enough to last several endless seasons in hell, Victor stashed the spyglass in his pocked, turned quickly and went back inside Goblin Manor, closing the door quietly behind him lest the sound of it attract Erra's attention, causing that wrathful deity and his bloody brood to return for him. But he suspected that Erra knew exactly where he lived and what experiments he conducted, just as Satan knew. *But why have they not bothered me*? Perhaps Satan did indeed protect his favorites, as Napoleon himself once explained to Victor.

Walking into the elegant Victorian Era parlor, Victor saw his friend and assistant, Quasimodo, still entertaining his new-found love, Madame Marie Lenormand, who was once a famous French cartomancer, a reader of Tophet Cards.

A petty fortune teller, Victor told himself, a note of disdain and disgust in his mental voice. *Poor Quasimodo, forever pining away for his lost Esmeralda. Is she in New Hell or did she find salvation and attain heaven*? Just as he had searched in vain for his beloved Elizabeth and his family, Victor knew that the Hunchback of Notre Dame had searched long and hard for his lost Gypsy girl, for whom he murdered the priest who lusted after her.

Victor listened while Madame Lenormand read her cards and told the hapless hunchback's fortune. Quasimodo sat across from her at a small table set in the middle of the parlor, mooning and cooing over her. She was beautiful, to be sure, dressed in a crimson gown that reminded him of the vault hanging over hell.

What he found most fascinating was that Quasimodo had forsaken the wearing of one of his silly costumes in favor of a nicely-tailored black tuxedo, complete with top hat and tails.

Idiot! *King of Fools, indeed*! Victor thought, shaking his head in disgust. But Quasimodo was enamored of the woman and could not be faulted for such feelings.

"The Purges, floods, plagues and Flux will soon pass," Madame Lenormand told Quasimodo as she turned her Tophet Cards over, one at a time, to read their message.

Victor stifled a laugh. He believed in no such parlor games as palmistry, rhabdomancy and reading the tea leaves at the bottom of a cup. An eternity ago he briefly met the mystic when she managed to crash a party at the Hellview Golf and Country Club. In life, she was powerful and charismatic enough to worry Napoleon. Thus he had her tossed out on her ass upon her arrival at the club, for he had always believed her to be a fake and a spy.

"Fortune and fame await you, *ma chérie*," the fortune teller intoned. "Hell is only a beginning, not the ultimate ending."

Victor bit his tongue lest he call the woman out for being the dangerous charlatan he believed her to be, as Napoleon himself had always believed.

"What more? What more can you see?" Quasimodo asked eagerly, almost drooling over the red-haired, green-eyed beauty.

She winked at the hunchback and set down another card.

Victor's stomach lurched. *Disgusting*!

Born Marie Anne Adelaide Lenormand in 1768, by 1790 she was already a celebrated teller of fortunes. She predicted to the unfortunate Princess de Lamballe her horrible death at the hands of an infuriated populace. Robespierre and other leaders of the French Revolution consulted with Lenormand, and even Czar Alexander begged for her services. Empress Josephine also put great faith in Lenormand's predictions. Unfortunately for the sibyl, she did not content herself with telling Josephine's fortune but instead ventured to predict a future, replete with influences, to the Emperor himself. This was why Napoleon loathed and distrusted Lenormand. Nevertheless, she died a wealthy woman at a ripe old age. Napoleon divorced Josephine and married Marie-Louise of Austria, who had left Purgatory to remain in hell with him. As for Lenormand, upon her arrival in New Hell City, she immediately resumed her former trade but barely managed to keep her head above water.

What need have the damned to have their fortunes told? Victor wondered.

"I see that soon you will find true love and happiness, dearest Quasimodo," Lenormand said after studying her cards for a time.

The hunchback smiled lovingly at her, took one of her hands and kissed it.

Gag me with a pitchfork! Victor said to himself.

"So, my future . . . is it bright?" Quasimodo asked hopefully.

Lenormand nodded. *"Oui, mon petit kumquat.* Your future is so bright you will be forced to wear the Faustus-Rant sunglasses."

Victor had seen and heard enough. "You have no future, you humpbacked little whale!"

Quasimodo took no offense, knowing how quickly the mercurial Frankenstein's moods could change. "Our future is eternal, my friend. *C'est la vie*, as we French would say."

"Such is life?" Victor raved. "We're dead, you imbecile!"

"Dead we may be, but still I have plans."

Victor sighed; his friend was such a hopeless romantic. "You still wish to find and ring Hell's Bells with the hope of learning the location of the Get Out of Hell Free Card?"

Quasimodo puffed himself up with pride. "Yes. Indeed I do. Am I not the greatest and most athletic bell ringer who has ever lived and died?"

"Without a doubt, Quasimodo. But there is no such card. It's all myth, legend and lies upon lies. Don't waste your time."

"Time in hell is all I have, Victor my friend. I have an eternity of it."

Madame Lenormand coughed to clear her throat. "I hate to interrupt this philosophical discussion, Quasimodo, but we really must be going." She hastily gathered up her Tophet Cards and rose to her feet.

Victor ignored her and addressed Quasimodo directly. "Where are you going?"

"To Hell's Kitchen," Quasimodo told him. "We have the reservation."

Clenching his fists in barely-controlled anger, Victor said, "Well, return by five, Quasimodo. Mister Turing will be here tonight with our test subject and we must prepare for the work that lies ahead of us."

Lenormand shot Quasimodo a look, one eyebrow slightly raised. The hunchback blushed and lowered his gaze.

"Yes, master," he said to Victor, rising from his chair. He and Lenormand then turned and left without bothering to say goodbye.

"How utterly rude of them!" Victor said as he headed toward his laboratory, stopping briefly to stare at himself in the dirty, full-length mirror hanging on one wall.

The Creature whose body he had constructed, given life to and now inhabited stood about eight feet in height and was proportionally large. Despite Victor's intentions, the beautiful creation of his dreams had turned out to be hideous, with watery white eyes and skin that barely concealed the muscle tissue and blood vessels underneath. However, he was no longer repulsed by his reflection, although the stocking cap looked ridiculous. *I really must find another hat.* With a smile, he removed a handkerchief from a pocket and polished the bolts on either side of his neck. After all, company was coming.

*

Through the grimy glass windows of *Nick's Czar and Grill*, located near the intersection of Basilisk Boulevard and Judas Drive in downtown Port Boil, the patrons inside watch the Prophets of Doom proclaim the fall of Satan and the rise of Erra and his Seven Sibitti as the New Lords of Hell. Damned souls carry signs that read *Raise Hell, Not Hope* and *Repent? It's Too Late to Repent*. Others chant slogans such as *To Hell with Everything* and *Make Hell Hate Again*. The noise and commotion are almost unendurable, but the customers of the Russian tearoom are accustomed to such madness. This *is* hell, after all.

Pouring himself a cup of Charnomile tea, Grigori Yefimovich Rasputin, the Russian mystic and self-proclaimed holy man, studies the room and the patrons around him, and then stares out the window, ignoring the companion sitting at the table across from him. A pair of tormented lovers stroll down the other side of Basilisk Boulevard when the man abruptly dissolves into sand. The woman screams hysterically and runs down the street, seeking shelter lest she, too, be purged. A Plague Zombie brushes up against the window of the tearoom, smearing it with his melting necroflesh as he moves on.

Rasputin clutched the leather thong hanging around his neck, which was attached to an unholy talisman concealed beneath his Siberian peasant's shirt. *More victims of plagues. Not even I, who once healed Czar Nicholas' hemophiliac son, can help such afflicted ones.*

Once upon an eternity ago, Rasputin had been a member of the Czar's court and a favorite of his wife, Alexandra. He wielded great power and influence over the Czar and Czarina and was seen by many to be a visionary and a prophet. But as

Russian defeats in World War I mounted, he, Nicholas, and Alexandra grew increasingly unpopular. Involved in a paradigm of political struggle, Rasputin was accused of various misdeeds, from an unrestricted sexual life to political domination over the royal family. Nobles in influential circles around the Romanovs clamored for Rasputin's removal from the royal court. A peasant woman even attempted to assassinate him by stabbing him in the stomach outside his home. Then on December 30, 1916, at the Moika Palace of Prince Felixovich Yusupov, he was fed tea, cakes and wine laced with cyanide. When that failed to kill Rasputin he was beaten and shot three times, once in the forehead. Two days later a pair of workmen retrieved his body from the half-frozen waters of the Malaya Nevka River; it appeared as if Rasputin had tried to claw his way out of the ice. It was later determined that he died of drowning.

The door swung open and Madame Marie Lenormand sashayed into the tearoom, ordered a cup of Cadavender tea and promptly sat down across from Rasputin and next to his companion.

She nodded to Rasputin and then kissed his companion on the cheek. "*Bon après-midi, mon chér*, Joey," she told him.

The man grunted and toyed with his cup of Jasmented tea. "Where have you been all afternoon?" he asked in a slight, Italian accent.

"That circus freak Quasimodo insisted on buying me lunch at Hell's Kitchen," Lenormand replied. "The food, of course, was most horrendous."

Rasputin turned from the window and stared at the French teller of fortunes. "What more did you learn from our little friend? Is true?" he asked, speaking with a Russian accent.

"Yes, Grigori. It's all true."

"Robots, indeed! *Ridicolo!*" said the Italian.

"Cyborgs, dear Joey. Cyborgs," Lenormand explained. "But it's a waste of time trying to borrow money from Frankenstein. He's as destitute as we are. Quasimodo told me that Howard Carter can no longer afford to finance the doctor's experiments."

"Bah!" Rasputin said, a note of frustration in his voice. "I still not understand. The Devil, he knows all that happens in his realm. Why does he not put end to Doctor Frankenstein and his attempts to build creature with both organic and biomechatronic body parts?"

"Perhaps His Satanic Majesty no want to," said the Italian.

"What do you mean, Joey?" asked Lenormand.

The man she referred to as "Joey" was none other than Giuseppe Balsamo, alias Count Alessandro di Cagliostro—*the* Cagliostro, once dubbed the Prince of Quacks. In life, he'd been an adventurer and self-appointed magician who was welcomed at the royal courts of 18ᵗʰ century Europe, where he pursued psychic healing, alchemy and scrying. He also claimed to have studied the Kabbalah and the Dark Arts. His personal history was veiled in rumor, propaganda and mysticism. He had a religious education, was expelled from the Catholic Order of Saint John and then became a pharmacist on the isle of Malta. Later he married seventeen-year-old Loreza Seraphina Felciani and forced her into having a sexual affair with a forger and swindler in exchange for being "shown the ropes" in all kinds of illicit activities. A charlatan and imposter, one of his critics called him; Cagliostro was a man of amoral values.

While on a visit to Rome, Cagliostro met two people who proved to be spies of the Inquisition. Some accounts hold that his wife had betrayed him. He was soon arrested and sentenced to death on the charge of being a Freemason. His sentence was later changed to life imprisonment and he died at the Fortress of San Leo in 1795.

Now he sat in *Nick's Czar and Grill*, a chubby little man with a high forehead and graying hair, smartly dressed in a black Crooks Brothers' suit that had seen better days. He pursed his lips and nodded at Lenormand.

"*Mi scusi, signora,*" he said. "What I mean is, perhaps Satan does not want to stop Doctor Frankenstein. Maybe the Devil finds some amusement in the antics of the mad doctor and his hunchbacked little gnome."

"What about Erra?" Lenormand asked.

"That *bastardo* of Babylon knows what Frankenstein does. Of this, I am certain."

"Then why does Erra not stop him?"

"Perhaps Erra, too, is amused by Doctor Frankenstein and his little clown, Quasimodo, who has eyes only for you, Marie."

"Eat cake and die!" Lenormand said with a laugh. "He's just another paying customer. And a good one, too. Can I help it if he has a big mouth and a small hard-on for me?"

"You are not one to put away old habits, are you, Signora?"

"Old habits are difficult to break, my dear Count—especially when there's a good chance of financial reward."

Rasputin sat there, quietly listening to Lenormand and Cagliostro talk about their afterlives, the floods, the plagues, the purges and the Flux. But his mind was on other things.

After an endless tenure of trying to persuade, cajole, con, bribe and threaten their way through the ever-shifting maze that is hell, he and Cagliostro decided that leading a simple Afterlife was the best course to traverse. They now wanted nothing more than to own a humble establishment, a lodge and gathering place for all the mystics, prophets, magicians, fortune tellers and psychics in hell.

The Infernium Club was the name they had chosen for their establishment.

Trouble was, as it was in Life so it is in the Afterlife, starting and operating such an organization required money, and they were all but destitute. With hardly a diablo to split between them, what they needed was a financier, a wealthy patron, a silent partner. In short, they needed seed money for their start-up venture. This was all Rasputin and Cagliostro wanted: wealth and a place of their own, a place to call home. As for Lenormand, while she managed to eke out a peasant's income, she was hungry for more. She was out for whatever and as much as she could get.

Rasputin decided to rejoin the conversation. "If Satan know all and see all, then why he not lock us in cages and torture us until end of time?"

Cagliostro nodded. "This is, I tell you, not the hell I was told of in my childhood."

"*Da,*" said Rasputin. "And if Erra is so much powerful, then why not he destroy Satan, conquer hell and rule like czar?"

"The ways of gods and monsters . . . they are truly mysterious, *mio amico,*" Cagliostro told him.

"Do you think Satan truly cares about what we do in hell?" Lenormand asked.

"I am certain he does," said Cagliostro. "He knows, too, that much of what we do often amounts to no more than a plate of meatballs."

Rasputin slurped his tea and wiped his mouth on a sleeve. "Perhaps we are but peasants and pawns in game where only they know rules."

"There is but one rule in hell," said Cagliostro. "And that is, there are no rules."

"And that is beetle in borscht," Rasputin said.

"But we abide by our own rules, do we not, Grigori?" Cagliostro asked.

"Is truth, *tovarisch*."

"And what *are* your rules for continued existence in hell?" Lenormand asked.

"To keep low profile and avoid Reassignment," Rasputin told her. "Even though there is no true death in hell, still we fear it. We mourn passing of friends who must go to be reassigned. A most unfortunate thing. It is difficult for us to shed old habits and emotions."

Lenormand sat back in her chair. "What about hopes and dreams?"

"We all know in hell there is no hope," said Cagliostro. "It is senseless to have big dreams. Such things, they are . . . how you say? Exercises in futility."

"This very true," Rasputin agreed, having learned long ago that there is no hope for the hopeless, no dreams. Only nightmares.

"Yet still we hope, still we dream," said Lenormand.

"Hell is big paradox. All we want is money to live like czars of old Mother Russia."

Cagliostro reached for and kissed Lenormand's hand. "And that is why, *la mia bella donna*, we came seeking your help. Your ambitions are much like our own. We thought you could help extort or borrow money from Frankenstein and his little *stronzo* of an assistant."

"Blood cannot be squeezed from turnip," said Rasputin.

"Is there no wealthy aristocrat you know who you can hypnotize into giving us money?" Cagliostro asked the Siberian peasant.

"*Nyet.* Plague, pestilence, flood have reduced all to status of peasants." The Mad Monk barked a laugh and told Cagliostro, "Hypnosis not always work in such a way. Perhaps your own skills work better."

"Perhaps," Cagliostro said thoughtfully.

"I'm very sorry I could not help you, my friends," Lenormand said.

Cagliostro kissed Marie's hand again. "*Il mio amore,* do not worry. We shall think of something and you will be part of it."

"Oh, Joey," she said. "Your soul may be damned but it is nonetheless sweet."

Rasputin ignored the Italian con artist and the French fortune teller to pursue the path of his own thoughts. He knew there had to be someone in hell who had managed to hang onto their fortune. Someone slick, clever and cunning. A con artist much like Cagliostro, only better . . . and that's when it hit him like a blast of lightning from the blazing sword of one of Erra's seven Sibitti Cossacks.

Rising abruptly to his feet, Rasputin said, "Forgive me, comrades. I must go look for one I know, who has recently been reassigned."

With a sharp, penetrating look in his eyes, Cagliostro scrutinized his Russian sidekick. "You have thought of something?"

"What is that strange look I see in your ice-blue eyes, Grigori?" Lenormand asked. "Where are you going?"

Rasputin tapped the side of his nose, a half-smile curling one side of his mouth. "To see dog about man."

*

Sequestered in his secret lab deep below Goblin Manor, Victor and Quasimodo watch Alan Turing fiddle with knobs, flip switches and rotate control dials on a massive computer he built when he worked for Psychodyne Industries, Inc.

Unlike his laboratory in life and the others Victor had here in hell, this is a surprisingly more modern and sterile environment. Heat lamps, sun lamps and lanterns whose sole purpose is to provide cold, white illumination are strategically placed all over the lab. Metal chairs and desks, workbenches and operating tables, plus huge vats and a vast array of chemical and electrical gadgetry fill the brightly-lit chamber. Not a speck of dust or a single cobweb can be found. The floors are spotless, the walls freshly red-washed, and cooling fans hang suspended from the black ceiling among the electrical conduits and PVC pipes.

"Are you certain it will work this time?" Victor asked.

Alan Mathison Turing, so elegantly attired in a turquoise shirt, dark blue suit and light-green tie from Hellview Road rolled his eyes at Victor. He wore a holster with a Bolt .45 pistol for protection against Plague Zombies, fascists and homophobes. "My good man, how many times must I remind you that I invented the Enigma machine that successfully broke the Nazi code during the Second World War? I was influential in the development of theoretical science, algorithms and computation. Why, my Turing Machine is considered the very first computer." He huffed in a manner Victor often found to be most annoying. "Of course it will work!"

"My apologies," said Victor, choosing to ignore Turing's arrogance.

"Apology accepted," Turing replied, returning to his work.

"But on the off chance that it *won't* work, Alan, we'll have to find another specimen and then give it the old college try once again," said Victor. Already dressed for that eventuality, he wore black work pants, shirt and leather apron. He took pride in his appearance, even though there was little he could do to conceal his scarred face and bulging brow, although his neck bolts were brightly polished, as were his thick-soled, hobnailed boots.

"That's something you're quite adept at, I'm sure," said Turing.

"We have mastered the art of the body-snatching," said Quasimodo, his sense of hearing having been restored to him by Gorgonous in a rare moment of mercy during his only trip to the Mortuary. Having changed out of his tuxedo, the former Hunchback of Notre Dame now looked spiffy in his 1970s, lime-green leisure suit, brown cowboy boots and a yellow T-shirt emblazoned with the words: *Disco Sucks*! "Even those two sons of the bitches, Burke and Hare, cannot compete with us. Is that not correct, *mon ami*?"

"True enough, Quasimodo," Victor told him, remembering how the two body snatchers had tried to cheat him when he needed their help in building a new body for Joseph Merrick, the Elephant Man. But Frankenstein evened the score by sending them both to Slab A. Sadly, his dream of helping Merrick went up in smoke, as had all his dreams in life, as well as in his hellish afterlife. But that misadventure gave birth to a new idea and a new venture.

"We shall succeed, of this I am certain," said Quasimodo. "Madame Marie assured me that we shall succeed in the building of our cyborg."

Victor's monstrous face turned red. "You *told* her of our work?"

"*Oui*. So I did."

"I'd damn you if you weren't already damned, Quasimodo. You and your silly fortune teller, bah! Love is not only blind, it is deaf and mute, as well. I can't stop you from seeing that woman, but you are forbidden from ever bringing her here again. Understand? And *never* discuss the family business with outsiders, no matter how much you trust them. Got that?"

Quasimodo nodded and hung his head in shame. "I shall do as you say, my friend."

But Victor wasn't quite finished with his rant. "Damn right you will! Erra and his seven Sibitti are still running amok with their punishments, the plagues are evolving, the floods continue to wreak havoc throughout hell, and you waste your time consorting with fortune tellers while we have important work to do." He shook his head. "My word, Quasimodo! I think your brain's been rattled from all those years spent ringing cathedral bells."

"Will you two stop bitching like a couple of aging queens and let me work in peace?" Turing shouted.

While the father of the computer kept checking his settings and Victor prepared his instruments, Quasimodo waited patiently, if not silently, for the doctor to give him his orders.

"They tell me you prefer the men over the women, Mister Alan," said the hunchback. "And for that, you were damned for eternity?"

Turing sighed in frustration but replied to Quasimodo's question while he continued to work. "No. Satan's counterpart cares nothing about who we love and with whom we have sex," he said, having chosen chemical castration as an alternative to prison after being prosecuted for homosexual acts. "It was my Enigma machine that damned me."

"How do you mean?"

"Breaking the Nazi code may have helped win the war for Britain and her allies, but it also cost the lives of many German soldiers who were just doing their duty," Turin said.

"But your machine helped to *save* lives!"

Turin sighed once more. "Apparently, even in war it is better to be killed than to kill. The sixth commandment leaves no room for interpretation. It is what it is."

"Well then," said Victor. "Let's have some fun, shall we?"

Turing clapped his hands. "I say that's a jolly good idea, old boy! Now, ready your instruments, if you please. Quasimodo, fetch the operating tables."

Quasimodo rolled the two operating tables into place, both draped in black sheets that covered what appeared to be bodies. He noticed a particular instrument he had never seen before. This had a visual monitor, much like a computer. "What is this machine?" he asked.

"That, my dear boy is called an electroencephalograph," Turing told him. His knowledge of automation and computer science had been of great value to Victor when they first began their little experiment. "Here, try this on for size." He handed Quasimodo a strange-looking cap that had wires and electrodes attached to it."

"What is this material?" asked the hunchback.

"A biaxially-oriented, polyester film made from stretched polyethylene terephthalate," Turing explained.

Quasimodo placed the cap upon his head. "This is all the mumbo-jumbo to me."

"It's Mylar, Quasimodo. *Mylar*, like those silly balloons you love so much," said Victor.

Although the Hunchback of Notre Dame nodded like some bobblehead doll, it was quite apparent that he was as lost in the realm of science as a soul lost in hell. "But what does it do?"

"It records the electrical wavelengths of the brain," Turing told him. "Here, sit down and let me show you." When Quasimodo sat in the chair next to Turing, the professor then connected some wires and switched on the encephalograph. The monitor buzzed to life and projected all sorts of squiggly, zig-zag lines moving across the screen.

"Those are alpha waves, dear boy. That is the rhythm of an active thought process . . . your brain when it's awake. Delta waves display the rhythm of a sleeping brain. Even though we're dead, our brains and our hearts continue to function. Illusion? Maybe. But I think not."

"I find it most illuminating that Quasimodo actually *has* an active thought process," Victor quipped. "Sometimes I wonder about him."

"You are in a most jocular mood today, *Docteur*," said Quasimodo. "But still I believe the soul is in the heart."

Victor wagged a finger at his assistant. "The soul is in the brain, you ninny! We've been through all this before and no doctor or philosopher in hell could reach any sort of agreement on the exact location of the soul. But I have experimented with the dead and I know better. While I could jump-start a dead heart and keep it beating, I could not reanimate the dead without a usable brain that can be reawakened to function on some cognitive level."

"Quasimodo's correct," said Turing, removing the Mylar cap from Quasimodo's head. "The soul is located in the heart."

Victor put his hands to his ears and shook his head. "Oh, please, Alan! Not you, too?"

"See? I *do* have the active thought process," said Quasimodo.

Victor heaved a long sigh of frustration. "Yes, yes, yes—so you've demonstrated."

He turned to a pile of charts and graphs lying upon his desk. "Well, for now, we've accomplished arrested evaporation or suspended dissipation, if you prefer. However, there's still much work ahead of us."

"Yes, we've managed to keep our test subjects from dashing off to the Mortuary for a limited time, once the brain has been removed from the body," said Turing. "Our goal now is to turn that temporary suspension of dissipation into a permanent state of arrested evaporation." He winked at Victor. "See that? I managed to incorporate both your terms into one sentence."

"Brilliant," Victor said with a trace of sarcasm in his voice. "And by the way, I like to call what we are aiming to do here *Halted Reassignment.*"

"Dissipation, evaporation . . . each is a euphemism for death, as we know and experience it here in hell," said Quasimodo. "And Reassignment is but an infernal version of resurrection, is this not so, *mes amis*?"

"Quite so, Quasimodo," Victor said to him. "I'm very impressed with your thought process. One would almost think you truly *have* a working brain."

"Perhaps I am much smarter than you think," the hunchback retorted.

"Or do you think you are much smarter than you actually are?" Victor replied with a laugh.

"Gentlemen, that's neither here nor there," said Turing. "What I find rather paradoxical is that while we're all dead and perfectly aware of it, we keep thinking in terms of life and death."

Victor nodded in agreement. "I see no other way of thinking about our existence here in hell. In the afterlife, we do our best to avoid Reassignment, just as we did our best to avoid an untimely death when we were alive."

"And what we do here, you and Monsieur Turing, is very much the same as what the Undertaker and Gorgonous do in the Mortuary," said Quasimodo.

"Quite so, Quasimodo old boy. Quite so," said Turing.

"But I won't call it Reassignment," said Victor. "I made up my own rather nice term for what we do, what I have always tried to do: *Necrogenesis*—transforming death into life."

"I think I understand," said Quasimodo. "Whereas once you created life through death and constructed a living being from the bodies of the dead, you are now attempting to reassign people by transforming them into robots."

"They're called cyborgs, Quasimodo," Victor said, exasperated.

"May I ask again why we are trying to build a cyclops?" asked the hunchback.

"To see if we *can* do it!" Victor snapped. "And it's cyborg, Quasimodo. A *cyborg*, for hell's sake! How many times must I tell you that?" Taking a deep breath and exhaling slowly to control his temper, Victor said, more kindly this time, "Now please, let's get started, and do stand by to assist when called upon."

Quasimodo bowed and replied in a slightly mocking tone of voice, "Yes, master."

*

Grigori Yefimovich Rasputin, lost in deep thought, strolls with a purpose down Belial Way. The street-corner Fear Mongers and Doom Sayers all scurry to get out of his way, his smoldering, blue-eyed stare chilling the damned down to the grimarrow of their moribones. No one dares cross his path or even remain on the same side of the street.

Maybe is chance he has money, Rasputin muses. *We need his kind of big money—and we need it before some other hellizen purchases old Hellstrom House.*

Plague Zombies shamble down the streets of Port Boil until they melt into steaming pools of liquefied necroflesh and moribones which soon vanish, only to reappear in the Mortuary to face Reassignment. Others, suffering great pain, confusion and anger, go after uninfected souls, biting and tearing them apart like a herd of resurrected, hungry corpses attacking the living in some ancient horror film. Some of those bitten are immediately stricken by the contagion, while others run screaming down the street. Of these, some return to their homes and wait to fall prey to a host of symptoms, while many commit suicide, which everyone in hell knows is a pointless endeavor.

If not for plagues, wealthy friends not flee New Hell in search of refuge.

When Rasputin reaches Libertine Lane and turns the corner he spies a platoon of demons using automatic weapons to take down Plague Zombies before they can attack and infect others. These demons are the Uncubi, all the unpublished writers who had ever lived, would-be authors in hell who wound up in the netherworld because the Muses they thought they were courting were, in reality, hell's own Nephilim.

The Uncubi look like flickering, three-dimensional images that emerged from an old, black and white television. Infernal hybrids of Man, Woman and Pteranodon, they're naked and without genitals, and have wriggling worms for fingers; their weapons, the Hexum-9 assault rifles, have been customized exclusively for the demons' hands. Because of their congress with the Nephilim, the Uncubi have the distinct honor of visiting the Mortuary immediately upon their arrival in hell, whereupon the Undertaker and Gorgonous turn them into a new breed of androgynous demons not indigenous to hell, as are the Kigali.

Although the Uncubi are indistinguishable from one another, what with their lack of apparel and their pointy, almost triangular heads, Rasputin recognizes their leader by the Union badge hanging around his neck. This Uncubus is known as the Unknown Poet but is more commonly referred to as Mister Up. In life, he'd had an eidetic memory, and while he never published a single poem, he remembered every word he's ever written. In hell, however, he remembers nothing of those poems. Not only is the Unknown Poet the hetman of these New Breed demons, but he's also their Union representative and reports directly to Jimmy Hoffa.

"Gospodin Up!" Rasputin called out to the Uncubus. "What goes?"

Mister Up walked over to Rasputin and they bowed to each other. "The Boss called us in to do crowd control," he told the Russian. "The Plague Zombies are growing in number and getting out of hand, infecting Old and New Dead alike. We're trying to stem the tide of the contagion."

"You not worried about getting sick?"

"No, my friend. We Uncubi are immune to Erra's plagues. But many of my tribe have been swept away by the floods and Flux ravaging hell."

"Be careful and be safe, *tovarisch*." Rasputin bowed to the demon.

Mister Up bowed in return. "You do the same."

With that, the Unknown Poet took off to rejoin his platoon.

Continuing on his way, Rasputin headed down Libertine Lane and then Dead Man's Curve. As he approached Crud

Alley the sounds of whimpering and moaning made him pause. He peeked around the corner of an old warehouse and into the alley, and as fate and hell would have it, saw the very soul he was looking for: the Orange Ogre.

They hit Ogre and kicked him. They whipped him with motorcycle chains and beat him with baseball bats. But Ogre did not fight back. Instead, he cried out for help—a cry that went unheard or simply ignored—then fell into the muck and mire of the alley.

Having seen enough, Rasputin stepped into the alley. "Stop!" he shouted, his voice edged with eerie and unsettling power. "Turn. Face me, swine!"

Almost immediately the young punks stopped beating Ogre's diseased body and turned around to confront the Siberian peasant with the wild and crazy blue eyes.

"Who the fuck are you?" one of the gangbangers dared to ask.

"One you must obey," said Rasputin. He stretched out his left arm and pointed his index finger at the street gang. "Drop weapons. Come here," he added, curling his finger inward.

As if hypnotized in a flash, the three punks dropped their weapons and walked towards the Mad Monk like a pack of mindless Plague Zombies.

"Remain here. Move not," Rasputin commanded them.

The gangstas did as they were told, not moving, not even blinking.

Rasputin hurried over the where Ogre lay curled in the fetal position next to a garbage dumpster on the slimy brimstone pavement of Crud Alley, staring wide-eyed at his savior.

"You hurt?" Rasputin asked.

"A little, but I'll be okay," Ogre replied. "Say, don't I know you? Wait—don't tell me. I think I remember." His eyes went wide. "Vladimir?"

Rasputin ground his teeth. "*Nyet!*"

"You sound like some foreign-born immigrant."

With a sigh of frustration, the Mad Monk said, "We are all foreigners in hell. I am Grigori Yefimovich Rasputin."

The light of memory and recognition flared in Ogre's eyes. "Greg!" With Rasputin's helping hand he rose to his feet. "That idiot Undertaker and his pervert of an assistant . . . what's his name?"

"Gorgonous."

"That's the asshole! They keep screwing with my brain."

"All memory of who and what you were in life is gone. Erased. Obliterated. No damned soul has memory of you. Not even I, Rasputin, can undo what has been done."

"More recent memories I can remember," Ogre explained. "Like, I was in Lost Angeles, in Hellywood, to secure a deal to be the host of a hellivision surreality show when the plagues began. I got sick but made it back here to Port Boil when the floods started. I think I drowned. Then I woke up in that Mortuary wearing these monkey hands. Not sure how long I was there."

"Time is irrelevant in hell." Rasputin looked at the Ogre. "You are mess. Need doctor."

"Yeah, I'm sick and my body's pretty messed up, all right. This really sucks. But at least I still have my money. Plenty of money. I love money. Who doesn't love money?"

Rasputin furrowed his brow. "You are like czars of old."

"I don't know what that is, but I have lots of money. Big money. Huge money!"

He still has money! This was exactly what Rasputin had been hoping for. "Where you going, *tovarisch*?"

"The Worst Irrational Bank."

"That some bank, that bank."

"It's the worst there is, Greg. I pay ninety percent interest fees, but I can afford it. Besides, no other bank in New Hell will do business with me."

With his reputation, I understand, Rasputin told himself. "Why you go to bank?"

"I want to make a withdrawal so I can pay to have someone find out who's responsible for all these plagues and floods. I can't remember. Do you know who's responsible for this mess?"

Before Rasputin could answer, a loud crack of thunder echoed from one end of Port Boil to the other. He glanced at the crimson vault hanging over New Hell and then saw them gliding across the blood-red sky on invisible wings: eight majestic figures, dreadful in their dusty raiment, with cloaks of human skin decorated with braided scalps. These personages shimmered, with eyes aglow and swords in hand.

"They are responsible," he told Ogre, pointing at the sky.

At that moment hellizens began screaming and rushing about, looking for somewhere to hide. When a bolt of lightning struck and obliterated the street thugs standing as still and silent as statues near the mouth of the alley, Rasputin grabbed Ogre and dragged him behind the dumpster, where together they knelt, cowered and covered their heads with their arms.

A chasm opened in the middle of the street and hundreds of hellions tumbled into it. More turned into ice and then shattered into numerous pieces when they toppled over and crashed to the ground. Others were mowed down and mutilated by a rolling juggernaut of sharp, glistening blades. Lightning blasted untold numbers of the damned. Lost souls by the score crumbled into sand. Holy fire caused others to burst into flames, turning them into black ash. Winds howled and raged with tempestuous violence. A rainstorm from the crimson vault above caused more flooding, fear and commotion. Mayhem and destruction struck fast and furiously, and then it was over as quickly as it had begun.

"I think I remember now," said Ogre. "Some bastard named Arrow is behind all this fucked up shit."

"Erra. Not Arrow," said Rasputin. "Erra and his seven, the Sibitti."

"Erra. Arrow. Error. What in hell's the difference? That asshole and his little jet boys have to pay for what's been done to me. They all have to pay, *everyone*—even Satan and those two vermin in the Mortuary."

Rasputin understood the Orange Ogre, who wanted nothing more than revenge against every soul in hell who had ever mocked, laughed and turned against him. Vengeance boiled within the Ogre, consuming him, festering in him like an open wound. It was the desire of a simple-minded soul, petty and futile. The Russian mystic was certain there was some way he could turn Ogre's hatred to his and Cagliostro's advantage.

"I want to get even with them all!" Ogre shouted.

"Ever been in army?"

"I don't remember."

"Military school?"

"School? School is hard!"

Rasputin tugged on his beard. "Ever fight in war?"

"Not that I recall. Why would I do that, anyway? That's what poor people are for. They're born cannon fodder." Ogre shrugged. "But since I'm dead and in hell, what can be worse than the Mortuary? I'll take my chances."

"Then would you fight enemies?"

"That's a good question, Greg. My enemies can destroy me with ease. They can twist and bend and break my body, then put it back together any way they see fit. Oh, if only I had a body that could not be hurt, not get sick or fucked with."

"How do you mean, Ogre?"

"Well, like a suit of armor. No, not really a suit of armor, I want to be some kind of indestructible mechanical man."

"Like robot?"

"Yes! One of those exterminator things, equipped with blasters and ray guns and Martian disintegrator pistols. Nothing could hurt or stop me then!"

An idea exploded in Rasputin's head like a blast of lightning from a Sibitti sword. "You come with me. Now."

"Wait! What are you talking about? You want to help me?"

"*Da*. But will take much money to do this thing."

"Of course it will take money. Everything takes money. Money talks, bullshit walks. You're not bullshitting me, are you, Greg?"

Rasputin ground his teeth together; he hated to be called *Greg*. "Gospodin Ogre, how hot does revenge burn in your heart?"

The Orange Ogre rubbed his big orangutan hands together as a wicked grin twisted his pumpkin-face into a nasty-looking mask. "I'll pay anything to even the score and show Arrow and Satan who's the real boss around here!"

"*Erra*," Rasputin corrected the tangerine troll.

"Whatever! If you're loyal to me I'll make it well worth your while."

Rasputin stroked his beard and smiled. "Then come. Now. We talk more."

"Where are we going, Greg?"

"For cup of tea."

*

While Quasimodo scurries off to see to his part in the experiment, Victor wheels over to the supercomputer a large medical instrument of his own design, one he calls the Prometheus Bonesaw. Built of bright, shiny metal, this device resembles a dental drill crossed with an X-ray machine; it was constructed for him by the sinister and secretive Bumbershoot Corporation. (Many of the damned still accuse the Bumbershoot executives of being in league with Erra and having concocted for him the contagions that still inundate the nether regions. But this is a blatant fabrication and an outright lie, for the Babylonian god is more than capable of creating his own pandemics and pestilential fallout.)

Doctor Frankenstein sets his machine in place, plugs it in and begins adjusting its settings.

Meanwhile, Quasimodo removes the white sheets covering the two metal operating tables. Lying upon the first is a cyborg made out of dark blue metal and bearing a striking similarity to a suit of medieval armor. Upon the second table lays a man dressed in an elegant dark suit, white shirt and black tie. He's laid out like a corpse in a coffin, eyes closed and hands folded over his breast. Of course, he isn't "dead," for if he was, his body would have already gone to the Mortuary to be reassigned. Alan Turing had abducted the damned soul lying on the table and administered the Hexoroform to put him to sleep.

"Who is he?" Quasimodo asked.

"Some asshole United States senator," Victor replied.

"Which party did he belong to?"

Victor threw his hands into the air in frustration. His patience often ran thin where the hunchback was concerned. "The birthday party! How the fuck would I know and why the fuck should I care? I was dead and in hell long before this asshole arrived."

"Will you two please shut up?" said Turing. "I'm ready to begin."

"Then let's get the show on the road," said Victor, glad to get underway. He pressed a button on his Prometheus Bonesaw and it immediately began to hum and cause the floor to vibrate. A bright blue light emanated from the point of the machine's drill and burned four holes into the man's skull. There was no mortisblood whatsoever because the incisions had been instantly cauterized. Once this had been accomplished, Victor shut off his brand-new gizmo.

Just like old times, he told himself, feeling energized by the promise of what result this experiment would yield.

Next, Turing inserted four tiny netherchips into the holes in the man's skull, which corresponded to the location of the frontal, parietal, temporal and occipital lobes of the brain; these were connected by wires attached to his computer. Then he flipped a toggle to the ON position. Lights flashed. Sparks sizzled and flew about the room. Circuits hummed and ghostly wisps of blue smoke floated towards the ceiling. The body of the damned soul trembled and writhed for a few seconds, then fell still. Turing switched off the toggle, carefully removed the wires attached to the netherchips and tossed them aside.

"*S'il vous plaît*, what is next?" Quasimodo asked.

"The netherchips each contain a special battery designed to provide continuous electrical stimulation to the brain," Turing explained. "If my theory and my calculations are correct, the chips will keep the brain active after it's been removed from the skull of our senatorial guinea pig over here." He rubbed his hands together in a most theatrical manner. "Your turn, Victor."

Frankenstein recalled how he had wanted to transplant the Elephant Man's brain into a new body, but wasn't sure he could succeed. An eternity ago in Brimstone, Hellizona, in a bizarre experiment, Merlin the Magician had successfully switched Victor's brain with the brain of the creature he called Adam. But whatever strange magic Merlin had employed was far beyond anything Victor was familiar with. Although he had tried to find Merlin, the magician had not been seen or heard from since the coming of Erra and his Seven Sibitti. Now, however, with Turing's knowledge and assistance, Victor was confident that an active brain could be successfully transplanted from one body to another, even though the host body was inorganic, a thing made of metal and electronic circuitry.

Victor adjusted the settings on his hi-tech Bonesaw and placed his hands on the controls. "While I enjoy using a hacksaw or chainsaw, they're too messy for an operation of this magnitude."

Next, he adjusted the settings on the control panel of his device and swung the extension arm into position. Closing one eye, he took aim, licked his lips in anticipation and maneuvered the tube head into position above the neck of the comatose senator.

"Quickly now, Quasimodo! Grab your glove and get over here," said Victor.

Snatching a catcher's mitt hanging on a wall, the Hunchback of Notre Dame scampered over to stand at the head of the operating table.

Taking careful aim again, Victor switched on his Bonesaw and watched as a crimson beam from the machine's barrel-like nozzle began slicing through the neck of the unconscious senator.

"It's working! It's working!" he cried.

Moments later, the head rolled off the table, but Quasimodo caught it in his catcher's mitt. Once again, there was no messy mortisblood to mop up afterwards.

"Nice catch!" said Turing.

"Place the head on the towel on top of that cart over by the wall and bring that cart over here," Victor instructed his hunchbacked assistant.

Quasimodo quickly did as he was told and wheeled the cart carrying the senator's severed head over to Victor. The infamous doctor then used his surgical instrument to cut off the top of his patient's skull. He shut down the Bonesaw, pulled a Hexacto knife from his apron pocket, delicately removed the bulbous grey matter from the skull and cut the brainstem free of the spinal cord. Only a small amount of mortisblood and spinal fluid dripped onto the towel. He set the brain with its four embedded netherchips next to the head of the nameless senator.

"*Toutes nos félicitations*, my friends," said Quasimodo, pointing to the table where the senator's headless body reposed. "You have succeeded. Look!"

Victor and Turing glanced at the table: the politician's torso had not shimmered and faded and gone off to the Mortuary.

"Eureka!" Doctor Frankenstein shouted. "Your netherchips work, Alan. The brain thrives! It thrives! *Oh, it thrives!*"

"This proves your theory," said Turing.

Nodding excitedly, Victor said, "As long as the brain continues to function, the body will not dissipate and dash off to meet the Undertaker." Gently he picked up the still-active brain and carried it over to the metallic figure lying on the other operating table. "Quasimodo, if you please . . . flip the lid open so we can install and link the brain to the automaton's circuitry."

Popping open the top of the helmet-like head of the lifeless robot-knight, Quasimodo stepped aside so Victor and Turing could go to work. Together the brilliant scientist and the equally gifted physician inserted the brain into the cyborg's head, connected its nerve endings and brainstem to circuits and wiring. They finished their task in a jiffy. Quasimodo closed and secured the lid of the cyborg's head and then scampered away as if the thing was going to suddenly spring to life, reach out with one arm and strangle him.

Turing checked a small, drop-down screen on his computer's monitor. "The brain is active but still slumbers, lost in dreamland," he said. "Quasimodo, be a good chap and kindly step aside while I attempt to awaken the brain."

"*Excusez-moi*, Mister Alan," said Quasimodo. "How will you control this cyclamen thing, once you have awakened it?"

"For damnation's sake, Quasimodo—this is not a plant!" said Victor. "It's a cyborg, you apish buffoon! A *cyborg* got it?"

Quasimodo's eyes darted back and forth over Victor, Turing and the cyborg. "I hope its brain is in a most reasonable frame of mind."

"If not, we'll just have to reason with it," said Victor.

"Tally ho!" said Turing, flipping a switch and pressing two buttons on his computer.

A weird sound echoed from inside the helmet-head of the cyborg; if a machine could sigh, it would have sounded like that.

"The voice box you designed seems to be functioning," Victor said to Turing.

The two eye slits in the knight's helmet began to glow with violet light.

"Vision is working, too," said Turing.

Slowly, the cyborg sat up, stretched its arms, shifted its position and swung its legs over the side of the table. An electronic yawn emanated from the cybernetic knight. The steel hulk lowered its arms and looked around the chamber.

Victor was so elated that he stammered. "It's . . . it's—"

"I believe the word you are looking for is *alive*," Turing said with a grin.

The cyborg focused its attention on Victor and Turing and then spoke in a computerized simulation of a human voice:

"*Where am I? This doesn't look like the Mortuary.*"

"That's because it's not," said Victor. "You are in my home—Goblin Manor."

"*And who the hell are you?*"

"My name is Doctor Victor Frankenstein, and these are my two associates—"

"*What the hell?*" The cyborg glanced down and saw his metal chest, arms and legs. "*What's happened to me?*" Raising its head, the thing stared at Victor. "*What have you done?*"

"There, there, my good man, there's no reason to become so overwrought," said Turing. "We have simply made you powerful and invincible. Never again will you experience the cessation of existence, the horrible dissipation and torments of the Undertaker's cold slab, and the unsettling disorientation and agony of Reassignment."

"We have made you a god among men and demons," Victor told the cyborg.

It was then that the cyborg noticed his torso lying on the other operating table, and his empty, disembodied head sitting on the cart.

"*That . . . that's me!*"

"Why, yes. As a matter of fact, it is," said Victor.

The cyborg roared like a hadesaur made of steel, hopped off the operating table, turned around so he was facing it and then pounded it into scrap metal with his huge fists. Then he picked up the mangled table and threw it across the room, where it crashed with a clang and a clatter against the far wall.

"Ungrateful little bitch," Turing remarked.

Swinging around, the damned cyborg howled and moved menacingly towards Victor, Turing and Quasimodo.

"Talk about *déjà vu*!" said Victor.

"I am afraid there is no reasoning with this thing," said Quasimodo. With a shrug, he flung himself upon the cybernetic monster and started beating it with his fists.

"Quasimodo, no!" Victor shouted.

The cyborg seized the hunchback with its metal hands, lifted him high above his head . . . and abruptly collapsed to the floor, Quasimodo landing atop him. A bluish smoke floated from the now lightless eyes of the cyborg and quickly vanished. Quasimodo picked himself up, dusted himself off and walked over to where Victor and Turing huddled together like a pair of frightened chimpanzees.

"That was very brave of you," Turing said to the hunchback.

"I hope you're not hurt," said Victor.

"Thank you both, but I am fine," Quasimodo replied. Then his eyes went wide. "Look, my friends. The head, the body—they have vanished!"

"Back to the Mortuary with our senatorial friend, I see," said Turing.

Victor's hopes and dreams crashed and burned. "We have failed, Alan. Failed, I tell you!"

"No, we haven't," Turing told him. "We succeeded. My netherchips *did* work, if only for a short time, and your theory is proven. We *can* build a cyborg using the necro-brain of a damned soul. What ruined everything are the laws of hell, of cessation and Reassignment. You can't beat the devil, but we made a damn good show of it, what?"

"*Oui*," Quasimodo agreed. "You two fine gentlemen managed to keep the brain working long enough to make it part of that demonic cyclone."

"You mean cyborg," Victor said. "But it certainly was a cyclone of demonic temperament." The spark of an idea suddenly flared in his fevered brain. "Quasimodo, do you recall the conversation we had with Burke and Hare when we approached them regarding the purchase of new limbs for Joseph Merrick?"

"That I do indeed," Quasimodo replied. "I am most familiar with that look in your eyes, my friend. You have come up with a new idea?"

"Of course I have!" Victor said with a laugh. He cracked his knuckles and grinned mischievously. His brain was on fire with renewed hope, and his customary tenacity reasserted itself. "Listen. We are but lost souls inhabiting necroflesh forms that are fabrications, mere imitations of the bodies we had in life. Correct?"

Quasimodo nodded and shrugged.

"Victor, whatever are you talking about?" Turing asked.

"We are not native to hell and thus our bodies are not real and have no actual substantiality. Not in the same way they would be if we had *originated* in hell," Victor explained.

"Do you speak of demons?" Quasimodo asked.

"Yes indeed, my funny little asinine," Victor replied. "We use the brain of a demon."

Turing's eyes opened wide. "Please don't tell me you're thinking of abducting one of the Kigali. Oh, Victor, if you were to do that there would literally be hell to pay."

Victor shook his head. "I'm talking about the Uncubi. I think we may be able to persuade one of them to take part in our little experiment."

"As the guinea pig?" Quasimodo asked, rubbing his chin thoughtfully.

Turing chewed on a fingernail. "I don't think any Uncubus would agree to that."

"Then we'll just have to kidnap one or two of them," said Victor. "Shouldn't be too difficult to do, I'd say."

Quasimodo gasped. "But they are our friends! We cannot do such a thing."

Victor shook an angry fist in the air. "In the name of science and research we can!"

"He's right, Victor," Turing agreed. "Besides, the Uncubi may indeed be demons but they are *not* native to hell. Remember: once they were human until the Undertaker turned them into demons. Your idea won't work."

"Fiddlesticks!" said Victor. "There's always a bat in the belfry to muck things up." *There has to be a way*, he thought, undismayed. *There* must *be a way*!

"And yet, *mes savants amis*, I think I may have discovered the thing that causes the bat to fly about the bell tower," said Quasimodo.

"Do you mean to say you know why we failed?" Turing asked him.

The Hunchback of Notre Dame nodded and took a long pause; whether for dramatic effect or not, Victor didn't know, but the doctor quickly lost his patience.

"Don't just stand there like one of your gargoyles, Quasimodo. Tell us!" said Victor.

Quasimodo blushed but did not hesitate to speak up: "You may have had the success keeping the brain active, if only for the short time, but the heart . . . the heart must be kept functioning, too, I am thinking."

Victor and Turing turned to each other and grinned like two mischievous schoolboys.

"Exactly," said Turing. "Like the Tin Woodsman, our cyborg needs a heart."

Victor and Quasimodo exchanged glances and then shrugged. Neither of them got Turing's reference, but Victor did catch the gist of his meaning.

"I think I understand," he said. "Our hearts, once they stop beating or whatever it is our hearts do when we're dusted and sent off for Reassignment, are the key."

"I'm no physician, but I think we've been going about all this in the wrong way," said Turing. "Once the heart ceases to function, the brain also ceases to function. Thus, the body dissipates and shuffles off to the Undertaker's grim parlor." He scratched his chin. "As our sweet little hunchback has suggested, the heart must be kept beating."

Victor glanced at Quasimodo. "Are you certain about your idea?"

"Yes, I am dead certain of it," Quasimodo suggested, irony in his voice.

"Then by Jove, that's it!" Turing shouted. "The brain and all this technology won't keep a heart beating if it's not integrated with the body of the cyborg. The heart has to be placed inside the cyborg and attached to the circuitry of the brain. The two must be *in tune* with each other, just as they were in life."

"I wish you had thought of this sooner, Quasimodo," said Victor. He couldn't believe that he of all people, who had conquered death during his lifetime, had overlooked this one simple fact. *Hell must finally be getting to me.*

Quasimodo grinned and thrust out his chest. "So if the heart is the key, then it must certainly follow that the soul is located in the heart."

"Don't start in on that again, you misshapen lump of clay!" Victor told the hunchback. Then he turned to Turing. "Alan, how many cybernetic bodies do we have left?"

"Two, including this now useless one lying over there on the floor," Turing replied. "But the other one is merely an empty shell. No circuitry, wiring or fiber optic cables. No electronics whatsoever. And neither of one of us has the money to purchase what we need to conduct another experiment."

"That freaking Monsieur Howard Carter can no longer provide the gold we require to fund our experiments," said Quasimodo. For a short time, he had managed to procure body parts from his friend Gorgonous, Deputy Assistant of the Mortuary. The hunchback then gave those body parts to Carter and Ernst Haeckel in exchange for gold to help finance Victor's experiments. But then, suddenly and without notice, that source of revenue dried up.

"And fuck that King Midas and his shitty Buttcoins, too!" Turing added.

"Yes, yes! Screw them, curse them and damn them both, I say!" Victor ranted.

"They are already damned, my friend," said Quasimodo.

"Screw you, too!" Victor shouted, his temper getting the better of him. "Where will we ever find another benefactor, another lost soul who's bored and has a lot of money to throw around?"

"Do not worry, *mon ami*," said Quasimodo, grinning and winking at Victor and Turing. "I have the *hunch* that something will turn up. Is this not, after all, hell?"

"Oh, how utterly droll," Victor told him.

*

"So, Gospodin Cagliostro and I wish to have place of our own where friends can meet," Rasputin tells the Orange Ogre.

He, Ogre, Cagliostro and Marie Lenormand gathered together in a small, backroom of *Nick's Czar and Grill*. The Russian tea room is crowded at this time every Sinday, so for privacy they used the chamber for their meeting.

"How much money are we talking, here?" asks Ogre, the hairy fingers of his orangutan hands tapping the tabletop as if they're using an old-school calculator.

"The way we have it figured—" Cagliostro starts to say, as he's interrupted by the arrival of their waiter, a rotund bald man who had once been the premier of the Soviet Union. The former Russian dictator brings in four cups of Sindemon tea and a plate of stewed, rotten turnips and onions, sets them on the table and then removes one shoe. He bangs three times on the table with his shoe, slips it back on his foot and then leaves.

"What's up with that?" asked Ogre.

"Old habit from former life," Rasputin replied.

"So, let me get this straight," said Ogre. "You want enough diablos to open this exclusive golf course and by giving you what you want, I get what I want?"

"Not golf course. Private club," Rasputin told him. "But *da*, one hand wash other."

"The money must be given free and clear, like a gift," said Lenormand. "No fee, no interest, no reimbursement."

"That is the offer we make," Cagliostro said.

"Okay, but what's in it for me?" Ogre wanted to know.

Rasputin clutched the unholy talisman hidden inside his shirt. "You will become most powerful soul in hell. No more fear of torture and pain. No more to be threatened by plague and flood. Your body will be made of metal. Indestructible."

"Like a robot?" Ogre asked.

"*Oui c'est correct*," Lenormand assured him. "But you will be better than a robot. You will be a cyborg. The first of its kind in hell."

Ogre picked his nose. "Awesome! I'll be like some powerful monster in a horror film. I like horror films. Do you like horror films? I don't like to be scared, but horror films are a fun kind of scared." He leered at Lenormand. "You know, you're really quite a hot-looking broad. I like foreign women the most. You and I should—"

"Don't even think about it," she warned him.

If looks could dust a damned soul and send him or her to the Mortuary, the look Cagliostro shot the Orange Ogre would have done just that. "She is my *compagno di sesso femminile*—my woman," he said. "Say no more or I will cut off your balls and give them to the Sibitti."

"Okay! Okay!" said Ogre, holding up his orangutan hands. "You Italians certainly play rough, don't you? Now, where were we?"

"Fifty thousand diablos," Cagliostro told him.

Rasputin shook his head. "One-hundred thousand, *tovarisch*. We must consider cost of remodeling, license fee, appliances, supplies, furniture and such for our venture alone. Plus, we must take into account Doctor Frankenstein's fee."

Cagliostro winked conspiratorially at the Siberian peasant. "Ah, so it is. *Mama Mia*—my brain, it often forgets."

"No sweat," said Ogre. "That kind of money is pocket change to me."

"*Da*," said Rasputin. He planned to split fifty-fifty with the infamous doctor, and he was certain it was an offer that would not be refused. He knew and liked the maker of monsters, had great respect for him and would never think of cheating him. Cheating the Orange Ogre, on the other hand—a narcissist so wrapped up in a cloak of vanity that he wouldn't know a Kigali from a tea kettle—would not bother the Russian's conscience at all. As for convincing Ogre to undergo the surgery involved, the Mad Monk had a plan for that as well.

Lenormand took out her Tophet cards and placed them on the table. "Pick three cards and lay them face-up on the table, Ogre."

Ogre wiped a booger on his shirt sleeve and then selected three cards from the deck: the Burning Soul, the Laughing Devil and the #13 card.

"Interesting," Lenormand remarked. Then she selected three cards and placed one on top of each of the other three: the Hanged Demon, the Pit of Fire and the #666 card. "*Very* interesting," she added, giving Cagliostro a quick wink.

"What's it mean?" Ogre asked eagerly.

"Good news," she told him. "All your hopes and dreams will be realized. Out of the ashes of defeat will come the resurrection of a victory long denied."

"That sounds great. Really great! I hate losers. I'm a winner. I like to win. Don't you?"

"All of us, we like to win," said Cagliostro. "And so it is that we shall."

Ogre rubbed his big, hairy hands together. "So what else do I have to do to become a cyborg? Will I be able to use fire and fury to bring down Erra and his gang and kick Satan's ass right outta hell?"

By hell, this pumpkin head very stupid, Rasputin said to himself. "Without doubt."

With a sudden frown, Ogre asked, "Is this Frankenstein a liberal? I hate liberals."

"Of course he is," said Lenormand. "He is a man of great intelligence."

Ogre frowned. "I don't like intelligence. It's dangerous, unless it's mine. And I don't trust people who read books, either. Reading books is for losers. But I'll do whatever it takes to bring a hell down upon Erra and Satan the likes of which no one has never seen."

"And so you shall, *tovarisch*," Rasputin told him. "So you shall."

"Then what's the holdup?"

Rasputin glanced at Cagliostro, who tapped the side of his nose in reply. They were trying to reel in the big fish, but would he take the bait once he was told about the operation? Or would he swim away? No matter, though, for the two mystics were prepared to make sure their catch would be unable to wriggle free of their net.

"It's a simple operation," Lenormand told Ogre. "First, you will be put to sleep and then your brain will be placed inside the body of the cyborg."

"Wait! What?" Ogre said. "You're going to take out my big, smart brain and stuff it inside the head of some robot?"

"Cyborg, *ma chérie.* Cyborg."

"I don't give a rat's ass what you call it. I'm not gonna do it and you're not gonna get my money!" Ogre crossed his arms over his chest and sulked like a little boy.

"But my friend, this is an offer you cannot refuse," said Cagliostro. He seized the Ogre's arms, pulled them apart and forced them down upon the table.

"Screw you, you dumb dago!" said Ogre.

"Hold him down!" Lenormand shouted.

Cagliostro's eyes flared menacingly. "Look at me, Ogre. *Look at me!*" Ogre looked into the eyes of the Italian mystic—and his orange face turned white. "You *will* take Marie and myself to your bank and withdraw the money we have asked for. *Capisci?*"

"I . . . I'm not sure. I don't know about this," said Ogre. His eyes slid towards Rasputin. "What should I do? Help me!"

Ready for this, Rasputin smiled at Ogre and removed the talisman hidden inside his shirt. It was an inverted Crucifix made of cedar, pine and cypress, like the one true cross. The number 666 had been carved into it. He held it up by its leather cord and let it swing like a pendulum.

"Concentrate. Stare only at object in my hand," Rasputin told Ogre. The hepatitis-orange eyes of Ogre darted back and forth, mimicking the movement of the unholy object. "You do as we say, Ogre. Close eyes and think only of my command. Sleep now. When I snap fingers you will wake and obey us as peasant obeys czar."

Ogre closed his eyes and immediately nodded off. Rasputin tucked the inverted cross back inside his shirt, counted to thirteen and then snapped his fingers.

The Orange Ogre opened his eyes and looked at his companions. "Now what is it that you want me to do?"

"You get money. I go meet with Frankenstein," said Rasputin.

"Then I can become this all-powerful cyborg?"

"*Si,* then you will settle all debts with your enemies," said Cagliostro.

Ogre made the "OK" sign with the fingers of his right orangutan hand. "I'm in!"

Rasputin was pleased. He had hoped it would be easy to get Ogre to agree, although for a moment there he feared he had underestimated the ginger troll. But all had gone as planned and soon he and Cagliostro would have the money to open their Infernium Club.

"Soon Colossus of Hell will make hell his own," said the Mad Monk of Russia.

*

Sitting at the table in his Goblin Manor parlor, Victor pours a round of drinks for Turing, Quasimodo, Rasputin and himself.

"This is a synthetic blend of my own concoction," Victor tells Rasputin. "My friends all say it's quite palatable, but having no taste buds myself, I wouldn't know."

Rasputin tastes his drink and smiles. "Is good. Like Russian vodka."

This pleases Victor. Everyone who samples the beverage declares it a fine beverage, although it has a different flavor for anyone who tastes it. "Thank you, my friend."

"Victor, old friend, I have always wondered why Erra and Satan leave you alone," Rasputin says. "Why they not punish you?"

"Good question," Victor replies, "and one that may forever go unanswered. It's a discussion with no possibility of a true conclusion."

They nurse their drinks in a thoughtful silence so dense you could stab it with a pitchfork.

Finally, Turing nodded. "I think we each serve a purpose here in hell. Whether to slave and suffer, to hope where there is no hope, to strive in vain when only failure and frustration await us, each one of us has some role to play. But such things aren't for us to know."

"And what do you think is *our* role, Alan?" Victor asked.

"To serve and to suffer, of course. All of us who have been damned to an eternity in this asylum of paradox and pain serve the Devil in some fashion. Therefore we are all subjects and servants of His Satanic Majesty. We are merely pawns in Satan's game of eternal woe."

"*Da*, if I knew such answers I would be czar sitting on throne of heaven," said Rasputin. He paused then suggested, "I think Devil is silent partner to Almighty Above."

"Could be," Victor agreed. "At one time Lucifer *was* the Almighty's favorite angel."

"And now Satan is Almighty's henchman, as Daemon Grim is Satan's henchman."

"*Oui*, this is true," said Quasimodo. "The Devil, he does the work of heaven so the *seigneur* upstairs never has dirty hands."

"Yes," Turing said. "Satan works for heaven, if you consider it from that angle. The Almighty could have destroyed Lucifer but instead banished him here to hell, exiled to Perdition where he labors to punish the wicked. But I think Satan has grown somewhat lax in his duties, so now Erra and his Sibitti, the Almighty's new enforcers, have been sent to show the Devil how it's done."

Victor closed his eyes for a moment and sipped his drink, not for the flavor of it, but to wet his throat. "Did you ever consider the fact that the Almighty and his Adversary may actually be two sides of the same coin?"

"Interesting theory," Turing admitted. "Dual identity. Split personality. Multiple personality disorder. While I don't subscribe to this theory, one never knows. Perhaps we'll never know."

"Just as we'll never know why Satan and Erra allow me to continue with my experiments," said Victor.

"That is because we are forever doomed to fail," said Quasimodo.

"Screw you!" Victor told the hunchback. "A little more positive thinking around here is what we need. And this time I *won't* fail!"

Quasimodo sat back and shook his head. "But all I am saying is—"

Turing interrupted the argument. "What we *do* know is that heaven is displeased with Satan, thus Erra and his Sibitti were sent to shake things up, and the Babylonian god has certainly done just that."

"And it may very well be that our time has not yet come to pass when Erra turns his eyes upon us," said Quasimodo.

A chill scurried down Victor's spine, cooling his temper. "A most sobering thought."

"Indeed," said Turing. "But Ogre's a fool if he thinks he can go up against Satan and Erra."

"Foolish and stupid, *da*," said Rasputin. "But loss of identity and consigned to hell in obscurity made him lose sight of all reason."

Quasimodo rubbed his one good eye. "He is hungry for power. That is a certainty. Why should we care what he does and what happens to him?"

"Quasimodo's right," said Turing. "Now, I think we should set aside this discussion and return to the business at hand."

Rasputin explained the plan he and Cagliostro had concocted. "Simple, no?"

"It should be," Victor agreed. "But tell me, Grigori, how did you first come to hear about our experiments in cybernetic technology?"

Rasputin finished his drink, helped himself to another and said, "Quasimodo tell Madame Lenormand, who then confided in Cagliostro, who in turn tell me."

A grim look darkened the hunchback's malformed face, a look of pain and betrayal. "Cagliostro, *ce bâtard!*" he mumbled under his breath.

Victor frowned. Quasimodo's infatuation with the woman had been of some concern to him lately. "Well, Grigori, since you've come to us with this generous offer of fifty-thousand diablos I shall overlook my crookback assistant's slip of the tongue—this time." He shot Quasimodo a warning glance.

A thin smile played about Quasimodo's lips. "*Merci, mes amis.*"

Fifty-thousand in hot cash will more than cover the cost of what's needed to complete the other cyborg, with enough left over to finance future experiments, Victor told himself. "We've always been honest and forthright in our dealings, you and I," he said to Rasputin, "and I think we can call this a done deal."

"Is good," said Rasputin. "Ogre will want effective weapons, of course. Like those." He pointed to where the Hellraiser-13 and the Grimm-666, also known as Satan's Left Hand, hung on the wall.

"Naturally," said Victor. "He can have those and plenty of ammunition, too."

"Does Ogre have any idea what will be done to him?" Turing asked the Siberian monk.

"*Da.* His brain go in cyborg body."

"Not only his brain but his heart, as well."

Rasputin shrugged. "What Ogre does not know will not hurt him."

"How soon will we get the money so we can purchase what we need to finish building the cyborg? And how soon do you wish to begin?" Victor asked.

"This day, money is yours. After that, when is convenient for you."

Turing glanced at Victor and then asked Rasputin, "What if we fail and Ogre dashes off to the Mortuary?"

"Not problem. We keep money."

"Sounds good to me!" Victor said, rubbing his hands together. "Quasimodo, looks like your hunch paid off," he added with a wink.

"Now who is the one being droll?" asked the hunchback.

Turing raised his glass. "Gentlemen, shall we toast to a new age of demons and monsters?"

Victor took note of the fact that Quasimodo didn't join in the toast. The hunchback just sat there in silence, stewing in his anger and jealousy.

*

Computers buzz. Electronics purr. Medical instruments hum. Machines grumble and whine and growl. Tiny arcs of lightning crackle. Transformers and generators spark and sizzle. Potions boil and bubble. Torches set in sconces chase shadows up and down the red brick walls of the laboratory. The sharp tang of ozone fills the air.

The carcass of the Orange Ogre lies on one of the two operating tables in Doctor Frankenstein's laboratory. Ogre's chest has been cracked wide open and the top of his skull removed. On the second operating table rests the shiny black, blue and red metal shell of a cyborg in repose. Victor and Turing have already completed the operation to remove Ogre's heart and brain, transplant them into the cyborg's body and connect everything to the intricate electronic components.

"So far, so good," said Victor, keeping an eye on the EKG. "Heart is still functioning normally. No sign of dissolution or dissipation of the subject's body."

"Encephalograph shows alpha waves are active," Turing added.

The Orange Ogre had been eager and ready to undergo the operation as soon as he, Rasputin, Cagliostro and Marie Lenormand arrived at Goblin Manor. Those three now sat on a bench along one wall, quietly watching the proceedings. Quasimodo sat in a helleather chair across from them, scowling at Cagliostro and Lenormand, who were holding hands like a pair of teenage lovers in hell. After administering the Hexoform to Ogre, which put him to sleep almost immediately, the hunchback had refused to take any further part in the experiment, preferring to sit and stare daggers at Cagliostro. The bogus Italian count ignored him and acted as if all was well in hell.

"Delta wave pattern is weakening. Alpha waves ascend to normal levels," Turing announced, flipping toggles and switches left and right.

"Good!" said Victor. "Our patient awakens."

Lenormand noticed Quasimodo glaring at her. "What's *your* problem?"

"You—and him," the hunchback told her, pointing to Cagliostro. "You deceived me, Marie. You betrayed me!"

"I did nothing of the sort," she said.

Quasimodo's knuckles cracked as he balled his hands into fists. "You made me believe you had affection for me, and I poured out my heart to you."

"My dear Quasimodo, you deceived yourself. I never gave you any indication that I thought of you in *that* way. You are my customer. At best, we are just friends."

"How can you say such things, Marie?" Quasimodo jumped to his feet. "How can you be the lover of this *goombah* charlatan?"

"Sit down before I knock you down, you ugly little *monstre*," Cagliostro told Quasimodo, not bothering to rise from his seat.

"Quiet!" hissed Rasputin. "Ogre soon wakes."

"But Marie, I love you!" Quasimodo said in anger and heartsick disappointment.

"Stop bothering our guests and get over here and assist me, Quasimodo," Victor said. "And if you can't behave yourself, please leave."

Cursing in French, the Hunchback of Notre Dame smashed his chair with his fists, rushed out of the laboratory and slammed the outer door shut behind him.

"Where's he off to?" Turing asked Victor.

Victor shrugged. "Who knows? But he'll be back. He always comes back."

The body of the cyborg began to stir.

"He awakens! He awakens!" Victor shouted in triumph.

Everyone fell silent as the cyborg once known as the Orange Ogre sat up on the table. Over ten-feet tall, the thing's eyes glowed with violet fire.

"Keep an eye on Ogre's body," said Turing. "Hope it doesn't evaporate."

"It won't," Victor assured him. "This time we've succeeded. This time we've won!"

"Ogre, how you feel?" Rasputin asked.

"Fantastic!" The cyborg spoke in a more normal tone of voice than had its predecessor.

Turing gave Victor a thumbs-up. "Voice box working even better than before."

"Of course, of course," said Victor. "And the body still shows no signs of oncoming dissipation. We've managed to halt Reassignment!"

Cagliostro applauded. "*Magnifico!*"

"I wouldn't have believed it had I not witnessed it," said Lenormand.

"Ogreborg, that's what you are," Victor told Ogre while he and Turing removed the wires and cables connected to the cyborg's body.

"Where are my weapons?" Ogreborg asked. He hopped off the table and stretched his mighty metal arms. "I want my weapons. I want them now."

Victor walked over to the wall where the Hellraiser-13 and Grimm-666 were hanging and removed them. "These are very unique weapons. Each one is equipped with a thousand-round clip of small but extremely powerful ammunition." Handing the weapons to Ogreborg, he added, "There are plenty of extra clips in the metal pockets of your legs."

"Nice feel to them," said Ogreborg, testing the weight of the weapons. "Now I can get even with all those who've scorned and ridiculed me."

"You do realize that the act of seeking vengeance in hell is pointless, don't you?" Turing said to the cyborg.

"If you dust your enemies they will only go to the Mortuary," said Cagliostro.

"And there they will be reassigned," Lenormand added.

"We'll see about that." Ogreborg walked up to the dirty mirror hanging on the wall and stared at his reflection. Then he turned to face the others. "I am the Colossus of Hell! Look upon me and weep, you turd burglars!"

Rasputin's mouth fell open and his eyes went wide. "Ogre, have you gone mad?"

Ogreborg laughed at him "I am *Ogreborg*, the awesome and frightening, and there will be *no* others like me in hell!"

With that, he fired one mini grenade from the Hellraiser-13 at Turing and Victor's banks of computers, machinery and medical instruments. Cagliostro threw himself upon Lenormand to shield her from the blast. Victor and Turing jumped out of the way only a heartbeat before the lab equipment exploded into a burning and smoking ruin. But Rasputin didn't move quickly enough and a huge piece of charred metal sliced his head in two; a moment later his body glimmered and vanished from the lab.

Turing rose to his feet, shouting, "You son of a bitch!" He drew his Bolt .45 from its holster but before he could even take aim, the Colossus of Hell squeezed off several rounds from his Grimm-666, cutting Turing's body in half.

"Alan!" Victor cried.

The Bolt .45 flew from Turing's hand and landed on the floor only a hellisecond before his body shimmered, dissolved and began its journey to the Mortuary.

"Who else wants a taste of this?" Ogreborg asked. Then, laughing hysterically, he ran towards the outer door, smashed through it and raced away.

Victor climbed to his feet while Cagliostro helped Lenormand to stand. "Poor Alan," he lamented. "I hope the Undertaker doesn't mess him up too much. This is his first time."

"Ah, but Rasputin . . . who knows what will be done to him in that morgue of mayhem and mutilation," said Cagliostro, sadly shaking his head. "Are you all right, *il mio amore*?"

Lenormand nodded. "Yes, Joey. I'm fine. Now what?"

"The Orange Ogre has finally gone over the top," said Victor. "We have to stop him."

"But how, Signor Frankenstein?" Cagliostro asked.

Victor had no idea what to do. He felt lost and helpless without Turing and Quasimodo. "I have no fucking idea, Giuseppe."

*

I am strong. I am unstoppable. No motherfucker is ever gonna fuck with me again!

Ogreborg runs amok throughout the Golem Heights, destroying buildings and vehicles, and blasting damned souls to smithereens with his Hellraiser-13 grenade launcher. Hundreds of hellizens flee from him, screaming and pushing each other out of the way as they try to escape. The damned cry out in agony as bullets from the cyborg's Grimm-666 rip them to pieces. He doesn't know and doesn't care what becomes of the lost souls he dusts. All he desires is the destruction of every resident of New Hell. He's having his cake and enjoying the taste of it. Each time he reloads his weapons, more damned fools explode into shimmering particles that dissipate and fade away.

I don't give a shit if they end up in the Mortuary. I'll just keep dusting them until there's nothing left of them to be recycled!

Ogreborg leaves a path of chaos and destruction in his wake as he makes his way down to Port Boil and Vile River. Buildings crumble and necroflesh bodies burst into glittering atoms that quickly disappear. Vehicles burn, windows shatter, pavement buckles and cracks. Towers and bridges collapse as scores of hellions are slaughtered and then vanish from the filth-laden streets. Ogreborg is a juggernaut of explosive firepower that terrorizes and tears apart the bodies and souls of the damned.

Must find Satan. Must find Erra. Must destroy them both!

That's his mantra. That's all he thinks about as he continues his rampage through the streets of Port Boil. He is now a mad, near mindless automaton bent on only two things: destruction and revenge.

Heading around the bend of Dead Man's Curve, Ogreborg spotted some panic-stricken hellizens fleeing down the dead-end byway of Crud Alley. Violet, robotic eyes blazing with vengeance, he stopped at the mouth of the alley and opened fire with his weapons, blasting men and women into glittering atoms. The alley turned into a ruin of fire, black smoke and burning debris.

When he spotted a group of men who reminded him of the gang that had beaten him, he turned his gunsights on them and fired away like a kid at a shooting gallery.

Bastards! *That'll teach you*!

"Drop your weapons and turn around slowly with your hands in the air," he heard, a commanding voice from behind.

Slowly, deliberately, Ogreborg turned to face a platoon of Uncubi aiming their Hexum-9 assault rifles at him. "And what if I don't?" he asked the leader of the Uncubi death squad.

The Uncubus didn't waste any more words and immediately opened fire on Ogreborg. The other Uncubi followed suit, their weapons popping with explosive sounds. Bullets ripped through the air and ricocheted off the metallic body of the cyborg, causing not one dent or scratch. Ogreborg laughed maniacally and retaliated, shredding the New Breed demons to pieces with rounds of bullets and exterminating them with grenades until nothing was left but red smoke.

"Fucking snowflakes!" he whooped, reloading his weapons and continuing on his wave of terror and destruction through the riverfront town of Port Boil.

*

Victor, Cagliostro and Marie Lenormand follow devastation left in the wake of Ogreborg's blitzkrieg. Fire and destruction point them in the right direction. Plague Zombies burn and crumble into sand and ashes. The fatally-wounded cry out in agony and then collapse into quickly evaporating particles of glittering necroflesh that Victor knew would soon wink out and be reconstituted in the Mortuary to await Reassignment. Cars and trucks collide and crash into buildings, pedestrians are run over as the drivers disintegrate the moment bullets or grenades take them down. Other vehicles speed off in the opposite direction to escape the wanton destruction unleashed by Ogreborg.

Port Boil swiftly turns into a Biblical hellscape of fire, torment and madness.

Wreckage of all kinds is strewn everywhere. Body parts lie scattered about or fly through the air before they shimmer and vanish. Victor wishes Quasimodo was by his side as he and his two companions run through the streets, ducking and dodging the shrapnel and debris flying all about them. Unlike every other damned soul who flees from Ogreborg, they head the other way, hot on the trail of the blood-crazed cyborg. Finally, they reach the banks of the Vile River, where hundreds of boats, wharf-side taverns, warehouses, homes and necroflesh bodies are burning in a conflagration that would make Dante proud.

"He must run out of the ammunition sooner or later," said Cagliostro.

"Not with the ammo clips I designed," said Victor. "This can go on for days!"

"Your experiment has proven to be a great success, Doctor," said Lenormand. "The fact that he's still running free to cause havoc and destruction shows that his heart and brain, even his body, have not been whisked off to the Mortuary. You cheated Reassignment."

"Yes, but at what cost?" Victor asked. "Once again I have created a monster that has gone on a terrible rampage."

"Then how do we stop such a *mostro orribile* as this?" Cagliostro wondered.

Quasimodo unexpectedly reappeared, carrying Turing's discarded Bolt .45 in one hand. "*Docteur!*" he called out.

Victor and the others were surprised to see him. "Quasimodo! I'm so happy to see you!"

"I come back to help if I can, *mes amis.*"

Pointing to the gun in the hunchback's hand, Victor said, "With *that? Against Ogreborg?*"

"No, this gun, it is for *them.*" Quasimodo raised the pistol, aimed it at Cagliostro and fired off two quick shots: the first one drilled a hole through the Italian's forehead while the second tore the top of his skull clean off. Cagliostro's body abruptly dissolved into glistening particles and quickly faded away.

"Joey! Joey!" Lenormand cried, falling to her knees.

Quasimodo then turned the weapon on her.

"No, no," she begged. "Please don't do this, *ma chérie.*"

"You betrayed me!" You lied to me!" Quasimodo growled. "When we had dinner at Hell's Kitchen you said you loved me!"

"I did. I mean, I *do* love you, dear Quasimodo. Just not in the way you want."

"No, you conned me, and that, *ma petite pute*, I cannot forgive. Revenge may be futile but it is no less sweet." Quasimodo raised the pistol and pointed it at Lenormand.

"No, not the Mortuary. Anything but that!" she pleaded.

"Quasimodo—no!" Victor shouted.

Click! Click!

The Bolt .45 jammed.

Lenormand fainted and collapsed.

A gust of wind howled and blew wildly through the ruined streets of Port Boil. The crimson vault hanging over New Hell trembled. Lightning flashed and thunder shook the firmament of the riverside town as damned souls screamed and ran seeking shelter.

At that moment Ogreborg emerged from the smoke and fire of destruction and marched towards Victor, Quasimodo and the unconscious Lenormand. "Are you here to join me or join all the other assholes I've destroyed?" Though his weapons were silent, they were smoking hot.

"This is insane, Ogreborg," said Victor. "Your rampage has caused panic and destruction. You have accomplished nothing here expect to make even more enemies for yourself."

"Screw all that! I'm in charge now and soon I'll control New Hell and every other hell in this fucking netherworld!" cried Ogreborg, raising and firing his weapons into the air.

And then, in the blood-red sky above them, Victor saw a beautiful but terrifying figure swooping down upon them on invisible wings. Draped in dusty raiment, the dreadful figure drew his flashing sword as he descended lower and lower . . . a lone Sibitti wearing a cloak of human skin decorated with braided scalps. People wailed and fled in terror, but Ogreborg didn't notice, his attention focused on Victor and the fiery destruction of Port Boil.

"Nothing to say for yourself, you piece of shit?" he asked Victor.

Fighting his fear of Ogreborg and the Sibitti, Doctor Frankenstein stood his ground. "I know you, Ogre. I know all about you."

Ogreborg took a step closer to Victor. "What did you say?"

Knowing how Ogre's loss of memory and identity tormented him more than anything else in hell, Victor told him, "I know who you are and who you *were*, you two-bit has-been."

"You *know* me?"

"Yes! And if you have the balls to discover the truth, look to the sky. Look, I say!"

Almost reluctantly, Ogreborg looked up and saw the Sibitti hovering in the sky not far above him. "Where's the rest of your terrorist cell, you loser?" shouted the cyborg. When the Sibitti did not answer Ogreborg aimed his weapons at Erra's #2 Personified Weapon. "I am Ogreborg, the Colossus of Hell. Prepare to be annihilated. Resistance is—"

The Sibitti's sword flashed once and a sizzling, white bolt of lightning struck Ogreborg, blasting him into a jigsaw puzzle of fiery pieces that the wind scattered in all directions.

Victor closed his eyes and stood waiting for the inevitable. *If this be it, then sobeit.*

But a second lightning bolt from that terrible swift sword never struck. Instead, flapping wings stirred and a powerful wind slapped him in the face. When he opened his eyes the Sibitti was gone just as quickly as he had arrived.

Then, from down the street, Victor saw the Unknown Poet leading a squad of armed Uncubi towards him. "Mister Up!" he shouted in surprise.

"That was close and you were lucky, Victor," said the hetman of the Uncubi. "But you must leave here soon before the rest of the Sibitti finish whatever business they have in Ki-gal and decide to return. Be grateful that only one was sent to deal with the monster you created."

"Did Ogreborg obliterate all those souls?" Victor asked.

"Obliteration is not yours or any damned soul's provence," said Mister Up. "His weapons merely sent them to the Mortuary."

"What about Ogreborg?"

"Obliteration or Oblivion. That I do not know."

"And your people?"

"We Uncubi may be demons, but we are not native to hell. We are still damned souls. My people will be reassigned."

"The Undertaker and Gorgonous will certainly have their hands and claws full."

"Indeed, my friend. And if you and Quasimodo wish to escape Erra's wrath and remain in good graces with His Satanic Majesty, the Mortuary is the safest place for you to be. I'd advise you both to get your asses over to Slab A—and *pronto*. There is much work to keep you busy and out of mischief for a long time." The Uncubus' strange-looking mouth in his pointed, Pteranodon-like face smiled. "And please, Victor . . . no more robots in hell. Okay?"

Victor was crestfallen. "But I like to build things!"

"Then buy yourself some Stinkin' Logs or a set of Killegos," Mister Up told him. "Beware, Victor. I know that look on your face. I know your brain is already concocting some grand new experiment. Just be careful. For now, you amuse and entertain Satan and may even serve some purpose of his. Erra himself may be tolerant of you for his own reasons, but for how long?"

The Uncubus shrugged his sharp-boned and crooked shoulders. "Neither of them confide in me. But I think part of your punishment is to suffer endless failure. And that may be why, for now, you've been left alone to do pretty much as you please. Just don't press your luck too far."

"I shall take your advice to heart," said Victor. But he'd never give up. As dogged and as fearless as ever, the infamous doctor remained undaunted and determined to find a way out of hell. That was his mission in the afterlife.

Bidding Victor farewell, Mister Up and his squad of Uncubi took their leave. Victor studied the crimson vault that teased and tormented the damned with the light and promise of Paradise. As of yet, no sign of Erra and his Seven Sibitti could be seen.

I guess Quasimodo and I should hightail it back to the Mortuary for another tour of duty there, once again helping to reassign all those poor souls Ogreborg took down.

Quasimodo walked over to Victor, carrying the unconscious Marie Lenormand over his shoulder like a sack of potatoes. "So we must return to the Mortuary to work again?"

"I'm afraid so, my friend," Victor told him. "Things could be a lot worse, of course." He nodded to Lenormand. "What are you going to do with her?"

"I am taking her to the Vile River, where she can sink or swim or be eaten by whatever lives in such filthy water. Tell me, Victor . . . what you said to Ogre? Do you truly know who he is and who he was?"

Victor winked. "What do *you* think?"

The Hunchback of Notre Dame laughed. "Meet you in the Mortuary." Then he scurried down to the riverbank with Lenormand, shouting "*Sanctuary! Sanctuary!*"

Strange Arts

Janet Morris and Chris Morris

"What strange arts necessity finds out."
Christopher Marlowe – Dido

"Someone's been a very naughty boy, and a stupid one." Christopher Marlowe heard a voice from the dark: sometimes a tormenter's voice, a lover's voice, a protector's voice. Never could he forget *this* voice, a spymaster's voice, scratchy and full of tongue. Speaking for the Elizabethan Privy Council, this voice had shielded Marlowe in matters to benefit their country, until his handler's death in 1590. With those protections gone to the grave, Kit soon followed, murdered on the 30th of May,1593. This voice he heard in hell's dankest crypt could be no other.

"Sir Francis?" Kit Marlowe croaked. His own voice was a phantom yet, comprised of memories best forgot, a vestige of a body sundered from its head, and both parts out of his control. Still, he tried again: "My good lord, is that you?"

"None other," said the voice.

Until his death at age 58, Sir Francis Walsingham had used Kit as a secret agent, paid for his scholarship and debauch while at Cambridge; funded him as spy, instigator, and bed warmer; even bailed him out of Newgate Prison and somehow secured him a Master of Arts, though Kit attended few classes. However, the truest arts came between them: love and betrayal in service to the Queen. Yet in hell, Kit had never encountered him. "Francis? I didn't mean it, any of it. I'm so sorry." His gurgled words must do for all that, an apologia centuries overdue, in this the direst of circumstances.

He had wronged his mentor.

What's past is prologue, he and Shakespeare had long agreed. While alive, and now in hell, Kit remained a spy, a brawler, a writer, a Faustian heretic and duelist—true to all things said of him, except "magician." He cared little what fools called him. He'd been a collaborator with Will Shakespeare, until Diábolos made an end to that with an edict that tore Kit's head from his body whenever *Macbeth* was performed.

"Be still, Kit," decreed the scratchy voice from the dark. Hell this must truly be, to leave Marlowe paralyzed in Walsingham's clutches.

He struggled once more to speak. He thought to sit up but had no more control of his body below the neck than of the head once attached to it.

Someone else spoke: a woman's voice followed by a second and a third's, soft and low, words unknowable.

Did Walsingham hear those voices too?

Kit saw a patch of light. He made it out to be woman-sized and ephemeral. He thought he could feel his feet, his hands, his torso; a palm on his brow. He tried once more to push forward, sit up.

To no avail.

The palm remained on his brow, oddly comforting as his interlocutors conversed in phrases he couldn't parse.

Then the touch fell away, and he was spinning, only Banquo's head and Banquo's body, surrounded by nothing but pain.

*

When Kit next woke, he could swallow, even grunt. More, he could move his head from right to left, and clench a fist.

The stony room around him held torturer's implements on racks. He well recalled those, and a gray face close to his, with breath that made him gag. The form hovering over him tugged a threaded needle: this specter was sewing him up, perhaps where his neck had been lopped from his body. Kit's jaws were jacked apart, held there for purposes he wished were beyond his ken.

He moaned when he could, grunted when he couldn't.

After a time, the gray man, if man he was, shuffled away, and Kit slept once more.

*

Prisoners cried out somewhere near. Rats and cats scurried hither and thither. One rat climbed onto the slab where he lay, scampered from his scrotum to his face. It used its clawed hand to pull down his lower lip and taste the blood and spittle in his mouth.

Basta!

This rat cocked its head, licked its own lips, and reached out to get another taste of him.

"*Get thee hence*!" He slapped at it, and it tumbled off him, onto the floor.

He hadn't realized he could move that arm, control those hands shackled with iron, or turn his head. Now he could do all of those.

Where he lay, he felt about him. He could see out of one eye, but not the other: That second eye hurt beyond tolerance, as if the dagger that killed him, Ingram Frizer's dagger, had found Kit in hell and once more made its home above his eye.

With care, he dragged his right hand high and felt for a dagger there. He found none. He explored his neck. The sutures there were clumsy. He could feel where they puckered his flesh.

He wanted to sit up. He was now sure he could, once he got his bearings.

This place had all the comforts of the Tower, and surely held as many ghosts. The slab under him was stone, sticky with too much blood to be his alone. A high arrow loop served as a window; from it a rufous light showed in rays.

As he summoned his courage and sat up, a screech of wood dragged over stone sounded louder than the one that escaped his lips. He heard metal rattling, maybe keys, preceding a group of people into the cell, for cell it was.

Walsingham, long and dark of hair and heart, strode toward him. "Good morrow, Master Marlowe. Stay seated."

He'd followed so many orders from Walsingham over his young life that he froze where he sat, iron bracelets abrading his wrists.

Beyond the spymaster he could now make out three creatures. Women or ghosts these might be, translucent.

And after them came . . . the exalted J, first writer of the Hebrew bible, with a shawl wrapped round her shoulders. Once within, she touched the cell's door; it screeled in its tracks, sliding shut, obedient. The three wraiths stepped aside for her.

"Kit," said J, whose words had brought Mercy in hell for many worse sinners than he. She glided to the slab where he sat. "Kit Marlowe, so nice to see you whole once more."

His good eye might have watered, or the sight of J might have brought tears to both his eyes. From beside her, Walsingham reached out to Kit. "I have a message or two for you, here where we can speak as we'll choose, with these sisters present to divine what is true and what's not."

Kit frowned when he looked up to meet those eyes that had consigned so many to their doom in life. Kit had no doubt the words Walsingham spoke were genuine and of the moment.

"Francis, I'm sorry. Let me try to explain—"

"Shh. There'll be time. Or there won't," said Walsingham.

"And J, I'm sorry," Kit said as he'd said before: sorry for all he'd done in life; sorry for trying to outwit fate.

And he was.

J floated beside the slate slab, so near that he realized he was naked and aroused at this most inappropriate time and place. She put a finger to his lips and said, "Kit Marlowe, in this netherworld of disorder, there remains much for you to do. If you can. If you will."

At that moment, the three wraiths said together, "Much to do, much to do, Christopher Marlowe."

Walsingham swept a bow toward the witches and turned back to Kit: "We bring a message from your friend Shakespeare. He is saddened by your plight but remands you into my custody. If you will accept our troth and plans, there is business to do in these latter-day hells, and few adroit enough to accomplish it."

Kit's mind churned. Was Wally telling the truth? Had he ever? Really recruiting him as of old? "As I told the Prince of Lies, I have nothing. What you may want from me, I no longer own: Not my soul, nor even my body."

"Offer your . . . heart, Kit Marlowe," said Walsingham. "Offer your time, turned to our cause. Hell will test you, as it tests us all. As it did in life."

"Love truth and plague the devil," said the three witches in unison, "and rest, in eternity, you will earn, Christopher Marlowe."

J nodded toward the Sisters, then looked hard at Kit. "Ahead lie trials and penance, yes, but truth can make you strong. Mold you. You have the ear of Diabolos and the god of plague and mayhem. Against these, add Walsingham, with his determined soul, and even the Fates will aid you, if you'll join us. And Mercy, of course, such as I can deliver."

"I have a thing yet my own, one thing the devil values not. That thing is love. Love as I have for Will and a story on the wing. Love as I have for you, sweet J, eternal, ever pure. For it will I labor, and dedicate to you what ravages I must endure. What the Fates may decree, and my own eyes see, will I add in the bargain." Kit's words came thick and full of pain. He knew what he was doing. He was not fooled. There was no escape from hell. He was sentenced to lose his head and his heart time after time, but here came the Fates themselves, offering something else, shimmering wisps of days to come.

And here came Walsingham, who had taken his part when alive, and might again.

Walsingham said, "And I must deliver to you the rest of Will's message: He reminds you of what wisdom you yet own, and promises he will do what he can to see you right."

Walsingham unshackled Kit's arms. One Sister stroked away the sutures on his neck. And as J took his hand and pressed it to her cheek, Will's message brought back to Kit how much he had done, on so many yesterdays and todays, and what he might do on his tomorrows.